Holeshot
2

Lynn Michaels

DEDICATION

To all the wonderful people who read Holeshot and waited, beyond patiently, for me to put this second book together. Thank you so much for your continued support.

CONTENTS

ACKNOWLEDGMENTS

Special Thanks

Beta Readers – y'all go above and beyond just reading for me. Thanks for your help and encouragement: Maggie, Amy, Laura, Melissa, and JP. Y'all totally Rock!

Thanks to Jay Aheer at Simply Defined Art – your covers and extras are just...amazing! I have no words for how wonderful it is to work with you. Thank you for all you've done for me.

Sharon Stogner at Devil in the Details Editing Services – you keep me straight with more than just grammar! I could never put out professional level books without you.

Brand Name Recognition and Disclaimer

This is a book of fiction set in the world of Supercross. Although much research has been done (and it was a ton of fun), facts and details have been changed and manipulated to fit this work of fiction. Many names and brands have been made up and some have been borrowed. Those borrowed brands do not belong to me. Recognition goes out to: Supercross, Monster Energy Drink, Alias, H&M, Nohow, Dolce and Gabbana, Ray-Ban, Fox Sports 1, Suzuki, Toyota, Yamaha, Kawasaki, KTM, Michael Kors, Aviator, Onia, Panera Bread, Versace, Ruger LCR, Thor, American Eagle, Abercrombie and Fitch, Ford Mustang, Todd Snyder, Hugo Boss, Levi's, Wrangler, Under Armour, HBO, George Foreman Grills, Uber, and Motocross University.

Chapter 1 – July, New York

Tate Jordan pulled his huge duffle bag out of the trunk of the cab and tipped the driver. Thankfully, it was stuffed with mostly clothes and not much racing gear. Exhaustion from the partying and celebrating with his friends and then the long trip home weighed him down. His shoulders sagged. For the millionth time, he wished he lived closer to Davey and Tyler, and he was going to miss them while they were on their honeymoon and during the off season. Friends like them did not come around often. He enjoyed their company and more importantly, he trusted them.

He drug his luggage up the short flight of stairs that led to the shiny black, front door of their apartment building, as he listened to the cab drive off, wheels grumbling on the cobblestone street. Home. He'd missed his boyfriend, Donny, and couldn't wait to get his lover in bed. They'd been apart too long over the race season. Donny not accompanying him to Davey and Tyler's wedding still irked him, but he didn't want to fight about it, so he stuffed it down with all the other things he wasn't too happy about. Part of being in a relationship meant you had to compromise. Tate didn't mind, really, but lately he'd been the one doing all the giving in, getting nothing in return, even with being gone so much, which really said something for just how fucking bad it had become.

Pushing the door open, he shouldered it to lug his bag inside then let it shut behind him. The old building was a relic from the past, but the owners kept it in shape. It had four flights in all, including the basement level with windows that looked out at the street, which made the building a bit smaller than most in trendy Soho. The red, gray, and black bricks nestled right up to taller buildings on either side and the only greenery came from one small tree planted in a square that had been dug out of the sidewalk in front of the building. The main hallway stretched out just past the mailboxes and ended at the stairwell. Two apartment doors bracketed the hallway on either side, but neither were his. He would have to trudge that heavy bag up another flight of stairs.

Tate liked the quaint feeling the place had about it and hoped one day it would feel a bit more like home, rather than the place he spent part of his year with Donny. The other half of his year, probably more than half if he included training away from New York, was spent chasing his Supercross dream.

At the top of the stairs, he shoved his key in the door and slid his bag across the floor and over the threshold. "Donny," he called out, anticipating a sweet, sexy reunion.

Donny stepped out of the bedroom, tugging at his buttoned sleeves as he walked. Tate had to reel in the urge to let his jaw drop. His boyfriend was dressed up and looking too hot in chocolaty brown slacks and matching vest with a salmon colored dress shirt. Tate had been corrected on the color before. He knew better than to even *think* it was pink, though he still wasn't certain of the difference or whether he really cared about it, other than the fact that it looked nice against Donny's tawny skin. Donny's tie was a darker shade of brown, as were his loafers that he wore without socks of course.

"Baby," Tate leered. "You look so good and I missed you." He opened his arms, stepping forward.

"Oh, you're home?" Donny allowed himself to be hugged, but only briefly before stepping away and adjusting his tie. "I, uh, didn't think you'd make it back until later." He'd shaved, but left his dark mustache and a trail of beard, just around his jaw line. His dark hair brushed back from his face with perfectly streaked highlights in a perfect style, not one lock out of place. Tate wanted to run his fingers through the thick strands, just to mess it up.

"I texted you my flight info." Tate leaned his hip against the breakfast bar that separated the kitchen from the rest of the open loft space, which earned him a scowl from Donny. He stood up straight and crossed his arms. Donny hated him leaning against the bar's slick gray granite. He took pride in his renovations of the apartment, and while Tate could appreciate that, he also thought Donny tended toward obnoxiously obsessive about it all.

Donny huffed, his disapproval very evident on his frowning face. "I guess I just didn't pay attention. You're never home." He slid his fingers into the pockets of his slacks and glanced at the clock above the kitchen sink.

"Going somewhere? Or did you dress up for me?" Tate knew the answer before he asked, but couldn't help himself.

"Oh, you know. I'm just meeting some of the guys across the bridge." He didn't seem like he wanted to tell Tate his plans. Worse, it didn't seem like he wanted to invite Tate along, either. Tate would need an hour to spiff up to Donny's level of dress including showering, shaving, and pressing something to wear, and he seriously doubted Donny would wait that long.

"Across the bridge?"

Donny pressed his plump lips together and put his hand on his stomach, as if inspecting the buttons of his vest. He had several bracelets on, some silver with stones, some plain, and a few leather wraps, all tight enough not to slide around, but just cling to his wrist looking fashionable.

Tate raised his eyebrows, questioning, waiting for his answer.

"Just a new club. It opened last week in Williamsburg."

Tate leaned against the bar with purpose. Fuck upsetting Donny. "Williamsburg?"

"So, what? It's *the* place right now. At least for hanging out. All the starving artist types are there..."

"When are you going? Do you have time for me to clean up?" Tate looked down at his own attire. He wore his H&M distressed jeans that tapered down to his ankles, looking cool against his beat up chucks that used to be some sort of bold color, but had faded to some kind of gray-blue over the years. His bright blue hoodie from Nohow gave him a pop of color over his faded, soft Thor t-shirt. He liked to be comfortable when he traveled, but still have some style.

Tate might not be as hipster suave as Donny, but he appreciated fashion as much as the next guy, maybe even a little more. He'd thought that had been one of the few things he had in common with Donny. "I'm sure I have something to wear." Though, Tate had no intentions of looking through his closest for something he'd have to press.

It'd been a long trip, and all he wanted to do was climb into bed, preferably naked with Donny, but since that didn't seem likely to happen, he figured, he'd provoke his boyfriend a bit. Maybe he'd feel guilty about ditching Tate, but Tate doubted that. What he wanted from Donny and what he actually got never seemed to match up.

Tate grabbed his duffle bag and lifted it, not wanting to garner the wrath of Donny should he scratch the tile. Donny had spent a lot of money remodeling the place, so Tate couldn't blame him. He'd done a fabulous job and their loft apartment was sleek and modern, but really it was Donny's apartment. Tate hadn't ever felt like it was home and his name wasn't on the mortgage anyway. One more thing they'd fought over that he didn't want to bring up. Again.

As he hauled the bag toward the bedroom, Donny cleared his throat. "Tate...you won't have fun. You don't...fit. This is a trendier, more fashionable crowd. You're just going to be bored out of your mind."

Tate dropped the bag by his side of the closet and turned to face Donny. To say his words hurt was an understatement. Tate had been away and hadn't seen Donny in at least a month, not since before the last few races of the season, and then he'd gone straight to Colorado for the guys' wedding. He missed his boyfriend, and now...now Donny was going out with friends without Tate on the night he returned. "Why'd you make plans?"

Donny's bottom lip trembled slightly, the only sign that there was going to be a fight. Donny was going to act like a bitch about it.

Tate had learned to just give in and apologize fast, rather than listening to his shit ad nauseam. "Look...I didn't mean it like that."

"How did you mean it?" Donny asked. "I'm supposed to just sit here and wait for you to come home?"

Tate wanted to go off. He'd texted his flight the day before. They'd talked on the phone the day of the wedding. He knew exactly when Tate was due home. Even though he'd started poking at the issue, he didn't really want to fight. *Too fucking tired.* "I said I'm sorry. I'm home now. I'll be home for at least a month." He needed the down time and hoped to spend a good bit of it in bed with Donny, making up for lost time.

Donny narrowed his eyes. "Too little, too late, Tate. See?" He shook his head, but not a hair fell out of place. "I can't do this anymore."

"Do this? Do what?"

"Don't make it harder than it has to be. I think...you know, just, when we first got together it seemed cool. Dating a motorcycle racer. But, we really come from two different worlds. You don't fit into mine and yours is..." He waived his hand in the air. The bracelets didn't even clink together. "Out there somewhere."

"You can always come with me."

"No. You don't get it. I can't. This is my home. Here, in New York. I don't want to follow you all over the place, across the country, to every disgusting dirt track in the nation."

"Disgusting?"

"You know what I mean. It's dirty." He lifted one eyebrow as if to imply by association, Tate was dirty as well.

"This is just fucking great," Tate mumbled and ran his hands through his long blond hair. It had grown to a shaggy length and needed a cut, but Tate kind of liked the wilder look. He'd hoped Donny would like it too, but apparently, Donny wasn't liking anything *Tate* at the moment.

"Fuck you, Tate. I don't need this shit either. I'm trying to be nice about it."

Maybe the jet lag had scrambled his brain, or maybe he was just tired of everything. "Nice? Do you know what that word means?" Tate didn't know exactly what prompted him to let those words fly out of his mouth, but there they were.

Donny took a step forward and shoved Tate in the chest in one fluid motion. The momentum that carried him pushed Tate hard and he fell back into the closet, taking down a handful of clothes yanked from their hangers with him. He landed hard on his tailbone on top of a small pile of shoes, but the worst was an old pair of racing boots. They were hard from the plastic shin guards and hurt his ass. "Fuck me!"

"That's not going to happen again," Donny snarled. "I want you out of my apartment." He pointed to the door, as if Tate was going to just get up and walk out because he said so.

"Damn, Donny, for real, let's just talk about this."

Donny wasn't listening to a word, he talked right over the top of Tate. "I've had it and I don't want to see you anymore. I really was trying to be nice, Tate. But, you've got to go. I mean it. Now!"

Tate picked himself up off the closet floor. He wasn't going to let Donny, or anybody, intimidate him. Even though Donny was about the same height as him, his shoulders and chest were bigger, his build overall larger, and he probably outweighed Tate by a good thirty pounds. It didn't matter. He wasn't going to let anyone shove him around. Not ever.

He stepped right into Donny's space. "I said we need to talk about this."

"There's nothing to talk about." His dark eyes turned hard and unforgiving, leaving Tate to wonder just where their relationship had gone this wrong.

"Yes, there is. We need to discuss logistics." Judging by Donny's actions and irrational temper, as well as his own feelings that they'd been heading downhill fast, Tate couldn't bring himself to fight for their relationship. There was nothing left worth fighting for, but space and time were important.

Donny stepped back, shooting a decidedly evil glare at Tate, and pulled his cell phone out of his pocket. He turned away from Tate and started tapping his phone.

"Don't fucking ignore me!" Tate snatched the phone out of his hands.

Donny gasped, "Oh my God. You didn't just do that. You're such a drama queen."

"Me? Donny. For real, you are the king of drama queens."

Donny lunged forward, trying to grab the phone back, but Tate pulled it back and up, out of his reach. "Listen to me," he growled in Donny's face, but his boyfriend—ex-boyfriend—wasn't going to listen. He shoved Tate in the chest again. Without the same momentum, it didn't push him off balance physically, but something inside him snapped. He shoved Donny back. Hard. "Stop it."

"Give me my phone."

"Or what?" They both yelled, angry, not fighting over the real issues, but Tate couldn't calm down enough to care.

"Or fuck you!" Donny screamed in his face, spittle flying out and hitting Tate's cheek and chin. Tate shoved Donny's chest again to push him away. He was thinking about the damned phone, not giving it back, and the spit in his face.

Donny pulled his arm back and let it fly, punching Tate in the jaw.

"Mother fucker!" Tate threw the phone across the room. It smashed into the wall.

Donny's mouth fell open, slack jawed, as he turned and stared at the phone. He bent over for a closer inspection when Tate took the opportunity and booted Donny in the ass, hard.

He fell forward, following the path of his phone, and yelped. "Fuck Tate! Get out!"

Tate stalked across the room and yanked his mountain bike off the wall where he'd installed a rack to hold it. Then, on his way out, he grabbed a heavier coat out of the closet, yanking it violently from the hanger, and put it on. He dragged his unopened, unpacked duffle across the floor. This time he hoped like hell it scratched up all that shiny dark tile.

Behind him Donny cried, dramatic sobs. Tate turned to see him still on the floor, but leaning against the wall, cradling his broken phone, as if it represented their broken relationship. Tate wasn't going to feel sorry for him. Not one fucking bit. In fact, he was pretty sure that when his adrenaline dropped, his jaw was going to hurt like hell and that thought pissed him off even more.

"I swear to God, Donny, if you fuck with my things, I'll really hurt you. I'll have someone come pick them up later and you better not fuck with me. Got it?" He emphasized his point with a finger in the air, aimed at Donny.

Donny mumbled his answer and it sounded a lot more like, "get the fuck out," than, "yes, Tate," but Tate did not care about that either. He pushed through the front door of their loft—Donny's loft—for probably the last time.

Once he wrangled his bike and his bag down the stairs, he pulled out his own phone to call for a cab. He couldn't haul all his shit across town, so he requested a vehicle that could accommodate his bike. He leaned against the black wrought iron railing that protected the stairs that lead to the basement apartment to wait.

After what seemed like forever, but was probably only twenty minutes, Donny slammed out the front door. "You still here?"

"Not for long."

"Good. Give me your key." He held out his hand.

"Not until I get the rest of my stuff."

"Oh, fuck no! Not after that scene, baby," he huffed. "I won't mess with your shit or keep it from you, but I'm not having you just come barging in whenever you want. You can call first. Key." He wiggled his fingers, expectantly.

Reluctantly, Tate pulled out his key ring and worked the key off of it. He honestly didn't think Donny would fuck with him. He was just mad, even though Tate had no clue what the hell Donny even had to mad about. They just needed to be over. That part was obvious, even if Tate hadn't wanted to admit it before the fight. He slammed the key in the palm of Donny's hand, hoping it hurt. "Don't make me regret this."

"Just don't be here when I get back."

Tate watched Donny walk away in those brown pants, clinging to his ass and thighs in all the right places, tailored just right. He could admit Donny had a fine ass...and he'd been right about one thing. They didn't belong together. They were from different worlds. Donny was high fashion and drama. Tate was down to earth and gritty. They'd done nothing but fight in their relationship. Often the makeup sex was the best part of the day, but seriously, it seemed like that had been the crux of their existence. They fought and made up and fought some more. Surely, love wasn't supposed to be like that, wasn't supposed to be so difficult. Davey and Tyler didn't act like that. Sure, they bickered now and then, but for the most part, they couldn't keep their hands off of each other. They looked at each other from across a room, as if it was killing them to be so far apart, as if more than a breath between their lips was too much. That's what Tate wanted. Someone that wanted him just like that.

Tate managed to find a decent hotel near the park for about two hundred bucks a night. He wasn't going to be able to stay in New York long at those rates, but he didn't know what else to do. It would work until he figured it out, though. He just needed somewhere to crash for a few nights.

Once he checked in and got up to his room, he stripped his clothes off and jumped in the shower. He turned the water hot enough to really steam up the bathroom and just let the tension go as it beat against his shoulders and back.

His jaw ached; he would need to put some ice on it. His ass hurt where he'd landed on his boots, too. He momentarily wished he'd also picked them up, but it hadn't been practical. He'd have to find someone to go get his stuff for him later. He didn't want to see the place again. He didn't want to see Donny again either, for that matter.

After his shower, he pulled on his new Under Armour jogging pants that were cuffed at the ankle, but loose around his hips and wandered down the hall for ice, then made his way back to his room. The hotel blanketed him with a hushed silence and smelled like Lysol and some fake scent that was probably supposed to make things feel fresh, but only covered the stale air with the acrid tinge of rubbing alcohol. Flopping down on the bed, he pressed the ice to his jaw and wondered just how he'd let himself get into this situation.

The only damned thing he regretted about the break up was that he'd sold his place when he'd moved in with Donny. That had been a colossal mistake. In fact, looking back on it, his entire relationship had been a colossal mistake. What had he been thinking, anyway? Donny hadn't ever been supportive or loving. The sex was hot, but after a while that wasn't even great and certainly not worth sticking around and putting up with Donny's bullshit drama-fest.

Tate stared up at the popcorn ceiling and thought about what Donny had said. Donny said New York was his home, but it really wasn't home to Tate. He hadn't had a real home in...a long damn time. No, he did have a home. Any dirt track was home. On the back of his bike was home.

He needed a plan.

He sat up and grabbed his cell phone. Only one person in the world would pick up every time he called, no matter what time of day or night, his manager, Mark Osgood, aka Oz. Not too many people in Tate's world could be counted on, could be trusted, but Oz could. Always.

Oz picked up quickly. "What's going on Tate?"

"How soon can you get me registered in a camp? I need to ride."

"Dude! Take a break already. Season just ended."

Tate didn't need or want a break from riding. He needed to get back on the track as soon as possible and going to one of the camps would mean he could put off looking for a place to live for a while longer. "I need you to get someone to get my shit from Donny's, too."

"Whoa, what?" His deep voice rumbled through Tate's head, feeling solid and comforting.

"We broke up."

Tate listened to the silence on the phone for a moment, not needing to fill it, just waiting.

Oz coughed. "Uh...that's probably a good thing. I never really liked him."

"Me either." Tate laughed, realizing how true the statement was. He wasn't brokenhearted at all over this shit. He didn't like Donny or how he'd been treated in their relationship. He'd only really liked how Donny looked, how classy he seemed, but he really wasn't that at all. "Listen, I'm cool, but I need to be on a track." *Need to get home.*

"Really, you're okay? Where are you?"

"Crappy hotel."

"Fine. I'm flying in. Text me where you're staying and I'll let you know when I'll be there."

"Oz," Tate groaned. "I don't need a babysitter." Tate knew that Oz managed a few other people besides him. He had teams on flat track, drag, and MotoGP for Morley-Stapelton Racing—the MSR team. MSR had their hands in almost all types of racing involving motors and wheels and some things that didn't have wheels. He'd heard they had race teams for speed boats, too. He couldn't monopolize Oz's time and he didn't really need to. "I just need to get my ass on a track. Seriously."

"I'll hook you up, T, but we're taking a meeting first." He hated it when Oz pulled out his pro-card and got bossy on him.

Tate liked to think he was in charge. In fact, looking back on his relationship with Donny, he figured that had been the biggest problem. Tate wanted to be in charge and so did Donny. Tate could never let Donny have complete control. He could only give in on unimportant bullshit that would save him the hassle of listening to Donny bitch, but Donny wasn't strong enough to control their relationship. Well, that was over.

"Fine," he answered curtly. He didn't have anything else to say. At least he had some kind of plan in motion.

"You want to go to that Moto Club in North Carolina or you want to try one down in Florida? We can hook you up with a private trainer."

"If you can get me in Moto that'd be cool. They have a great track. I don't need a trainer there for now. I know the routine." They both knew it was too early in the off-season to worry about trainers.

Oz grunted and they said their good byes. Tate texted his hotel information and put the ice back on his jaw.

Chapter 2 – July, Denver

Pilot tuned out the noise of banging weights, the soft chatter of conversation, and the low hum of treadmills in the gym around him and focused on his muscles, feeling them pull and flex. He slowly lifted the bar over his head, contracting his traps, pecs, and shoulders. He didn't fully extend his arms before he slowly brought the weights down, tightening his muscles to get the most out of the move. He ignored the sweat on his brow and the pull along his oblique muscles that stretched under his faded Go Army tank.

Then he saw his best friend, Johnny, walk into the gym. He let the weights clang as he eased them all the way down and grabbed his towel. He wiped his face and pushed the sweaty hair off his brow. "Johnny! Man, what's up?" he blurted out, a little loud so Johnny could hear him.

Johnny raised his hand as he walked over. "Hey, man. How's it going?" He was dressed in a pair of baggy sweat pants and an old t-shirt with a faded logo of a big green TSS over a trident for Trident Security Services, Johnny's Uncle's security company, on it. Pilot could guess he had running shorts under the sweatpants; he usually did when he hit the treadmill or ran in the park, ready to strip down when he got too hot.

"Good. You going to work out with me?"

Johnny rolled his eyes. "I'm going to work out. But, I'm not lifting with you, oh king of the gym rats."

Pilot laughed. He had to; Johnny wasn't far from the truth. "It's not going to make you pump up like this." He flexed his arm showing off his guns.

"Yeah, I know. That's why I'm not doing it." He winked at Pilot and turned to head toward the treadmills like he always did, but then he stopped. His shaggy hair brushed across the top of his glasses, as he turned back to face Pilot. "Hey, Uncle Gary wants you to call him."

"What?" Pilot reached over for his phone sitting with his water bottle next to the equipment. He flipped it on and watched as the lights flash on the screen.

"You don't have to call now. It's not urgent."

Pilot looked up at his friend. They'd known each other so long that Pilot couldn't remember them not knowing each other. Johnny might as well be his brother and Uncle Gary was like a father to him and had supported him in a lot of ways, particularly with his job. Johnny and Gary were the two most important people in his life. So, when he said jump, Pilot jumped. He owed the man so much more than that. "I'll call him now. Could be important."

"At least take your gym rat ass out of here, Sean," Johnny said, thumbing toward the front door.

"Yeah. Whatever." Pilot hated it when Johnny called him by his given name. He was the only person who did, or could get away with it. Sometime after basic training, he'd become Pilot, trading in Sean Mahan for good. He wasn't going to get into all that with Johnny in the middle of the gym, though. He flipped through his contacts and took a long drink from his water bottle and headed outside.

He found Uncle Gary's number and tapped his screen just as he walked through the front doors. The heat of a typical Colorado July swamped him, and he yanked the legs of his sweats up to his knees, exposing his calves, hoping to cool down some.

"Trident, Gary Killebrew."

"Hey Uncle, it's Pilot." He leaned against the cement block wall that stretched out along the sidewalk.

Gary chuckled. "Hey, hey man. Guess Johnny caught up to you?"

"Yeah, he said you needed me to call."

"Didn't mean drop everything. It's not urgent. I would have called you if it was urgent."

Pilot shrugged it off. "So? What's up?"

"I know you just got back, but the folks from Apex called and they want you to do the Supercross route again next season."

"Wow. That's great." He loved working with the Supercross guys, and they'd given him a nice bonus at the end of this past season, too, which only made him like them more. Johnny invested that money, since he was the accountant. It'd go a long way toward their goals. "That was a decent gig."

"Doesn't start till January."

"January through May, right?"

"Right. So, come on in Monday and we'll get you set up on a plan to keep you busy for the next few months. Gotta keep a guy like you busy."

"What's that mean?"

"Keep you out of trouble and all that."

"Sheesh. I'm no trouble." Pilot guffawed, though he didn't really take

11

offense to Uncle Gary's teasing.

"Yeah, yeah. Now get back to the gym."

"How'd you know I'm at the gym?"

Pilot could hear real laughter. His Uncle was always cutting up with him, teasing him, and Pilot loved it. "You're always at the gym, Sean." Well, maybe there were two people that could get away with calling him Sean.

"Right. I could be lifting a few pounds instead of taking this shit from you," he joked.

"Yeah, yeah. Get out of here!"

"Later, Uncle G."

His uncle grunted and hung up. That was typical. Pilot was happy about the call and not just for the lighthearted teasing. The Supercross job with Apex would be bank, plus he'd loved working with Davey and Tyler the past season. He'd gotten along well with them and he'd even been invited to their wedding. It would be a great job working the whole season. The traveling that long would wear him down, but he had nothing or no one special to stay home for.

Chapter 3 – South Carolina

Bryce tore into the dirt around the turn on the practice track. He laid on the throttle hard and flew over the next jump, taking massive air. His coach probably wouldn't like that since he was supposed to be practicing taking the jumps low and fast, but he couldn't help it. In that moment, Bryce wasn't riding for practice or time, he rode for the joy of it. Dirt flew out behind him as he roosted through the softer spots. It was as if even the track felt his delight.

His bike thrummed happily between his legs as he slowed, back at the start of the track, where his coach Reuben, flagged him down. "What the hell, Bryce? What was that?"

He pulled his goggles off and slung them over the handle bar. "That was major air, dude." He couldn't help the stupid grin stretched across his face.

"Not funny."

"I know, but I've been at it for hours and just needed to cut loose. Relax. Want me to go 'round one more time?"

Reuben put his hands on his hips and gave Bryce a stern look, but then he shook his head. "No. That's fine. We'll get this at the camp. You *are* going to the camp, right?"

"Of course." Bryce knew he was going to the camp in North Carolina where his team wanted him to start practicing. What he didn't know was whether his parents would be tagging along. If he could help it, the answer would be no. He knew the team would be flexible and accommodate them, but Bryce didn't really want them there.

"Fine. Get out of here and we'll see you at camp."

Bryce tossed his cell phone on his dresser. His manager, George, said he had all the approvals ready, now he just had to get his parents to let him go. Alone. He ran his fingers through his dark hair contemplating what he would say and imagining all the different scenarios of how the conversation would go. If only he were eighteen already...

He groaned and forced himself to get up and get on with it. He paused at the door to pull off his favorite hooded pajama top. He often wore it for comfort and he loved the tiger ears sewn on the hood. The soft and cozy pjs always made him feel better, but he'd look like a kid wearing them. He needed to look mature, so he tossed it on his bed and ran his fingers through his hair again, pushing that purple lock out of his eyes and tucking it behind his ear.

"Mom? Dad? Can we talk?" Bryce made his way to the living room where they were settled in to watch some program before bed. Bryce rarely watched TV with them anymore. He had a million other things to do, and would rather sit in his room with his ear buds in, listening to music and imagining his next ride, than waste a minute on a stupid sitcom.

"What's going on Bryce?" his dad asked, turning the volume on the TV down with the remote.

"Uh...So, I just got off the phone with George."

"It's not time yet. You still have a few weeks before you have to be seriously practicing, don't you?" His mother looked over at him. He got his blue eyes from her.

They didn't understand how much more intense the Supercross 250 was going to be for him than the other divisions he'd raced in. "No. Not really. Not anymore. Moving up to Supercross means I need to stay on top of my skills. He wants me with Reuben as soon as possible and I can do that easier at the camp. He has me set up already." His parents didn't respond. His mom sat there, lips pressed together tightly. His dad's forehead wrinkled with his frown. "On Monday. He's arranging everything, but I'll need to bring my bike. Just for the first week or so, until they get my new one out to me."

"Can't you just wait for the new one? We hardly get to see you—"

"You hardly see me when I am home." He shrugged. He'd finished school, taken the tests and passed everything. She had home schooled him the last couple of years so he could spend more time racing and now he finally got the tap to move up that he'd been waiting for. He signed to a Supercross team. His life was dirt bikes.

"Bryce," his dad started in with a grumble. "This is probably your last year at home and once the season starts? Isn't the local track good enough? We just want to spend time with you first."

"I know. I get that. But, I'll always be your son, but I need to do this now. I need to be at my best. That means no distractions. Supercross isn't going to wait for me. I have to grab it. Don't you get it?"

"Okay." His mom always seemed to cave first. "When do we have to be there?"

"I don't need you to come with me. I can drive the pickup."

"What?" His dad crossed his arms over his chest. "Isn't this the camp in North Carolina? We can stay in town."

George had actually promised he could get them in a private cabin on camp grounds, but Bryce didn't want that. He didn't want them there at all. "Listen. This is hard core training. Working out, riding. They have a cafeteria and staff—"

"You're not ready."

"Mom. Really? I'm almost eighteen. Plus, if you're worried about me getting into trouble, don't. Everyone there is all about racing and training. They're just as...uh, I don't know, single minded? Yeah. One focus. Plus the staff is capable and—"

His dad stood up. "You're not eighteen yet. You've been sheltered from a lot, being home these last few years. I don't know."

Bryce huffed and sat down in the recliner. He wanted to yell and stomp his foot, but a tantrum wouldn't get him what he wanted. "This is important."

"We'll think about it." Usually, when his mom said that, he'd get his way. He tried not to look too happy. They still hadn't said yes, officially. Yet.

Bryce had his bike loaded and strapped down the night before, so when he got up at five in the morning, he started his day with jumping jacks, pushups and sit ups to get his blood pumping. Then, made a couple of breakfast burritos with egg, leftover chicken breast, and chilies and ate them on the way to the track. He hoped like hell his folks would finally give in and let him go to camp without them, but all those thoughts were shoved away when he arrived at his local track.

Bryce had been coming to this track his entire life. His cousin had first got him into bikes when he was five years old. He had been the only kindergarten kid at school that rode a little mini motos bike on the weekends. He moved up to an 80cc bike before he turned eight. By the time he was in middle school, he was riding five days a week. His folks realized he had talent and let him keep riding, even after his cousin had sold his own bike and moved on to other things, namely girls. Bryce had no interest in chasing after girls, though. He kept racing—and winning.

He got his bike on the track and took a few practice laps. It felt good to ride without the pressure of Reuben watching him. He needed to relax and enjoy this moment, knowing there wouldn't be too many more of them. Once he got to camp, it would be hardcore practice time and *getting it right*.

After a while Bryce's arms ached, so he stopped before they started shaking. He'd spent more time on the track than he realized, so he started packing it up for the day. After he had the bike loaded back on the truck, he checked his phone. His mother had sent a text for him to meet her for a late lunch in town. It would be on the way home, and he would have just enough time to make it there. He knew he was in for a grilling, but if he wanted to go to camp without her, he'd have to face it.

It'd been a great day riding and he didn't want to blow his mood thinking about it all, so when he got in the truck to leave, he connected his MP3 player and cranked up the volume. His playlist rocked hard. He loved bands that mixed a killer horn section with electric guitars and hard percussion. He flipped through his list until NOFX came on. The song focused more on percussion and horns and the lyrics felt appropriate for his funky mood. Nodding his head to the beat, he mouthed the words.

He drove into town and parked at his mother's favorite diner. Bryce liked the place too, because he could get good healthy food, stuff that wasn't fried, yet served up pretty fast. He made sure to park his truck in the front, as close as he could get to the restaurant, so he could watch it out of the big windows. He didn't want anyone messing with his bike. He looked forward to tinkering around on it when he got home, to tune it up a bit.

When Bryce walked into the restaurant, he spotted his mother in a booth next to the windows where he could see the parking lot. "Mom. Hey!"

"Go get cleaned up. You're filthy."

Bryce frowned, but headed to the restroom just the same. When he looked in the mirror, he saw she'd been right. Dirt smeared over his face and cheeks, hiding his freckles. He washed up and then lingered a minute, looking in the mirror. What did people see when they looked at him with his big blue eyes and purple streaked hair? He wanted another piercing to go with his gauges…eyebrow maybe, but that wouldn't be practical with motocross, and nothing in his life was more important than riding.

The diner wasn't one of those old fashioned places that served burgers, fries, and milkshakes. It seemed a bit more modern, and although it wasn't a Panera Bread, either, it did have decent food. The decor was simple, clean, and functional. He passed beige tiled floors, light brown tables and chairs, and Warhol style prints of various menu options on the walls.

He sat down across from his mother and took a glance at his truck.

"I'm watching it, Bryce. Everything's fine. Oh, I ordered you grilled chicken and salad."

"Dressing on the side?"

She huffed and clasped her hands together on the table. "Of course."

"Thanks."

"I do get it, Bryce."

"I know, Mom. I'm not trying to be mean about this, about any of it. I just want to find my own way. I'm not a kid anymore." He took a sip out of the glass of water sitting in front of him. Cool and refreshing. He wished his life could feel like that.

His mom sighed. "I know that too. It's not always easy. You haven't had a…normal childhood."

"What's normal?"

"You know what I mean."

"I guess." Bryce shrugged. He did know what she meant. He'd given up public school, dances, and pretty much having friends to ride motocross. He home schooled and he rode bikes and he worked out. He didn't have time for anything else or any one, but he didn't care. He probably would have missed out on a lot of that stuff anyway. He wouldn't have had dances and friends, because he was gay. So, he missed out on drama and being bullied. That shit had started before he left school and he didn't miss it. On the track, the only thing anyone cared about was how good you rode, how fast your bike was, or how much air you got on that last jump. Giving up high school for motocross was more than worth it. "I don't think I really missed out on all that much."

"Maybe, but we can't go back anyway. I just want to make sure you're good. Safe. Going forward."

"You can talk to George. Ask him what it's like at camp."

The waitress showed up with their food. The salad looked fresh and he could see the grill marks on the chicken. He dabbed on just a little dressing. His mom had the same thing, but her salad had been smothered in delicious honey mustard dressing. Bryce knew it would be good, but stuck to his own vinaigrette, used sparingly. He didn't need the extra calories. The waitress left, satisfied that they had what they needed and Bryce dug in. "I'm so hungry. I probably should order an extra chicken breast."

"You can. Want me to call her back?"

"Nah. It's good." He shoveled in another bite and chewed.

His mother hadn't started eating. "So, Bryce. I don't need talk to George. Your dad and I agree that you're mature enough to handle camp on your own."

Bryce looked up quick. It wasn't what he had expected her to say. He thought he'd have to fight harder for it. Maybe they were coming around after all.

"But. You will call and check in with us and if things aren't going well, you will let us know. Plus, we're coming up on the weekends, just to make sure you're okay."

He didn't really want them checking up on him, but he knew he needed to make a compromise. "Okay. I can live with that. I need to bring the bike, just for the first week or two."

His mother sighed again. "Your dad is going to want to drive up with you, then."

Bryce could see her jaw clenching. She thought he was going to fight her on that, but he wasn't really ready to drive that far by himself and he knew it, so giving in on that demand wasn't so hard. Besides, Bryce wanted to surprise her too. "Good."

"Good?"

Bryce nodded and gave her a small smile. His mom smiled back and picked up her fork. Finding his independence would be a challenge, but he was happy they were willing to compromise with him.

Chapter 4 - New York

Tate sat down hard in the seat across the table from his manager. They didn't venture far, choosing the cafe just down the street from the hotel. As always, Oz had dressed impeccably, suave and cool with his ever present fedora and silk tie tucked into a gray vest. His suit was probably Versace or some other just as famous designer. He sure as hell didn't look like a motor sports manger. When he'd said that in the past, Oz gave him a sideways look and reminded him that he managed people not sports. Just a coincidence that the people he managed all happened to be pro-racers. Regardless, he was the classiest man Tate knew, even when he took off his hat and showed his bald head, shiny and brown like an acorn.

"Tate, my man. You don't look so good."

"Did you get me in?"

Oz poured Tate some coffee out of the carafe the wait staff had left on the table. That was one of the best parts of the cafe. Endless coffee. "Thanks man," Tate muttered, looking up at Oz with questioning eyes.

"Yes, yes. You're in. You leave in two days. That fast enough for you?"

Tate gave him his wicked smile with only one side of his mouth turned up. "No."

"Shut it, kid," Oz shot back.

"Seriously, though. Thanks, man. I really need to be on the track right now."

Oz gave him a grunt then asked, "So, what happened with Donny?"

Tate didn't want to talk about it. Donny was just the last mistake in a long line of them. "I need someone to go with me to get the rest of my stuff and get it into storage."

"Yeah, you said that." Oz shifted his focus to the pastry in front of him, leaving his words hanging in the air between them. Tate waited. He was pretty sure Oz had more to say. When he was good and ready. After chewing a bite and swallowing, his dark eyes traveled across the table and met Tate's gaze. "It's hit social media. In that short time since you called me, there's been a huge buzz. Have you seen it?"

Tate shook his head. He had disconnected and let himself wallow in self-pity for the past day or two. "It hasn't been that long."

"Long enough."

"So? What's he saying? Am I going to lose sponsors?"

Oz shook his head as he wiped his hands on the linen napkin, then tossed it on the table. "No, no. Nothing like that. There's a big difference between this here and what happened with McAllister. We've done some damage control." He waived his hand in the air, as if the news were nothing.

Tate lifted his eyebrows. Davey McAllister and his boyfriend at the time, Tyler Whitmore, had been outed with a picture of them getting it on in an alley outside a bar during last season. They turned Supercross on its head and managed to gain hate-fan stalkers. Donny bitching about him all over social media could only be a close second to what had happened to them. "What's the fall out then? That bastard." He wondered if getting his stuff back would turn into another fiasco.

Oz sighed and picked up his coffee cup. It looked like tiny toy china, like his cousins used to play with, in his big paws, but he sipped at it daintily. Oz was an enigma, a mass of contradictions. The big black man was so muscular, it almost seemed as if his muscles were growing on top of other muscles. He looked like a brute when he worked out, sweat dripping off his bald head, ready to take on Tyson, but sitting across from him at a fancy cafe table, dressed to the nines, and sipping coffee with his pinkie out, he was gentle, caring. He let that soft caramel center show, and it was exactly that soft center, and his competent management style that made Tate enjoy working with him. Oz meant more to him than just a manager, more than a friend. Oz had taken care of Tate when he had nothing and no one else in the world.

With lowered brows and a slight scowl, Oz finally answered. "All we have here is an asshole saying you dumped him. No pictures, no evidence. Just a ton of speculation and that'll blow over, so let them speculate."

"Okay, so he's lying? Sort of. That's normal relationship perspective bull shit. So, why the damage control?"

Oz set his cup down. "He said you hit him. That we disputed."

"Fuck no. The bastard hit me." Tate wanted to take Donny's head off. "That's why I want someone with me to pick up my shit."

"Drink your coffee, Tate." Oz motioned with his eyebrows. "Don't let it get cold."

"Forget the coffee. What—"

"No, nothing. We're not going to address this *picking up your shit*," he mocked, but Tate knew he did really care, and that's what made the difference. "How's your jaw, Tate?"

"Hurts. Bruised, but I'm fine. You can't even tell it's bruised with this." Tate scratched at his two day growth of beard, coming in darker than the hair on his head and tinted with just a hint of red. "I'm fine. Physically."

"Good. We'll go get your stuff so we don't have any more issues. Don't reply or respond to anything about this on social media. Just go ride your ass off at the track. You have a few weeks or so and then we'll send a trainer to join you at the camp. We're working on lining up a new guy for you."

"Okay." Tate exhaled long and slow. This wasn't going to touch his career and he'd have free time on the track to get his head straight before dealing with his new trainer. That's what really mattered.

"Don't worry. Even if this was more of an outing, Supercross folks already got their gay-feet wet. McAllister did you a favor."

"I've never been in the closet. But, yeah...Davey hadn't meant for all that to happen, though."

"Well, what did he expect? Fooling around with a competitor's mechanic. Bound to blow up. I'm just amazed at how his team handled it all. He really bounced back."

"Well...you know his attitude...he's all about *win the championship and fuck the rest!* No way would he *not* bounce back, man." Tate could acknowledge that oversimplification, at least to himself, but it didn't change anything.

Oz chuckled. "You'll get your shot, Tate. Be patient."

Intellectually, Tate understood the situation. He'd only raced in the elite 450 event for two seasons. With Davey and Chad Regal dominating the field, he'd be lucky to pull third place this next season. It would be Davey's last season, maybe Chad's too, so the following year, Tate would be in line for the championship, if he kept up. Winning the championship in his fourth year would be an accomplishment. His team didn't expect him to win until his fifth year. In his heart, he wanted to win every race, every time, and he wanted the championship *this* year. He'd train and push like he was going to win, regardless of expectations.

"Tate. I see that look on your face. Relax. No pressure."

Tate laughed, but there was no humor in it. "There's always pressure, Oz. Always."

21

Chapter 5 - Denver

Pilot lived on the northwest side of town, inside of the main metro area of Denver. When he wanted to go out for the night, it always involved picking Johnny up and driving to the Jefferson County station and taking the bus into town. Johnny came down the driveway wearing painted on skinny jeans in black and a ripped up t-shirt. His hair had been styled in a purposeful mess that flopped over one eye and made him look younger than he was, especially since he'd ditched his hipster glasses.

When he got in Pilot's old Mustang, he had to pull hard to slam the door and he cussed under his breath.

Pilot chuckled softly. "You trying to get laid tonight?"

"Shut up. Just want to look good. That a crime?" Johnny snarled back.

Pilot put the car in gear and it roared as he accelerated away from the curb. "You've sure been cranky lately."

"I *need* to get laid. Doubt that's happening tonight, but it's been too long." Johnny gripped the *oh shit* handle as Pilot took a curb a bit too fast. "Fuck, but there are no decent gay men here."

Pilot couldn't help smiling at his friend. He knew Johnny was right on one level, but he also knew Johnny had been working too many hours trying to get their dream going to even look for a decent man. He also knew Johnny wasn't interested in starting a relationship with any of the men he would find in Denver. It wasn't an ideal situation. He wanted the best for his friend, his brother, and he was in the same situation, but they had to keep the right attitude about it all.

He parked at the station and they waited for the bus into the city without much conversation. Johnny kept rubbing his arms like he was cold, but in July, it wasn't cold at all. He fidgeted around until they were settled on the bus. "What's wrong with you, J-man?"

"Oh, fuck off, Sean. Don't call me that stupid junior high nick name."

"Don't call me Sean, then." There wasn't any heat behind his words.

This was the same old tease they always went through, just following the motions. It started when he came home after his discharge. Pilot had no desire to answer to his given name. Why should he when his parents weren't ever going to call him and his siblings were shit? Even if that strain had loosened over the years, he still didn't much care for the name or anything that too closely attached him to his given family. "Seriously, John. What's going on with you?"

Johnny sucked in a long deep breath and released it just as slowly. "I'm just lonely and over worked." He rubbed at his arms again. "And no pockets or anywhere to tuck my hands." He laughed as he realized what he'd been doing.

"'S'allright, Johnny, but you do know you can talk to me. Right?"

"Right. Always." Johnny smiled, obviously trying to reassure Pilot that everything was fine, but the smile didn't reach his eyes and a real knot of concern for his friend twisted itself around in his gut.

After a brief silence between them, Johnny finally confessed. "So, your asshole brother showed up at work this morning."

"What? What the hell?"

"Yep. He demanded I do his taxes for him. Figure out his big fucking cluster fuck of a mess. At a discounted rate, no less. Then he dropped a three inch thick folder of bullshit on my desk."

"I'll kick his ass. He's not doing that to you. Don't worry about it." Pilot's gruff words were probably meaner than the situation called for, but they both knew there was more to it than just trying to get nepotistic favors.

"You know he's not going to let up until I do it."

"If you do it, you're charging him extra. He's taking advantage."

"Soooo...you want me to do them?"

Pilot thought about the situation. He didn't want Johnny inconvenienced, but his brother could be a total dick. He didn't really want to deal with it at all, despite his earlier outburst. If he had to kick Colin's ass, it would get really ugly with his family, and they'd just started acting like a family again. His sister and his mother seemed to finally accept him, but he didn't want to push his luck. He hung his head and bit at his lip, trying to decide what to say.

Johnny snapped at him, "What the hell? Are you afraid he's going to go rub your gayness in your parent's face if you don't do what he wants? You going to let him hold you hostage over it?" Johnny, as usual, knew exactly what he'd been thinking.

"Damn, Johnny. Seriously. It's not—"

"It is."

"Fine. But, you know...fuck it! I'll pay the difference. Just do his damn taxes," Pilot grumbled, resolved to find a more diplomatic way out of the situation. Colin was just as big as Pilot and worked out just as much, even if he didn't really know how to use that muscle. He was a mechanic with a string of brokenhearted women behind him. He was determined to sleep his way through Denver, the miserable bastard. He never had anything to do with Pilot, but he'd harass Johnny any time he could, as if he blamed Johnny for Pilot being gay, for joining the military, for coming back a changed man, or for being so entrenched in Uncle Gary's security company. None of it had anything to do with Johnny, except maybe the security company. That was their dream, together, to buy out their parts of the company from Gary. It was Johnny's legacy and one both Killebrews had generously let Pilot share when his own family had turned on him.

Well, just fuck Collin. He'd have to get his sister involved. She was the only one with sense and she'd come down hard on the asshole.

"No. That's not fine." Johnny muttered. "At all. Sean, damn it. I'll do the taxes, but he's paying fucking extra."

"Okay."

They got off the bus and walked the two blocks up to the club, Trip Chill, in silence. When they got to the door, Johnny started grumbling. "Why do we always come here? I hate Trip Chill. Can't we go to the Apollo? Just once, for Christ's sake?"

"Stop bitching. Give me an hour or two, then we'll go to the Apollo."

Johnny's eyes narrowed as he stared at Pilot. He knew damn well what Pilot was up to, but he wasn't going to say anything, and Pilot was glad of that. He didn't want to argue with Johnny, but he needed to see a few people at Trip Chill. He knew the club was trashy. He knew Johnny preferred the classier Apollo, but he'd have to wait. Pilot had needs.

Once they got inside and parked their asses at a high top table near the rear of the bar, Johnny relaxed a bit and slid out on the dance floor. Pilot watched him. This was the regular MO—Pilot staked the table, Johnny danced, and drinks flowed. He ordered two rum and cokes and sipped on his own, watching Johnny gyrate against some taller guy wearing purple pants and a silver vest. It showed off two full sleeves of colorful tatts over bulging biceps. Not Pilot's type at all, but Johnny seemed to go for the bad boys. Purple pants had earrings in one ear that dangled down and swung against his cheek as he moved on the floor. He was certainly Johnny's type, which worried that knot in his gut just a little more. He sipped his drink, trying not to be too concerned.

Soon enough, the reason for his visit to the tawdry club sauntered up to his table. "Pilot!" he called out over the music and stuck his fist out. Pilot bumped his own fist against it and nodded for the guy to stay. Pilot didn't know his real name and he didn't care. Everyone he knew called him Booker for good reason.

"Got anything?" Pilot asked loudly, leaning into Booker so the man would hear him over the pounding bass.

Booker nodded, his dark unruly rat's nest flopping around his head. His hair was a mess because he probably never brushed it; it was nothing like Johnny's styled chaos. Booker's eyes were practically black and glistened with possibility as he met and kept Pilot's gaze while simultaneously digging his wallet out of his back pocket. His jeans looked like they were crusted over and able to walk away from the table on their own, they were so dirty.

Finally breaking eye contact to look at his back pocket, Booker pulled out a card and slid it over to Pilot across the table. He held up two fingers. Pilot knew that meant he had two spots open.

The white card had a phone number on one side, printed in standard type. The other side was a handwritten date and time with an address below it. Pilot nodded and tucked the card in his own back pocket.

"Good to see you, as always," Booker barked out, tipped a two finger salute, and then left.

Pilot exhaled letting out anxiety along with his breath. He couldn't stand Booker, the slob, but he was the best way to get what Pilot wanted. With that part done, he tossed back his drink and let his eyes search the dance floor.

The fight he set up was for Saturday night, so he'd have a week to train. He'd be living in the gym for the next seven days, but he would be ready. The payoff would go into funding their dream, but it wasn't the money that had him making arrangements with scum like Booker. Nope, it was the fight, the thrill, the adrenaline. Nothing in the world matched up to punching some asshole in the face.

"Speaking of assholes," he grumbled to himself, as he saw some dick harassing Johnny on the dance floor. The guy had his hands on Johnny, around his arm, and he pulled him like he was trying to get Johnny to go with him, but Johnny had other ideas. He shook his head and tried to pull away. Pilot wasn't going to have that shit. Why did assholes think any slim dude on the floor wanted to get fucked in the bathroom? Johnny just wanted to dance and maybe meet a few new people. He didn't want to hump every guy grinding on him.

Pilot stood up and took a long drink out of Johnny's untouched glass, then marched out to the floor before his friend got dragged off. He grabbed the guy's wrist and shook it a little. "Let go!" he roared at the guy. This guy was almost as big as Pilot. He wore cowboy boots with faded jeans and a Florida Georgia Line t-shirt with their name and motto scripted in a circle in fancy writing. Pilot didn't care. He looked into the guy's face. He had a scruffy beard and a mustache and an incredulous look on his face like he was used to getting his way and had no idea why Pilot would be interrupting him.

"Mine," the cowboy mouthed, gripping Johnny's arm harder, making him squeak.

Pilot shook his head and yanked Johnny back, inserting himself between them. "Fuck off, dude. He doesn't want to go with you."

The guy let go and took a step backwards. He held his hands up in front of him in a peace offering, like he didn't want trouble. His face softened and he seemed to be saying it was a misunderstanding with his body language.

Pilot gave him a curt nod, content to let him walk away. He started to turn to Johnny when the guy yelled, "Hey!"

Pilot flinched back and the asshole cowboy took a swing; his knuckles clipped against Pilot's jaw. Pilot rolled with the punch. He took a step, re-balancing, and then swung back. His punch hit the guy's face, full force. Johnny hollered out something unintelligible and grabbed Pilot's shoulder. The cowboy hit the floor. Pilot kicked out at his prone body. "Asshole!" Even wearing a pair of L.L. Bean loafers, Pilot could do some serious damage. His legs were no joke, either, bulging in his Levi's.

Johnny tugged at his bomber jacket. "Come on."

He turned to leave with Johnny, but they weren't fast enough. He pushed right up against the bouncer, and this guy was bigger than Pilot. That was rare. Broady was the only guy he knew that came close to intimidating Pilot with his size, but they were partners and worked together. This bouncer was a different story with his face mashed into a scowl that screamed out his desire to crush something. Either that or he wore his underwear too tight.

The guy grabbed Pilot by the shoulders. "Out. Now," he growled into Pilot's ear. He could have fought the guy, could have made a bigger scene, but the music had stopped and most everyone had vacated the dance floor, choosing to stand around it staring and waiting for more entertainment. Nope. Pilot wasn't going to give it to them.

A second bouncer had his hand on Johnny's back, gently guiding him out of the club beside Pilot and his own bouncer. "It's cool. I'm gone." He let them be escorted to the front of the club and out the glass doors without a fight. Possibly getting arrested wasn't worth it and Pilot had accomplished his task anyway.

Out on the street, Johnny shoved his brown and blond highlights out of his angry face. He wore his contacts so Pilot could really see his expressive eyes, and his thin lips pressed into a frown that dragged his cheeks down. The center of his face was wide with his eyes set kind of far apart with high, sharp cheek bones, and a long, strong jaw. "Can we go to the Apollo now? I wasn't done."

"Done?"

"Dancing. You fucker. Why do you have to pull shit like that?" He started marching off, not giving Pilot a chance to answer. "Did you book a fight? I saw you talking to that dirty fucker."

Pilot didn't answer, just grunted and followed after Johnny.

Johnny kept moving, kept talking. "At least you didn't have your gun."

Pilot lifted the tail of his button down shirt and flashed the butt of his gun. "I'm always armed." He had his .38 Ruger LCR, or lightweight concealed revolver, in his tuckable holster on his front right hip. In social situations, it was almost never needed, but he'd never go anywhere unprotected. After four years in the service and a good hard year working for Uncle Gary, he knew better.

"I should have known," Johnny said with a sly smile. "I'd felt your back earlier and you'd never have gotten in the club with one at your back."

Pilot winked at him. Not too many people carried in the front, but Pilot had practiced this and knew what he could get away with in most situations. "I know what I'm doing J-man." He was licensed to carry concealed, but clubs don't allow guns there and Pilot couldn't blame them.

"Oh, don't even fucking call me that." Johnny flipped him off and marched off. "Fuck the club. Let's get milkshakes and just hang out."

"You okay?"

"Yeah. I, uh, don't feel like dancing any more. That's all. Come on."

They made it back to their side of the city early, and after dropping Johnny off, Pilot called his sister. He put her on speaker phone when she answered. "Hey, sis. You up?"

"No, jackass. I had to answer the damn phone anyway. What the hell do you want at this—. Shit, it's two in the morning, Sean."

"Pilot."

"What-the-fuck-ever. At two a.m., I'll call you whatever the hell I want." She sounded sleepy and grumpy, but he could also hear the affection she had for him. It was nice to hear that from family again, even when she was bitching him out.

"Okay. So, uh, can you call Colin and get him to back off of Johnny?"

Sheila groaned. "That couldn't wait until a reasonable hour? He's always fucking with Johnny."

"He showed up at his work demanding discounted services."

Sheila laughed like she couldn't believe what Pilot had just said. "Wh- What? Fuck! What kind of service?" Pilot could tell she was holding back some smart ass comment. His sister was a no-nonsense, foul mouthed, hard assed, bitch, and he loved her beyond reason. He could live without the other assholes in his family, especially Colin, but not her. Pilot could bet his entire savings that getting his family to come around to accepting him had been all Shelia's doing, one hundred percent of it.

"Sis. I'm serious. He can't keep doing this and if I have to deal with it, I'm just going to shoot the fucker."

"Okay, okay," she sighed. "I'll take care of it. I suppose he wants help with his business mess?"

"Yes, but instead of asking nice, he just barges in. Demands. At a discount. And I know for a fact his mess is worth extra if Johnny sorts him out. Colin can't even keep his shit straight. I'm surprised that dive hasn't closed yet." His brother Colin owned a small, very small, auto shop. He had good people working for him, though and he paid those people well and never fell behind on his suppliers, but outside of that, he was a mess. If his staff didn't carry more than their share, he would have gone under years ago. It wasn't Pilot's place to judge, though. At least his brother had a somewhat successful business and really, he wouldn't mind Johnny helping him, but only the right way.

"Fine. I'll talk to him and get him to apologize. We done?"

"Yeah."

"Okay, love you baby-boy." She hung up before he could answer, but he didn't blame her. Sheila knew he loved her. He didn't need to say it. Sheila was the only one of his family that didn't change toward him when he came out. She took it in stride, like she'd known all along, and she probably had. She was ten years older than him, and had been his primary caregiver as a child. Hell, his parents had never really been there for him *before* he came out, so it didn't surprise him that they weren't there since. He went a long time without speaking to them since that day and had only started those conversations back up recently. Thanks to Sheila.

He pulled into his dark driveway and cringed. Johnny's parents hadn't been much better. In fact, worse, they assumed that he and Johnny were boyfriends. *Ugh! Nightmare.* They were too much like brothers for anything romantic to ever happen. At least Johnny had his uncle, and well, Pilot did, too. That thought made him smile as he went into his lonely, empty little house.

Chapter 6 – August, Moto Club, North Carolina

"It's really important for you to train on a different track, Bryce. This will give you some time with different dirt and different configurations." Reuben waved his hands around. He always talked with his hands. Bryce was learning that the gestures sometimes meant as much as the words, though.

"Okay. So, what's the plan?"

"Today, it's just getting a feel for the track. Don't push too hard. Take a few easy laps first."

"I did that yesterday when I got here."

"Do it again." Reuben's hand fisted on his hips. That meant he was serious.

Bryce gave him a nod and pulled his goggles over his helmet. "Anything else, boss?"

"Don't be a smartass. Go." He pointed to the track, so Bryce went.

He took two laps at a moderate pace before Reuben called him over. He glided over and hit the kill switch. "Can I go faster now?"

"Listen up, East Coast."

Bryce practically groaned at the nickname his manager, George, had given him, but he didn't want Reuben to think he didn't want to listen, so he sucked it up. "Yes, coach?"

"Stepping up your game and taking your ride to the next level is about getting out of your comfort zone. It's setting your goals and taking things one step at a time."

"Okay?"

Reuben pointed at the track. "You've been around this thing a few times now. It's comfortable. But, the next time you're on this track, it might be different. You have to react quickly to the obstacles. Don't think about the layout, just react and move in time with it."

"Yes, coach."

He pointed to the other side of the camp. "We're going to go get on a different track now."

"The 450 track?"

"It's not about the size of the bike, Bryce. But, yeah. We're going over there and you're going to open it up on a different track. So, you can react to it. You've not been on that one yet, right?"

"No, sir. I haven't."

"Okay. Let's go. I have it booked for about an hour, but then I want you to ride during open track time. This is about reacting. Got it?"

"Uh. I think."

Bryce pushed his bike along beside Reuben, as they made their way to the other track. Once they got there, Reuben grabbed the handle bars. "Walk the track. Look for the ruts and soft spots." He gestured with his hand in the air. "Take your time, but not too much time. Again, I want to see your reactions."

After a walk around the track noting the obstacles, Bryce slung his leg back over the bike and pulled his goggles on.

"Treat it like a race. Go." Reuben flicked his fingers.

Bryce took off.

He opened it up for the first time, pushing on the throttle, but it didn't take long before he found himself slowing down. He had gotten comfortable with the first track. This one had a different feel, a different set up. He loped through the whoops section, trying to keep the bike as straight as possible, thinking more about form than speed. He always had a difficult time getting through the whoops with the small mounds close together. He leaned back and up shifted, and got through them, decent enough, but had no time to congratulate himself, because the track turned sharp ahead and the dirt had many deep ruts.

Bryce picked his way through the more difficult areas and opened up when he could, but still didn't like his time through the first two laps. The third time around, he stayed on the throttle, determined to pick up speed. He pushed too hard and nearly wiped out around the turn with the deep ruts. It didn't surprise him to see Reuben waving him over.

"If there had been others on the track, that could have gotten you wrecked or hurt. Don't worry about speed. Just react to the track."

After a few more laps, other started joining him on the track, and the challenge increased. With others so close, some passing, some being passed, it mimicked a race and his reactions had to be spot on.

At some point, Bryce stopped thinking about the jumps and turns ahead of him and the other riders around him. He simply felt the flow of the track and the speed of the bike. He tuned in to the hum of the other machines around him and the vibration of his own ride. He moved with a rhythm all his own, yet still in sync with the track, almost like hitting the off-beats in the Ska music he loved so much. He fell so hard into the ride, that he almost missed Reuben flagging him down.

"That's a lot better, Bryce."

"Cool."

"Go get cleaned up and get some lunch. The cafeteria has your diet plan. Then meet me in the gym in about two hours."

"We're done riding?"

Reuben laughed. "You have no idea how long you've been out there, do you?"

He shook his head, because he didn't know. "Hour?"

"Try two. And that's just since the others joined you out there."

Bryce noticed many of the others heading back to the garage. He really had been into the ride. He shrugged and headed off to the garage. The mechanics there would clean up his bike for him, while he took a shower in the barracks. Before he even got that far, his stomach started growling. "Hope that diet has a lot of food on it."

Reuben just snorted and walked away. It seemed strange to let someone else take care of his schedule and his diet, but that's the way the team worked it. They paid for the coach, the camp, the mechanics, and sometime in the next week, they would be sending him a new bike. All of this because when Bryce got in the zone, he could really ride; he could win races. He smiled to himself, knowing that his talent would only take him so far, but it had gotten him to this point. Now, he had to show them he could commit. He just hoped he'd have some free time to have fun, too.

Tate wasted no time once he finally arrived at camp. He dropped his bags on his bed and dug out his riding gear. The only thing that stopped him was getting a good look at the new KTM bike his team, Morely-Stapelton Racing or MSR, supplied him. The thing practically sparkled. The mainly white body was fine, but it had black and bright neon yellow accents. The rear fender practically glowed in the neon yellow, even with the sponsor logos stickered on it. Tate sighed. He hoped like hell it rode a bit more bad ass than it looked. He didn't have a choice about the colors and stickers. That was up to MSR, but if it didn't perform, well that was another matter altogether.

The club mechanic waltzed over as Tate checked out the bike. "Hey, Jordan!" he called out and lifted a hand for a high five. Tate gave him one. Brett was one of his favorite mechanics at the club and had been around for as long as he'd been training there.

"You see this?" Tate asked, leaning the bike away from him with the handlebars.

"Sure. Got the beast all gassed up and primed. Ready to go for you. It came in yesterday." Brett eyed the bike with appreciation, while wiping his greasy hands on a rag.

"Beast? Yeah. I hope it's a beast on the track. Sure is ugly."

"I don't know. I kinda like it." Brett's cocky grin told him that he didn't really mean it.

"Tease all you want, but these KTMs are killer on the track."

Brett shrugged. "I don't think it matters what brand you're on Jordan." He shook his head a little as he spoke. "As long as it's in good shape. I've seen you ride, dude."

Tate let his mouth form a smirk. It felt good to get compliments, but it meant little if he didn't win races. "Thanks. Guess I'll find out in a minute."

Tate pushed the new bike out to the 450 track. He had it reserved for a few hours of private riding. He knew he needed that just to unwind after the flight in from New York, and the break up with Donny. *Fucking Donny!*

Tate refused to give the bastard any more thought time. After Oz and a hired moving crew went in and got the rest of his stuff and unloaded it at his storage bin, Tate put the relationship behind him. The only thing left to bother him was the fact that he had no home. Yet, Donny's place hadn't really been a home anyway. It had felt like he was pretending and it probably ended way later than it should have.

With one last exhale, Tate pumped the kickstarter twice and brought the bike to life with a roar. Instead of walking the track, like he should have done, Tate rode the bike around the loop slowly to get the lay of the land. Not much had changed since the last time he had been there, but he needed to make sure he knew the track features and layout before opening the bike up. That first round also allowed him to get a feel for the new bike.

The second lap was faster, but still not up to racing speed, but by the time he finished the circuit, he was ready to go all out. He pulled on the clutch and shifted gears with his foot and let the bike fly as he throttled up. The red-brown dirt flew behind him as he tore through the first straightway and he dug into the turn. He took the table tops with an effort, pushing the bike into the jumps. The machine buzzed in his ear as he dug into the ruts of other riders that had been there before him. He liked the wider bars and higher seat on the bike; it felt like a better fit for his body type, and it also let him shove the bike around the track a little bit harder.

After a few laps, Tate felt really comfortable with the bike and he let it rip through the course. He throttled hard to see what it could really do when he went all out. He found he was impressed with the speed and handling when he let himself go. Joy bubbled up in his stomach as he flew over the jumps, gunning for as much air time as he could grab. The loamy smell of dirt and pine mingled with synthetic motor oil and gas. That made him feel more at home than he ever had in Donny's perfumed condo.

Tate gave up counting the laps and just listened to his body. His back stretched and his thighs burned, particularly when he plowed through the whoops McAllister style, really pumping for speed. He'd learned that trick from his friend. Being taller than other riders would allow him an advantage, if he learned to use it. He missed racing against Davey at The Ranch, his friend's home track. That had been fun and educational. Even though The Ranch would be better than the race camp, it was still one more thing he couldn't control. Davey and Tyler were honeymooning on some tropical island, while Tate dug into the ruts of the camp track. He wanted to feel jealous and bitter, but he loved the dirt too much.

When his arms started tingling and feeling weak, he decided to stop. He slowed the bike around the last stretch to wind down. When he stopped, back at the beginning, another racer waited there for the track. Tate hit the kill switch, silencing his machine and stared at the other rider.

"Hey, nice riding." The guy was tall, but not as tall as Tate, with pitch black hair that had one thick lock of purple hanging over his eye. He had decent size gauges in his ears, bright blue eyes that stood out against that dark hair, and a smattering of freckles across his wide cheeks. He held his helmet under one arm and the handle bar of the bike he straddled with his other hand. Goggles hung backward around his neck. All and all, a pretty cute guy, even though Tate out grew the urge to crush on other racers.

Tate pulled off his own goggles and helmet. "Yeah?"

"Yeah. Nice to meet you. I'm Bryce Nickel," he said as if Tate should know who he was. The kid seemed a bit too young to have that kind of ego, but this was motocross and every rider needed that self-worth just to compete consistently against other riders with egos just as big or bigger.

"Tate Jordan," he answered smugly, knowing the kid really would know who he was.

Bryce's eyes widen with excitement. "No shit!"

"No, no shit," Tate laughed. He still wasn't used to the strange responses he got from fans, not that Bryce was a fan. He was just some kid coming up through the ranks.

"Oh, wow. I'm, uh, uh, just starting. I'll be riding in the 250 West this next year."

Tate nodded. "Really? How old are you?"

"I'll be eighteen before the season starts." He flipped his head back, knocking that long purple strand out of his eyes, just to have it slide right back down. His jaw tightened with more of that self-important attitude, but Tate kind of liked it. "I'm really good."

Tate wondered if Bryce was still talking about racing with the way his eyes cut through him. "I'll bet," Tate answered with a wink. "Wanna race?"

Bryce nodded, eager to show Tate what he had on the track. Tate wanted to play with him on and off the track, but safety was always first, so he made them ride the track slowly as he pointed out deep ruts and soft spots. Bryce seemed to appreciate the tips. Then, back at the start, he took off, gunning it hard down the straightway. Tate laughed and followed quickly. He had a bigger bike that was more powerful than Bryce's, so he caught up quick and passed him on a jump. The rest of the lap, Tate played cat and mouse with him, but took notice of Bryce's skill. He hadn't been exaggerating, the kid was good, and in a couple years, he'd be up on the 450s for sure.

The second lap, Tate didn't fool around. Despite his muscles getting sore, he drove himself harder. He could feel the pressure of Bryce following behind, hungry to show his skills. If the kid had been on a bigger bike, he would have really given Tate a challenge. When they finally stopped, Tate felt compelled to tell him. "You were pretty good out there."

Bryce pulled off his helmet and shoved his goggles in them. "You ran circles around me."

"Yeah, but I'm on a brand spanking new KTM 450. What are you riding?"

"Two year old Yamaha. It's all I can afford. At least until my team sends up my new bike." Bryce looked down at his bike, frowning.

"Dude. It's a two year old 250. There's no way you could keep up. But, you put on a damn good show. You've got skill. I'm shaking in my boots." He kicked one up to show him. "In two years, you're going to be gunning me down hard on a 450."

One eyebrow lifted under that purple hair. "You think?" Bryce looked so vulnerable and sincere, Tate wanted to kiss him. He shoved that thought down hard, though. It would be pretty stupid to have a fling with another racer right then.

"Yeah. I totally think." His stomach growled hard, interrupting the conversation, making Bryce laugh out loud. "Yeah, I'm starving. Wanna go grab some chow? Or do you need to keep practicing?"

"Nah, let's go eat. I'm not even supposed to be here." Bryce gave him a sly smile, making those deep blue eyes twinkle. "I heard some hot shot Supercross star was going to be around, so I gave my coach the slip and stalked the track."

Tate's stomach fluttered with Bryce's admission. He was totally getting under Tate's skin with his cute freckles and arrogant little smirk. "Let's go then."

Chapter 7 – August, Denver

Pilot plopped his feet up on the desk beside Johnny at the Trident office. The doors were locked and the receptionist had long since gone home, but Johnny had some investment numbers to crunch, and that almost always happened after hours, after his real job.

"Get those nasty boots off my desk, asshole," Johnny grumped.

Pilot slid the big combat boots to the floor with a clump. "Are you done yet?"

Johnny sighed, "I'd get this done faster if you weren't asking me that every two minutes."

"Are you done yet?"

Johnny laughed this time and smacked Pilot's thigh, then immediately cringed, holding his hand. "Your thighs are made of cement."

"Whatever. I'll need thick thighs this weekend." He stretched his arms then clasped his hands over his head, leaning back in the little office chair. The grip of his gun stuck out above his belt loop where he had his holster strapped in front. One tip of his boots touched the floor, keeping him balanced.

"Don't break that." Johnny eyed the chair as if he were afraid it would collapse under Pilot's huge frame. "And what do you mean you'll need them?"

"I lined up a fight for Saturday. What do you think we were doing at Trip Chill? Didn't we already discuss this?"

"Fuck. You're such a dick sometimes." He tossed a paperclip at Pilot before bending his head over the computer, shaggy hair falling in his face and hiding the edges of his glasses.

Pilot leaned forward, planting his feet once again firmly on the floor. "Come on, J-man. Come watch me fight."

"Oh, hell no. I can't stand seeing you get punched or kicked. It's not like security work, Pilot. They hit back in the ring. And don't call me J-man."

"It's not that bad. I'll win. Booker will put me on a good card because I've been gone a while."

"Good or easy?" Johnny narrowed his eyes. He knew enough about the underground fights to be suspicious and Pilot wouldn't lie.

"Good."

Johnny pushed the keyboard away from him and shook his head. "Anyway, I can't stand the blood either. Even if you're winning." He cringed as if seeing the blood behind his closed eyes.

"Okay. But, I'm planning on tearing somebody up. Sight to behold." Pilot winked, trying to stir Johnny up. He wanted to make Johnny smile and laugh with him. That seemed to be getting harder and harder to do lately, and Pilot didn't like where that negativity was headed.

"I'm sure. But I'm still not going."

"Johnny," Pilot pleaded. "It'll be fun."

"I understand why you do this—"

"No," Pilot interrupted. "You know, but you don't really understand. You can't. But, there is a reason. A reason why I do security work. A reason why I fight. A reason why I keep this nickname. Pilot."

"I...Yeah, I get it Pilot. If anyone does. I do. We're close. Always been close."

Johnny calling him Pilot concerned him. Suddenly the conversation shifted and became about him and he hadn't meant that to happen. "Okay. You don't have to come to the fight. But, you do have to find something fun to do, J-man."

"Don't call me that, Sean." He tossed another paperclip, but he smiled. "I'm going to watch a movie and crash. Then Sunday I'll come over and patch you up."

Pilot wanted to dig into that and find something more entertaining for Johnny. He didn't like the idea of him sitting around at home with the potential to sink into another depression. He looked over his friend, though. Johnny's lips turned up at the corners in a natural smile with no indication of a struggle. He didn't want to ask, because that would surely reveal things Pilot didn't want to know. That didn't feel like he was being a good friend, but he didn't know how to deal with Johnny's issues when he had such a hard time just dealing with his own.

Booker held the fights in a warehouse near Wazee, the historic warehouse district. People were asked to bus in, take the metro, or cabs so there wouldn't be too many parked cars around drawing attention to the event. They didn't have medics, refs, or rules. Pilot knew what he was getting himself into, though. He'd done it before. He would probably do it again and again. There was no better high than pitting himself against another fighter of equal caliber.

Inside the warehouse, an open area with a makeshift ring had been set up in the center with a cage around it. There were no backrooms to change clothes. The first fight had barerly gotten started when blood splattered across the mat. That worried Pilot a bit, because he had no idea if these guys had been tested and they sure as hell didn't share results if they had. Pilot had himself tested regularly, but it didn't stop anyone else from getting in that ring without it. He couldn't let himself focus on that, or he'd never fight.

He shucked his sweatpants and t-shirt off, stuffing his clothes in his duffle bag. He was left standing there in tight red and black shorts that kind of resembled swim trunks. He had his ankles wrapped, but his hands and feet were bare. This league was all bare knuckles, no gloves, no shin guards, no helmets. Just two men slugging it out the old fashioned way. Well, almost. Mixed martial arts called for real fighting skill in more than one discipline. They'd punch, kick, wrestle, and use whatever techniques they had to take the other guy down.

Pilot bounced up and down, trying to loosen up and get his body warm. He'd jogged a bit on his way in and wanted to keep that heat going. Adrenaline would kick in and get him rolling soon enough, though. Booker had him fighting in the second match, so he had to watch the first match before getting in the ring, and it had already started winding down.

The two rather scrawny guys pummeled each other. The blond got a good kick in to the other guy's ribs and sent the guy down. Blond guy was all over him then. It only took him seconds to get his opponent into a submission hold. The guy pounded his free hand on the mat to tap out.

For a second or two, Pilot didn't know if they'd stop the fight. Without rules and officials, they could let it go on until the kid passed out. Just as Pilot had decided to intervene and made a lunge toward the mat. A big guy wearing a tight black t-shirt that barely covered his bulging biceps did it for him. He had on black slacks and shoes, looking like maybe he'd been hired as security for the night and was doubling as the final ref.

The muscled guy in black pulled the scrappy blond off his opponent and raised his hand in the air. "Winner!" he yelled to the crowd, and they went nuts, screaming and cheering and jumping up and down.

The fighters left the ring. The blond went out with a bounce, though his face was going to be bruised up the next day. His opponent trudged out with his head hung low, but he had a super-hot chick consoling him, so it couldn't be too bad for the guy. At least he had someone. Win or lose, Pilot was on his own.

"Next fight!" the security dude yelled, obviously doing triple duty as announcer, too. He pulled a note card from his back pocket. "Joining us from south of the boarder...from Albuquerque, New Mexico. Welcome Jo-ose the Hombre...Mene-endez!"

From the other side of the ring, a dark haired, dark skinned man slid inside the gates of the fence surrounding the mat. He wore shiny blue trunks that ended just above his knees. He jumped around the mat and lifted his hands up and down to get the crowd pumped up. They obediently cheered for him. The Hombre was probably on a winning streak. He had a muscular chest and arms and wiry legs. He wouldn't be on that streak much longer.

"And our local boy come home, Pi-lot." The man lengthened his name with way too many syllables, but Pilot needed no other introductions or names. Anyone who'd been around awhile knew who he was. Even though it had been a few months since he'd fought, his reputation would still be talked about.

Pilot pushed passed a row of people and made his way around to the gate. Hombre kept up with the bouncing, and narrowed his eyes at Pilot as he slipped into the ring. Pilot was about the same height as his opponent and his shoulders just as broad. His thighs and calves, though, made him look like a giant next to this guy.

The hired security guy looked between both of them and gestured for them to meet in the center. "Rules are, there are no rules. Except when I say break it up. Then you fucking break it up. Got it?"

They both nodded.

"Meet your opponent and take a step back and we'll get this bitch started."

Hombre stuck his fist out, and Pilot gave him a knuckle bump before stepping back to the edge of the ring.

"Let's fight!" the security guy announced before stepping out of the ring.

Pilot and Hombre circled each other. Every match started that way. Sizing each other up. It didn't take long before Hombre dove right in, though, swinging fists and flipping up a quick kick meant for Pilot's head. Pilot dodged and blocked and then punched the guy in the stomach. Hombre started to bend at the waist from the impact, but danced back away from Pilot. The man moved quickly, but Pilot had taken down quicker. He bounced lightly on his toes, waiting for Hombre to attack again.

Hombre cocked his head to the side and started circling again, as if debating how to come at Pilot. He shuffled his feet to the right, and Pilot decided to take the decision out of his hands. He lunged forward on his right leg in a fake, pulled back, and then kicked Hombre in the left thigh. He threw his forearm to Hombre's throat with his left and another punch to the stomach with his right. Before Hombre could back pedal out of it, Pilot tangled his feet and pushed Hombre to the mat, falling after him.

Hombre landed with a thump and a rush of breath exhaled involuntarily, as he took all of Pilot's weight. Obviously, he hadn't done his homework. That was Pilot's signature move. He didn't waste time congratulating himself, though. Pilot pulled Hombre's arms, and tightened his hold on Hombre's legs. Sweat already poured off of their bodies, making Hombre's limbs slick and harder to get a grip on, but Pilot managed to secure the hold.

Pilot took a punch to his head, as Hombre tried to wriggle out of the hold. Pilot released him, ready to beat on him a little more. Before Hombre could get on his feet all the way, Pilot twisted his body to the right and landed a side kick to his ribs. Hombre's wince was unmistakable. As he turned to defend himself, Pilot stepped forward and kneed him in the stomach. This time, Hombre bent fully over. Mistake. When he leaned forward, Pilot grasped his hands together in a double fist and brought the hammer down on the man's shoulders, just below the neck.

Hombre stumbled to the mat, hands out in front of him. Pilot had no sympathy and planned to get as many licks in as he could before the security guy called the fight. He kicked Hombre in the face. Blood bust out over the mat from his nose. It was probably broken, and surely painful. Pilot expected him to go down.

He didn't.

He rolled toward Pilot and grabbed his legs, fingers digging into Pilot's calves. He leveraged his weight to pull Pilot off balance and the next thing Pilot knew, they were wrestling on the ground. Hombre made a hell of a grapple with him, despite the bruised gut and probably broken nose. The bastard wasn't going to give up easily. Pilot had to get out of the hold and off the mat. His punching and kicking were better than his wrestling. So, that's what he did, snuck in punches and knees and elbows everywhere he could. He took his share from Hombre too, but if they were counting, Pilot was winning.

After what seemed like ages of being tied up with the sweaty man, rolling around on the mat, Pilot managed to get an elbow to his nose again, and he heard a distinct pop. *Broke the nose for sure this time!* Hombre cried out. And even better, he let go.

Pilot jumped to his feet and commenced kicking the shit out of Hombre, connecting with ribs, stomach, neck, legs, the back of his head, until Hombre finally started pounding on the mat with the flat of his hand.

The pretend ref in black appeared in the cage in front of Pilot, as if by magic. Pilot hadn't looked away from Hombre for a second. He shoved Pilot back and grabbed his hand, lifting it above his head and hollered, "Winner!"

Pilot's adrenaline levels immediately started falling. He sprung out of the cage like a jackrabbit on crack. He needed to get out of that area before his high came crashing down. He knew from experience it would. He grabbed his duffle and pulled out his oversized t-shirt and sweats. He yanked them on quickly, and then stuffed his bare feet into his black slides with the sports logo on the top, glad it was still summer and he could wear them instead of sneakers or his combat boots.

"Pilot," Booker called out to him over the noise of the crowd. "Awesome fight, bloke!"

Pilot didn't bother to answer the pretentious flake. He merely stuck his hand out, demanding his pay.

"Yeah, I have your money, but do you want to go another card first? I think I have a no show in a bigger fight. Tougher opponent. Pays more."

He had to think about it for just a moment. He stared at Booker's ugly mug, but he saw Johnny's face and heard his sarcastic barbs. He didn't want Johnny to have to pull out the first aid kit, and he didn't think he should push it by adding a second fight...at least not yet. "Nope. I'm done. Give me my cash and I'm out of here."

"Next week?"

Pilot shook his head, making sweat fall from his bangs, into his eyes and down the side of his face. He didn't like the energy in the place anymore. Suddenly the little lightning tingles in his chest and on the back of his neck creeped him out. "Nope. I'm working. I'll hook up with you at Trip Chill in the next week or two if I have a night open."

Booker slapped an envelope into Pilot's still open palm. "Fine. If you weren't so damned good, you wouldn't get away with jerking me around, bitch."

Pilot growled, but didn't think Booker heard it over the crowd. "Fuck off!" That, he knew Booker would hear. He didn't wait for a response. Feeling the negative vibes, he tucked the envelope into his bag and zipped it up, then high tailed it out of there before the whole night went tits up.

By the time he made it to the sidewalk on the main street leading to the transit station, his hands were shaking and his cock was hard. Fighting tended to do that to him. The adrenaline made him want to fuck, but he didn't have anyone to go to. Pilot wasn't into one nighters or quick bathroom fucks. He knew he could get plenty of that, but it seemed so cheap and empty. Pilot needed emotional connection with his sex. Or at least that's what he thought he wanted, though he hadn't ever really had it. Still, just because he hadn't had that, didn't keep him from dreaming about it. He'd never owned a security company, either, but he lived and breathed that dream.

He thought about his lack of relationships all the way home. It didn't do much to soften his dick, though. Maybe imagining what it would be like for him only made it worse. At home, he jumped in the shower and soaped up quickly, more interested in getting off than getting clean. His soapy hand wrapped around his cock, stroking fast then slow, building it up as slowly as he could stand it.

Pilot didn't have anyone to think about as he fucked into his hand. No relationships, no crushes, but a super hard cock that wanted to plow something besides his sudsy hand. He squinted his eyes shut and pressed his palm against the wet tiles and let his mind wander. He needed something besides a faceless body to think about. In moments, a face came to him. One with a hot body and long legs. Davey McAllister.

He knew better than to think anything would ever happen with the Supercross star, and he really didn't want it to. The guy was nice but totally in love with his partner. But, damn, he was hot as hell, too. The Supercross racers were all pretty hot, even in their gear. Maybe especially in their gear. He couldn't wait for January with that thought. He imagined Davey with his blue and red pants shoved down to his knees, bent over his bike, and Pilot's cock pushing into that tight hole. He'd run his hands down those long, lean thighs and wrap his big fingers around Davey's slim hips, as he pounded hard. In and out. His balls slapping against Davey's ass. Back and forth. What would it look like? Pilot shot out like a rocket, cum splattering over the shower curtain as he imagined it.

He slumped against the tile, his shoulders bracing against the cold. Pilot had never thought about Davey like that before and felt kind of guilty about it. But, damned if it didn't work. He'd come hard and his buzz from the earlier fight was gone. He wanted to crawl into bed.

After a quick rinse and toweling off, Pilot did just that. He slid under his comforter, wishing he had someone to join him, someone to hold onto.

The next day he would give Johnny his winnings to invest. He'd make living expenses doing shorter security jobs over the next few months, but the real payoff would be the Supercross gig with Apex.

He'd get to spend all his time with Davey's partner, Tyler Whitmore. He really liked the guy when he wasn't being a hot head and getting himself in trouble. Otherwise he was very laid back with a great attitude and a wicked sense of humor. Let anyone fuck with Davey though, and his cool demeanor came unglued.

Pilot wanted that. Someone to rush to his defense, even if he didn't really need defending. It seemed so unlikely. Would the rest of his life be like this, wanting things he'd probably never have?

Chapter 8 - Moto Club in North Carolina

For the next few days, Tate and Bryce were almost inseparable. They ate meals together in the mess hall and practiced together on the track. Tate could see almost immediate improvement in Bryce's ride and was stupid-happy with that. All of that. He really liked Bryce. They never ran out of shit to talk about and just generally got along well. Tate tried to swallow down that higher level of attraction and just be the kid's friend. Knowing that he'd helped Bryce on the track made his chest warm, and he told himself that had to be enough.

As they pushed their bikes back to the garage, Tate swallowed down how proud he was of Bryce, but after they released the bikes, Tate clapped Bryce on the back. His hand stayed between Bryce's shoulder blades. Not wanting to move.

Bryce looked up at him with wide dark eyes and thick fluttering lashes, and whatever Tate had meant to say left him. "Uh," he stammered completely and totally ineloquent. His hand slid slowly down Bryce's back. "Want to come to my room? Uh, to hang out?" He was pretty sure he'd mentioned that he had a private room, so when Bryce bit his lip and gave an almost imperceptible nod of his head, Tate's cock shifted behind his track pants, trying to harden. So much for not thinking about Bryce that way.

Tate finally moved his hand and they shuffled off toward the bunk rooms where four or five guys shared three or four bunk houses, each with shared bathrooms and showers. Bryce bunked in one of those, but Tate's team paid for one of the eight private rooms. MSR always went all out. The little mini-houses lined up four each on both sides of the common bunks. Tate led Bryce to his and used the keypad to punch in his code and unlock the door. The camp made it easy to remember the number—two nines plus his race number, *87*.

Inside the front door was a small room, not unlike a hotel. It had a queen sized bed against one wall and a big screen TV on top of a chest of drawers on the other. A small desk with a rolling chair was next to the dresser. Next to what passed for a kitchen, was a bathroom. At least it was private and had the basics: sink, toilet, and shower. The small kitchenette with a mini fridge, a microwave, and a two burner stove top also had a small sink and a few cabinets if he wanted to put some dishes in there. He didn't have any dishes, but there were two boxes of dry cereal that he'd picked up from the little town down the road. If he could actually call it a town. It wasn't much more than a handful of store fronts.

Bryce pulled out the rolling chair and sat in it, looking up at Tate, expectantly. Tate sat on the bed and leaned toward him, grabbing the chair by the arms and pulling it forward. His thighs pressed against Bryce's knees, trapping his legs between his own. That purple hair hung down in his eyes, making Tate want to push it away. Bryce bit his bottom lip again and lifted his chin. The look on his face, full of want, made Tate's brain fizz out. He heard white noise and his vision narrowed to focus solely on Bryce. Nothing else in the world existed.

He leaned forward and pressed his lips, gently on Bryce's, then pulled back slowly and waited. His heart beat twice before Bryce opened his mouth and leaned into Tate.

Tate's hands pushed through Bryce's thick, dark hair as his tongue plunged into Bryce's hot, wet mouth. Bryce slid his tongue back and forth against Tate's, a bit nervously, but that little timid move drove Tate nuts. He needed more. He leaned forward, trying desperately to get Bryce closer. He wanted their clothes off, hot, bare skin pressing and sliding together.

The kiss continued; Bryce's tongue flicks grew braver and more demanding by the second. Tate reached down between them, barely skimming over the bulge in Bryce's track pants. And damn if Bryce didn't look hot in those blue and white Alias pants. Bryce moaned softly into Tate's mouth, encouragingly. Tate pulled at the tab and belt that held them together, and Bryce jumped back. The chair wheeled farther away, out of Tate's reach.

"What?" he asked. "I mean. We don't have to." Tate didn't want to push him, didn't *mean* to push him. He normally dealt with older guys who knew what they wanted, but Bryce might not know, might not be ready. He seemed like the kind of guy Tate could wait for, though.

Bryce's eyes widened and his gaze darted all over the room, landing on the door. His body hummed like a rabbit ready to jump. Tate could feel the energy rolling off of Bryce like lightning.

"It's okay. I'm sorry. We don't have to do anything," Tate repeated, holding his hands up, but it was too late.

Bryce darted out the door without looking back, without even closing it behind him.

"Damn it," Tate cursed himself and flung his body back on the bed. His cock still pressed hard against his own track pants. He'd blown it for sure. He'd forgotten just how young Bryce really was. He probably shouldn't have even kissed him. Bryce was still a boy and obviously in the closet.

Bryce ran.

He couldn't catch his breath, but it didn't stop him. He ran through camp and straight to his bunk. He climbed up and smashed his face into his pillow. Noises came out, muffled but still frustrating, sobs and screams alike. What had he done?

After spending every free moment he could tagging after Tate, following him around like a love-sick dog, when he finally got that moment he'd been waiting for, what did he do? Chicken out. He ran away. Tate must think Bryce was some kind of prick tease. He didn't want that, but didn't want to move so fast either.

It had been difficult negotiating his time between his coaching sessions and work outs with Reuben and his time with Tate, but he'd been doing it, and it had been so worth it. Tate had been so nice to him, giving him tips and talking to him like he mattered. The electricity between them had been a heady thing.

And that kiss.

Tate's hot tongue in his mouth, dancing around his own. It was like their mouths were meant to be pressed together. His heart leapt like he'd taken a big jump on the track. His stomach quivered. Nothing else existed in that moment, but Tate's mouth on his. Tate. The rock star of Supercross. Tate Jordan like-liked him...Bryce...just one of a hundred kids at the camp vying for a spot on a Supercross team and he hadn't even got his race bike yet...and how did any of that even matter?

Bryce rolled over on his bunk and gently touched his lips with just the tips of his fingers. Tate's lips had been right there. They still felt warm. Why did he have to pull away? He could have just asked Tate to slow down, but when Tate had tugged his belt, he knew what it meant. Tate wanted to fuck him. Right there. Oh and boy did a part of Bryce really-truly want that. Yet, another part of him didn't.

No. That wasn't right. He wanted it. All of him wanted it. But, if Tate only wanted him for sex, it would break his heart and that's sure what it felt like. As soon as they'd made the first moves, Tate jumped ahead to the sex part. He was older, more experienced. After Bryce had followed him around with his moony-eyes, Tate probably expected Bryce to do it. But, it had been Bryce's first kiss, first real kiss. He put his heart and soul into that kiss.

Damn. Bryce was acting like a baby. But, after the way he freaked, he couldn't face Tate. Couldn't imagine how mad Tate must have been. He bolted out of there so fast, it could have been a damn holeshot on the track. Tate couldn't *even* have caught him.

Bryce had broken his own heart. He turned over and sobbed into his pillow again. He'd done this to himself. Tate had been nothing but nice, and would have slowed down for him, but now it was over. Bryce couldn't go back and change it; he'd just have to live with it, even if he didn't want to.

Tate dragged himself through the next few days with an excruciating numbness. He went back to riding alone. Worse, he saw Bryce everywhere else around camp. He'd see him in the large community center where other riders hung out, played games, talked about racing, and sometimes watched track footage on the big screen. Tate would stare at him from across the room until Bryce's gaze met his own. Then, they'd both turn away. He'd also see Bryce in the cafeteria, usually sitting with a few other riders his age. He pointedly ignored Tate, but still Tate caught a flash from his dark eyes, every now and then, reminding him of what he'd lost. More than sex or making out, Tate had lost his friendship.

Tate reacted by spending more time on the track and less time in the common rooms, logging his hours in the dirt. He wouldn't have the luxury of riding whenever and however he wanted for much longer. Oz had said he would be sending a trainer soon enough. Tate hoped it would be Tim Albright. That man was sex on wheels and an out gay man as well. He was someone Tate could be interested in. Tim was older, but not too old. Even if he was, Tate could see Tim as a sexy, silver fox. Maybe that would get his mind off of Bryce.

Tate pushed his bike back to the garage after riding really hard in a useless attempt to get Bryce out of his head. His limbs ached, tired in a good way, and he hoped to just go get a shower and crawl into bed. Once the trainer came, he'd dictate everything right down to when Tate could sleep and for how long. He might even tell Tate what the hell to dream. Until he got there, though, Tate would sleep when he wanted and hopefully, that would mean sleeping late.

"Hey, how's the bike running?" Brett asked, taking the machine from Tate's hands.

"Pretty good. I can't complain. Haven't broken it yet, but I'll keep trying." Tate only half joked. He did like to run bikes into the ground and was thankful for MSR for always replacing them quickly. During the racing season, he had two race bikes at the rack at all times, plus a practice bike stored at whatever track he practiced at between races. Tate tended to ride hard, although he had lightened up a bit since training with Davey.

He turned the bike over to Brett, fighting his urge to stay and talk. He knew he was lonely, but he couldn't let that emptiness take control. He needed to focus on riding and training. That meant taking care of himself, too. Paying attention to his body's need to rest, he waved bye and got a quick wave in return, as Brett refocused on the bike. He didn't really want to talk to Tate anyway.

There wasn't anything else to do but head for his bunk. As he was punching in his code, another racer approached. He hoped it was Bryce, but turned to see someone else. Warren Tanner. He'd been coming to this camp for a long time. He spent almost as much time in the chapel trying to convert everyone as he did on the track. He was a big guy, bigger than most riders with broad shoulders, and too bulky to be a really good racer. That was probably why he never made it to the pros. He was about the same age as Tate, in his twenties. Tate figured he kept coming to camp to hang on to something he'd never really had a shot at.

"Tate," he said, his voice low. "I've seen you around mooning over that kid. You don't even bother to acknowledge anyone else."

Tate figured this was the start of his conversion speech. "What are you talking about?" His door popped open, and he held it as if holding on to his last refuge in a world of conflict.

"You know what I mean. What's his name? Bryce?"

Tate narrowed his eyes, unsure of what Warren was getting at. "What about Bryce?"

Warren sneered, his wide nose scrunching up in his long face. He wasn't bad looking. His brown hair leaned toward golden and his smile was usually broad and welcoming, but not at this moment. His distaste warped his pink lips into a mask of disgust. "I know what you want. I can give it to you. You don't have to go following him around like some lost puppy. I got what you need." He grabbed his crotch and raised an eyebrow.

"Uh, I don't think so, Warren. You know, uh, I'm here to ride. Whatever you think you saw between me and Bryce, well, uh, you're wrong." He took a step inside his room, pushing the door open just enough to get in.

Warren stepped closer, leaning in. He put his hands on Tate's shoulders and shoved him into the room, pushing the door closed behind them with his foot. Tate's heart pounded. This was new.

Warren stepped into Tate's space and breathed down into his face. He was just a little taller than Tate, but used the height difference to loom over him. "I know what I've seen. I know what I've heard. It's true isn't it?"

"What? What are you doing here?"

"I know you want it and I can give it to you." He reached down and tugged at the fastener at his waist.

"What? Why?"

"Fuck! Shut up, Jordan. Get your pants down." Warren's own pants dropped down to his thighs, and he shoved his jock strap down. His fat cock flopped out, half hard. Warren started stroking it with one hand and reaching for Tate with the other. "Come on."

Tate stood there with his mouth hanging open. He didn't know what to say or do. Warren was big and suddenly demanding. He grabbed at Tate's shoulder and shoved him toward the bed.

"Pants. Now." Warren grabbed Tate around the waist and pushed him hard, flinging him to the bed and yanking him up on his hands and knees. He reached around and fumbled at the fastener of Tate's pants, pulling the strap out with clumsy fingers. He yanked and pulled and had Tate's pants and jock down to his knees in a quick minute.

Warren's dick rubbed up and down Tate's crack, and damned if his own cock didn't respond.

"I've got a condom," Warren growled, moving away from Tate's body. Tate wanted that heat back. Wanted some kind of personal closeness, even if it was from Warren.

"Lube. You need lube."

"Right."

For a long drawn out second, Tate wasn't sure if that *right* had been agreement or sarcasm. He waited, confused.

"Uh, you have lube? Where?" Warren muttered. Tate twisted to the side and looked over his shoulder. He didn't know what Warren saw in his face, but Warren's face scrunched up like he'd bit into a lemon slice. "Dude. I'm not an asshole. This is me being nice. Damn."

"I don't get you. This."

Warren groaned and stomped into the bathroom. Tate could hear him rummaging through his things. "This?" he asked, finally coming back into the room.

Tate had no words, staring at Warren holding up a bottle of lube, his cock jutting up and wrapped in a condom, ready to go, like some twisted present for him. He nodded and turned around.

"This is good, Tate." He squirted lube down Tate's crack and followed it with a blunt finger, pushing into his hole. "Look. Works for both of us. You want this and I'm horny. My girl is a thousand miles away. So..."

Tate didn't respond to his *any port in a storm* philosophy. It did make Warren an asshole, but with his fingers in Tate's hole, jutting in and out and circling the rim in turns, Tate's brain stopped understanding any other language than what his own body was making. His hips thrust forward. It had been too long and Tate was too lonely.

Then, Warren abruptly shoved his shoulders down onto the bed, and Warren 's hard cock breached his hole with a shove. "Damn! You are tight. And hot. Like an oven."

Tate's face was smashed into the mattress. Warren had one hand between his shoulder blades, holding him down, the other was gripping his hip as he fucked Tate without mercy.

Tate tried to relax, but he hadn't been ready. He tried to shift his hips to get a better angle, but Warren was in command and not letting him move. "Hold still, damn it," he growled out.

The mattress muffled Tate's cries, but he could feel the tears on his cheeks. It hurt and he couldn't relax. His erection softened. He hoped the brute would accidentally brush against his prostate, but Warren's cock didn't seem long enough. Thick, yes, but squat like the rest of him.

Finally, Warren called out, a grunt and a "Fuck!" and then he pulled out, leaving Tate on the mattress empty. He shuffled into the bathroom. Tate heard the toilet flush. "Thanks man. Catch you later." The door opened and shut.

The silence hung in the room like an accusation. A cold hole opened up in his chest. What had he just done? The truth hit him hard and fast. Despite all of his confidence on the track and his perceived bravado, Tate knew damned well, that deep inside him, in a place he never let anyone see, hid an insecure kid that just wanted to be loved. That kid, yeah, he'd do anything if he thought he'd be loved for just a few moments...

Tate curled up in a ball and sobbed.

Chapter 9 – September, Denver

"Tell me again why we're going to Sheila's?" Johnny grumbled.

Pilot answered without looking at Johnny, keeping his eyes on the road. "We were invited."

"Everyone's going to be there, aren't they? Your parents? Colin?"

"Yes," Pilot sighed, pulling the car to a stop at the sign on the road that turned down to Sheila's house. She lived in the suburbs on the north side of town near Thornton. Their subdivision was over crowded with ranch style houses of various sizes. At least she lived on a cul-de-sac which gave her a bit more space and room for her kids to play, should she ever have any. They'd been trying for a while with no luck. They wouldn't bring that subject up at dinner.

"You know I love Sheila." What he didn't say was how much he hated Colin and how bitter he was toward Pilot's folks. They'd been really shitty to both of them over the years, but they were family and maybe they were coming around. Not as well as Johnny's uncle, but it was still better than when he first came out. Sheila had promised they'd behave or he wouldn't have consented to coming. It'd been a good long time since he'd talked to any of them besides Sheila, so maybe it was time for a change.

"It'll be all right." Pilot turned his car down the cul-de-sac and parked in her driveway. "Come on. Let's get this over with."

As they approached the front door, they could hear arguing inside. Most of it from Colin. Pilot wanted to knock him out. He couldn't tell what all was being said, but he caught *faggot* a few times. He pushed the doorbell, as if he hadn't heard a thing and gave Johnny a weak smile. Of course Johnny rolled his eyes and crossed his arms over his chest.

The door jerked open. Pilot's mom stood there. She was a stocky woman, but not fat. She had light brown hair that was sometimes a bit more red or a bit more blonde, depending on what color she wanted to dye it with that month. Her eyebrows pinched together. "Well, come in then."

They followed her into the open living room/dining room combo area. When they'd bought the house, the kitchen had been closed off, but Sheila's husband, Jim, was handy and tore down the walls, installing a huge island in its place. Currently, Colin and Sheila were the only two at the bar.

Sheila had a glass of wine that she sat on the counter when they entered. "Hey guys!" She came around the island from the kitchen side and hugged them both. Colin leaned against the island and leered at them.

Sheila smacked Colin's arm. "Tell them."

"No. Fuck you," he growled.

They started in on each other, both voices rising over each other. Pilot had no idea what they were going on about until Sheila grabbed Colin's ear. "Tell him you'll pay extra. Now!"

"Fuck-fuck-fuck!"

"Tell him!"

Pilot's mom came around them and smacked Colin upside the back of his head. "Knock this shit off. I told you. You will not take advantage of Johnny. End of story."

"Fine. I'll pay extra."

Johnny snorted. "Thanks, ladies. But, I already knew he was paying extra."

Pilot was pretty sure of that. Johnny always found a way to get what he wanted.

"You done with them then?" Colin snarled.

"Not yet. Come by next week."

Sheila had gone back into the kitchen and filled two more wine glasses. "Good boy, make him wait." She said as she handed one to Johnny. "Dad's in the lounge with Jim, if you want to watch the sports stuff."

Colin took that opportunity to slink out, but Pilot and Johnny stayed in the kitchen. Jim, was nice enough, but he wanted as little to do with his dad as possible. Colin took after their dad in most ways. They looked similar with thick dark hair, almost black, though his dad's had started to do that salt and pepper thing. They both had wide set eyes, also dark brown and set on either side of noses that had been broken a time or two. In Colin's case, due to his mouth. He didn't know about his dad, but it was one of the things that had made him afraid of his dad growing up. That big offset nose in a gruff face that only ever seemed to have criticism for him.

Johnny, Sheila, and his mom chatted familiarly as Pilot sipped his wine. All of them together like this was a rare occasion. Pilot couldn't help but think how nice it was that Johnny seemed to fit in with them, at least a little. More than he did himself. They generally treated Johnny like family, like one of them. He wasn't going to get jealous that Johnny was more a part of the family than he was; he was going to be happy about it. At least he told himself that, sipping on the wine.

Johnny had been hurt a lot in his life by family and lovers alike. Finally, having some solid people around would be good for him. Pilot considered both himself and his sister in those buckets, as well as Johnny's uncle. He'd love to put more people in there with them, but he really couldn't see it happening. At least not yet. Pilot had no idea how to find more dependable people for himself, let alone Johnny.

Eventually, Sheila put food on the table and sadly, Jim, Colin, and his dad were called in from the other room to join them. Sitting around the table with his family wasn't the worst thing that could happen, though. Mostly, everyone quietly enjoyed the food. Sheila and his mom could put on a nice spread when they got to cooking together and this meal was no exception with rich pot roast and veggies, homemade bread and his sister's deluxe mac and cheese. The Syrah wine Sheila poured went well with the roast and everyone seemed to enjoy it. His dad and Colin drank beer instead, but still seemed to enjoy the food.

As the meal wound down, conversation started to pick up, which Pilot always thought was dangerous in this company. Where Colin was purposefully rude, his dad tended to be unknowingly uncouth. Sheila and mom were loud and didn't take their crap, but like Jim and Pilot, Johnny generally tried to stay out of it. Until Colin or Dad provoked Johnny, which was often. Pilot couldn't keep track of his family's disposition from one moment to the next. They loved Johnny with one breath and with the next they were at odds, but that was how they treated Pilot and Colin as well, so he shouldn't be surprised. Only Sheila was immune to their mercurial nature.

"Pass the mac and cheese," Colin demanded.

Sheila handed him the bowl, snarling back, "You're welcome."

"Wha—?" he asked.

Mom and Sheila started in on him and his manners, while the other men in the room tried to quietly turn invisible. Until Colin growled out, "I'm not putting on extra for the faggot. Damn, it's just family here."

Sheila's mouth dropped open, but had no sound coming out of it. Mom huffed, but also failed to respond. Pilot's eyebrows drew together as he stared a laser beam across the table at his stupid brother.

"Oh, Christ. Are we on about that again? Faggot this, faggot that. Give it a rest." His dad growled the first words out of his mouth the entire evening. "Seriously, why don't you two just do us a favor and get married already and we can stop acting like the boy's any different than the rest of us. Or at least like Sean…" His dad was always harassing Pilot and Johnny like that, as if they'd have to be a couple because they were gay.

Sheila finally came alive and piped in, "He's not different than any of us, anyway. He's already part of this fucked up family. What the hell?"

While Pilot simultaneously growled, "Are you kidding me?"

Johnny's back slowly straightened, his shoulders squared. Pilot looked at him, watching as his friend practically grew two inches just sitting there. He was a gorgeous guy with his brown-blond hair stylishly pushed behind his ears and swooping off his forehead. He wore his black Dolce and Gabbana frames that didn't look very different from a stylish pair of Ray-Bans to Pilot, and yes, they'd had that conversation. The glasses sat on his lean nose, which was just a bit wider at the bridge and almost looked like it was meant to be that way just to keep his glasses on. His cheekbones were so sharp, they'd cut a bitch. He sucked his bottom lip in between his teeth and his face turned tomato red. Pilot couldn't tell if the change in hue was due to embarrassment or anger, but Johnny was doing a great volcano impression, and Pilot felt it necessary to diffuse the situation before his best friend exploded.

"Shut up. Johnny and I are best friends. Not dating. Not ever. He's like a brother to me, so yeah, he's the same as everyone else. God damn. We're both just people. Family. So, shut up already."

Pilot's dad turned toward him. "You're very sensitive about it, Sean—Pilot."

A long sigh escaped Pilot's lips. His dad catching himself on the name thing, surprised him. He usually didn't, and his words didn't sound sarcastic or teasing either. Pilot let a small smile creep over his lips. "Sorry. Thanks. But, if Colin would just learn how to be a human, too—"

"Fuck! Don't blame your queer-bate shit on me. I didn't make you gay. Your faggot-ness is not appreciated--"

Johnny stood up, apparently unable to contain himself any longer, and let his lava flow. "Colin. You piece of shit. It's not like you're really a homophobe or you wouldn't—oh, never mind. My God! You just say whatever flits through your brain with no filter. That doesn't excuse you. None of it does. I've never done a damned thing to you—"

"You turned my brother queer!"

Johnny started laughing hysterically. He dropped his napkin on top of his plate and grabbed his sides, he was laughing so hard. Sheila and mom smiled, ready to join in on a bit of humor rather than have the tense argument continue, but Pilot knew it wasn't over.

"Ah...shit, Colin," Johnny gasped between bouts of laughter. "You say the stupidest shit. I'm not even going to bother..."

"Johnny?" Pilot asked, pushing his chair back.

Johnny reined his fit in enough to say, "Thanks, Sheila. The meal was delicious." Then, he headed for the front door without another word.

"Colin, you're a dick," Pilot growled. He really wished he could just un-holster his gun and unload a round right in the asshole's face, but shooting family at dinner wouldn't be tolerated by Sheila.

Chapter 10 – September, Moto Club in North Carolina

Tate laced up his Puma trainers and jogged in place, warming up. Determined to not think about Bryce or Warren or any other fucking man, sex, or hedonist distractions; he headed for the gym. Cramming his feelings down and ignoring them seemed like the best idea when he couldn't do shit about it anyway. Keeping busy and working out was the best way to go. If he ignored it long enough, maybe it would go away. Besides, the camp had a decent facility, but unless a rider got in early, it would be packed. Unlike the tracks, no one set down a schedule; it worked first come first served.

He sprinted over, between dorm buildings and past the cafeteria building, before dawn even thought about rising, just to get on a rower. Thankfully, one was open when he got there, but other riders had already snagged two of the three top of the line machines. They all dressed similarly to Tate with Under Armour t-shirts and sweatpants or joggers low on their hips, and all manner of sneakers.

He only admired them for a second or two and with a quick nod, Tate sat on the pad of the machine and set the resistance to *low* for his warm up. He concentrated on his abs and core with each stroke, feeling the pull and willing his body into submission. After a few minutes, he cranked the resistance higher and set the timer on his phone. He didn't want to think about counting his reps, just feeling his muscles work. He set a decent pace and it wasn't long before sweat broke out on his forehead and dripped down his back.

"Jordan!" a husky voice called out, interrupting his blissful moment of not thinking. He looked up and saw the camp manager, Mr. Wylie. The man was old enough to be his grandfather, but still ran the camp with dedication, endurance, and respect. His jeans were baggy and his camp t-shirt faded, but he owned the place and walked with his back straight and tall, carrying the confidence of a man in a three-piece suit.

"Hey! Mr. Wylie, what's up?" Tate stopped rowing and grabbed his towel, wiping his forehead and hands.

"Your coach is here." He thumbed behind him, just as a tall, thin Latin man entered the room. His black hair shined under the fluorescent lights of the gym. A friendly smile stretched his mouth that was surrounded by a black mustache and goatee. Tate liked the crinkles that appeared around his eyes. His shoulders were relaxed, but didn't hide his self-assurance.

The man held out his hand. "Joseph Cruz. Call me Joey."

"Hi," Tate squeaked, grasping the man's rough hand. They were about the same height, but Tate could see Joey was older than him, not nearly as old as Mr. Wylie, but definitely in his thirties. Still, he was hot, and Tate had to fight himself not to look for a ring and wonder what he'd look like out of that Henley shirt and gray slacks that hugged his hips and thighs just right. His new coach could prove to be an even better distraction than just working out.

Joey pointed at the rower. "I don't want to interrupt your work out, but when you're finished, we should talk."

"Sure." Tate couldn't think of anything else to say. He felt like he'd swallowed his tongue, but that was better than letting it hang out to drool all over his new trainer. "MSR sent you?" What was Oz thinking, sending him such a sexy coach?

That smile again, glowing brighter than the lights. "Yeah. They did. I'm qualified."

"I don't doubt it." There was no way the man could be gay. Tate couldn't be so lucky.

One dark eyebrow lifted as the man stared Tate down. "I trained Chris Bowie, 250 East Champion, last year," he said, as if proving his quality.

"Oh?"

"He's staying in the 250's another year. I wanted a, uh, a bigger challenge."

Tate finally returned the smile. Obviously Oz and the executives at MSR considered Tate challenging, but he wasn't sure if that was good or bad. Yet, they both knew that everyone wanted to be in the 450SX division, so what did it matter?

Before Tate could respond, Joey cleared his throat and spoke in a growly, commanding voice. "MSR expects you to finish third in points this year."

Tate's face fell. He didn't understand their lack of confidence in him. Just because his love life resembled the third level of hell, didn't mean he couldn't race his ass off. He was better on a bike than anywhere else.

"I'm here to make sure you don't. I expect you to win."

Tate stared at the floor. He didn't know what to say. He mumbled,

"Thank you," but wasn't sure Joey even heard him.

"I know you're friends with McAllister. But that doesn't mean you can't beat him on the track."

Davey was the man to beat, at least Joey had done his homework. Tate looked at him again, from a professional point of view, putting aside his hormonal attraction. "You think you can help me do it?"

"Yes." He had no smile this time. Joey's face was a mask of strength and determination with pinched brow and lips and a slight wrinkle around his pert nose.

"Well, let's get some breakfast and talk about it. I'm starving."

Black brows lifted above his dark eyes, "Aren't you training?"

"I'm not on a specific schedule. Yet." Tate winked at him. He couldn't help himself. The guy was gorgeous, especially with his serious face.

"All right. I'll get your diet sorted out with the cafeteria and we'll get you on a schedule. Ready?"

"Hell, yeah." Tate was more than ready. With Joey here, manipulating his time, he wouldn't have a moment to spare thinking about Bryce or that fucker Warren or his break up with Donny or sex or any number of other things that had him constantly stirred up. He'd be able to do what he'd come to the camp to do in the first place. He'd train and ride.

Joey put Tate through the paces over the next few days, not only on the track, but in the gym and on a bike—the pedal kind. Tate loved that. He'd left his own bike in storage in New York, but the camp bikes were in good shape, so they rode through the North Carolina country side. They spent a lot of time riding through the trails around the camp and enjoying the scenery with lots of pines and evergreens that gave a lush backdrop to the changing colors of the oaks and maples and other upland hardwoods. The weather most days provided clear warm temperatures that hovered around seventy. The fresh air blowing across his face while they cruised down a hill or pedaled hard to crest one went a long way to healing his heart. Fuck-all if he was lonely; Tate didn't really need anything else but training and riding. As sweet as the bicycling was for his soul, it was nothing compared to motoring his KTM on the dirt.

Even though Tate enjoyed all the extra activity, his head still wasn't in it enough. He knew he wasn't giving enough, but no matter how he tried, his string of failures kept haunting him. No matter how busy his day was, his empty bed reminded him of what he couldn't have. He wasn't even good enough for that bastard, Warren Tanner.

It wasn't just the camp guys, Bryce and Tanner, it was also Donny and half a dozen others before him that hadn't even given him their time or respect and half the time, not even their names. He could remember a few names, Clay and Jerome, and even more faces. They skated through his brain as he rode his bike through the dirt, and ironically what the dirt was supposed to be distracting him from only distracted him from focusing on his ride.

He missed a triple jump, landing on the front side of the third mound. The shocks in his machine absorbed the contact, but the hard hit still reverberated through Tate's fingers and thighs. He gunned the bike and pushed it hard through the next turn, but by the time he came up to the whoops, he was tired and he loped through them at a moderate pace, essentially obliterating what could have been his best advantage on the track.

As he came around to the front of the course, Joey waved his arms over his head. When Tate drove up the hill to him, he stopped, killing the bike engine.

"Tate, man? What the hell? I'm not fucking here to babysit you. I'm not gonna coddle you. What?" He held his hands up at his sides, begging Tate to answer him, but Tate didn't have an answer. Joey balled his hands into fists and planted them on his hips. His face scowled and he shifted his weight to one foot. "This isn't going to beat McAllister. This performance? What the hell have you been doing here? Lollygagging? Hiding?"

Tate huffed, but still didn't answer.

Joey glared at him. "This isn't going to cut it. You're better than this. Your time today makes it seem like you haven't been on this track before. Hell, it looks like you've never made it to the 250s. I thought you won a championship, Tate?"

"Yeah." He had a trophy and a tattoo to prove it. Joey was right, though; his current performance on the track didn't prove anything. "Sorry."

"I don't care how sorry you are. I care that you're doing everything you need to do to win, to be a champion. You should be getting faster, stronger. You should be able to push that bike all over the track, not the other way around." He made some kind of swishing motion with his hand in front of him.

Tate pulled off his helmet, ready to confess his distractions, but Joey wasn't listening.

"Look, Tate," he scowled. "Oz said you like to ride to get over your shit. But that shit should have been over last week. Your head needs to get in the game now. I want you at the Rhythm event next month. I want you to win it."

Tate wanted to win too, but he couldn't help wonder what Oz had shared with his new trainer. "What do you mean, Oz said?"

"That's all you got out of that?"

"Uh, no."

"Damn, Tate. I'm tired of this shit. Too old for this shit. I want to train with winners, not love sick puppies." Joey turned and stormed away, his hands animated and flashing around like lightning emphasizing his rage.

Love sick puppy? Tate ground his teeth together. Heat raced over his face. He flung his helmet down the hill, only slightly wishing that it had been thrown at the back of Joey's head.

Chapter 11 – October, Denver

It made Pilot antsy to wait for three other fights to finish before his own card could start, but when he finally entered the ring, he wanted nothing more than to take the other guy down. He didn't know his opponent and it didn't matter. Once the preliminaries were out of the way, Pilot jumped on the guy. Their stats matched up equally, much better than his last fight. They exchanged a few blows and a few holds that the other broke out of relatively easily. Indeed, the fight would be close, but Pilot would still put the man down. Pilot needed to get the violence out of his system, and he also needed the money. His cut would be bigger for winning, so he intended to do just that.

Deep into the second round, both fighters had worked up a sweat, but neither showed signs of weakening. Pilot managed to slam his elbow into the guy's gut a few times, but the dude didn't give in. Yet.

In his peripheral vision, Pilot caught odd movements of the crowd, something going down around him, and he lost his focus, shifting toward the audience. That never happened, but the other fighter took advantage of it and clocked him in the head. Pilot staggered back and shook it off. Then he roared.

He jumped toward his opponent like a spider monkey on crack. This guy had to go down. He wrapped his foot around the guy's ankle to pull him off of his feet, but before the guy fell, others jumped in the ring and grabbed him, pulling him back away from his rival. Pilot's blood surged through his veins, driving him on. He lunged forward and kicked, the top of his foot connecting with soft stomach just below the guy's ribs.

Voices around him screamed and yelled. Arms grabbed at him. Pilot yanked away, needing to go after his challenger again, but the man had been pulled out of reach and men in black uniforms surrounded him. Pilot stopped and spit out his mouth guard. The black and grey plastic hit the mat and bounced. "What the fuck?" he snarled.

Amateur fight clubs were not illegal. Betting on them was, but the fighters weren't involved in that. Not really. They just came to fight. Being manhandled by cops was not a part of the package, but that's what they did.

They yanked at Pilot's arms, and it took three of them, but the cuffs clinked into place, cinching behind his back. "Really? What the hell?" They shoved him around to face another cop against the side of the cage with his head tilted back, grabbing his nose.

"You have the right to remain silent," one of them started reading his rights.

"What? What for? What'd I do?"

"Sir, you're being arrested for assaulting an officer. Now, again, you have the right to remain silent." This from an older man, obviously telling him to shut up.

"Fu—" Pilot groaned. It finally started registering in his brain. He'd been so hyped up on adrenaline that he'd barely noticed elbowing the guy. His elbow started throbbing, now that he thought about it. He sure as hell hadn't meant to hit the guy. He'd never hit someone that didn't deserve it, but what the hell? They came in behind him in the middle of a fight. "This is just bullshit," he muttered, garnering another glare from the older cop.

Taking the hint, Pilot shut up and let them take him out of the cage. The other fighter pulled track pants on over his fighting shorts. "Can I get my sweats, man?" Pilot asked, but the cops ignored him. His opponent didn't look like he was being arrested, which just pissed Pilot off more. He wondered if he'd just lost his payment for the match. The day had just turned to serious shit.

The cops tucked him, half naked, into the back of a cruiser and hauled him down to the tall glass fronted, gray building that passed as the police station on 46th. Orange paint desecrated the walls of the lower levels and stood out in the night, lit by spotlights. The cruiser circled around to the back where the paint job appeared a bit more non-descript. The officer pulled him out of the car and shoved him toward a big steel door. It took a long time to get him booked, fingerprinted, and sitting down in front of a phone. Pilot didn't worry too much about it. He called Uncle Gary. The man had connections and lawyer friends and Pilot was pretty sure it would all go away, but so would the fighting. No way would he be able to keep it up now, after having to be bailed out.

They brought Booker in while he waited for Uncle Gary. He gave Pilot a quick nod. "It's all good," he drawled.

Pilot opened his mouth to say something, but Booker shook his head. They couldn't really say anything there in the middle of the police station. He'd have to wait and see about the money, but regardless, Pilot knew the fighting had come to a screeching halt. Gary would make him promise and he'd never break that kind of promise. Not to Gary, anyway.

A few hours later, Uncle Gary showed up to get him with the bail paid. "So, where's your car?" The pit of his stomach felt hollow.

He'd parked at the share ride and took the transit into town, so Gary pointed his old pick up in that direction without much conversation. Before they got there, he cleared his throat. "This shit has to stop, Sean."

The tone of his voice made him sure Gary was more pissed off than he thought. "Yes, sir."

"Don't sir, me. This is not the kind of trouble you need. Johnny is going to kick your ass." That was too true. "This is going to cost you more than you made at the fight, boy." That hole in his stomach rolled with acid.

"Yes, sir." He'd screwed up, but really it wasn't his fault. He was trying to do the right thing, or at least he had been trying to do something.

"Plus, you didn't need that extra money anyway. Johnny takes care of your finances, Sean. Damn. Plus, you have a big gig coming up."

"Supercross isn't until January."

"Wrong again." He shook his head a little and bit his lip, as he pulled up beside Pilot's mustang.

Pilot could have bought a better car, but he didn't really need one. His baby still ran and he only used it for running around town. Why pay out extra for something he didn't need. Johnny didn't even have a car.

Pilot opened the door of the truck and stepped out. The night chill bit him to the bone, still dressed in nothing but his fighting shorts. Uncle Gary hadn't brought him anything and he had no idea what happened to his bag. He could only be grateful that he'd left his gun in the car for once, safely locked in the truck.

"Hey!" Uncle Gary got his attention. "Did you hear me?"

"Sorry, I'm tired." He tried to smile, but only grinned weakly.

"Listen. There's a Supercross special event coming up at the end of next week. Apex wants you there. So? You going to do another fight and go to jail or look out for your boy? You can't do that if you're in freakin' jail, Sean."

His boy? Oh! He meant McAllister. Yeah, that was important and lucrative. "Yeah, you know I'm in. Thanks, Uncle. I'm done with the fighting, okay?" He knew he didn't have a choice about that anymore anyway, and Gary hadn't been kidding when he said Johnny would kick his ass.

"Promise?"

Pilot knew that would be a requirement, and he supposed he was ready for it. He had to be, but he still felt like he'd just lost something important in his life. "Yeah. Promise."

"Okay. Go home and get some rest. I'll take care of it." Pilot had no doubt that he would. He wondered again how he'd been so lucky to have Uncle Gary on his side. And Johnny, who was going to kill him.

Pilot knew quitting was the right thing, but he had no idea how to move forward without the fights grounding him and giving him the release he so desperately needed.

Chapter 12 - X-TS Event

Tate loved the added event, sponsored by X-Top Energy drink. They called it the X-Top Energy Straight Event, which rapidly became known as the X-TS Event. This was not a typical race or race track, for that matter. No, it was head-to-head, straight out, wide open race down a half a mile stretch of rhythm section. Whoops and dragon backs and table tops all stretched out in one shot—no turns. The racers went against one opponent at a time in an elimination bracket style tournament. The gates had been designed more like horse racing than for motorcycles, but Tate liked that, too. It allowed him those few last seconds of headspace before tearing through the dirt. The top sixteen Supercross riders would be there to compete for the honor and the money along with some few others from other motocross leagues. The excitement of seeing Davey and Tyler again would be second only to barreling down that track—and winning.

Bryce would be there too, racing in the Lites class for the smaller 250cc bikes. Tate wasn't sure how he felt about that. Ignoring the boy at the camp had been hella-hard, but at least here, at this massive event with thick crowds, he might not even see Bryce at all. Bryce wasn't even in the same class as Tate. Likely, they wouldn't run in to each other at all, yet his body thrummed just knowing Bryce would be there somewhere. The real question tumbling through Tate's head was whether he *wanted* to see Bryce. Was he ready to be something for Bryce? A friend? He wanted more, but Bryce deserved better. Tate had let that caveman, Warren, have him like some kind of slut. All of it was Tate's own fault. His own fault about Warren, and moving too fast with Bryce. What could he do about any of it? *Too many questions.*

He pouted, unable to answer himself and headed out from the RV that MSR had provided for the weekend to find his mechanic and his bike. He didn't like not knowing who was working on his machine, but MSR had complete control. Tate didn't know if he liked that or not. He realized handing over a lot of that kind of control was probably better. That way he didn't have to worry about much else, and it left Tate with the surety of the one thing he knew how to do. Ride.

At his pit, an awning stretched out from the side of a huge truck with his number, *87*, and his sponsor names plastered all over the place. The mechanics had huge tool boxes wheeled out and the bike up on a stand. When he stepped farther into the area, he noticed Joey sitting in a chair, tipping up a bottle of water. Yeah, it was damned hot in Southern California, even in October. "Hey," he called out to the guy leaning over the seat of his bike.

The guy stood and turned. Andrew Hansen. Tate let out a relieved breath, knowing Andrew was one of the best mechanics on the MSR team. "Hey, Tate. You're going to love this ride."

Tate offered his best smile, usually reserved for the podium. "I'm sure, Drew. Glad you're on the team today." He held out his hand, but Andrew held his up in the air, showing the coating of grease that had turned them black.

"If today goes well, I'll be on the team, leading it, for the season."

"Great!" Tate couldn't be happier with that setup. Andrew meant quality craftsmanship. He wasn't Tyler Whitmore, but that mechanic was booked. Davey wouldn't be letting his man work for any other riders, even Tate. "Looking forward to it."

Joey stood up and handed Tate a bottle of water. "Oz should be here shortly and there'll be fans to talk with. Drink now. Make sure you stay hydrated today."

"Yes, boss." Tate knew the man was right, he just didn't like taking orders. What could he say though? He may be the star, but not the only one on the team. MSR made sure to surround him with the best, knowing it took everyone to make it work. Joey was the best trainer and Oz the best manager. Now, Andrew would join the team. Tate couldn't complain. Nope, with help from the team he could easily get through any bullshit until he hit the track. Then, nothing would matter but the dirt.

His first set of races would be against Cole Lindt, who had helped that asshole, Parker, fuck with Davey and Tyler last season. Tyler had been Cole's mechanic until some ass posted that picture on the internet of Davey and Tyler engaged in a sexual act. They never figured out who had snapped and posted the pic, but most suspected Parker. It had damaged their reputations in the beginning and had gotten Tyler fired from the team.

Cole's loss.

Tate wanted to make sure it would be Cole's loss in the first bracket as well. They'd be going head to head, best two out of three runs advancing. Tate could not be knocked out in the first round; he just couldn't let that happen. He had learned a few things from Davey about leveraging his longer legs and handling the bike over the jumps. He'd learned a lot from his coach about jumping with speed, low over mounds. He had every intention of using all of that knowledge and his natural instincts to decimate Cole Lindt.

"Clean that bike up," Oz roared. He stormed into the pits wearing cargo shorts, a red polo and a white straw hat. You'd never see him in a jersey or the team uniforms. He always presented a classy front.

"What's up, Oz, man?" He grasped Oz's hand and they shared a chest to chest bro-hug.

"I've got a reporter coming to interview you in a few minutes. We'll do it right by the bike. I want the number front a center. Let's go," he commanded with a clap of his hands.

Andrew gave him a quick salute and finished up whatever he'd been doing, then grabbed a fresh towel, to wipe down the bike.

Tate bumped into Oz's shoulder. "Yeah, hello to you too, Oz."

"No time, no time, my boy. This is race day. I don't care if it isn't a point's race. It's still important. We want you to win this."

Tate snorted, knowing that his sponsors didn't think he'd do better than third in points this year and that probably included the X-TS event. "I plan to." He did. He planned to show them all.

He glanced at Joey, who wore the same smirk. Yep, at least he knew his trainer was in his corner. Despite their somewhat rocky start, the man had gotten Tate's head and racing where it needed to be, on the track instead of in his pants.

Joey slapped a hand down on Oz's shoulder. "Relax. Tate's got this."

Oz pointed at Joey. "You, I trust. All right." He jerked his head to indicate the production rolling down the pavement toward them. "Hey, grab one of those hats."

Tate rolled his eyes, but grabbed a hat anyway. It had his colors, the main hat was yellow with black and white stripes across the brim, and a KTM logo on the front. He tugged it on and tucked his long hair behind his ears and gave a goofy smile that made Oz and Joey laugh.

"Shit. Behave, Tate," Oz laughed, just as the reporter with her gear stopped outside the awning.

"Good morning, Mr. Osgood." The reporter had long brown hair pulled back into a ponytail and a fresh face. Her voice rang like a bell.

"Oz, please." He shook her hand and gestured for her to enter the domain of Tate Jordan, *number 87.*

Behind the reporter, a camera man and a helper pushing a cart pressed in. Joey and Andrew took that moment to disappear out the other side. They weren't the ones that the sponsors wanted to see on camera anyway.

Tate knew the drill; he turned on his winner's smile. "Hello."

They shook hands before the woman spoke. "Nice to meet you. I'm

Amy. May I call you Tate?" She had a nice smile and confidant stature.

"Yes, sure, of course."

"Great. So, I'm just going to introduce you and ask you a few questions."

Tate nodded. "Sure. Fine."

After she fussed with her crew for a minute, Amy pulled a set of headphones, huge black cups strapped together with an antennae sticking up on one side, over her ears. Her assistant handed her a big mic with a box wrapped around it with the X-Top Energy logo on one side and the network station on the other. "Ready?" she asked.

Tate smiled and uncrossed his arms. Oz had instructed him numerous times to keep his hands at his sides during an interview unless he was holding something with a sponsor logo. Empty handed, he clenched and unclenched his fists but kept them at his sides.

"I'm here this morning with Tate Jordan, one of Supercross's best riders," she started. "Tate, you qualified eighth today, putting you up against Cole Lindt, who also did not qualify as well as expected. What happened out there?"

"Uh, I can't speak for Cole," he chuckled and Amy chuckled with him. "But for me, it was just getting used to the track. It's different than a regular Supercross track without the turns, so getting the feel for it just took me a minute, but I've got it now."

"So, you think you're going to eliminate Cole in the first round?"

Tate plastered his winner's smile across his face. Ear to ear, he knew it outshined anything else around. "I don't think. I know."

"I love that confidence. You finished well in points last year, but with the likes of McAllister and Regal consistently leading the board, how do you think you'll finish this next season?"

Tate laughed. MSR probably told them not to ask that question. Over Amy's shoulder, he could see Oz scowling. He knew it was a sore subject. No one expected Tate to win against those two, especially Davey. "It's any man's ride, right. I mean, yeah, they're great racers, but being on the track with them only makes me better, and if I can take the lead from any other racer, I'm going to. I'm going to finish in points in the best place I possibly can."

"Even if that means beating Davey McAllister? He *is* your friend, right?"

"Oh, we're friends," Tate nodded.

"Haven't you been training with Davey McAllister during the off season? Is that why you're getting better?"

Tate smiled again, knowing that Amy was asking all the questions MSR wanted to avoid. He didn't care. "I haven't been with them yet during *this* off season, though I have trained with Davey in the past. Yeah, it makes me a better rider. Of course. He's the best."

Amy gave a sly smile. "Why haven't you been out with him, yet?" she asked, probably already knowing the answer.

"Davey started the off season on his honeymoon. You'll have to ask him about that." Tate winked at her. Being charming had always gone a long way for him in this game. He knew how to work it.

"Indeed. We wish you a lot of luck today on the track." She turned and smiled at the camera and Tate took a subtle step back. "That's Tate Jordan folks. Ready to prove he's got what it takes." Amy paused just a moment before adding, "Cut. That's a wrap." She turned back to Tate. "Thank you. Really, you did very well."

Tate shook her hand again and watched silently as the camera crew left to make their way down the row to another competitor.

"She's right. Good job, Tate," Oz practically purred. Yep, Tate had handled her questions perfectly. "You're getting good at this."

"You shouldn't have worried, boss." In fact, Oz had nothing to worry about. Tate intended to do better than expected here and during the regular season.

Tate examined the brackets for the event. McAllister had qualified first and Regal second. Surprisingly, Shannon Parker was in the event with new sponsors and qualified fifteenth and was up against Regal as the second qualifier in the first round. Davey would have to race the final qualifier, a guy named James Brunswich. It was Brunswich's first year in the 450SX division, having won the 250SX West two years prior, and had a great season the year before. Nice, but Davey would blow him away.

After Tate beat Cole, he'd have to race the winner from another bracket, either Robin Owens or Perry Schmidt. Both were decent racers that landed in the top five regularly over the last few years and both were hungry for some wins, but neither were a match for him. After that round, he'd be racing McAllister for the final spot, since they were in the same bracket. Regal had ended up in the opposing bracket. All things holding true to talent, skill, and history, it would be either Davey or him facing good old Chad Regal in the final battle. Tate felt better about his chances against Regal than he did against Davey, truth be told. If he could get past Davey, he'd win. He knew it. He liked and respected Davey, but if he could beat the guy on the track, he would.

"One race at a time," Joey said, handing him another bottle of water.

"You reading my mind now?"

"Don't have to. I see you staring down the brackets, as if that alone were enough to win. Seriously, don't underestimate Cole Lindt."

"No. No, I'm not. Just because I don't like him, doesn't make him a bad racer. Same as Parker. I'd rather see him in jail than on the track, but the fucker has skill and here he is."

"Don't sweat it. Parker isn't yours to deal with right now. Regal will send him packing first round."

Tate snorted. "Damn straight."

Bryce stood back in the crowd gathered at the MSR pit. Some news lady had a mic in Tate's face, asking about the upcoming event. Bryce blushed and sucked his bottom lip in between his teeth. His heart sped up, irrationally. It was a total fanboy moment hearing Tate's voice again so close. Yet, he might as well be a world away. Bryce still couldn't have him.

Tate's confident answers amazed him, and he talked about Davey McAllister as if they were best friends. Sure, Bryce knew that they knew each other, but Tate hadn't said anything about them practicing together at McAllister's place. How amazing would that be?

It just made Bryce feel like some star-struck kid. No, it would be better to just walk away than to let Tate see him standing there mooning over him.

The reporter shook Tate's hand, and their voices lowered. Other people started walking away, thinning the crowd. Tate would see him, if he just looked up. For one slow heartbeat, Bryce wished he'd just look up. Then, his manager jumped in and jostled Tate around, breaking the spell. Bryce had his own shit to worry about, anyway.

He turned with a sigh and walked away. Tate wasn't meant for him, but he could still feel the heat of Tate's lips against his own, as if it had just happened moments ago, rather than weeks.

Pilot stood in the back of the mechanic's area, leaning against the big semi-trailer with his arms folded across his chest. The ground in front of the truck was covered with plastic and above their heads, a huge awning stretched. All of it tastefully covered with Apex, Kawasaki, and Cam Top Oil logos. Even the red metal tool boxes that had been rolled out between the bikes had logo stickers on them. Doing his job meant staying out of the way and watching everything. That meant watching Tyler Whitmore-McAllister buzz around directing the work being done on both Davey's bike and a new bike that the new girl, Sarah Bolster, would be racing.

Trident Security sent Pilot with a partner, Broady, to protect the Apex team. Last year Broady had worked well with him, so he returned with Pilot. He let Broady shadow Davey while he attended interviews and signed autographs, leaving Pilot to watch Tyler who made sure the bikes were ready to go. He bee-bopped around, humming some song, and every now and then, he stopped to shake his ass. Pilot found it quite amusing...and distracting. He needed to be watching out for issues, not Tyler's ass shaking. He smirked to himself, thinking he'd rather watch Tyler dance around. The man was hot as hell. And taken.

Not that Pilot would have made a move on him anyway. He wouldn't. Why bother? He was not in a position to be starting shit with Supercross kids that traveled around nine or more months of the year. He'd have fun traveling around with them this year, but home was Colorado, not in a trailer or hotel room.

He sighed and ran his hand across his buzzed hair. He'd had it done just before catching his flight out to the coast. He figured it would be hotter than he was used to in Southern California, and he'd been right. He was already sweating through his soft t-shirt and it wasn't even eight in the morning. *Damn! Supercross racers started early.*

He heard a commotion outside of the area and perked up, more alert. He peered out the side of the tented space and saw Davey and his group approaching with Broady's big body shadowing him. When Davey turned and came a bit closer, he put his finger up to his lips like a kindergarten teacher, begging with his eyes for Pilot's silence. Pilot gave him a quick nod and stepped back. Broady followed him in and reached out for a quick, but quiet fist bump.

They both watched Davey sneak up on Tyler. He grabbed at the mechanic's sides, and Tyler squealed and turned, raising his hands in the air above his head. "Stop. Stop," he protested with much laughter. "I'm all greasy." He stretched his neck up to kiss Davey, who wrapped arms around Tyler's wide chest and back.

Something tightened inside Pilot's own chest. Jealousy? Not of either man in particular, but jealous of what they had. Something he didn't think would ever be a possibility for him. He'd never really wanted that before anyway. He had Johnny as a close friend and he could find a hook up every now and again for sex. He didn't think he needed anything else, but seeing Davey and Tyler so openly loving each other, he reconsidered. Maybe he did want that. Maybe he wanted Johnny to have something like that, too. He deserved to be happy. Hell, they both did. What the hell were they working so hard for, just to have an empty lonely life? What would it mean to reach their dream, buying part of Uncle Gary's business, if they didn't have any one they loved to share it with?

Pilot stifled a growl. He wasn't supposed to be thinking about relationships or watching Davey and Tyler play with each other. He glanced over at Broady to see if he'd been busted. It looked like his partner was looking beyond the awning, but he couldn't be certain since he couldn't see his eyes behind the dark sunglasses. Well, beneath his own dark Ray-Bans, Broady probably couldn't see what he had been watching either.

The guys busied themselves with the bike, getting serious and talking about Bolster's bike and performance. She would be riding a little later in the day. Their seriousness in their business made it easier to ignore them. Pilot only had a passing interest in their sport. He didn't need to be a fan to protect his charges.

He focused on the perimeter, so he wasn't surprised when a shaggy blond head popped in. The tall racer smiled from ear to ear, doing a better job at lighting up the space than the sun had done. He smelled like dirt, grease, and citrus-fresh. Pilot inhaled as he passed, wanting more of that scent.

"Davey, Tyler!" the racer called out. He was long and lean like Davey and sexy as hell in his racing gear. Pilot remembered him from last season, but not his name. He hadn't been important then. Why was he now? Davey and Tyler turned and greeted their friend with half hugs and glad-to-see-ya's.

Tate.

They called him Tate.

His sea-green eyes danced around the pit and when they landed on Pilot, something leaped up his throat from his chest, making Pilot stop breathing. Tate smiled. The world stopped. "Hi," he said with a plump bottom lip, perfect for kissing and biting. His upper lip was thinner, but just as perfect.

Pilot stood up straighter, dropping his arms to his sides and desperately searching for his voice. "Hi. I'm Pilot," he finally croaked out.

"I know." The sea in his eyes sparkled, looking like eternity.

Tate continued his conversation with Davey and Tyler, but those eyes kept sliding back to Pilot. He wanted more than Tate's eyes on him. He wanted that mouth and his hands and maybe those long-long legs wrapped around his waist. Pilot swallowed hard. He didn't believe in love at first sight. Lust at first sight was apparently a yes, though. He'd never been this attracted to anyone. Ever. Want swam around in his gut and stirred his cock.

Tate had to go. He needed to get his bike and get up to the track, but he didn't want to leave his friends. Davey and Tyler were so cool to hang out with and he'd missed them, but Tate knew they were just his excuse. What he really didn't want to leave was Pilot's hot gaze on him.

For the hundredth time in five minutes, Tate slid his eyes over to Pilot's handsome, glowering face. He'd met the body guard previously, but he hadn't registered much on Tate's scale aside from being a mountainous hunk of scowly man. Yet, now he found him attractive in an animalistic sort of way and could seriously imagine doing all sorts of dirty things with him.

None of that mattered, though. Tate had a job to do and couldn't afford to get in trouble with his team. Oz would kill him if he didn't move his ass.

He said his goodbyes to the team and hauled ass, forcing himself to ignore Pilot as he raced off. He could hear Oz admonishing him as he got on his bike. "Stop being so boy-crazy. Pull your head away from your dick. Get a grip and get on the bike." Okay, maybe some of that was Tate's own inner voice rather than Oz, but all of it was truth.

Lined up at the gate, throttle revving, Tate mentally dropped all thoughts of sexy body guards. Cole was in the next box, though he couldn't see the man. The gates had canvas dropped on both sides that looked like faux wood, playing up the fact that horses used to race on this track. Tate didn't give a shit. He watched the gate in front of him, ready to take off the instant it dropped. He needed to beat Cole twice, back to back. If the man got an inch, it wouldn't be pretty.

The gate dropped. Tate took off, flying out of the gate. Dirt exploded up around him. Staying low on the bike, he pushed hard over the first set of table tops. He focused on the track, ignoring the other racer. The whoops section had been designed to knock lesser skilled racers off their game. Tate's bike hit the top of each mound, front tire then back tire, front tire—back tire, as if he were skimming rocks in a pond. He flew over the next few jumps and across the speed break. The dragon back, a set of dirt mounds set close together that consecutively got higher—uphill—as they went along, loomed ahead. This dragon back followed dual table tops and made the first whoops section look like training wheels. Tate used his powerful legs to pull the bike along them.

Ignoring Cole felt impossible. A tightness pulled in his chest, but he ignored it, too. Until the final jumps, Cole raced alongside him in his peripheral vision. Then Tate pulled ahead. As he flew over the final jump across the finish line, he angled his bike sideways. When his tires came back down and hit the ground, he knew he won the first round. He pumped his fist in the air. *Victory. Take that, Cole!*

He had to wait for another set of racers to take their turn before taking the track again, but Tate was determined to take the second race too. He lined up like before and blasted out of the box. Cole pushed him the entire way, so close he practically breathed down Tate's throat. He used his taller body to pull his bike ahead by inches, but those few inches were all that mattered. Tate only won in the last second, by a hair, but he won. Once he saw Cole had pulled off the end of the track, Tate did a quick donut before exiting.

He had to give an interview as the winner of the bracket before going back to his pit. He gave a quick, happy and hopeful answer, wondering why anyone cared how he would feel about racing against his friend, should he have to face off with Davey. Yes, they were friends. On the track though, any track, they were competitors first. Tate respected Davey like no other, but he still could beat the man. Tate had something to prove.

He let those thoughts ruminate as his mechanic jumped on the back of his bike, and they rode together down to the pit. He killed the bike and handed it over to Andrew. "Don't mess with it too much. She ran like a fucking dream, man."

Andrew nodded and pushed the bike up on the stand.

A throat cleared behind him. "Great race, Tate." Tyler.

Tate couldn't help the smile that stretched across his face as he turned around, but as soon as he had Tyler in his sights, he also had Pilot there. He towered over Tyler, arms crossed, sexy mouth frowning. Tate's heart stopped. He forgot how to use words. The man's arms were thicker than the seat of his bike and busting out of his tight shirtsleeves like water from a hydrant. His thick muscles curved around his shoulders and arms, unmistakably hard, even under his t-shirt. You just couldn't hide muscles like that, and Tate had never found a man with such a physique so sexy before. Pilot's dark eyes caught his own, making him feel like some kind of trapped bird with his heart pounding fast like beating wings. Finally finding his voice, he croaked, "Hey."

Tyler reached out and patted his shoulder. It felt more like sympathy than congratulations and had Tate wondering if Tyler could read his mind. Or maybe he just noticed Tate rolling his tongue back up into his mouth. A man like that made it a lot easier for Tate to forget his own bullshit.

"You ready to take on Davey?" Tyler quipped.

Tate nodded, still staring at Pilot who cocked his head to the side as if trying to figure Tate out, or maybe he was thinking of something else entirely. Tate wanted to find out, wanted to push for more. He forced the edges of his mouth to turn upward. "Yeah," he said. Real intelligent. So much for flirting.

Tyler laughed and started to say something, but stopped and rubbed his hand against his mouth before starting again. Tate didn't have a chance to wonder what he had planned to say, before Tyler blurted out words that completely distracted him. "So, you broke up with your dickhead boyfriend, right?"

Simple words, but spoken while Tate continued to eye-fuck Tyler's bodyguard, caused his head to spin. He made some kind of noise and nodded dumbly, causing Tyler to laugh again. Pilot didn't laugh. His lips pursed together so hard the pink temptations turned white. What did that mean?

"So, that means you're single. Not seeing anyone?"

"Uh...right." Tate looked down at his hands, realizing he hadn't taken off his gloves. His goggles still hung from his neck. When had he even taken off his helmet and where had he put it? He looked around the pit area, but didn't know if he was looking for the allusive helmet or an escape hatch.

"Cool, so after Davey kicks your ass on the track, meet us for a celebration."

"Oh, you think?" Nothing like a racing taunt to jump start Tate's brain. "You and your bodyguard are more than welcome to celebrate my victory, but Davey will be so beaten, he'll have to crawl there."

Pilot made some kind of straggled noise that sent blood racing through Tate's body, straight to his cock. He wanted to hear that sound again.

Tate pulled his gloves off and tossed them on top of one of the tool boxes. "Hell, Ty, you'll probably have to have Pilot carry the man." He stared straight at Pilot and winked.

"Fuck you! Davey's going to leave tire tracks on your ass," Tyler joked.

"What kind of shit talk is that?" Tate chuckled. "Nobody's going near my ass."

"Sadly."

"Shut up." Tate could feel the heat flare across his cheeks, as he realized what he'd said.

Pilot's little pink tongue darted out of his mouth. Tate wanted more of that too.

Tyler bumped his shoulder against Tate's. "You're still welcome to come hang out with us." He wiggled his eyebrows a bit. Tate realized that Pilot couldn't see Tyler's face. His friend just might be trying to hook them up. Tate was pretty sure he was down with that, if Pilot was. He looked up and smiled for real and watched as the corner of Pilot's mouth left his ever present scowl to give him half of one back.

Chapter 13 - X-TS Event, After the Race

Tate won his next bracket with ease, then found himself facing his friend, number one ranked, Davey McAllister. Determination to win boiled in Tate's blood. He gave it all he had. But, Tyler's prediction came true. The race against Davey had been a tough one. He'd won the first round, but Davey won the second. Even though he psyched himself up to beat him on the final try, the best out of the three went to Davey. Barely.

Tate was not going to sulk over it. He ignored Oz and Joey and hung out with the Apex crew, cheering Davey in his final set. Oddly, Davey would be up against Jack Benson, a racer from Arenacross that they didn't know much about. Benson surprisingly took out Regal in their bracket, but Davey wouldn't care about that. Tate never saw him getting hung up about his competitors, who he had to beat, he just rode hard every time. He had to be the fastest bike down the track. That's it. Tate simply enjoyed watching his friend. Nobody rode like Davey did.

He made his way to the track where he would watch with Tyler and Pilot and the rest of the Apex crew. The pits had been set up on the inside of the original horse track and the stadium seats for fans were on the other side of the straight track. They got situated near the end where they couldn't really see much of the start of the race, but watching the end was better. You wanted to see who took that final jump. The announcers would tell everyone, but seeing it with your own eyes was way more exciting. The only thing better was being on the bike that won.

As he found his friends, he heard Tyler grumbling to their manager, Stewart. "I still can't believe this isn't the same old battle with Regal."

"If he wouldn't have screwed himself..."

"How's that?" Angel asked. She was the dark haired beauty that had pulled the Apex team out of the crap, against all odds. She was a photographer, but she apparently had other skills as well. She lifted her camera with the gigantic lens, pointing it at the other end of the track.

Stewart snorted. "He didn't do well through the whoops and landed wrong on the jump that follows the speed break. You know? He just had a shitty run. Very unlike him."

Tate agreed and shook everyone's hands. He knew them all from hanging out with Davey. They'd all been to the ranch. Tate suspected they felt almost like family. He wasn't sure about that, since he didn't really have a family and hadn't for a long time. His experience with family wasn't good anyway. They drop kicked you when you needed them most, so maybe he didn't want the Apex team to be family. Maybe it was better to have great friends instead.

He enjoyed watching Davey race with them, except for the constant uncomfortable tension caused by wanting to crawl into Pilot's arms and set up house there. The man probably wasn't gay. Probably had zero interest in Tate. Surely, Tate must be reading the man wrong, but if he wasn't?

The crowd roared. Davey sailed over the final jump, fist in the air in his typical win-style. Tyler jumped up and down, grabbing Tate and shaking him, letting go and grabbing Stewart and shaking him. When he went to grab Angel, she pointed her finger at him and he held up his hands in defeat.

Tate wanted to grab Pilot, but no one was about to grab that man and all his muscles. He stayed next to the other bodyguard, a step or two back from everyone else. Tate couldn't help looking at him, wanting him.

The celebration didn't last long. Most of the Apex crew took off early. Their new female rider, Bolster, who ran in the Light class, did well, but didn't win. Tate got the vibe that she felt bad about it and consoling her was like walking through field of land mines. It put a damper on Davey's celebration, but that man ought to be used to winning anyway. So, later that evening when Davey and Tyler went back to their trailer, accompanied by their driver and the other bodyguard, Tate found himself alone with Pilot in the Apex pit and quite unsure how it had happened.

Pilot sat on top of the last giant red tool box that hadn't been loaded into the big truck yet. Mickey Hun, Tyler's second mechanic, said he'd be back for it in a few hours. He'd left with a few others to have a drink or two in the nearby town.

"So, what? You're off duty now?" Tate asked him.

Pilot smiled for the first time that Tate had seen. His dark eyes twinkled, sending happy glitter-sparkles through Tate's veins and down into his stomach where they danced with butterflies. *Fuck I'm an idiot!*

"Yeah," Pilot answered with a nod.

"Uh, so is Pilot your first name or your last?" Tate asked with a laugh. He didn't expect much of an answer.

Pilot licked his lips and said, "Neither."

Tate had to push that line of questioning. "So, what's your name then?"

"I don't know you well enough. Only my closest friends, family…or lovers get that out of me." His deep voice resonated in Tate's chest and the way he said *lovers* made Tate's knees quiver.

"That can be arranged," Tate said with a wiggle of his eyebrows. He couldn't keep himself from flirting.

Pilot's face morphed into that familiar scowl. "What?" he asked.

His reaction disappointed Tate, but he had nothing else to lose. He wouldn't hold back because of fear. Hell, Tate wasn't made like that. "The lovers part." He wanted to keep it light and flirty, but his voice sounded serious, and he was. Serious and raw.

Pilot laughed, softly. "You're really trying too hard, Tate."

Tate blew out a slow breath. "Nah, really. I'm just kind of lonely. You know?" He gave up the silly flirting. Pilot didn't seem to respond to that anyway.

Pilot looked at him long and hard until Tate squirmed from the intensity and wondered what he was getting himself into. Pilot was so severe.

Finally Pilot said, "I know what you mean. But, don't sell yourself short. Or too quickly. It's better to hold out for the real thing."

"Real thing? You mean love?" Tate asked with a grunt.

"Yeah. Love. Don't you believe in love?"

Tate shrugged. "I don't know. Maybe for some. But, with my life…" He held his arms out, indicating the pit they were sitting in, but also Supercross as a whole. He traveled half the year and trained the other half. "Hell, Pilot! I don't even have a home right now. This is it. A fucking hotel room at every track." Tate was surprised at his honesty. He hadn't even been honest with himself because that was the truth of the matter, the ugly truth that he didn't want to acknowledge. Failed relationships. All his relationships. None of them ever had a chance because Supercross was Tate's first love and he'd never, never cheat on her.

"That's a harsh life, but it's what you chose. Would you do anything else?"

Tate shook his head with a chuckle at how Pilot echoed his own thoughts. "Hell, no. This is me. I bleed dirt and I breathe jumps."

Finally, the smile that had vanished returned to Pilot's face where it belonged. "Yeah, I see that." His eyes traveled over Tate's body, up and down, giving him delicious little tingles. "Truth is, uh, I don't know. I've never been in love. I don't know what that's like and I don't have time for it either. I work. Work. More work." His words sounded cynical and Tate thought the man was just as lonely as he was.

"Doesn't have to be all work. You know what they say about Jack."

"Fuck your cliché Tate. Besides..."

""What?" Tate took a few shuffling steps toward Pilot.

"Time for that later. For now, I only have time for occasional, very occasional, hookups."

"Yeah? That's apparently all I can get anyway." Tate wanted more—a lot more, but Pilot had the right idea. Tate would focus on racing until he couldn't race anymore and then maybe, if he were lucky, he'd find someone he could have more with. The bitter end to his last relationship proved that. The way he'd searched the track earlier in the day for Bryce, proved that again. He didn't find him and didn't have his number to call. He did get the news that Bryce had lost in his second bracket and that he hadn't raced against Bolster. That was it. No Donny. No Bryce. Not even a piece of shit like Warren Tanner to fuck him unmercifully.

"Hey!" Pilot cut into his thoughts. "Come here," he commanded and Tate obeyed immediately, stepping between Pilot's legs.

He felt a shudder thrill down his body when Pilot put his gargantuan paws on his shoulders. The man's hands were as big as a helmet, rough like a tire tread, and comforting like wrist cuffs tied to a bed. Tate's half-hard cock sprang to life, plumping out fully and caused him to lean into Pilot, wanting to hump his leg.

"Easy, boy. I'm armed."

"You sure are," Tate practically purred, wanting to get more of Pilot's hands on other parts of his body.

Pilot shook him back. "No. I mean it. I'm carrying."

Tate's eyes went wide. "You mean like a gun?"

"Yeah," Pilot answered, but his voice was low and sounded like a growl. Tate tilted his head up to better see his dark eyes.

Pilot moaned softly and leaned down, bringing their lips together. The press was soft like velvet and sent his heart off like fireworks. Tate had no control over his tongue, as it slipped out to lick at Pilot's mouth. The motion must have been encouraging, because Pilot slid off of the toolbox and went in for a dominating kiss, devouring Tate's mouth. He wrapped Tate up in his python-worthy arms and pulled him against a hard chest.

Tate lifted his hand and tentatively touched Pilot's shoulder, feeling the hard muscles. "Wow," he said, pulling out of the kiss. His hands slid over the rounded flesh. "Your shirt's stuffed with boulders."

Pilot's laugh was low and throaty and as precious as diamonds. "Let's go back to my hotel. I-I want you, Tate."

Another wow moment for Tate. His name on Pilot's lips was like honey on biscuits. "Please," he muttered. His eyes fluttered closed as Pilot kissed him again. Tate wanted their naked bodies pressed against each other. "Uh...I, uh, I bottom," he choked out. Pilot had him feeling nervous like some young, inexperienced kid.

"Good." Pilot guided him out of the pit area.

Tate barely remembered the drive to the hotel, but thanked God it didn't take long. Once inside the room, Pilot's hands became wild, out of control. They were up and down his back, in his hair, grabbing his ass, and pulling off the rest of his gear. They fumbled at the strap and buckle of his pants, but Tate helped him and in record time he was standing there in his jock strap. Pilot yanked his shirt off, over his head and Tate was surprised he hadn't ripped it in his haste, but didn't care as long as it was off.

Pilot's lack of shirt also revealed the top of his gun holster. Pants and gun came off almost simultaneously. Tate had never thought much about weapons, but everything about Pilot was hyper-sexy including the firearm. Pilot stopped to secure it in his suitcase, tucking the luggage in the small closet. "Can't be too careful," he muttered. Again, Tate didn't care as long as the man continued with the de-clothing process.

Tate sat on the edge of the bed and trembled as Pilot stalked across the room toward him like some kind of muscular jungle cat. The man was more than bulk, he was coordinated, graceful. Tate grabbed his crotch, squeezing his dick, trying to get a grip. He was so hard. He couldn't remember ever being this turned on. Not with Donny, even when they'd first met, and not with anyone before or since. Nope. This super hard cock was for Pilot alone.

"Mine," the man growled and grabbed Tate around the waist, shoving him farther up the bed. He had both Tate's jock strap and his own briefs off before Tate could even squirm against the man, and then Pilot was on him. Their bare chests pressed against each other, hands roaming and exploring each other and hips thrusting desperately.

Tate noticed tattoos in the dim light and ran his fingers across the one on Pilot's chest. "What's this?"

"My bird." Indeed, it was an eagle with something clasped in its talons.

"What's he got?"

Pilot snickered and kissed down Tate's neck before finally answering, "A snack." That was when he bit down on the top of Tate's shoulder.

"Ahh..." Tate groaned and thrust his hips against Pilot. He rubbed his cock against the man's rock-hard thigh.

"I have a few places that would feel better to rub against."

"Please," Tate whispered and grabbed at Pilot's triceps. Digging his fingers into the muscles, he tried pulling Pilot closer.

Pilot chuckled and pulled away. "So eager." He flipped Tate over onto his stomach.

Tate loved how Pilot manhandled him. It was enough to let him swallow all thoughts of that asshole Warren down. He responded to Pilot by sticking his ass up. Maybe he was just a slut, but he wasn't going to live his life hiding just because of one mistake. He wanted to move on, and he wanted it with Pilot. He wiggled his ass, enticingly.

Pilot was taller and carried heavier muscles. Tate was lean and strong, tall for the sport at five-nine but not the tallest. Davey was taller. Still, Pilot had to be over six, maybe even six-three. Tate worked out all the time, strength as well as cardio, but Pilot's muscles put his to shame. With Pilot massaging his ass, pulling the cheeks apart, lifting his hips, then finally licking across his taint Tate didn't give a damn about whatever the hell he'd been thinking about. Pure pleasure ripped through him as that soft tongue circled his hole, and then poked into it.

Tate heard strange noises coming from his own mouth, but didn't even know what they were or how to stop them. It wasn't often he got rimmed. In fact, he could only remember one time, and he wasn't about to start thinking about that now. He buried his face into the hotel pillow and shoved his ass up, silently begging for more attention.

"Mmm..." Pilot hummed, continuing with his tongue fucking. Tate hoped it would go on forever, but all too soon, Pilot pulled up. "Tate, damn, I don't have any condoms."

"Fuck, no!" Tate flipped back to his back. "Pilot?"

"There's a drugstore on the corner..."

For a moment neither of them even breathed. "Why didn't we stop on the way here?"

"Wasn't planning to...you know."

Tate groaned and pulled the pillow over his head. "Wasn't planning? What the hell did ya bring me here for?"

"I thought we'd, you know. Rub off or blow jobs or whatever, but not—"

"I need more than that now. Jesus Christ!"

"Hey, don't say that."

"Say what?"

"Jesus Christ. I don't like that."

"Well, then...fucking Easter Bunny. Go get the damn condoms and lube if you need that too." He threw the pillow at Pilot, who caught it easily enough.

"Don't you fucking move, Tate." He dropped the pillow to the floor and grabbed his jeans, yanking them on commando.

Tate held up his hands. He couldn't even believe this. Pilot's tongue had been in his ass just three seconds ago and now this. He was a bit pissed off and if he weren't so fucking horny, he would have told Pilot to take him home. He watched Pilot's ass, snug jeans that were practically bursting at the seams running down his muscular thighs. Pilot had Tate wanting him like nobody else every had. Nope. Not going anywhere.

Pilot couldn't believe it. He felt like the biggest dick in the world. He had a naked Supercross star in his bed. Well, the hotel's bed, but still...and he had to leave to go get condoms. Fucking crap!

He really hadn't planned to go that far, but he couldn't resist. Tate was all long, lean muscle with not an ounce of fat on him. When he'd had his hands on that body, he'd literally stopped thinking. Tate didn't have much hair, just a thin blond happy trail from his belly button, leading down to golden blond hair, trimmed neatly around his long cock. His mushroom head was purple on top of a reddish-pink shaft. He had every intention of sucking Tate until he screamed Pilot's name. Then his body wanted something else. He kept hearing Tate stuttering out that he bottomed and Pilot needed to get his hands on that ass.

Tate looked good in his riding gear but even better out of it. When Pilot had that ass in his hands, he needed to taste. When his tongue plunged into Tate's hole and he pushed back, Pilot knew he had to fuck. He wanted Tate and would do anything to get him. Including leaving him in his hotel room with his loaded gun stashed in the closet. He hurried, hoping Tate would be trustworthy enough not to mess with it.

Damn! Pilot had lost his mind. Maybe it had just been way too long since he'd been laid.

He bought two packs of condoms and a bottle of lube and raced back to the hotel. He stabbed the key card into the slot and jerked the door open. Tate was still naked, still on the bed, but his erection had deflated. Well, Pilot's had too, but he figured they'd get them back up in no time.

Pilot emptied the bag onto the bed beside Tate's stretched out legs. Damn! They went on forever. Pilot's hands followed his eyes from Tate's ankles, up his shapely calves, and over his lean thighs. His legs were lightly covered with golden hair. "Fucking gorgeous!"

Tate huffed. "Easter Bunny! Took you long enough."

The kid was ridiculous. "How old are you anyway?"

"Shouldn't you have asked that earlier?"

"Huh, shows what you know." Realizing how bad that sounded he quickly added, "Tyler promised me you were legal."

"Yeah, just. I'm twenty one." He sat up in the bed, leaning closer. Pilot noticed Tate had his own tattoo.

"What's yours, huh?" He pointed at the marks on Tate's upper arm.

"Oh, for the championship I won at the 250 level. Can't wait to get another one."

"Tattoo or championship?"

"Yep! Hey. You have another one, too."

Pilot flexed his arm, showing off. The tattoo was a black and gold star with U.S. Army written under it. He'd gotten it between signing his papers and heading off to basic.

"You were in the Army?"

"Yeah."

"Huh. Is that where you picked up your nifty nickname?" Tate tucked his hands behind his head, elbows out, and leaned back down on the pillow stack he'd created. His blond ruffled hair smooshed out across the linen.

Pilot crinkled his nose and dropped his pants, toeing off his sneakers. He wanted more touching and less talking. He grabbed Tate's ankle and dragged him down the bed, just because he could. He loved the way Tate squealed. He planted his knees on the bed, straddling Tate's chest, knowing his cock was almost in Tate's face. "Take a hint, race-boy."

"Easter Bunny, Pilot! You have no finesse!"

Pilot plunged his hands into Tate's shaggy hair, gripping hard and tugging his head back. He watched Tate's throat work as he swallowed. He opened his eyes and Pilot could see the black eating up all that seafoam. "Think you're funny? Huh?"

Tate's smile had Pilot's insides coming undone. Instead of answering, Tate opened his mouth, sticking out his tongue a little, making it flat. Pilot's cock knew it wanted in there, and fully hardened in a hurry. He rubbed it across Tate's tongue, the head sliding back and forth, wet and spongy, then Tate's lips circled around his dick and he sucked. Pilot couldn't stop his hips from thrusting in and out. If he kept going, the need for his trip to the drugstore would be obsolete. "Want to fuck you, Tate."

"Mmm," Tate hummed around his cock.

"Oh, Jesus!"

Tate pulled away from his cock, laughing. "Oh, no! You don't get to use it if I don't. You're supposed to say Easter Bunny!" He laughed again and licked at the underside of the crown of Pilot's cock.

"Tate," he growled, pushing Tate back down on the bed and dragging him toward the head of the bed where they'd started.

"Is it okay that I like hearing my name like that?"

Pilot didn't know how to answer Tate's shy question, so he kissed him instead. His tongue thrust in and out, just like he'd done to his tight, little hole earlier. He scraped his teeth across that plump bottom lip, then licked at it. "Want you," he said again.

Tate answered the same way he had the last time, "Please."

Pilot was inclined to give Tate anything he asked for as long as it involved coming and having Tate in his arms. He popped open the lube and started the process of opening Tate up by sliding his slicked finger where his tongue had been earlier.

Tate pushed his ass up toward his hand. He really wanted it. Pilot just hoped it was him that Tate wanted and not just quick hot sex. Why that mattered to him, he didn't know. But, his brain had stopped working right from the first second he saw Tate. And smelled him. He pushed his face into Tate's belly, smelling that citrusy skin. He wanted to smell and taste every bit of this man. He stuck his tongue in Tate's belly button, making him wiggle.

Pilot added more lube and another finger and wrangled Tate's body around to where he wanted it, sliding him down a little so he could attack Tate's mouth again. First, he licked his long neck and behind his ear. Tate giggled and squealed at Pilot's snuffling. Playing with Tate made him ridiculously happy. He could almost feel the joy in his chest like a tangible thing. Yet, it wasn't something that could last even if he wanted it to. Did he want it to?

Tate's hips flexed, as he tried to get more of Pilot's fingers, so Pilot gave him more.

"I want your cock, Pilot. Gah! Fuck me, bunny."

Pilot snorted at the name, but he really didn't care what Tate wanted to call him. He pulled his fingers away. Tate groaned and thrust his hips again, making the edge of Pilot's mouth quirk up. He hadn't smiled this much since he was a kid and maybe not even then. Sex had never been such a delight. It had always been about getting off, but with Tate it was more about the fun and just being together. He didn't kid himself, though, it was also about getting off. Yet, he wanted to see Tate come, more than he wanted to come himself. That was entirely new.

He ripped open the condom and rolled it on, pinching the tip. Tate leaned up and squirted the lube on his cock, and stroked it several good times.

"Now, please."

"Why such a hurry? Damn. Give me a second."

"I just...ugh! Pilot. My last time wasn't so good. I want to replace those memories with something better. You're better." He laid back on the bed and spread his legs, knees up and wide apart. "Way better. Please."

The sight had Pilot almost losing it right there. He grabbed the base of his cock and squeezed. "I hope so."

Tate squirmed beneath him, probably anticipating the fucking he was about to get. Pilot didn't want to keep him waiting and he really liked the idea of being a good memory for Tate. A part of him deep down wanted to give Tate tons and tons of memories, but he couldn't go there. He shoved those thoughts down and lined up his cock and started pushing. The mechanics worked out quickly enough, and he was completely inside Tate, holding still, and waiting for Tate to get used to him.

"Go. Now. Move. Gah! Please," Tate moaned and rolled his head against the mattress.

Pilot started out slowly, pulling out and pushing back in. Tate panted, eyes squinted shut. "Are you okay?"

"Yes, just, uh, keep moving," Tate said, as he canted his hips a bit. And just like that his expression changed to pure bliss.

"Did I get it?"

"What's your fucking name?"

Pilot laughed a bit as he picked up speed. He didn't want to give up his secret. He just wanted to fuck. In and out, he slid through Tate's ass, hopefully brushing the prostate. He wanted Tate to feel good. "You like?"

"Yes, faster. More."

Pilot stretched over Tate, wrapping his arms around his rib cage. He pulled Tate up off the mattress. Tate's legs wrapped around his waist. "I've got you," Pilot said with a breathy voice. He wanted to be as close as possible. Tate wrapped his arms around Pilot's neck. He still wanted closer; he pulled Tate tighter. "Want you."

"Pilot," Tate groaned. "Fucking's never been like this." He worked his thighs, pushing up and back along with Pilot's own thrusts.

He agreed with Tate. He'd never felt this intimate with anyone before. Tate opened his eyes, locking gazes with Pilot. In that moment, he was pretty sure Tate could see his soul.

"What's your name?" he asked again.

Pilot was no longer capable of keeping the secret. He turned everything over to this man. "Sean. Sean Mahan." He thrust faster and harder.

Tate groaned loudly, "Sean! Mmm...Fuck, me, now!"

He dropped Tate's shoulders back down to the bed and dug his knees into the mattress, aiming for better leverage. He fucked Tate with everything he had, feeling his orgasm building slowly, tingling in the small of his back and slowly traveling up his spine and into his stomach. He started grunting, uncontrollably, needing just a little more.

"Now, now, fu—" Tate called out, just seconds before his face contorted and his cock spewed out between them. Tate opened his eyes in the very last second. They were dark with huge pupils and just a slim line of mossy green circling, but beyond their color, they were pleading for something Pilot didn't know if he could give.

He sucked his bottom lip between his teeth and with a groan, his orgasm raced over him, locking him up. He grunted, feeling momentarily paralyzed as he released into the condom.

Pilot stretched out in the bed and pulled Tate up against him. He didn't want to get dressed and drive Tate back to his own hotel. He didn't want Tate to leave at all. Ever. The thought scared him, mostly because he knew it wasn't possible. "What'd you mean about not having a home earlier?"

"I meant I don't. Everything's in storage except a suitcase."

"So, where are you going tomorrow?" The race was over. Pilot couldn't imagine not having a home base to return to and the thought of Tate on the street had him squirming.

Tate shrugged, cuddling into his side. After a minute or two, his breathing evened out, and Pilot thought he'd fallen asleep. He was okay with that, so he snuggled Tate closer, contemplating whether to ask him to go home with him.

Tate yawned loudly. "I may go hang with Davey out at The Ranch. Or go back to the camp in North Carolina." His words were sleepy.

"What camp?"

"They have a track and a gym. I can stay there. MSR pays for it." Tate rolled over, shoving his ass up against Pilot. He couldn't resist and rolled toward Tate, spooning him. He'd never cuddled a hook up before. Tate was somehow more than that already.

"Davey will let you go out there?"

"I'm pretty sure. Don't worry about it."

Pilot grunted. He worried. A little.

They lay there quietly in the dark. Pilot listened to Tate's breathing. "I like you, Tate," he whispered softly, nudging Tate's ear with his nose.

"Mmm." Tate wiggled his hips a little, his bare ass and legs rubbing against Pilot, causing a little friction against his cock. It started to stir with the movement and Pilot considered going another round.

"I wish things were different, Tate."

Another hip wiggle. "Different how?"

"Our lifestyles make it hard to be anything more than friends."

Tate twisted in his arms. Their cocks bumped against each other like the giraffes fighting for mates that he saw on National Geographic, both immediately thickening. He looked down into Tate's face, open and teasing. "Maybe friends with some benefits?" He wiggled his eyebrows.

Pilot wanted to laugh and cry at the same time. Instead, he leaned down and kissed those crazy eyebrows and rubbed his nose against Tate's. "Yeah," he sighed, wrapping his arms around Tate's shoulders. "I'd rather keep you close."

Tate's face pressed into Pilot's neck. He could feel his eyelashes fluttering against his skin. Then his tongue licked. "How'd you get your nickname, Pilot?"

"You just want to steal all of my secrets, don't you?" Pilot rolled, pushing Tate onto his back beneath him. He snapped his hips, making their cocks battle again.

"Yes. Gimme."

Pilot wasn't sure if he meant his secrets or his cock, so he chose the latter. He reached down between them, grabbing both of their cocks in his hand. Tate thrust up like a little rabbit and made huffing noises as he chased after his orgasm. His cock rubbed against Pilot's with quick strokes. Pilot didn't try to keep up, just let Tate get his. When he came, squirting all over Pilot's cock and fingers, Pilot groaned and his own orgasm came just a few pumps later.

Chapter 14 – Clermont, Florida

Shannon Parker walked into the short, squat cinder block building. It had been painted a horrible blue that stood out against all the brown dirt, but wasn't nearly as bad as the trailers lined up closer to the track. The offices of Florida Sharkpark Motocross had been designed for utility, not luxury, and every bit of that showed.

How many racers had drug dirt in on their boots over the years? Hundreds? More? Shannon's own boots had brought in plenty. Evidence of it stained the linoleum in the front office area where two old metal desks and a couple of folding chairs stood in as a reception area. Shannon would never use the word fancy to describe this place. He snorted at his own musings and crossed his arms over his chest, hooking his fingers under his chest armor.

A moment later, Mr. Desani came stomping down the hallway. "Good, Parker, you're here. Come on back. I have a room set up for you." He ran the park, kept it moving, kept the schedules running, kept the bulldozers working the dirt, and he did his job well. Shannon could respect that, but the man wasn't good for much else.

"Thanks." He followed Desani down the hall.

He opened a door and gestured for Shannon to go in. He swallowed down the butterflies trying to escape his stomach by flying up his throat. Bastards could drown in the acid first. *Fuck being nervous!*

The room had been cleared of everything except a long folding table with a few chairs around it. Sunlight streamed into the room through a tiny window with a cement sill underneath the glass, making it look sturdier.

Two suits sat behind the table, one had wide spread legs and leaned back with an expression of interest, but no concern on his face. He held his arms loose at his sides, waiting comfortably for the entertainment to start.

He had dark hair, a mustache and a firm jaw.

The other guy had his hands folded together resting on top of the table in front of him. He had plain brown hair, slicked back and plain brown eyes. Nothing interesting about the guy, except the tense wrinkles on his forehead and the scowl taking up the rest of his face. Shannon knew that guy...Gavin Peri. He used to represent the Honda factory team, but he'd been lured away to the newest start up BikeMax Toyota Team. Shannon expected him, but he didn't know who the casual suit was or why he was there at his sponsor meeting.

"Come on in, son." Gavin Peri motioned him forward.

"Who's this?" Cutting straight to the point was Shannon's style. *Fuck 'em if they couldn't take blunt.*

Peri blew out a loud and dramatic exhale. "Right. This is Jack Wolfe. He's interested in sponsoring a racer and since we haven't finalized your deal..." Peri waved his hand in the air. "So, he's here to meet you." He put his hand in front of him on the table again, his face went back to his natural scowl, but his eyes asked if Shannon had a problem with that.

Nope. No problem. Shannon stepped forward and reached out his hand. "Nice to meet you."

Wolfe leaned forward and shook his hand, then went right back to his casual sprawl. This guy reeked confidence.

Shannon smirked right back at him. He'd be surprised to find out that Shannon didn't give a fuck about his confidence. "So what are you offering?" He turned back to Peri.

"Nothing. Why should we offer you anything? You're trouble and you bring trouble. You're too aggressive on the track and we don't think you can win."

Shannon pulled out another chair and plopped down. He stretched out his legs and propped his racing boot up on the table and folded his hands behind his head. "Who else do you have? No one. You're wrong about winning. I'm a winner. I can be up there in the top five every race, but I have issues...with certain faggot racers. That a problem for you?"

Peri stood up and put his hands on his hips. "I don't care what your problem is." He leaned forward, his scowl deepening. "You win or you don't. What do you want?"

"I want cash up front. Fifteen grand for the first two races. Plus all the normal expenses you'd have anyway. That's all." He rolled a hand in the air, gesturing for Peri to get on with it. This was his show.

"Why should I give you a damn dime? You haven't proven yourself—proven anything. Tell you what...you place in the top five, no, top ten in the first race and I'll give you your money. Place top five in the first five races just once and I'll give you double again. But if you don't..."

"What? If I don't finish well, you'll break my knees?"

"Nope. I'll kick you to the curb. This is a trial basis, Mr. Parker. Trial. If you fuck up, you're out. Plain and simple, that's it, the end. Got it?"

"I won't fuck up."

"I don't care one way or the other… Now, get out."

Shannon stood up. That hadn't gone exactly how he wanted. He wasn't leaving with a big fat check, but the promise of more cash than he'd asked for and maybe even double it? He could wait. "I did pretty good at the X-TS. I'm gonna wipe that McAllister faggot off the track." He pointed at Peri. The man knew it, or he wouldn't be offering him anything.

"We'll see."

"I still have to train. Practice." Shannon held his hand up to indicate the track. "This place costs dough."

Wolfe stood up and snorted. He buttoned his jacket, tucking in his silky tie. He looked like he was made from money. He hadn't broken a sweat in the Florida heat, even with his fancy suit on. "Wolfe Real Estate will pay for your track time. If you can win, I'll buy you a fucking track. But, let's get one thing clear right here."

Shannon held his hands up.

Wolfe stepped around the table and slid his hands into his pants pocket. "I don't care for your attitude. I don't care for your *issues*. And I don't want Wolfe Real Estate's good name wrapped up in a public media shit storm. So, you better just make sure you're one hundred percent positive. If the camera is on you…you better be Mr. Loving-Everybody-Ball-of-Sunshine. Got it?"

Shannon let Wolfe's words wiggle around a bit in his head. He knew the guy was probably talking about the problems with McAllister last season. He'd come off looking like a villain or something. Hell, he hadn't done a damn thing that a million others would have done too, if they had the balls. Hell, if Cole Lindt had the balls and hadn't backed off, running away from it like a scared baby, he would have been the hero. Well, fuck him and fuck Davey McAllister and the rest of his sissy-crew. What he planned wouldn't ever make headlines and wouldn't ever be traced to him, but he needed the money to do it. He even had a 250 racer, Ethan Bowers, ready to do all kinds of shit for the right price. A real southern boy, that one. Shannon could make it work without getting his hands dirty at all. "Yes sir, Mr. Wolfe." He held out his hand. He could be charming too. He could play their game.

Wolfe didn't shake his hand. He turned and looked at Gavin Peri. The look on his face said he'd hold Peri accountable if Shannon screwed up and that gaze was fierce. He wouldn't want to be on the bad end of that. He had a feeling Mr. Wolfe wouldn't hesitate to kick someone's ass.

Peri nodded and Wolfe turned back to Shannon. He smiled coldly. "Don't make me regret this. I don't deal with regret very well."

Shannon put his hand down and smiled. He didn't give a shit what cocky Mr. Wolfe could deal with as long as he paid the bills and kept him racing. He kept smiling to himself like a crazy loon as the two men walked out the door. He watched them go, only half pleased with the turnout, but the contracts would come as soon as the first race started and so would the money. What he needed to focus on now was training. He followed after to search for Desani to set up some extra track time, now that he knew it'd be paid for.

Chapter 15 – November, The Ranch

Tate stretched out in a lawn chair, soaking in the sun with his sunglasses and new Michael Kors swim trunks on. They had a cool tie-die looking stripped pattern and fit him better than most, hugging his ass a bit. The hot New Mexico sun beat down on his bare chest. He loved the peacefulness here at Davey's estate that they called The Ranch. They did not have livestock, unless you counted Tyler. He chuckled softly at his own little inside joke, thinking he might use it later if he got the chance.

What Davey did have was a sprawling ranch-style house decorated to look like a Pueblo on the outside, but was modern and spacious on the inside and included multiple guest rooms, a full gym and sauna, and a completely decked out kitchen. The huge pool and outside deck with a grill, where Davey was grilling up some chicken for lunch, made the outside even better. The best part about The Ranch though, had to be Davey's track. Yep, he had his own personal dirt track where he could practice and the three of them had been riding on it every day.

Tyler and Davey had their own bikes. They rode Kawasaki. Tate had to have MSR ship his practice bike over. Oz had not been extremely happy about it, but they knew two facts that they couldn't ignore. The first was that it would be cheaper to train here with Davey than at the camp, because...free. And second, training with Davey made Tate better than if he trained alone. Something about training with another rider always made Tate push harder, especially when that rider was Davey Mc-fucking-Allister.

Cold water splashed over his warm chest and thighs, making him jerk up to sitting. He glared at Tyler who pulled his dripping wet body out of the pool. Tyler was curvy in all the right places with rounded muscles defining his arms, a flat stomach, and thick thighs. He looked even better than he had the last time Tate had been here. Tyler smirked as he walked over, as if he knew what Tate had been thinking.

"Brat," Tate called out.

"You know, Tate, I can get his number." He flicked more cold water at Tate before grabbing a towel.

"I'm not calling him up like some stalker, dude."

"I can't believe you guys didn't exchange numbers." Tyler plopped down in a lawn chair beside him. "I thought it went well."

Tate rolled his eyes, but Tyler probably couldn't see them behind his dark Ray-Bans. "Apparently, not that well."

"You stayed the night in his hotel."

Tate shrugged. "So? It just can't be more than that. Besides, if he really wanted to talk to me, he'd call here. He knows where I am."

"So, maybe he doesn't want to call *you* up like some stalker." Tyler snapped the towel at him. It made a snicking sound, but missed his leg by a hair.

Tate pushed his sunglasses up on his head to give Tyler the full effect of his glare, but before he could give him another smart-assed comment, Davey called out to them. "Come on you two. Foods on."

Tyler practically cheered as he jumped up and headed to the table by the grill. Tate followed him over, thankful it had an umbrella to block the sun that he probably had already gotten too much of. Thank God for sunscreen.

Davey placed a platter of chicken breasts, grilled to perfection, on the table and Tyler speared one popping it on Tate's plate and then went back for his own. Davey sat beside him and looked over at Tate. "Hey, man. Don't listen to this guy. He knows nothing about pursuing a man."

"And you do?" Tyler asked, plopping a third breast onto Davey's plate.

"I got you didn't I?"

Tyler scoffed at that. "Seriously, Tate. You probably shouldn't listen to either of us. I don't know how we finally ended up together. Hell, we managed to fuck this up three ways to Sunday before getting it right."

Tate swallowed his chicken and took a swig of water. His friends made a cute couple and he could not imagine them not being together. He knew he wanted something like that too, but they had been lucky and if Tyler wasn't in the same industry, they probably wouldn't have worked out with Davey's crazy Supercross schedule.

"It's different with Pilot. He may be working for you now, but he's not Supercross. He doesn't get it and he's not going to just traipse all over the country with me. Hell, I don't know when I'll ever see him again."

"I do," Tyler said. "January in Anaheim for the opener. He's going to be with us the entire season."

"Huh. Well." Tate didn't know what to say to that. He'd been hoping to hear it, though he wasn't going to ask. He wanted more of Pilot, but it was dangerous. He'd already spent the entire plane trip from the X-TS Event to the Four Corners airport bawling his eyes out. When Pilot had dropped him off at his hotel and kissed him goodbye, it really was goodbye and it broke his heart. He'd let himself want too much, too fast, and they both knew better. They couldn't have more. It wasn't practical. Pilot had his own life back in Colorado and Tate...he had no life, just Supercross.

He cut off another piece of chicken and stabbed it with his fork. Suddenly, the meat tasted dry.

He saw Davey nudge Tyler with his shoulder. "Leave it alone, Ty," he said softly, adding one more thing for Tate to be grateful to the man for.

Silence surrounded them as they ate for a few minutes, giving Tate time to shake it off. He refused to think about Pilot, or anyone or anything else that made him unhappy. "Hey, so, thanks for letting me stay here awhile. I, uh, appreciate it. So, like, yeah. Thanks."

Tyler knocked his knee against his, but Davey answered. "Hey, we like having you here, Tate. Training with you is better than training alone." He shrugged and stuffed chicken in his mouth.

"So, what are you doing for the holidays, Tate?" Tyler asked.

Tate wished he hadn't asked. He had no idea. He shrugged and ate the last piece of chicken on his plate. Before he had time finish chewing, Tyler asked him if he wanted more.

"No, thanks. I think I want to get a nap in, before we head to the track this afternoon."

They let him drop the subject, thankfully. What he owed these two seemed to be mounting by the minute. He helped the guys clean up before heading to the guest room where he lay on the bed staring at the smooth plaster ceiling. He needed to do something about his lonely life. Maybe he could get a rent boy and a hotel room from Christmas to New Years.

That's when he heard noises coming from the living room. Grunting and what? Was that squeak from Tyler? He got up and quietly opened the door. He couldn't see the living room from where his room was, so he crept down the hall. Before he got to the end, he heard more noises. Definitely sex noises. A clear cry of, "More!" That had been Tyler. More grunting and a shushing noise. They were trying to be quiet, but they weren't. They were fucking in the living room.

Tate turned around and rubbed his hands over his face as he went straight back to his room and shut the door. Carefully. He didn't want them to know he'd heard.

Damn! His friends were so hot and he could imagine what he'd heard but not seen. Davey plowing into Tyler, if he'd gotten the sounds right. His cock plumped up, tenting his swim trunks. He dropped them to the floor and crawled up on his mattress.

Lucky Tyler.

Tate stroked his cock, base to tip, remembering Pilot plowing into *his* ass. It had been simply scrumptious. He still couldn't believe the amazing sex they'd had. Fucking, jacking off together. Tate had woken up to those sexy lips on his cock. The man had his mouth on every inch of Tate, including his tongue in Tate's ass, which might have been the best part.

After some slow teasing, Pilot had fucked Tate again that morning. Pilot tossed him around like his own personal toy, and Tate had loved every minute of it. Pilot brought out a different, more playful side of Tate that even he hadn't really known he'd had, but he liked it. Maybe too much.

He had enjoyed Pilot lifting Tate's hips off the bed so high, his knees had left the mattress. Then, Pilot stood beside the bed and fucked him senseless. Tate's hands had gripped the mattress, merely for balance, until he had come—like lighting. The memory alone overwhelmed him, and Tate rolled to his side and grabbed the hand lotion off the nightstand, squirting it in his hand. Thinking about Pilot made his cock even harder.

He'd never deny wanting Pilot, wanting him to fuck him again and again. He hadn't wanted the night to end. The memories would have to last a lifetime. Even if they saw each other again at the racetrack, they probably wouldn't get together again. It'd been a onetime deal for sure.

His cock demanded he not think about that. Instead, he thought about what they'd already done. Pilot face-fucking him, rimming him. Tate's hands all over his chest and arms, his tongue licking that tattoo on his chest. Tate groaned and stroked his cock faster. He grabbed his balls and tugged with his other hand. It wasn't enough. Turning over, he got on his hands and knees and imagined Pilot fucking him again, as he jacked off.

More grunting came from down the hall, and he swore he heard the couch move across the floor. He almost laughed, but the image of Davey fucking Tyler *that* hard, had him finally shooting off all over his hand and the bed. Damn, now he'd have to wash the sheets.

Chapter 16 – November, Denver

Pilot slid his soapy hand over his cock. His shoulders pressed against the cold tiles of his shower. He needed relief. He'd never jacked off so much in his entire life. Thinking about Tate had him going crazy—sex crazy. He suspected something else was behind it, though. He wanted more than the great sex they'd had. It really had been so exceedingly hot, but the cuddling in between and the crushing weight on his chest when he left proved it.

He wanted a relationship, a companion to share things with. He wanted Tate every way humanly possible. The perfect place for his hands was on Tate's body. But they weren't there. Nope. They were in Denver, in this shower, stroking his own cock that seemed to have a mind of its own, and its thoughts were all about Tate.

He focused on imagining what he'd do if Tate was with him. He'd push the man against the wall and lift his hips as he fucked him, pumping in and out of that tight little hole. Tate had a way of clenching his sphincter that made Pilot's head explode. He tightened his grip and stroked faster until his shoulders came off the wall and he shot out all over his fixtures. He grabbed the handheld shower head to rinse himself and the shower walls before finally getting out.

He seemed to have started every day since they'd parted this same way, getting off to thoughts of Tate. He knew Tate was at Davey's place, so he was safe and secure. He'd also texted one of their managers, Angel, to check on things. He needed to know Tate wouldn't be spending Thanksgiving alone. She'd confirmed they were having a huge gathering at Davey's cousin's place and that Tate had been included in that. Then she promptly invited him. He turned her down and asked her not to mention it to Tate. He trusted she wouldn't.

He wanted to jump on a plane and fly straight to New Mexico, but he couldn't. He had to spend Thanksgiving with Uncle Gary and Johnny. What he had to be most thankful for was that he got a pass from his own family this year. His parents were eating with friends and his sister's family went out of town. The only other family was his dickhead brother and Pilot just couldn't bring himself to care what Colin would be doing.

After dressing in jeans, an American Eagle t-shirt with a denim button up over it and his old combat boots, he grabbed his leather jacket and his keys and headed over to Uncle Gary's house. There was no getting out of it, but honestly, the only thing that would make him want to get out of it would be spending the day with Tate. He shoved that thought down hard. It wasn't happening. Maybe it made him an asshole, but pursuing Tate could not end well.

Uncle Gary had hired the best lawyer, and they'd managed to postpone the court day for his bogus assault charges. Everyone felt confident that it would either be dropped or end in a fine. Hopefully, before he had to appear in court, sometime in January or February. He needed that to be the case. He had to be in Anaheim in January and it would take an act of God or death to stop him from getting there. His motivation had nothing to do with the job, as much as he liked the gig and liked his clients. Nope. His passion was all about seeing Tate.

Johnny greeted him at the door and let him in with a half hug and back pat. Pilot felt comfortable here. This was the best part of his family. He wondered if Tate would fit in with them. He wondered why he even considered that question, but he didn't stop thinking about it. All through dinner and on to pie, Tate was his constant companion in his mind. It was unsatisfying. He wanted more.

"Why the scowl?" Johnny asked, sipping his coffee.

"I always scowl."

Johnny put the mug down on the table. "You're more scowly than usual," he accused, scooting his chair sideways to look at Pilot.

"Well," he sighed, not really wanting to have this discussion, but not really being able to get around it either. He figured he'd better at least give Johnny something, and then maybe they could move on. "I met someone at that Supercross event last month and I can't stop thinking about him."

"What? What the hell? You got a hook up and didn't tell me?"

"He's more than a hookup."

Johnny punched him in the arm and immediately cradled his hand. "Ouch," he cried out.

"Told you not to do that, bro."

"Don't bro me," he huffed. "More than a hookup? My God Pilot, that makes it worse."

Pilot got up from the table and crossed the kitchen to pour himself another cup of coffee. He held up the pot silently asking Johnny if he wanted more, but Johnny shook his head. "I want to hear more about your mystery man. Fuck the coffee."

"Nothing to tell." Pilot made his way back to the table with his full cup.

"I'd hit you again, if I didn't already know how bad it'd hurt." He shook his hand. "Fucker. Give! You know I'll get it out of you and don't give me that *nothing to tell* BS, either." He mocked Pilot with a sarcastic sing-song voice. "Obviously, there's more to tell."

"Obviously," Pilot echoed.

"Give it up."

"Fine." Pilot sighed again and rubbed his hand through his hair. It'd started growing back from the buzz he'd given it before, but was still nowhere near as long as Tate's messy blond locks. He loved diving into those golden strands.

"Sean!"

"All right. His name is Tate Jordan."

"OhmyfuckingGod!"

"What?"

Johnny's mouth hung open and his eyes grew wide. "Tate Jordan? *The* Tate Jordan? Number *87* Tate Jordan?"

"Since when do you follow Supercross?"

Leaning back, Johnny crossed his arms. "Since you started working for them and Tate Jordan? Yeah, he's hands down *the* hottest one. Did you see him in his racing outfit?"

"Gear."

"What?"

"Gear. It's racing gear, not an outfit and yeah." Pilot couldn't stop the grin that spread across his face, remembering Tate in that sexy-as-hell racing gear. "I peeled him out of it."

"OhmyfuckingGod!"

"Stop saying that and wipe the drool from your chin."

Uncle Gary walked back in the room. "What's going on? Don't make me break you two up."

"Sean has a new boyfriend and didn't tell us."

"Tattletale."

They ganged up on him at that point and spent the next hour grilling him about Tate until he'd had enough. "Okay. Fuck you both. I'm leaving." His words were light, but true.

Uncle Gary stopped him at the door as he put on his jacket. "Hey, Sean. All kidding aside. This guy sounds nice and if you like him, go for it. For once in your life find some happiness. You've had it hard and been too lonely. There's more to life than being a workaholic, crotchety old man like me."

Pilot leaned in and hugged him. "Thanks, Unc. You've always been

97

too good to me."

"Remember that when I get these assault charges dropped. Seriously, though, you deserve it. You deserve happiness, too. He'll be welcome here. You know that."

"Okay."

He thought about those words all the way home. Maybe Uncle Gary was right. Maybe he needed to try harder. He thought about the upcoming holidays and wondered what Christmas would look like for Tate. He wanted to keep loneliness and cruelty from hurting his man. His man? Maybe he was getting ahead of himself. But maybe not.

Chapter 17 – December, New York

Tate stood in the window of his hotel watching the snow fall. Christmas was coming up fast and he'd have another lonely ass time by himself in his hotel. Joey had invited him over, but he felt it was imposing. Christmas didn't mean anything to Tate, but it meant something to Joey's family. His trainer had been great to him and they'd gotten to know each other a bit more. He spent two weeks with him at The Ranch and then at the training in Jacksonville. That only gave Tate more reason not to take him up on the offer.

Tate had nothing to do until the week between New Year's and Anaheim. That week, he'd be at another camp with Joey. This one was more serious and private and in Florida. Tate kicked the toe of his sneakers against the baseboard. He didn't want to go to Florida, to some hick town that he'd never heard of. He wanted to go to Colorado. He wanted to find Pilot and climb back into his arms, because that was the one place where all the pain stopped. The one place where he could relax and not think about Donny, Bryce or Warren or anyone else.

He pushed those unproductive thoughts away and contemplated going out to find a hookup. He was in New York. *Jesus Christ—Easter Bunny!* He laughed, remembering how he'd teased Pilot.

Sean Mahan.

That was Pilot's real name. He'd told Tate while they were fucking. Tate had hoped it meant something. He'd hoped Pilot—Sean—wanted more. Maybe he'd been way off on that assumption.

His cell phone rang, interrupting his thoughts and pissing him off, especially since the generic ring tone was the one that meant he didn't know who was calling. He ignored it.

A few minutes later and the message notification beeped. He didn't care.

It started ringing again. Whoever it was must be determined. Probably a reporter. They tended to be tenacious. When it stopped ringing, he tapped on his voice mail notification and entered his password as prompted.

The voice on the message was low and gravelly. "I hoped you'd answer when I called." Silence. "I miss you." Beep.

Pilot.

Tate gasped as psycho butterflies started churning up his stomach. His bird-heart beat its wings, desperately trying to break out of the cage.

It rang again. Same number.

Tate gulped and answered it. "Pilot?"

"Yeah. It's me." He sounded nervous.

"Hi." Was that breathy sound Tate's own voice? "Uh, did you say you missed me?"

"Yes. I miss you."

Silence.

Pilot laughed softly. "Are you smiling?"

"Yes." That was the truth.

"Good. I love your smile. I want to see it again. Do you have plans for Christmas?"

Christmas? "Uh, no. Not really. I don't normally *do* Christmas."

"What's that mean?"

Tate let out a loud exhale. Had he been holding his breath? "I don't like, uh, have family. So, that whole Christmas thing, just doesn't mean anything to me. I'm not religious and all that, either."

"Doesn't matter. No one should spend Christmas alone, especially you."

What? More silence.

Pilot cleared his throat. "Come spend it with me."

"Seriously?" Tate couldn't imagine anything better or anything worse. He had already become too obsessed with Pilot and his sexy brooding eyes, and his soft cinnamon colored hair. "Pilot. That's family time. I'm not—"

"Stop. I wouldn't be able to enjoy any of it, knowing you were alone."

"Don't even feel sorry for me. I'm not feeling sorry for myself. Seriously. It's a fact of life. That's all."

Pilot didn't seem to want to give up so easily, though. "I need you here for my peace of mind. Has nothing to do with you or feeling sorry for you or whatever. Cause I don't. I just, uh...need. You. Here."

Tate couldn't answer for a minute. He took a deep breath, just adjusting to what the man was saying. "Look, Sean. This isn't smart. I mean..."

Pilot made a noise that sounded suspiciously like growling. "I'll buy your plane tickets—"

"No," he barked out. It sounded way too harsh. "I'll buy my own damned tickets. Just pick me up at the airport."

"Great. Text me your flight info."

"Fine. When do you want me to come?" Tonight. Tomorrow. Forever?

"Well, I have work and stuff, uh, until the twentieth. Can you come then? Stay through New Year's?"

"Okay. What airport?"

"Denver International."

"Okay. And, uh, Sean...if you're not there, so help me, there will be hell to pay."

"Tate, I am serious. I'll be there."

"Okay, then."

"Okay. Bye."

Tate didn't even say goodbye, just hung up. Wow. He stared out at the snow, reflecting in the light. It would be snowing in Colorado too. He wasn't a huge fan of snow, but if it meant spending a few days cuddled up to Pilot, he was all in.

Wait—how did the man even get his number?

Tate flipped through the contacts on his phone and tapped on Tyler's number. His cute face popped up on the phone screen before he answered. "'Lo?"

"Tyler," he grumbled, "did you give him my number?"

"What? Who?"

"You know who." Tate scowled at his friend, even though he couldn't see Tate over the phone. "Pilot—that's who. Did you?"

"No." Did he sound so innocent on purpose?

"How'd he get it then?" Tate asked.

"Shit! Did he call? That's great."

"How?" Tate wasn't letting him off the hook.

"I swear, Tate, I haven't talked to Pilot since we left X-TS."

"Text?"

"No."

"Ty! Come on!"

He heard a guilty little chuckle. "Well, I did give your number to Angel."

"Angel?"

"Yeah, you remember Angel? Our photographer-slash-manager extraordinaire. She's that little chick with dark hair—"

"I know who she is." Damn, that sneaky man, going through Angel. Tate guessed it made sense though.

"Hey, Tate. Man, does it matter? He asked for it. He called you. That means something right?"

"Something. Yeah." What that something was, Tate didn't know, but he wanted to find out, even if it cost him a broken heart. Not like he hadn't

101

had one of those before. Not like he hadn't been living with one for several years now, ever since his parents disowned him.

"I didn't mean to upset you. I really thought it was a good thing."

"It is. Really. I'm not mad. I'm just, uh...you know? I guess I'm anxious about it."

"About what?" Tyler chuckled. "You already had sex, right?"

"It's not the sex. It's the other...stuff."

Silence.

"What other stuff?" Tyler asked.

Tate wasn't sure how to say what he needed to say. He hoped Tyler would give him some advice or something, as his closest friend. Maybe friends didn't do shit like that. How would Tate know when he'd had so few of them? "He invited me to his house for Christmas. That's family stuff. And I—"

"Oh! My gawd! I thought you meant like whips and chains and kinky shit. Damn, Tate, why didn't you just say that?"

Tate giggled. "You're stupid, Ty." Whips and chains he could probably handle. The emotional stuff, nope, not capable of handling.

"Seriously, though, Tate. Just go for it. See if it works or not. You don't know if you don't try and it sure as hell beats flirting with guys who are either physically or emotionally unavailable."

Tate had told Tyler about Bryce and that other asshole, Donny, and why they'd broken up, though he never mentioned what happened with Warren at camp. That one was totally on Tate, anyway. He didn't want to think about it, let alone bring it up. Tyler had been pissed enough that Tate hadn't called him when he'd left Donny's, even though he'd been on his honeymoon. He swore he would have dropped everything to help. That's what Tyler thought friends were for. Tate had never had friends like that before. He wasn't sure he understood any of it. "Yeah," he finally answered, unsure of what else to say.

Tyler breathed deep on the phone. "I'm worried about you. Pilot is a good guy. So, don't over think it. He hasn't asked you to move in or marry him. Right?"

"Right."

"So just enjoy, man."

Christmas would be interesting this year.

Chapter 18 – December, South Carolina

Bryce stared out his bedroom window. He had his kindle in his lap and a blanket over his shoulders. It was a cool fifty-eight out, but nowhere near cold enough to snow. Maybe it would be better if it did snow, or if he could go somewhere that snowed. As it was, his view of his back yard was brown grass, dried up and brittle with a few piles of leaves that he should probably help his dad rake up, but he didn't feel like it. He didn't feel like doing much. He couldn't even concentrate on his book and it was one of his favorite yaoi novels, Maiden Rose. The sexy soldiers in the story usually held his attention, but not today, not this close to Christmas.

The only thing holding his attention was wondering what Tate would be doing for the holidays. He probably would have a fabulous celebration with a fabulous family and a fabulous boyfriend. Later they'd ride together on some dirt track and then make out in front of a fire on some bear-fucking-skin rug. And *he* could have had Tate and he'd just tossed it away like a baby, like a brat.

"Bryce!" his mother called. "Come help me."

He tossed his kindle on the bed and dropped the blanket on the floor. He grabbed his hoodie with the tiger ears, pulling it over his head as he made his way to the kitchen.

"Here. Peel." She handed him the vegetable peeler and a potato. He started sheering the skins into the garbage can. "Why are you so mopey today?"

"I don't want to talk about it," he huffed. Again like a brat, but he didn't want to discuss it with her. She already had her nose too much in his life.

"Okay. So, are you planning on going back out to the bike camp or somewhere else to practice before the season starts?"

"Not the camp. I don't know for sure. I have to call George."

For a few minutes, the only sound in the kitchen was the click-click of the peeler and his mother clanging through pots and pans. "Why not the camp?"

Why did she have to push? He just shrugged a little and made a non-committed grunt.

"Seriously. I thought it went well there."

"It went fine."

"So? You can go back."

"I'm not going to that camp. Geez, Mom!" He tossed the peeler on the counter and stormed off. Why the hell did she always want to be in his business?

He slammed into his room and dropped onto the bed. Great—another temper tantrum. He *was* just a baby...a kid. Tate would never want him back.

He opened his laptop and clicked open his email. He hoped to find some team news to get his mind off of the bullshit his life had become.

Then he saw an email that he wasn't expecting. He opened it. It was Warren Tanner.

I know where you are. I know what you want. I told everyone about you and that dick Tate. Next time, you should get on your knees when I ask you to...or maybe next time I'll shove you down and take what I want. You'll love it too, bitch.

He deleted the email without a second thought. That Tanner had been a bully at the camp and was only one of the reasons he didn't want to go back. He had threatened Bryce, but Bryce wasn't about to give in to him. Bullies backed down when you stood up to them. Wasn't that the going theory? Maybe Tanner backed down, maybe not. It sounded like he made good on his threat and spread his dirty lies all over the camp. Bryce wouldn't be able to show his face there again.

He didn't want his mom to know about any of it. "I'm not a kid," he said out loud. He had to handle it himself like an adult, but he didn't really know what to do about it. He pulled his hood up over his head and shut his laptop.

Chapter 19 - Christmas Holiday, Denver

Pilot picked Tate up from the airport as promised. He even carried Tate's heavy bag and rolled his smaller one behind him, as he lead Tate into the parking lot and up to his car.

"Woah! Pilot. My God. This is your car?"

"Yeah," Pilot answered, popping the trunk. He was slightly worried that Tate's massive bag wouldn't fit. "Classic *69*. Restored her myself with the help of a great mechanic." He shoved the bag in and shut the trunk. The smaller bag and Tate's carry on would have to cram into the back seat. He hadn't expected Tate to have so much luggage. The Mustang was a sports car after all.

He looked up just in time to see Tate running his hand down the top of the front fender. His obvious appreciation had the corner of Pilot's mouth quirking up. His car was a sleek bitch complete with Shaker hood scoop and spoiler wing on the back. The paint was a shiny black that had cherry red metallic flecks throughout, making it gleam with a red sheen in the sun. A bad ass V8 hid under the hood. It was still an old car and seemed like it always needed some work or other, but he loved it and couldn't get a grip on how happy it made him that Tate seemed to love it, too.

"This is the sexiest car ever." Tate groaned like he'd just had his cock sucked.

"Get in and I'll take you for a ride, Tate."

"Yes!" he called out and scrambled into the passenger seat. He practically had an orgasm when Pilot finally cranked it up.

"I wasn't sure I'd be able to bring her this morning. It was so cold and she didn't want to start, the old bitch."

"Don't talk about her like that," Tate whispered, running his hand over the cracked dashboard. Interior work was more difficult. The torn seats had covers over them until he could get them reupholstered. "He didn't mean it, sweetheart. You're the best."

"I'm glad you like my car, Tate." Pilot chuckled as he circled out of the parking lot to the booth where he paid for the parking.

Tate bounced in the seat all the way home. Pilot had to remind himself that he was young. He was very mature for twenty-one, but he'd never been in combat, never held a real job. As far as he knew, the only thing Tate had ever done was race dirt bikes. It made their few years difference more significant. Yet, most of the time Tate seemed much older. Seeing Tate all excited and unable to sit still made his heart hurt a little. Both of them had grown up fast. He set his mind to making sure Tate enjoyed his visit as much as possible.

"When can I drive?"

"When the ice melts."

"What?" Tate asked, turning quickly to him. "That's like months away, isn't it?"

"Sorry, man. I've seen how you ride that bike of yours." Pilot shook his head.

He pointed his finger at Pilot. "Nah, that ain't right," Tate complained.

They bantered back and forth about racing and cars the rest of the way home. It felt comfortable, as if they'd known each other forever. It also settled Pilot's nerves and second thoughts. He'd worried that it'd been a mistake inviting Tate home, and he worried that they wouldn't have anything to talk about out of the bedroom. Sex was one thing, but relating on a personal level wasn't always something Pilot was good at. Tate made it easy. Maybe too easy.

Once home, they hung up the coats on the coat rack and hauled the luggage inside. Pilot had originally intended to give Tate the guest room so he could have some privacy, but that had been a nerve-based excuse and he'd always been more straightforward. So, he dragged that huge bag all the way to the back bedroom. They'd already spent a night together and shouldn't have to dance around the issue. He dropped the bigger bag on the floor at the foot of the bed and glared at Tate, challenging him. If he'd been expecting some sort of protest, Tate disappointed him. He dropped his carry-on bag on the bed and gave Pilot his bright room-lighting smile.

Pilot melted. His heart turned to goo, but his cock hardened. He closed the distance fast and pounced on Tate. The kiss in the airport had been a chaste peck as they hurried out of the congested building. This one was nothing like that. It was juicy, hot and insistent. Pilot grabbed a handful of Tate's hair and used it to maneuver his head into the position he wanted, as he devoured Tate's mouth. Their tongues slid against each other and made strange things move around in Pilot's gut. That simple pleasure swirled through his blood, making him want to take Tate right there were they stood. "Are you tired?"

Tate skimmed his lips down to Pilot's jaw. "No," he whispered against

Pilot's skin.

Pilot's hands found their way under Tate's soft t-shirt, claiming soft, warm skin. He wanted more. He pulled the shirt off and pulled Tate closer. He leaned down to find Tate's throat with his lips.

"You too, bunny," Tate complained, grabbing at Pilot's button up dress shirt. Damn, why'd he wear the medieval torture device with all its distracting buttons? Tate pulled away from him and fumbled with the buttons, but it was taking too long. Pilot helped, by pulling and yanking and by the time they got the beast off his back, several buttons had skid across the floor, bouncing on the carpet. Tate laughed. "Easter Bunny! Impatient, much?"

"Yes!" No sense trying to hide it. "I've waited too long to have you here." Pilot was pretty sure there were innuendos that needed to be made based on that comment, but neither of them were capable of making them. Their mouths met and their bare chests slid together, tight muscle against hard flesh. Tate's frame was smaller, but lined with muscles, just as solid as Pilot's. Pilot knew from his job with Davey, that Supercross racers never stopped working out.

Tate unbuckled Pilot's belt and popped the button of his jeans open. There was only one kind of workout Pilot was interested in doing.

Tate wasn't wearing jeans, but some kind of dressier slacks with a weird side button. "Don't you wear normal pants?"

That got Tate laughing, as he unbuttoned his own pants and slid them down his skinny legs. "They're Todd Snyder and so comfortable."

"More comfortable off." Pilot didn't want to comment on the designer or any designer. Levi's or Wranglers were Pilot's thing; he knew nothing about designer brands. "They look better on the floor, too."

Tate's pants hit the floor, exposing his shiny gray boxers, tight to his legs with neon yellow lettering across the waist band proclaiming them to be *Under Armour*. Pilot commented, "Sporty!" He wore just plain tighty-whities. He should have bought nicer underwear.

Tate didn't seem to care. He just smirked and yanked them down, so Pilot followed his example. He took just a second to look at Tate's lanky body, liking all of it and needing to feel it against him. He reached out and grabbed Tate around the waist. His long fingers stretched around his back and his thumb rested under his ribs. Pilot pulled Tate against his body, and then the next moment, pushed him down on his bed.

Tate bent his knees and planted his feet flat on the mattress, then spread his legs, giving Pilot the best view ever. He could spend hours just looking at Tate's hard cock, all pink and twitchy with that darker head. His balls pulled up tight beneath his shaft. His pubic hair glistened golden and had been neatly trimmed, tight but not waxed. Pilot liked that, too. Waxing seemed to go too far. Pilot loved what he could see, but he couldn't leave it at just looking—not an option. His hands flinched, wanting to touch everything and his own cock begged for more contact as well.

He palmed Tate's balls, giving them a little squeeze that made Tate shiver. He leaned over Tate, between his knees, and looked down at his pretty face. His mouth hung slightly open, his top lip looking like a perfect little bow, almost the same pink as his shaft, but his plump bottom lip begged to be sucked, and it stood out a darker red, probably from his teeth scraping over them. Tate did that again, sucking the flesh between his teeth. Pilot had to taste, so he did. When he licked across that lip, Tate opened wider, giving him more, and Pilot took it greedily.

Tate's cock was silk sliding over steel in his hand, familiar and yet totally different. He wasn't very big around, but he was long. He stroked Tate with a firm grip, his tongue fucking into Tate's hot, wet mouth. The dual sensations had his body demanding more. His cock bumped against Tate's thigh, and his hand left Tate's cock to travel up that same long thigh, stroking through the light hair. He held himself up with his other arm, but he wanted both of them around this fine man.

"Shift," he commanded and flipped Tate over. As Pilot rolled to his back, Tate slid on top, his cock digging into Pilot's stomach, and his tongue sliding across Pilot's collar bone and down to the tattoo on his chest.

Tate gave his eagle plenty of attention, while Pilot grabbed Tate's firm ass. He remembered it from their last encounter. Tate's ass was unforgettable whether it was naked or wrapped in race pants or whatever those soft blue things he'd worn were, but hands down, naked was best— pun intended. He gave them a squeeze and pulled them apart a little. "I want in here, Tate."

"It's all yours."

"I hope you want it because it feels good and not because you feel obligated. That's not why I asked you here."

Tate sat up and straddled his stomach. "Let's not pretend, Pilot. I know why you asked me here. Yes, you were being kind and you wanted my company, but you also wanted sex."

Pilot started to deny it. The way Tate put it sounded ugly and there was nothing ugly about this thing between them.

"No. Pilot. It's okay. I wanted the sex too. Hell, having sex with you for a week is a hella better way to spend this stupid holiday." His shaggy hair bounced around his head and his eyes stared down at him from his open face. Pilot thought he was entirely too lovely.

He reached up and circled Tate's neck with his hand, his fingers wrapping around the back and his thumbs brushing along his face. Tate had just a little stubble around the edge of his jaw and chin, but his cheeks were smooth. He slowly pulled Tate to him, and leaned up to plant his lips on Tate's again. He didn't think he could even begin to define the lust that bubbled up in him. If Tate felt it too, then he'd not apologize for it.

The kiss turned hot as they exchanged tongues. Tate's hips rolled forward, rocking his cock harder into Pilot's stomach. Pilot's hands traced down Tate's shoulders and back to find that ass again. Tate's skin was soft and smelled fresh, faintly of oranges and warm spice. His throat tasted like hot skin, slightly salty, and all Tate.

He wanted that moment to last forever, naked bodies sliding together, luscious skin under his tongue, but his own hips started bucking without finding any friction. Tate's legs rubbed beside his own. "There's lube and condoms in there." He pointed at the side table, and groaned as Tate leaned over him to get at them, squishing his dick hard into Pilot's stomach with a grunt.

After grabbing them, Tate laughed, that smile lighting up the room and Pilot's own dark heart. "Give me your hand," he said, holding up the lube bottle and shaking it. He flicked open the cap and squirted the sticky goo all over Pilot's fingers.

"Come here," Pilot growled and Tate knee walked up his body. Pilot repositioned Tate's knees on either side of his head. He licked under Tate's balls and flicked his tongue against his taint.

"Oh, God Da—Easter Bunny! Come on!"

Pilot couldn't help but chuckle at Tate's comment and his smart-assed way of covering up his cursing.

"Hey, are you like Catholic or something?" Tate asked, just before Pilot slid his finger into that puckered hole. Tate squatted down farther, opening himself up. "God more! Fuck." He moaned, giving up all pretense at not cursing, as Pilot slowly fucked him with his finger. "So damn good."

Pilot loved seeing Tate squirm down on his hand; wanted to give him just what Tate begged for. The position was odd and he needed more lube. Reluctantly, he shifted Tate around again, tossing him on his back and then flipping him to his stomach, grabbing his hips to lift them off the bed. Tate giggled at all the shuffling around, so Pilot swatted his butt before grabbing the lube.

"Hey!" Tate protested, but it sounded like a half-hearted protest to Pilot.

"What?"

"Feel free to do that again." He giggled. So, Pilot did it again before dumping more lube on his fingers.

He licked at Tate's balls, tasting the excess lube, as he push two fingers inside his hole. Tate groaned and wiggled and Pilot felt it quivering in his gut.

"Hey, you know. I play with a dildo. A lot. So, I'm ready. Please."

Pilot snorted. "I'll tell you when you're ready." He didn't want to rush it, but it wasn't just about not hurting Tate. That was definitely part of it, but the other was the joy of seeing Tate like this, coming undone from just his fingers and tongue.

He continued his fucking and licking until Tate was practically screaming, "Fuck, please-please-please!"

"Put this on me," Pilot ordered. His hands were covered in sticky lube.

Tate huffed, but shifted around and grabbed the condom off the bed and ripped it open, dropping the wrapper over the side of the bed. His adept fingers rolled it over Pilot's hard cock. When he finished rolling the rubber down, Tate splayed his fingers over Pilot's thighs. "How do you want me?" he whispered, voice husky with desire.

Pilot's answer was a grunt as he hauled Tate up over him, but he got the message and grabbed Pilot's cock, aiming it perfectly. Tate set his own pace as he sunk down until he was seated all the way on Pilot's dick.

"Wait," Pilot said. He leaned over, almost unseating Tate, and flicked the bedside lamp on. Tate blinked at the unexpected light, as Pilot re-balanced him with hands on his hip and thigh. "Okay?"

"Why the light?"

"I want to see you...clearly."

Tate smirked down at him and lifted up with his thighs a bit, only to sink back down. He repeated the action, raising up a bit higher with each new stroke. Pilot watched his face, as the different shades of ecstasy played across it. "God, you're gorgeous."

That earned him an eye roll and another smirk before Tate continued fucking himself on Pilot's cock. The heat and pull of Tate's asshole was incredible and had his damned brain short circuiting. He'd thought the heat had been scorching with just his fingers as he'd remembered the last time they were together, but with Tate riding him and controlling the pressure and pace, it felt more like a nuclear reaction. "Your hole is going to set my dick on fire," Pilot murmured.

Tate laughed and pushed his hands into Pilot's upper thighs as he moved. Pilot couldn't keep his hands off of Tate, rubbing them up and down his thighs, through that golden hair, and tracing a finger up his hip bone as he flexed. Tate rotated his hips a little on the down stroke with a deep moan that seemed to come from his chest and bubble up through his throat. Pilot could see the intensity on Tate's face, his eyes, the way he licked his lips. It made him want to do so much more. He watched, his cock begging for release, until he thought he was going to lose his mind. He grabbed Tate's waist and flipped him over, trying not to break the connection, but he slipped out anyway, his cock slapping back against his hard stomach.

It only took a second for Pilot to shove Tate's legs back, exposing his ass. He shoved his cock in and snapped his hips forward.

"Fuck, Sean!" Tate called out.

Pilot didn't want to hurt him, but his real name rolling off of Tate's lips and tongue, did something crazy to his head. He never let people call him that. He'd left Sean behind when he joined the military. During basic, Sean all but disappeared. Now, only family could get away with it, and sometimes not even them. Yet...Tate could call him anything and particularly *Sean*, especially when he made that deep-throated groan with it. "You okay?"

"God, yes. Fuck me."

Pleased with Tate's answer, Pilot let his body take over, rolling his hips, and fucking into Tate hard and fast. He knew he'd worried for nothing when Tate squeaked and called out, "More, more!"

Yes, Pilot could give him more.

"Sean!"

Yes, again. Pilot fucked hard and fast. The noises Tate made assured him that he'd jabbed that special place, bringing Tate with him. Tate's hole clinched like a hot glove, squeezing him so hard, he had to stop moving. When he tried to move again, the orgasm hit him all at once like a ton of bricks. No slow build up for this one. It slammed him, bursting out and filling the condom as his vision flickered to white.

It took a moment, but when he started to breathe again, his concern was for Tate. He glanced down. Tate's legs had fallen to the sides, spread apart and the lamp light glowed on his ripped abs, making them look golden brown and sticky, covered with come. His eyes traveled up Tate's body and back to that wonderful face. Tate's eyes were closed and his mouth was slightly open with the tip of his tongue sticking out. "You look satisfied," he said.

One eye peeked open. "Mmm..."

Pilot wanted to capture that moment forever. He needed to hold it in his heart and never let it go. The strange thought had his throat closing up. He couldn't breathe. He moved and his cock slipped out, making Tate grunt and hiss. "Sorry," he choked out.

"Oh, no, bunny. Don't be. Not. At. All." Tate's voice was all sex-rough and adorable. Pilot wanted to keep him. He'd never wanted to keep anyone. Why was the first one someone like Tate? He was wild and free. He lived his life on a dirt track, following the Supercross series, not settling down with someone. Those facts were obvious—blatant. Tate didn't even have a home. He'd said he was either at the race camp or in a hotel room. A nomad, his Tate was a gypsy. And Pilot?

He never wanted to let the man out of his bed.

Pilot scooped rocky-road ice-cream into two bowls on the counter and then squirted chocolate syrup over the top. Tate walked into the kitchen, halting the yummy construction, and Pilot turned to look at him. He was barefoot, wearing track pants slung low on those sexy hips and a long sleeved t-shirt with the outline of a fox face on it. He scrubbed a towel over his wet hair. Freshly showered and looking cozy, Pilot wanted to cuddle up to him. Instead, he tossed a handful of mini-marshmallows into each bowl.

"Here," he said, stretching out his hand with one of the bowls.

Tate cocked his eye. "Uh...guess we didn't talk about food. I can't eat that."

"A couple of bites won't kill you." Pilot shook the bowl.

"I can tell you're going to bad for me. Is that frozen yogurt? Low fat? And chocolate?" Tate bit his lip and tossed the towel over the back of one of the kitchen chairs.

Pilot looked at the ice-cream. "You're going to make me eat both of these?"

Tate shrugged. "Put one back in the freezer for later. I can't. Really. Okay, maybe just one bite." He changed his tune and opened his mouth as Pilot held out a spoonful of chocolate goodness. He moaned at the taste, but pushed Pilot's hand away.

"Okay. No more for you. Let's watch some boob-tube." He put the second bowl in the freezer, but he could see a bit of longing on Tate's face after having one small bite. He leaned in and whispered in Tate's ear, "It's okay, I'll share some of mine."

Tate laughed and shoved at Pilot's shoulder. "One bite is going to have me doing an extra half hour at the gym. Oh God! Tell me you have a gym." The horror and worry in Tate's eyes concerned him. Pilot hadn't even thought about Tate's physical requirements. "Pilot. I'm an athlete and Anaheim is only days away. I can't just stop, uh...everything. You know?"

"Sorry. I hadn't thought about it, but don't worry. I'll take care of you." The last of his words came out husky and full of more meaning than he intended, but the look on Tate's face was worth it.

They spent the next few hours fighting over the remote like an old married couple. Tate wanted to watch sports and was horrified that Pilot kept changing it back to Nick at Night during the commercials. Facts of Life was on and he hadn't seen that episode.

"Damn, Pilot. Don't you have HBO or anything like that? We can watch something a little more adult," Tate teased.

"No," Pilot whined.

"Then, can we at least watch Cartoon Network? Sheesh…this old crap is way too cheesy."

Pilot tossed a pillow at Tate's head, but he ducked, calling out, "Hey! Watch it."

"That's why they're called throw pillows, Tate."

That's when Tate pounced, jumping on him and attempting to wrestle him down, but Pilot out muscled him by a lot. Pilot lifted weights for bulk and strength, Tate lifted for endurance, so he was stronger than he looked, but not strong enough. He weighed nothing and it made Pilot's cock plump up in his sweatpants, just thinking about shoving him around in bed.

It only took a minute to pin a wiggling Tate down on the couch. "Mm…like this," Pilot purred his words against Tate's cheek. He hadn't shaved when he showered after their earlier go-round, but his stubble was soft, not too prickly, like Pilot's own. He nosed his face into Tate's neck. It was long like a swan's and just as soft as down. His tongue tentatively licked out against that creamy skin and Tate stilled and then groaned when Pilot sucked that skin into his mouth. The thought that he would leave a big purple mouth-shaped mark thrilled Pilot to no end. He never thought he'd be so caveman, but he wanted to mark Tate. Yes, toss him on his bed, mark him, fuck him, and have him in every way imaginable.

Tate's hips bucked up and Pilot could feel how hard he was. Momentary disappointment flitted across Tate's face when Pilot stood up. He changed it quickly enough when he grabbed Tate and threw him over his shoulder, smiling at Tate's giggles, as he hauled him into the bedroom.

The need for him, his lover, his Tate, hummed through him as if it were a physical thing. It danced across his heart, stomped through his belly, and flowed hard into his cock. Tate had only been there for the afternoon and evening…it was still his first night, the clock just now passing into morning, and Pilot didn't want to ever let him go. *Mine.*

Tate spread his legs, looking up at Pilot like he was everything, the magnet that kept him moving. Pilot would do anything to keep that look on his face.

Pilot slowly pulled Tate's track pants down like unwrapping an expensive gift. He rubbed his thighs and calves, worshiping every slender muscle and memorizing every inch of skin and hair. Needing to taste, he mouthed at the top of Tate's thigh, right below his lovely hip bone. He traced his tongue around until he was between Tate's legs, licking at his taint.

Tate's knees fell to the sides. "Oh, God. Fuck me."

"Working on it, baby." Pilot leaned up and over Tate's prone body to grab the lube and condom off the side table. He returned to work lube-covered fingers in Tate's hot hole.

"I'm gonna need another shower," Tate groaned as Pilot slid two fingers inside him

"I'll join you." Pilot kissed Tate's belly, sticking his tongue in the little divot. He ran his nose down Tate's happy trail. Tate's hands roamed across Pilot's head, feeling the soft hair that was just starting to get a little length to it since he'd shaved it for the Supercross event.

The hot and heavy had been replaced with slow and sensual. They touched each other as if they couldn't help it. When Pilot finally pushed into Tate, he used long, slow strokes, just wanting to enjoy this feeling of being so intimate with him.

He stared into Tate's wide, bright eyes. His mouth hung open and Pilot swore it was the least Tate had moved since he'd gotten there. Tate gripped his own knees, pulling them to his chest and offering himself to Pilot. Whatever was happening between them was bigger than just having a good time, bigger than he'd ever thought he'd have in his life. Pilot decided right in that stolen, precious moment that he would take whatever Tate offered him.

He made love to Tate, sultry and breathy with Tate's name sliding from his tongue. The heat between them scorched his soul. Pilot wanted to ask Tate to stay with him forever, but he swallowed back the words. It was a ridiculous thought. Even if they wanted to stay together after the holidays, Tate would be racing practically nonstop until May...five solid months.

Squinting his eyes tight, he picked up the pace, drowning all thought in Tate's pulsing ass. When they both came, calling each other's names and God's, Pilot sighed and collapsed beside Tate on the mattress and peppered gentle kisses along his shoulder and upper arm.

"Let's shower and sleep. I have to get up early."

Pilot scoffed, "What the hell for?"

"To work out, asshole. Didn't we already talk about that?"

Pilot groaned. He hadn't realized how life changing having Tate over for the holidays would be. "Okay. Shower, sleep, work out, and then we'd better go to the grocery store. I'm sure I have nothing you can eat here."

Chapter 20 - Christmas Eve, Denver

Christmas would not be an excuse even while he was with Pilot. No, Tate stayed with his training. He bought a George Foreman grill and a ton of chicken, despite Pilot's protests, because he just had to have it. Pilot made sticking to his diet difficult enough with his love of late night ice-cream, but Tate couldn't afford to slack off.

He got up every morning and dragged Pilot to the gym, kicking and screaming. Once they got there and started working out, Pilot relaxed. He spent more time on the weights and doing fifty million crunches, but damn his body showed every minute of lifting in every rock hard muscle.

Tate had to spend as much time on cardio as the weights. He usually started on the row machine, worked with Pilot on weight training, which was drastically different than Pilot's routine, and then moved to the treadmill or bike. He probably only finished half his cardio before Pilot finished and headed to the showers. After, he would run out to get protein shakes for both of them. Most of the time Tate finished before he got back.

The routine worked and Tate felt content. The sex was beyond amazing. The only thing they lacked was a nearby track. If he had that, Tate might never leave. At least, he'd never want to leave. He had no idea if Pilot would want him to stay and that made all the difference.

It seemed like they had a deeper connection, something more than casual fuck buddies. Tate hoped he was right about that, because his fragile heart would end up shattered if he was wrong, but he wasn't going to let that stop him from falling. Even if he could stop it; he wouldn't. Every second spent with Pilot healed up his wounded heart and kept him from thinking about other opportunities he'd missed out on, like Bryce.

The day before Christmas Eve, Tate convinced Pilot to take him to the mall. Not that he really wanted to go shopping in the crazy crowds, but hell if he was going to show up Christmas morning at Pilot's family's home without presents. Plus, he wanted to get something special for Pilot.

Roaming the overcrowded stores searching for the perfect gift showed just how little he knew about Pilot and made him sad. He thought they had a blooming relationship, but late night re-runs aside, he didn't know much about Pilot, proving that it wasn't a real relationship at all, just an affair, a fling. Tate wanted to change that, but Pilot had said from the beginning that Tate tried too hard. So, he just needed to get Christmas right. He needed to be serious, but subtle.

Pilot had been in the military, he liked guns, and his friend Johnny had told him that he used to fight in MMA style leagues around the city. When Tate thought about Pilot, he thought masculine. The man was a bodyguard, hired security. Nothing mushy would do here, he needed a manly gift. He started with the one guns and ammo calendar that didn't have half naked girls on it, from the booth in the middle of the mall that sold them. It wasn't enough. A Sports Authority gift card went into his shopping bag, but it still wasn't enough, wasn't personal.

After spending most of his time away from Pilot wracking his brain, he finally found the trinket shop that personalized nice stuff for gifts. He didn't think he'd find anything suitable, but he wandered in anyway. Surprisingly, he did find something. An upscale version of those cheap id bracelets kids bought. It had a leather band and a small silver slide. He had it engraved simply with *Pilot*. They finished it up with just enough time to meet Pilot at the food court.

The other gifts had been easier with Pilot's help. Johnny got a gift card to Abercrombie and Fitch. Pilot swore he'd go nuts over it. Uncle Gary was even easier. Pilot said the only thing he wanted was time on the gun range, so they stopped there on the way home from the mall and went in together to buy him enough time to last half a year.

Tate wanted to get stuff for the rest of Pilot's family, but Pilot wouldn't let him. He swore they had stopped exchanging gifts years ago since they all really could use the money more. His parents retiring and his sister preparing for a baby, if she could ever get pregnant, were major reasons, as well as Pilot saving up to buy part of his Uncle's business. That left his brother. Pilot said, "He's an asshole and I wouldn't get him anything anyway." So, they didn't. Their time with that part of the family would be drinks on Christmas Eve and that was all.

Tate had never met a boyfriend's family before. Donny had been like Tate, with his family disowning him, making his own family out of friends. None of his other boyfriends had ever been that serious. So, nervous didn't even begin to describe how Tate felt standing at Pilot's sister's door.

He rubbed his sweaty palms on his jeans. "What if they don't like me?" he asked, looking up to Pilot's dark, serious eyes.

He snorted. "What's not to love? You're the coolest person I know." He kissed the top of Tate's head and pounded his knuckles on the door, simultaneously.

A second later, a woman opened the door. She looked a lot like Pilot, with a large body frame, but she wasn't fat, just tall with wide shoulders. Her dark hair fell around those wide shoulders and her smile was warm. Her nose was softer than Pilot's but very similarly shaped. "You must be Tate," she said reaching out her hand.

"Hi," Tate said, shaking her hand.

"This is my sister, Sheila." Pilot reached in and hugged her, then she opened the door wide.

"Come in."

Tate smiled shyly and followed Pilot into the house. Sheila seemed nice, so he relaxed. They made their way into a large kitchen with a huge breakfast bar with stools in front of it. Pilot pulled one out for him, just as another woman approached him. She had the same dark hair and eyes. "I'm Sean's mom," she said, putting a glass of wine in Tate's hand.

He normally didn't drink, but he couldn't refuse and decided it would be okay to sip one glass.

"You can call me Mary or Mom, doesn't matter. All the kid's friends usually call me mom."

"Uh...thanks." Tate couldn't think of anything else to say. She was nice, but he didn't know if he could call her *Mom*. That was too foreign a concept for him. He hadn't seen his mom in ages and could barely remember what being his mom had even meant. Maybe he had never understood it.

Pilot put his hand on his shoulder, reassuring him, calming him. Tate melted into that warmth, wanting everything to be perfect. For a while it was. They snacked on cheese and crackers and laughed. Johnny showed up and hugged everyone, including Tate. He seemed a little tipsy already, but helped himself to a glass of wine. Pilot, noticeably wasn't drinking.

Sheila's husband and their father had been in the other room, but eventually joined them in the kitchen. Mary pulled out some kind of baked brie dish from the oven and Sheila cut up a loaf of fresh bread. Tate had one piece of bread with the warm cheesy concoction. It tasted of brie and honey and had to have a million calories in it. The food was too good, and Mary topped off his wine glass twice before he decided he couldn't drink anymore. It left him feeling warm inside. It'd been a long time since he'd felt the effects of alcohol. He'd never been a drinker anyway, since it wasn't included in his training plan.

Just when he thought the evening couldn't get any better, it crashed. Colin, Pilot's brother, showed up. Pilot hadn't lied about that one. Asshole didn't cover it.

Before even saying hello to anyone, Colin started stirring shit up. "Jonny? What're you doing here? Don't you have taxes to do? Like mine?"

Johnny rolled his eyes. "I'm not even getting into this with you right now."

"You're not getting anything into me, queer-bate."

Pilot huffed, but Sheila beat him to the punch. "Shut up or you're out of here, Colin."

"Can't you be decent for once?" Pilot asked him.

Colin popped the top on an aluminum beer can. "I'm decent. Always. Better than your faggy asses any day." He took a long swig. Then stared at Pilot, daring him to say more. "That's what I thought."

Tate could live with him being an ass to Johnny and shooting dirty looks at Pilot. It wasn't his family. Then, Colin noticed Tate.

"So, what's your story?" he growled, pointing at Tate around the beer can he still held.

"Story?"

"Yeah. What the fuck are you doing with Sean? He doesn't have money. What the hell? You just bend over for anyone?" Tate couldn't believe this guy.

His eyes flew wide open at his crass comment. "What the hell? You don't know me." Before much else could be said, Sheila came around the corner and swatted Colin on the back of the head.

Pilot's face turned red and Tate thought he might just explode.

"It's okay, Pilot," Tate said quietly, resting his hand on Pilot's thigh.

"No. No it isn't. Fuck you, Colin. You have no right coming in here acting like an ass to everyone."

His mom seemed sympathetic, but more interested in calming things down than in doing the right thing. She shushed Pilot and Colin. "Sheila stop hitting your brother."

Sheila wasn't backing down, though. "Bull! If he comes into my house acting like that, he's gonna get hit."

Their mom pulled her daughter into the other room, and Colin laughed. "You all must know I'm right or you wouldn't get so riled up. Seriously..."

Tate rolled his eyes. This guy was all about stirring up shit. Tate's grip on Pilot's thigh tightened, but it didn't do much good. Pilot stood and yelled at Colin and Colin yelled back. Tate felt like sliding under the table. Johnny slunk out of the room, leaving only the three of them. Tate hoped someone would come out and break it up, but the other guys in the house didn't seem interested.

"You have a lot of nerve bringing your fuck of the week home like this, Sean."

"You're a clueless dick. I don't have fucks of the week."

"This guy's trash." He flung his hand out at Tate. If he'd been meaning to hurt Tate's feelings, he missed the mark, but Pilot flew into a rage, and that's when Tate figured it out. This guy wasn't really attacking him or Johnny earlier; he was attacking Pilot.

"Pilot. Come on. Let's just go," he said, tugging at Pilot's arm. He just wanted to end this craziness.

Pilot shoved Colin and his voice dropped low. He wasn't yelling anymore and he sounded dangerous. He shrugged out of Tate's grip. "Tate is a Supercross racer. He makes more money in one race than you do in a year. He has more class in his little finger than you have in your entire fucking body. He is-is-he's everything and you're fucking nothing."

Colin backed up a step.

"Pilot. Pilot. Come on." Tate grabbed his arm again, turning him away from his brother. His face looked murderous for a second, then morphed into something softer, yet still angry. "Yeah. I'm done here. Let's go home."

They put their coats on and walked out to the car. "Can I drive? Please?" Tate really wanted to drive the sexy beast, just to drive it, but he also didn't want a pissed off Pilot behind the wheel.

Pilot tossed him the keys. "Know how to get back?"

"Eh. Kinda. You can navigate for me, bunny." Tate's happy attitude seemed to bring Pilot around and they climbed in the car. For a bit, the only conversation was Pilot directing Tate, until he was comfortable he knew where he was and how to get back to Pilot's house. Then, he decided he'd go ahead and break the ice before they got to the house. "Hey, Pilot?"

"What?" he answered, sounding sad.

"You know he wasn't really attacking me. He doesn't know me enough to attack me. That back there, you know, what your brother did? That was about you."

"What do you mean?"

Tate sighed. "He doesn't really give a shit about me or Johnny. He says that shit to get to you. You're his brother and he loves you, so he can't attack you directly, so he goes after your friends or lovers."

"Hm."

"I'm not mad or hurt or anything. So don't worry about that. But, you'd do better to stop reacting to his shit. Just like a bully, if he doesn't get the reaction he wants, he'll stop."

"You think?"

Tate shrugged. "Maybe."

"You're pretty fucking smart, Tate. I've been dealing with his shit storm since I got out of the service and hadn't *even* thought of that. You know, he's always been a dickhead, so..."

"I think there are more issues with Colin than you realize, and I'm not that smart."

"Turn here."

"Got it."

Pilot chuckled. "Okay. So? What makes you say all this?"

Tate thought about it for a minute, gathering his thoughts. He turned into Pilot's driveway and turned the car off, dropping the keys back in Pilot's hands. "I love this hot car," he murmured.

"Tate?"

"Right. I don't know. Maybe it's just easier to see from the outside."

"Come on." Pilot got out of the car and headed to the front door. Tate smiled to himself. Now that it was over and Pilot was happy again, he could acknowledge just how sexy a furious Pilot could be, even though he never wanted to be on the bad side of that rage.

Later that night, Tate crawled in bed and snuggled up to Pilot, happy and satisfied with his life for the first time since his parents had disowned him. Being able to take care of yourself and make it on your own was a bit overrated when you had to do it so young. Tate started down that *what if* path again for a minute: what if he hadn't had Supercross, what if he'd have come out sooner, what if... He stopped and cuddled his head on the pillow beside Pilot. It didn't matter and he wasn't alone. At least for now.

"Hey, what are you thinking about so hard?" Pilot asked, pulling him closer.

"Nothing. It doesn't matter. Hey, did I tell you how happy I am to be here?"

Pilot's lip curled up into a half smile. "No."

"Well, I am."

Pilot's eyes lit up "Let's open a present."

"No. That's tomorrow."

"It's customary to open one present on Christmas Eve." He got up and bounced up and down on the bed.

"What are you? Three?"

"Come on, Tate. It's Christmas Eve and, uh, I want to give you your present. Well, one of them. It's, uh, you know, personal. I want you to open it while it's just us here. Together."

Pilot was serious. He smiled, but it wasn't a good humor smile, just a happy, wanting smile. Tate was pretty sure he'd give Pilot anything he wanted as long as he kept looking at him that way. "Okay. I have one for you, too." He jumped up to dig through his duffle bag for where he'd hid

Pilot's presents and pulled out the small box with the bracelet in it. He hoped Pilot would like it.

When he crawled back on the bed, Pilot was on his knees on the floor beside the bed with his elbows leaning on the mattress. He held a small box in his hands. It was wrapped in shiny red foil wrapping and had a silver bow on top. "Here," he whispered, extending it to Tate with a shaky hand.

Tate handed his present over, but Pilot didn't open it. He waited, nodding for Tate to go first, so he ripped open the red paper and opened the box.

Two silver dog tag charms rested against black velvet. "What?" He picked one up. They both had "Tate & Pilot" engraved on them.

"I got one for both of us." He cleared his throat. "I want you to be my boyfriend. I want more of you, Tate. I-I can't imagine..."

"What?" Tate's eyes were wide and he had to force himself to shut his mouth. What was Pilot asking him?

"Since you've been here, Tate, I've realized how great it is and I don't ever want to be without you. I want you here with me."

Tate shook his head. "Are you asking me to be your boyfriend? Or move in with you?"

"Yes. Both. You're already here, so just like, don't leave. Ever."

Tate smiled. He would have never imagined how sweet Pilot was with his shy smile, his mile-wide protective streak, midnight ice-cream, and 80s sitcom reruns. And his sexy car. Tate raised an eyebrow. It would be so easy, wouldn't it? But, no. "There aren't any tracks here. I need to ride. I have to leave next week. I need track time before the season starts and that's barely a few weeks away. Joey has camp in Florida scheduled already."

"You sound like it's over before it's started."

Tate shook his head. "I don't know how to do this. I'm going to be gone. All the time. You know this."

"So, that doesn't mean we can't find a way to make it work. And there's got to be a track around here somewhere. Closer than Florida for sure. Can you look? Please?"

He was about to say no, but something in the way Pilot stared at him, made him stop. He didn't know what to say. He wanted it, wanted Pilot and everything he was offering. He wanted a home and this was the closest thing to it he'd ever had. Even when he was living with Donny, it hadn't felt so warm and he'd never felt this welcome. "I—"

"I'm going to be at every race anyway."

"This season. What about next?"

"I don't know, but if I'm not working for Apex, I'll be at as many of them as I can. Look. I get this Supercross thing. For the next five or six years, while you're on top, I'll sacrifice. Then, what? You come home and we settle down and find something else to do." He held up a hand like it was all settled.

Maybe it was.

"Tate? What are you afraid of?"

"I-I. Shit. I'm afraid I'll say yes and this will be perfect. For a while. Until you get tired of it. Tired of me. Then, I really will be brokenhearted. When Donny and I split up, it was hard. Not because of him. I never loved him. Hell, I didn't even like him much." Tate chuckled. "I missed having a home, feeling like I belonged somewhere. I never fit. Anywhere. I want a boyfriend. I want everything you're offering. But, more than that I want you and if we split up? I'm going to be shattered. I don't know if I could get over losing you and that's...I don't know...too much."

"Tate?" Pilot's eyes teared up, glistening in the low light.

"Shit. It's too late anyway. I'm already there."

Pilot leaned forward on the bed. "Does that mean?"

"Yes. I'll call Oz. I didn't want to go to Florida, and I have to call him tomorrow anyway."

Pilot jumped on the bed, tackling Tate, pushing his shoulders down on the bed. His mouth covered Tate's and his tongue probed, asking for more. Tate couldn't hold him back. Didn't want to. He opened for him. His mouth. His body. His soul.

Chapter 21 – After Christmas, Denver

Pilot pushed open the door to Trident Security and strode in like he already owned the place. He was on top of the world with Tate living with him. He hated going in to the office, just because he didn't want to leave Tate for a second, but that was ridiculous. He would just be happy that Tate would still be there when he returned home.

"Hey, bro!" Johnny called out walking in from the back office. "Wanna do lunch after your meeting?"

"Uh...no. Can't. Maybe later in the week." He hadn't told anyone yet about Tate not going back to New York.

"Why the hell not? What do you got going on?" The disappointment was plain on Johnny's face.

"Uh...it's just...Tate."

"What you have a phone sex date or something?" He held his hands up, fluttering the reports he had in his hands.

"No, uh...he's still here. He's, uh, we're...kind of going to try living together."

All kinds of emotions flashed over Johnny's face, but they ended with anger. "You're fucking crazy."

"Come on, J-man. I thought you'd be happy for me."

"Happy? Happy? What the fuck man. I thought—" Johnny pursed his lips together.

"Thought what? I mean I know I said he was going back to New York, or whatever, but he found a track close enough to practice from here. His trainer agreed to come too. And, I want him to stay. I'm happy."

"There's that word again."

"Johnny?"

"Nah. Forget it. I'm being stupid." He smashed his reports into Pilot's chest, wrinkling them, but he let go of them, forcing Pilot to catch them. "Here's your latest statements. Call me when you're ready to grow up." He turned and started walking off.

"Hey, wasn't it you that said this dream wasn't worth anything if we didn't have someone to share it with?"

Johnny stopped and turned around. "I didn't mean for you to take your hookup seriously. And what the fuck? How's he going to train with all the fucking snow? Huh? Don't they freakin' train in Florida? And they're on the road constantly when they're not training...you were last year—"

"And will be this year, too. Seriously, Johnny. Tate and I will be together more than not."

"Like I said. Whatever." He walked off again, and Pilot called after him, but he threw a hand in the air and kept going.

"Sean?" His uncle stepped out of his office.

"Yeah. What's up?"

"I don't know what all that was about, but I don't like y'all fighting."

"Yeah. Uh, he's pissed because I asked Tate to move in with me."

"Huh. Yeah. Well, maybe you just surprised him. I'm surprised."

Pilot held his hands up.

"Okay. We'll, deal with that later. First things first. I got the charges from your fighting escapades dropped, but you cannot do this shit again. No more street fights."

"Yes, sir." Pilot hadn't even thought about fighting since Tate had shown up in his life. He rubbed his wrist where the bracelet Tate gave him hung. "I'm okay with that." He'd be okay with anything that kept Tate in his life.

"Really? Because I didn't think even this arrest would stop this shit."

"I don't think Tate would like it."

His uncle lifted an eyebrow, but didn't comment. "Okay. Second. I have a couple of small jobs you can help me with the next few weeks until the Supercross shit starts. So, you ready to work?"

"Sure." What could he say? Uncle Gary came through for him as usual and he needed to be working. It made it a lot easier knowing Tate would be there at the end of the day.

Chapter 22 - First Race, Anaheim

Bryce should have been concentrating on the race. His heat was coming up and he needed to focus, but all he could think about was seeing Tate walking with that huge dude and wondering if they were together. He watched them go to the Apex tent. Knowing that they all had what he wanted boiled under his skin. Why couldn't he just get over it? Why had he freaked out so horribly when he could have had Tate Jordan for a boyfriend? One kiss and he was running for the door. In all honesty, it hadn't been the kiss. He could have kissed Tate on and on forever, amen! But, Tate had pushed for more than that and Bryce hadn't been ready. Still wasn't ready.

He'd been too worried that Tate only cared about sex and not him. But, he'd been such an idiot. Tate wouldn't have pushed too hard and he wouldn't have gone around telling anyone. Not like Warren Tanner had. That sonofabitch with his lies.

Bryce screwed his eyes shut tight. He didn't even want to think about how Warren had threatened him and when Bryce called his bluff, the bastard told everyone at the race club that Bryce had slept with Tate. So, not true. He only wished he'd slept with Tate. Sort of.

None of that mattered, because word got back to his parents and now they were watching him like hawks. They didn't care that he was gay, but they didn't want him ruining his career in Supercross by getting involved in inappropriate relationships. *As if!* That meant he wasn't *allowed* to talk to Tate or go anywhere near the Apex crew.

The worst part of it all was that he genuinely liked Tate. It had been fun hanging out with him and he'd loved the attention. Now, he couldn't have anything. Besides, Tate had never been anything but nice. It was that stupid Tanner dude that had fucked everything up with his threats and stupid emails. The fucker had even sent a few texts, and how he'd gotten Bryce's phone number, he had no clue.

"Hey East Coast, you all right?"

Bryce opened his eyes, hearing his nickname. George, his manager, had started calling him that recently, and it was sticking with others in the crew. He hadn't known it was odd for a racer from South Carolina to race in the 250SX West Division; it was just where they got him signed. It didn't matter to Bryce if he was in the East or West. With most of the races so far from home in the West division, he was thinking it might be a good thing. "Yeah, fine," he grunted.

"Okay, you have about twenty minutes 'til go."

Bryce gave him a curt nod and popped his ear buds in his ears and flipped to his favorite playlist. He wanted to just get into some tunes and focus. He had turned eighteen this past week and he could do whatever he wanted, but he didn't have the same kind of support Tate had. He still relied on his parents and breaking away from them wasn't going to be easy, but damn, he needed space before they smothered him to death. He'd manage it somehow and maybe even get himself a boyfriend—someone like Tate. But first, he had to win a race.

He nodded his head to the incessant drums of *Rancid* and mouthed the words. For the next twenty minutes, his music and his race were the only things in the world.

Bryce had been racing in smaller, less popular divisions for several years, but none of that prepared him for the chaos he was thrown into after getting on the podium in his first professional race. It wasn't even the main event, it was just the first heat race, and he didn't even win, he only placed second. Yet, there were microphones in his face, and people yelling questions at him left and right and the crowd cheering. He didn't know where to look or what to say.

George had told him that whenever a mic was pointed his way, his best bet was to thank his sponsors. Bryce couldn't argue with that logic since Suzuki put him on a brand new bike and TopSport Parts had signed on to be his main sponsor along with a few other minor ones. They paid him to do what he loved more than anything.

"How do you feel to have made it to the podium on your very first race?" A reporter shoved a *FoxSports 1* microphone up to his face.

Bryce tugged his Monster Energy hat back and forth across his head.

He had to make a show for the sponsors. "Feels great, but it's not my first race ever, just in this division. And, uh, I have to thank my team and my sponsors for this. You know? Without TopSport Parts, Suzuki, Camtop Oil, and uh, oh, Pro-hard Energy Sports supplements, I wouldn't be here in the Supercross 250 division. Without the TopSport crew working on the bike, making it work, yeah, I wouldn't be here. So, I'm thrilled, and ready to do it again in the Main Event."

"You heard it folks," the reporter said, turning away. Bryce hoped he gave them all they needed and tried to walk away as well, but other reporters stopped him first.

"I'm Cali from MotoMag. What's up with the purple hair, Bryce?"

Bryce shrugged. "I'm only eighteen. I like purple. It's fun."

"Are we going to see number 441 on the podium at the main event?" someone else called out.

"If I have anything to say about it," Bryce answered. He searched for a way out, for George, or someone to help rescue him. He'd had enough of the reporters. "I have to go," he muttered under his breath. He didn't know how the others, guys like Davey McAllister and Chad Regal, did it. They talked to the press all the time and made it look so smooth and easy. The lights blinded and the questions came at him from everywhere and worse, he had nothing else to say.

Bryce smiled and nodded while cameras flashed in his face. Someone handed him a X-Top Energy drink and he popped it open, drinking some of it. He almost never drank that stuff since he was on a very strict diet and exercise plan, but he was thirsty and he couldn't seem to get away. More lights flashed around him and people yelled out, and someone started chanting, "East Coast. East Coast." Bryce was already on an adrenaline high from the race, but his heart started pumping even faster and sweat dripped down his back. He pulled at the goggles hanging around his neck. He blinked furiously like his eyes had a will of their own and were trying to escape his face, only being held back by his sporadically winking lids.

A hand gripped his shoulder and he looked up to see George. "Come on. Good job, kid."

He let George lead him away, but figured the man had been behind some of the craziness. At least the chanting. It didn't matter, he'd do what he was told so he could keep racing.

As they walked toward the pit, his heart finally calmed down. He rubbed his arm over his forehead, wiping the sweat off and took a deep breath. "That was kind of crazy, man."

"Yep. For your first time, you looked pretty good. Next time, talk a little about the race."

"Okay." He hadn't even thought about that. Yeah, he'd heard other racers talk about the race and what had happened on the track. McAllister was really good at that. Bryce thought he should watch some more clips of him.

They walked on together until they approached the Apex pit and Bryce slowed down a bit. Just as they passed, Tate bounced out of the pit and almost ran right into Bryce. "Hey!" Bryce called out.

"Hey! Bryce? Hey." Tate's eyes flew wide, eyebrows practically exploding off his face.

"Yeah, hey, Tate. Good to see you." Seeing Tate felt a lot better than good to Bryce. It felt like seeing the sun for the first time after a month of rain.

"Did you race? Did you just race? How'd you do?" He seemed genuinely interested.

"Second."

Tate pulled Bryce into a hug. It felt warm and right and Bryce didn't want it to end, but Tate pulled back. He rubbed his hands along Bryce's biceps, lingering, as if he didn't want to stop touching. Or maybe Bryce imagined it. Tate couldn't still be interested in him. Yet, his touch felt like lightning zinging through his arm.

"I'm so proud of you. That's excellent!"

"Yeah, thanks. Hey, uh, you know about camp? I'm sorry."

Tate waived one hand in the air, as if saying it was nothing, but his other hand stayed on Bryce's arm. "My fault. Really. I'm sorry."

"I really need to talk to you about it. There's more you probably don't know. But, uh, this isn't the time."

Tate's eyebrow scrunched over his nose. His face was so expressive, Bryce could almost tell what he was thinking by just watching his eyes and mouth alone. Looking at his mouth was a bad idea though, because he remembered that one blissful kiss.

Stepping closer, Tate moved his hand from Bryce's arm to the back of his neck. His fingers flitted through his hair that hung loose at his collar. "Hey, we can talk. Anytime. Really. I-I want us to be friends, Bryce." Tate seemed concerned, as if he could sense Bryce's turmoil, and maybe he could. Maybe it was just as clear on his own face as Tate's emotions were on his.

"Yeah. My parents have been a bit smothering and it's all that Tanner dude's fault."

"Wait. What? What'd he do? That douche."

"Like I said, later. Can we talk later?"

Tate reached into his pocket and pulled out his phone, handing it to Bryce. "Give me your number, I'll text you after the Main Event when I'm free."

Bryce tapped his numbers in and put his name in as the contact and handed the phone back. Tate tapped at it and smiled. "Just texted you, so you have mine, too."

"Oh! What'd you send? My mom has my phone."

"Just said hi. Relax."

Bryce nodded. He overreacted. She wouldn't know it was from him anyway. It would be okay.

"Aren't you eighteen now?"

Bryce nodded again.

"You can do what you want, you know?"

"I know. It's complicated though. They've always been there and now, it's hard to push them away. You know what I mean?"

"Not really. My parents divorced me early on, I guess. Supercross is my parent. Has been for a while."

Bryce just looked at him and his gorgeous, blond hair that danced around his head, and those animated, green eyes. Tate was Bryce's Supercross god and he wanted nothing more than to kneel at the man's feet. He wanted one more kiss and anything else Tate would bestow upon him.

Tate's phone buzzed, and he lowered his gaze to look at it. "Yeah, I gotta run. My heat's up."

"Okay. Thanks, Tate. Good luck."

"Arg! Davey McAllister's the one that'll need the luck. Oh, Davey!!" Tate had raised his voice, and laughed as Davey came out of the pit, pushing his bike, his hot mechanic right next to him. "Hey Davey, Ty, this is Bryce Nickel, he's racing in the 250 West. I know him from camp."

"Nice to meet you," Davey said with a curt nod.

"Hey," Tyler, the mechanic waived, holding his greasy hand up, as if to say he'd shake hands, but they were too dirty.

"Yeah, hi! Nice to meet y'all."

Tyler smiled. "A southern boy. Nice! Why don't you hang out with us after the race?"

Bryce was pretty sure stars were glittering in his eyes at the thought of hanging out with his Supercross idols, but his parents would never let him. "I can't. Not this time, but maybe the next race." If he could ditch his parents, convince them that he didn't need a chaperone, maybe he could hang with them.

"You're welcome any time. Shit. Gotta go, Davey." Tyler directed Davey forward and they both climbed on the bike, as Davey started it up, and they drove away.

"Shit, me, too. Really, call me." Tate leaned in and hugged Bryce again, and then ran off.

Bryce looked up to see George staring him down. "You need to come talk to the mechanic about your bike. While it's fresh."

"Okay." He followed George the rest of the way back to the pit, but he wasn't thinking about the bike or the press or the race. Nope. He was thinking about crazy blond hair, a sunny smile, and a *win-it-all* attitude.

When they got to the TopSport pit, his parents were there chatting with the mechanics and a few other people under the awning. He really wished they'd not come. His mother saw him and jumped forward pulling him into a big hug. "I'm so proud of you, baby." Her cold hug and teasing words were nothing like Tate's hug had been.

Bryce pulled away from her. "Yeah, it was just the heat race, Mom."

"Still. It was important and you proved yourself." Bryce knew she was trying and he could have it a hell of a lot worse, making him feel guilty for questioning her affection. He worried his tongue against his back molar where he'd recently had his wisdom tooth pulled.

"Mrs. Nickel, good to see you." George stepped between them. "Let's have a chat while Bryce works with the mechanics." Bryce squatted down behind the bike, as George directed Bryce's parents out of the pit area. He peeked over the bike, watching them walk away.

"They're a bit intense," the mechanic said, looking down at Bryce. He had his hands in the bike, but Bryce didn't know what he was doing.

"Yeah, tell me about it." He rolled his eyes.

The mechanic chuckled. "So, how'd the bike run? What do we need to do?"

"It ran great. Hell, I took second."

"What do you think we should tweak?"

Bryce shrugged. He knew the basics, but not nearly enough about the mechanics of the bike. Even in the other division, he'd had help with that. "I don't know. It was just a little sluggish in the turns, otherwise, perfect."

"Okay, we can clean her up and do a few tweaks."

Bryce didn't want to find his parents and talk with them. Learning all he could about the bike would prove beneficial, so he took a deep breath. "Show me."

Chapter 23 - After the Race, Anaheim

Tate texted Bryce in the cab back to the hotel, letting him know that he could talk. He tapped on the door to the hotel room and Pilot opened the door and then his arms. Tate practically fell into them. It felt so nice to have someone there for him at the end of such a long weekend, someone supporting him, loving him. He hadn't really had that before. Sure, before his parents walked away, they were supportive and Oz was always there for him. Yet, they all seemed just as concerned with controlling him as supporting him. Maybe that wasn't entirely fair for Oz, but he was Tate's manager; he was supposed to be controlling. Pilot though? Pilot just loved him. Without judgement, without demands. It was new, but Tate never wanted to be without it.

"Missed you," Pilot said, kissing the top of Tate's head.

"Mmm...I need a shower."

Pilot shut and latched the metal lock at the door and shoved Tate toward the bathroom. "Go. Hurry up, snap to it."

Tate laughed and stripped on the way, toeing off his sneakers and letting his jersey and track pants land wherever they fell along the way. He'd left his racing boots by the door where he'd dropped them when Pilot dragged him in. Pilot leaned against the door frame, as Tate stuck his head under hot water.

"I have a thing in the morning," Tate said.

"What kind of thing?"

Tate dumped hotel shampoo on his head and rinsed before answering. "Some media promo shoot for next week's race. Shouldn't take too long or mess with our flight times. I'll be back before check out."

Pilot grumbled a little. "Was hoping we could sleep in."

Tate laughed and soaped his body up. "Uh, lazy bones. We can sleep in when we get home." Home. Tate practically wiggled at the thought that he finally had a home, somewhere that he could sleep in and snuggle with his lover and maybe have breakfast in bed or snuggle on the couch to watch a movie. Whatever they wanted to do—together. Pilot made all the difference. He touched the dog tag charm he never took off and smiled. "Davey's going to be there too. Why don't you know about it?"

"It's not a public thing. Guess they felt safe enough."

"Yeah. Okay."

Tate turned the water off and grabbed a towel to dry off. He didn't miss the way Pilot's eyes ate him up before he wrapped the towel around his waist. He loved the heat in Pilot's gaze and the way it stoked up his own fire. His cock started rising, tenting the towel up in front of him.

Pilot chuckled and grabbed his crotch. "Me too, Tate. Want you. All the time." He licked his lips and his pink tongue was an invitation Tate couldn't pass up. He closed the distance between them and tilted his head up, begging for Pilot's kiss. Pilot obliged, taking his mouth and owning it.

The percussion from UB40's Young Guns blared out from Tate's phone. "Oh!" He pulled back from Pilot. "That's Bryce. I need to take this." He looked at Pilot with pleading eyes, hoping he'd understand. He answered the phone and plopped down on the king sized bed. "Hey, dude. What's up?"

Pilot followed him into the room and quirked his eyebrow up, silently asking what the deal was. Tate decided he kind of liked that look and liked Pilot's concern.

"Tate, hey. Is this really a good time to talk?"

"Sure. Sure, no problem. So, what's up?"

Tate heard a long sigh and empty air before Bryce started in. "Okay. I'm just going to spit this out. So, uh...Tanner. Warren Tanner. That dick cornered me. He said he knew we were fucking."

"Oh! What'd you say?"

"Did you tell him that?"

"Fuck, no. He was guessing." Tate could feel the anger rising in his chest. Tanner had been an asshole all the way around.

"Okay. So, he said if I didn't bend over for him, he'd tell everyone about you and me."

There was a long pause while Tate decided what to say about that. He had regretted letting that asswipe fuck him before he'd even finished and left, but he'd never thought it would come back on Bryce. The fucker had a lot of nerve blackmailing Bryce, but worse, the thought of that fucker touching Bryce like that, taking him the way he did Tate, made his blood boil. "What'd you do?" Tate's words came out harsher than he'd meant. He was angry at Tanner, not Bryce. "Sorry. I'm not mad at you, whatever you did, Bryce. I just need to know."

"I get it. I guess. But." Bryce let out another sigh and Tate was afraid he was going to say he'd given in. "I couldn't let him touch me. I could barely kiss you. And I *like* you. So, I told him to fuck off. But, then he did it."

"Did what?"

"Told. Told everybody. So, everyone thinks I let you fuck me and that's why my parents are being so, uh, you know? Overprotective. Smothering. Really. I wish they'd leave me alone, but they don't think I can handle my shit."

"Damn. I'm really sorry, Bryce. I'm sure that's not how you wanted to come out. If you even wanted to."

"No."

"At least that fucker didn't touch you. I don't care what people say about me."

"Tate, how can you say that? You have a lot to lose."

Tate laughed at that. He knew rumors about his sexuality were not going to upend his career. It hadn't run Davey off and the rumors about Tate were already around before MSR signed him and when everything exploded last season, his name had been thrown around even more as he became associated with McAllister's camp. He hadn't lost anything. "Nah. I'm good. I'm more worried about you. Everyone knows about me. You knew about me, before, too. You know?"

"Yeah. I guess you're right about that."

"So? How are you? How are you dealing with this?" Tate's eyes followed Pilot as he paced around the hotel room. He picked things up and put them down. Packed a few things. Looked at Tate from the corner of his eyes. Tate fingered his dog tag charm. Pilot had nothing to worry about, even if he didn't know it, yet. Tate made a mental note to make sure he knew it, as soon as his phone call was over.

"I don't know. Mostly, I'm ignoring it. When I think I can just be myself, my parents are like right there. You know? I wish they'd leave me the hell alone, but then I don't know, I'd be like really alone. You know?"

Tate couldn't help making that strange grunting noise. He knew exactly what Bryce was saying. "I get it. Really. I've been through, well, most of what you're saying. Except, when I came out to my parents, I lost them. If you were honest with yours, and they're still around, even if they're a bit overwhelming, don't take that for granted. Obviously, they love you. Care about you."

"I know. I did and they do. I just wish they'd give me a little more space. I'm eighteen. I've got a career. I even got my high school diploma. A lot of racers don't get that, even when they're straight. I'm just ready to be a little more on my own."

"Well. I guess you have to tell them that. If it helps, you can tell them that we're just friends. I have a boyfriend."

"That big guy I saw you with?"

"You saw me with Pilot?"

"He's like a bodyguard, right? For Apex?"

Tate's eyes grew wide and his mouth hung open. Bryce had done his homework. Why? Was he still interested in Tate? He'd said he liked Tate, but Tate had thought that meant friendship, not lovers. "Uh, Bryce we're just friends. I mean, you and me. Pilot's my boyfriend. I-I don't mean to hurt—"

"No, I know. Just friends."

"—you. I want to be friends, though."

"I said I get it. I need a friend, Tate. No matter how I feel about you. It's, you know, a crush, or whatever. You were the first guy to ever kiss me and I'll cherish that, but I just need a friend."

"You've got it, Bryce. I'm here. As friends."

"Cool." He sounded relieved. Tate hoped he'd helped him sort through everything.

"Feel better?"

"Yes. Thanks, Tate. I mean it. This helped."

Tate smiled. It felt good to have helped Bryce. His heart warmed thinking about it. He didn't want to explore his feelings about Bryce any further than that, especially when Pilot stopped stealing glances at him and crawled up on the bed. He put his hand on Tate's leg, as if staking his claim. "You're welcome. Seriously. Call me anytime. If you need anything. I mean it."

"Thanks, Tate. Bye."

"Later, dude."

Tate put his phone on the side table. "He really needed a friend."

Pilot nodded. "You're a good man, Tate. Of course you're going to be there for him. Who is he, again?"

Tate scooted closer to Pilot, wanting his strong arms around him, reassuring him. Once he was snuggled up, he told Pilot everything about Bryce. Pilot held him tighter. "See," he said. "Like I said, you are a good man, Tate. I'm glad you could be there for him."

"Me, too." He tilted his head up for a kiss, and as usual, Pilot did not disappoint him. Their lips found each other and the electricity sizzled between them.

Tate stared down at his phone as he entered the warehouse-like area that had been set up for the interviews. Pilot had sent him a string of texts about how much he was missed and how much Pilot was enjoying that big bed all by himself. Tate texted back, begging Pilot to send him some pictures, but he wouldn't do it. It was probably just as well, since Tate didn't want to be giving an interview with a hard-on anyway.

"Tate! Here!" Oz called him over and handed him a cup of coffee.

"Thanks! Joey would kill you if he knew you were sliding me all this caffeine and sugar." He sipped at the treat and hummed his happiness.

"Yeah, well, what he don't know won't hurt him. Do an extra mile on your bike when you get home. Oh! By the way. I'm having a new practice bike sent to you tomorrow. You need to be there for it."

"Oh, why didn't you send it to the track?"

"They wouldn't guarantee someone could sign for it. They don't know us, really. Not yet. Getting set up at a new place can be challenging. Joey will meet you there Tuesday."

"Fuck. I guess I better go buy a truck."

"Your *boyfriend* doesn't have a truck?"

Tate lowered his cup of heaven and stared at Oz. "What the hell does that mean? He's got a muscle car, dude. That ain't gonna haul a bike."

"Are you serious about moving in with him? How permanent is this?" Oz sounded irritated, even more than he had when Tate had moved in with Donny. "Tell me this isn't because of your lack of housing. You have enough money to buy something, Tate. You don't have to—"

"Stop right there." Tate walked away to catch his breath and control his temper and then came back. Other racers stood around waiting for their turn for the interview and photo shoot, but none he knew well. They talked to each other or to their managers, ignoring Tate's drama completely. Tate sucked in his bottom lip, thinking about what he wanted to say and what he didn't want to say. He didn't want Oz in his private business, but if he didn't give him some reassurance, he would be. Oz was more than just his manager, even if Tate treated him like that sometimes.

The door at the far end of the space opened and Davey McAllister walked out with Angel, his manager. "Tate!" he called out and waved.

"We'll get back to this," Oz grumbled. Tate knew Oz wouldn't forget about their conversation but was happy enough to deal with the distraction.

"Davey! 'Sup?" They did a fist bump and Angel leaned in and hugged him. "Hey, sweet lady! Haven't seen you around."

"I seem to spend most of my time with the big wigs lately. I'd rather be closer to the track, though."

Tate had heard some of how Angel ended up in charge of the Apex team. She stepped up and helped out when Davey's previous manger, Stewart, couldn't because of his contract with Princeton. That shit storm didn't stop any of them and gave Tate hope. The way they handled Davey being outed made Tate want to be friends with them and after getting to know the team better, he really liked them. Everything about Davey McAllister screamed integrity, pride, and determination. That was the caliber of people Tate wanted to be around. He glanced over at Oz's scowling face. His own manager lived up to that standard, and Tate needed to treat him better.

He bumped shoulders with Davey. "So, how bad is this interview thing?"

A heavy set woman with bleach blonde, spiked hair and a clipboard came out of the room and roared into the large room. "Cole Lindt! I need your team now."

Tate hadn't realized Cole was even there. He frowned automatically, watching Cole cross the room, blatantly ignoring their group.

Davey cleared his throat. "Yeah, it's not that bad. They didn't ask many personal questions. Apex tried to get them to shoot this with Tyler, too, but no one else has their spouses or partners. We get what they want to promote, but damn..."

"They could give it a rest," Angel added. "There has to be some balance. It's equality across the board, not just homosexuality. If you keep shoving the gay around, it becomes an *us versus them* thing instead of being inclusive."

"Hadn't thought about it that way." Tate took another sip of his coffee. "Is that why you have a female racer in the 250?" He'd met Sarah and seen her around the track. Davey had been working with her and planned on starting her in the 250 East class this season. There had been girls racing before, but none seemed to be able to qualify.

"Sorta, but she's really pretty good. So, we need to get you down during the first break. You can bring Joey to help...and Pilot." He wiggled his eyebrows, knowing that they were living together.

"I'd have to. He's already grumpy because I left him in the hotel room for this."

Davey gave him a playful leering look. "I bet."

"Enough of that. Leave the boy alone." Angel tugged Davey's jersey sleeve. "Come on. We gotta go. See ya later, Tate." She nodded at Oz and he smiled back at her, politely.

Once they left, Tate sighed. He'd rather hang out with Davey's team than sit around this crappy warehouse, waiting to be shoved in front of the camera, or worse, discussing his love life with Oz. He shoved his bangs out of his face and glanced up. Oz studied him with creased eyebrows and a pinched mouth. "Okay, Oz. I get you're concerned. But, I really like Pilot and we're going to try and make it work. He's nothing like Donny. Trust me."

"It's not a matter of trust, Tate. I just don't really know this guy and you're moving awfully fast. I worry for you."

Tate sipped the rest of his coffee, emptying the cup. Cole came back out of the camera room and shot a quick grin as he passed Tate. It wasn't friendly, but it wasn't rude, either. Just an acknowledgment. Tate figured that was an improvement.

He walked across the room and dumped his cup in the trash, trying to avoid the rest of the conversation with Oz. The blonde woman called out for Tate, saving the day.

"Want me to go with you?" Oz asked.

"Nah. I got this. Relax. Seriously. About everything." He paused and gave Oz a hug, before following the assistant. He needed to remember Oz had his best interests in mind, always, even when he didn't get what was going on with Tate. He smiled to himself, realizing he needed to stop taking that for granted that.

Bryce had his earbuds in listening to some punk-reggae fusion while he packed the back of the sedan his parents had rented. Out of the corner of his eye, he saw a large man moving closer and he looked up. He pulled the headphones down and shut off his MP3 player.

The guy walking up to him was intimidating. Large. He couldn't keep his hands from shaking a little and he looked around, in case he needed to run. But then he recognized the guy. He was the big bodyguard Apex had hired, Pilot. The one he saw with Tate at the race. *His boyfriend.* Did he know what had happened at camp? Was he going to kick Bryce's ass for talking to Tate?

He stopped next to the car. "You're Bryce, right?"

"Yeah..."

The guy looked him over, making Bryce feel a bit unsettled. He could not even believe how gorgeous the guy was and if he really was Tate's boyfriend, Tate was so lucky. He stuffed his shaking hands into the front pocket of his jeans.

"You know Tate, right?"

Bryce gave a curt nod, not sure of what to say. "He's nice. 'Bout the only friend I have. This industry...hard to know who to trust." He wanted to trust Tate and his boyfriend. He liked the way the big guy looked at him, making his stomach flutter.

"You can trust us—trust Tate."

"Thanks, that means a lot." Bryce started to relax a bit. It didn't sound like the guy wanted to beat his ass or anything.

"Bryce!" He looked over at where his mom called him from their hotel room and rolled his eyes.

"That's my mom. She's great for my image."

Tate's boyfriend smiled and his eyes softened. "It's cool. Really. Call Tate if you need anything. Really."

Bryce nodded and put his earbuds back in his ears. He didn't really want to hear his mom calling him again. He turned and watched the guy walk back across the parking lot. Bryce wished he had a boyfriend like him or Tate.

Chapter 24 - Next Race, San Diego

Bryce's mechanic jumped on the back of his bike and rode with him over to the press area. His heart pounded a rhythm almost hard enough to play with the hard rocking bands he liked to listen to.

Second. He'd finished second in the Main Event in his second race. The mechanic took his bike from him when he got on the podium. His goggles hung backward around his neck and someone handed him an energy drink. Someone else put a hat on him before he could even see what it was. Bryce pushed the brim to the back just as the network shoved a bulky headset over his head.

The rest happened in a blur. Thanking his sponsors, talking about the race, thanking the network. Taking a long drink from the aluminum can. Smiling brightly...he pretended that he was Davey McAllister, so the butterflies would stop. He thought he had it under control, until he looked out into the crowd.

Tate Jordan stood there with his arms crossed and a smirk on his face. Bryce couldn't help himself. He yanked off the headset, shoving it at the nearest camera guy and raced over to Tate. "Did you watch? Did you see me race?" Despite being epically tired, Bryce had a megawatt of energy still thrumming through his veins.

"Yeah, yeah. I saw, wonder-boy." Tate pushed the hat off his head. "Hey, this is my boyfriend, Pilot."

"Hi, again. We've met," Bryce said, still bouncing on the balls of his feet. He raked his eyes over Tate's super-hot boyfriend. He was built like a professional wrestler, tall with bulky muscles; his thighs threatened to burst out of his jeans. He could have been a marine with his hair buzz cut and his dark expressive eyes, taking everything in around them with just a glance. He glowered at the world like he'd burn it all down in a second. Bryce swallowed down the slight fear the big man instilled. Although he definitely intimidated Bryce, he knew that if Tate approved, he had to be a good guy.

When he stuck out his hand, Bryce shook it without hesitation, and delighted in the electrical zing he got from Pilot's touch, even through his racing gloves. He couldn't help wonder what it would feel like to have the man's hands on him—bare skin to bare skin, touching every part of him. Bryce shivered and let go, catching a glimpse of a tattoo on Pilot's bicep. He wondered what it was, wanted to see more.

"Look, Bryce. We have to go get ready for 450s, but we're going to hang out with the Apex crew after the main event. Wanna come with?" Tate's invitation seemed sincere.

Bryce nodded quickly. To hell with his parents. He was not going to miss out on this. Not again. Tate wanted him around and he wanted to go. "Hell yeah, for sure. When and where?"

Pilot leaned closer and put his hand on Bryce's shoulder. "Just come by the Apex pit after the Main Event. We'll eventually get there."

Maybe Pilot wanted him there, too. It surprised Bryce. He would have thought the man would be jealous, but maybe he didn't know about him and Tate kissing. Maybe Tate hadn't told him anything. Or maybe he had, because they were really just friends, no matter how much Bryce wanted to pretend they had been more, or how much more Bryce wanted from him. Whatever Tate said or didn't say, Pilot had been surprisingly cool about it all—so far.

Davey McAllister won the race and Tate came in second with Chad Regal nipping at his rear tire for third. The results were exciting but not surprising. Bryce suspected the three of them would be duking it out every week for the rest of the season. They were the top three racers in the 450 class and unless one of them had a super bad week, they would continue to challenge each other. Bryce knew all three of them hated to lose. Hell, he hated to lose.

After the race, he made his way to the Apex pit area. His parents weren't happy with him, but he'd stood his ground. They physically slumped just before he turned and walked out on them. He stuffed the guilt down, though. Yes, he owed them more than the average son, but he didn't owe them his life. He was eighteen and he'd just had two major victories back to back and he wanted to celebrate. No, he deserved to celebrate— with his new friends.

McAllister, his mechanic-husband, and their two body guards, one of which was Tate's boyfriend Pilot, arrived in the pit area on a storm of chaos. Bryce moved to the back, out of the way. Another mechanic took the bike from them. He had dark hair and olive skin and an infectious laugh. They called him Mickey and Bryce made a mental note of the name. He wanted to get to know these guys, after all.

When most of the people and press left the area, Pilot came over and said hello. "Tate will be here in a few minutes. You know how it is."

Bryce did know how it went after a race. Tate would have to talk with his mechanic, his manager, his trainer, maybe even more press, before he'd be able to get away. All of that went on around him with Davey and his husband as well. "I know."

"He'll probably change too," Pilot said. He crossed his arms over his chest and leaned back against the huge eighteen wheeler truck, giving Bryce another opportunity to look him over.

It seemed to him that Tate had won the jackpot of boyfriends. Even though Pilot's build rocked that sexy military look, he also obviously cared about Tate. He was sexy, capable, and still really nice.

Davey's husband and the mechanic, Mickey, took care of the bike. Bryce couldn't remember what his husband's name was, but he was fine as hell, too. He had serious muscles but not as big as Pilot's, and an adorable face. His sexy dirty-blond hair looked like he'd just got out of bed as he ran his hands through it. Bryce remembered the scandal when the picture of the couple had been released to the media. They had gotten some hate comments, but the majority of people seemed to be okay with it. Bryce had stared at the picture for a long time when he had first seen it, hoping it might change something in his own life. Maybe it had.

Eventually, Tate showed up and hugged everyone. "Tyler!" he squealed when he hugged Davey's husband, finally giving Bryce his name. Then, he hugged Davey and Mickey and finally Pilot, who leaned down and gave him a kiss as well. Then, he fist bumped Bryce and for a second, Bryce thought he'd be left out of the hug-fest and his heart fell into his gut. But then Tate grabbed his wrist and yanked Bryce into his chest and his arms circled around him. His hug more closely resembled the hug he'd given Pilot than the ones he bestowed on everyone else. He held it just a little longer, his arms wrapped just a little tighter, and when he released him, Tate's hands slid across his arms. His heart leapt back into his chest and danced across his ribs like pounding through a woops section. "Bryce."

"Hey, um, Tate. Uh, hi." Bryce swallowed hard, sure everyone would see his overwhelming attraction to Tate. If they did, they didn't say anything about it, even Pilot kept quiet, acting like it hadn't happened.

After everyone was reacquainted and Davey had changed into jeans and a clean jersey, they all headed out. Bryce squeezed into the backseat of a cab with Tate and Pilot, his body humming with desire that he had to just squish. Davey, Tyler, and Mickey climbed into a second cab, and they left the arena.

They went to a family style bar, so he could actually get in. He was the only one in the group under twenty-one. It made him feel bad at first, but then he realized that none of the others even ordered anything alcoholic, just coke, water and food. They'd be getting wings, potato skins, chips and spinach dip, and southwestern egg rolls to share.

Tate and Pilot made him feel welcome, but Tyler and Mickey made him feel like a part of the gang. They laughed and teased him right along with the others. Mickey had a quick wit and a sharp tongue. He was also sexy as hell. They all were, but Bryce's gaze lingered over Tate and Pilot the most. There was an odd tension between them that he didn't understand. He chose to ignore it and have fun with his friends.

Davey and Tyler had been talking about superheroes until Davey slapped his hand on the table, getting everyone's attention. "I'll prove it, Ty," he said, looking around the table. "Bryce, if you could be a superhero, who would you be. Don't think just answer."

"Uh, Superman, or no...Green Lantern," he blurted out, happy to have been picked first.

"Right. Pilot?"

Pilot grumbled a bit before answering, "The Hulk."

Tyler complained, "That's not a superhero."

Mickey said, "Yes, he is. He's in the Avengers."

Tyler rolled his eyes, then Davey nodded at Tate.

"Uh... probably the Silver Surfer. He's rad," Tate said in a fake valley boy accent.

"Batman," Mickey chimed in before being asked, and then scooped some dip on a chip and stuffed it in his mouth.

"See? All the racers here picked superheroes that fly."

"The hulk flies," Tyler grumbled and Tate laughed.

"No. He jumps. That's different."

"So, Pilot's jumpy?" Tyler asked.

"That's not the point," Davey argued.

A wicked smile crept over Tyler's face. "Batman flies."

Davey groaned. "Not without help. He doesn't even have super powers. Just gadgets."

"He's still cool," Mickey complained. "That's why I like him. I'm a mechanic." He held up a hand, as if that explained everything.

Davey leaned back in the booth and stretched his arm along the seat back. "Also, not the point."

Bryce was enjoying their interaction, but also wasn't sure what Davey's point was, so he asked.

Davey leaned forward. "That we race because we want to fly."

Tyler laughed. "No. I think it means that you connect with flying more than the rest of us mere mortals and that's part of why *you* race Supercross and we don't, even though we also love riding."

Pilot grumbled again.

"What?" Tyler asked.

"I don't ride."

Everyone, even Mickey and Tyler, stared at him.

Tate chuckled, low in his chest. "Oh, that's it. Next week, you are coming with me to the track. You are so getting on a bike."

"I prefer cars."

"Nope. Sexy car or not, you're getting on a bike," Tate said and that was that.

Bryce's chest felt warm inside. He'd never imagined ever being included in a group like this.

Chapter 25 - After the party, San Diego

Tate threw his head back and it fell off the edge of the mattress, but it didn't slow Pilot's thrusts. He didn't break his stride in the slightest. Tate wrapped his legs around Pilot's waist, so he wouldn't keep sliding forward. He didn't like the idea of landing on the hotel floor.

The pounding rhythm continued, the heat building into an inferno. Sweat dripped down from Pilot's neck and Tate's hands grasped at the sheets. His shoulders slid down to the edge of the bed, and he thought for a moment he might fall off, but Tate did not want to stop. Pilot gazed at Tate with heat and want in his eyes, and Tate knew Pilot didn't want to stop either, but he did stop. Pilot reached under Tate and wrapped his arms around Tate's hips, hauling him back to the middle of the bed, shifting them to a more parallel position. With a grunt, Pilot's cock slipped out and he lined it back up. As he pushed back in, Tate let out a sigh. He needed to feel Pilot inside him, connecting them like nothing else in the world could.

Pilot canted his hips, finding a better angle that brushed across Tate's prostate with every thrust. Tate gasped with the first stroke and then his voice broke into a low moan that came from the back of his throat, his gut, and his soul, simultaneously.

A warm slick hand grabbed his cock, bringing Tate back to the moment, but only for a second. His orgasm knocked the wind out of him and all he could see was a field of shiny stars, as his eyes rolled back in his head.

Then Pilot grunted and his whole body went rigid. "Damn! God!" he called out with a series of grunts. He collapsed with his own sigh, right on top of Tate.

"Uh! You brute. You're too heavy. Get off," Tate teased. Pilot responded by leaning more into Tate's chest and tickling his sides. Their laughter broke the serious tone that Tate had felt only moments before in the best possible way.

"Come on. Let's get cleaned up."

They both jumped in a quick shower and then toweled off before getting back in bed. Tate considered all the snuggling up together a huge bonus. He had no idea he would love all this cuddly shit so much, but he did. "I'm not sleepy yet. Are you?"

"Nah."

"Cool."

Pilot tugged at Tate's blond hair. "Hey! I saw how you were looking at that boy."

"Huh? What boy?"

Pilot's body shook with laughter that he barely held back. It took him a minute to get it under control. "That kid, Bryce. I know you have a crush on him. Admit it."

Tate didn't say anything for a minute. He leaned up and looked at Pilot, trying to determine his level of seriousness.

"Come on New York! Admit it."

"New York?"

Pilot pulled Tate back down against him, so he could rest against Pilot's warm shoulder. "Yeah, because you think you're slick or something. You forget I know you, babe."

"Okay...Well, Bryce is adorable. Don't you think?"

"Yep. He's cute, New York."

Tate shoved at Pilot, but he didn't budge, just tightened his arms more. "You know I'm from North Carolina, right?"

"Oh? Didn't you live in New York?"

"Well, yeah. But, I'm not from there. Just ended up there."

"How'd that happen?"

In the quiet of the room Tate could hear the outside traffic and feel Pilot's heartbeat. He felt safe, protected, in Pilot's arms. "Well, my parents were rednecks really. They had me on a dirt bike before I was three. Back in the woods, it was just what we did. I rode four wheelers and big trucks and dirt bikes before I ever got a driver's license."

"I don't know what that's like. Did you like it?"

"When I was young I did. We hunted and fished and hung out in the woods. Just being a kid. I thought my dad was the greatest. Then he realized I was really good on a dirt bike and started putting me in competitions when I was about 10. I won a lot. Everything was cool, like I had the best life a kid could want."

When he paused, Pilot asked, "So how'd you get to New York? What happened?"

"Yeah, guess...same old story for a gay kid. By the time I hit 13, puberty reared its ugly head, and I started getting a little boy crazy."

"A little boy crazy?" Pilot asked with a teasing gleam in his eye.

"Okay, a lot boy crazy. I was in love with ever other racer on the dirt." Tate laughed. "But then there was this one guy. Chester."

"Chester?"

"Yeah, don't laugh. I know. But, he was really cute and had all these freckles all over his nose and under his eyes. And his lips were pouty and I wanted to kiss him every time I saw him. He was like a friend of the family, and we hung out a lot and he loved the dirt bikes. So, like, when I was almost seventeen, we were riding. I was smearing his ass all over the dirt. Hell, I'd already met Oz and he was signing me to the 250 division, and I'd already been racing Arenacross. And winning. Ha! I thought I was hot shit back then. You know how it is. Almost seventeen at the time. I thought I was invincible."

"Chester had no chance with you, Hot stuff."

"Ha! Right. So, I finally stopped and let him catch up. We took off our helmets and just grinned at each other like a couple of happy fools. I couldn't take it anymore. I grabbed his arm and pulled him closer and laid one on him."

"Did he punch you?"

"No. But he did say he wasn't interested. He said he liked me, but he liked Mary Beth more."

"So, he was bi? But not hot for you?" Tate smacked Pilot with his pillow and he retaliated by pulling Tate closer and snuggling his nose into Tate's neck. "Go on."

"I don't know what he was. I never saw him again, anyway. Uh, this is where everything really starts to suck."

"I like sucking," Pilot joked, obviously trying to keep the mood light.

Tate had never really talked about this much, even to Oz, but he felt Pilot should know. "My mom saw the whole thing. Well, the kiss anyway. She'd come out to the track for some reason, but I didn't know. So, when I got home she told me to cut that shit out. Asked what the hell was wrong with me."

"What'd you say?"

"I told her nothing was wrong with me, I just kind of liked guys." Tate paused and took a deep breath. Pilot held him and rubbed his nose up and down Tate's throat, letting him know he was loved. "My mom said that my dad would beat the shit out of me if he saw me kissing boys. I didn't have anything to say to that. You know? It's like stop being who you are, or your dad, who is supposed to love you unconditionally, will physically hurt you. I was being punished for something I had no control over. Well, I mean, I didn't have to go around kissing guys, but I couldn't stop looking at them. Hell, every sixteen year old boy wants to get laid like he wants to breathe. Not looking at guys was like telling my heart not to beat. It just wasn't going to happen."

Pilot shifted, pulling Tate around with him until they were situated with Pilot's arm around Tate's shoulders and Tate snuggled up against his muscular chest. He stroked Tate's arm with his other hand. "Go on."

"So, we didn't talk for a few days. I was hoping it would just blow over, but then, well, it was off season, so I spent most of my time on the dirt. My neighbor let us use the back of his property to build a small track. Up until the kiss, Chester would come almost every day to ride with me, at least for part of the day. But, after that I was alone. He didn't come out to ride again, but it didn't really matter to me. You know how I am. I put everything out there. In the dirt. So, I had a decent few runs around the track and headed home to grab some lunch."

Tate sat up in the bed and looked down at Pilot. His dark eyes held love and sympathy, but no pity. Tate was pretty sure that wouldn't change, even after his story. Pilot already knew the ultimate outcome, so he took another breath and kept going. "I don't know what I was thinking about. I remember that the sun was shining and birds were singing and I was sweating and the red dirt smelled like heaven. For that moment, I was just a kid with a decent, happy life. Yeah, I wanted a boyfriend and I wanted my parents to be cool about it, but it didn't really define me. I didn't know who I really was or who I wanted to be, but I knew it would be okay as long as I could keep racing. I guess that was a good thought to hold onto, 'cause when I got to the house, my mom had packed all of my shit into a few suitcases and brown boxes and had them sitting on the front porch."

Pilot sat up. "What?"

"Yeah. She, uh, had called Oz and told him to come get me."

"Just like that?"

Tate shrugged and sniffled. He didn't want to cry about this old bullshit. Pilot pulled him into his arms again and Tate settled between his legs.

"You know? It was hard. That hurt. They suddenly didn't like me anymore because of this one thing. It was like, 'Oh, I realize now that you have blond hair and we don't like blond hair.' That's how it felt. Maybe being gay is not as obvious a thing, but still."

They sat silently for a few minutes before Tate felt strong enough to keep talking. "She said that she had finally told my dad and he went nuts and if I wasn't gone before he got home from work, he'd probably kill me. So, even though she loved me enough to kick me out of the house, she didn't love me enough to stand up to him. Or maybe she was just using that as an excuse. I don't know."

"What happened?"

"A few hours later, Oz showed up with a truck, you know, one of them U-Haul trucks. He loaded my shit and my bike and gear in the back, loaded me in the front and drove off. I didn't even clean up or take a shower. I rode in my dirty gear the rest of the day. A lot of what happened after that was a blur. Oz made sure I got what I needed. Food. Clothes. He made sure I finished high school. He got a tutor and set everything up. He made me study when I wasn't working out or riding."

"He sounds like a good man."

"Yeah. He's been more of a parent to me than they ever really were. You know? Looking back on it. My dad thought it was cool that his boy was into dirt bikes and shit. It was manly. I seemed like a real boy-boy, playing in the dirt. But, he didn't really show any other concern for me. Mom just wanted me out of the house. They had already let Oz take over my schedule and seemed pretty happy they didn't have to deal with it. So, I'm pretty sure they sucked all the way around. If I hadn't been so into motocross, I'm not sure I would have survived into adulthood with those two." Tate laughed, but it didn't sound very humorous. He couldn't find much humor in the situation, even now. The pain of being rejected by his parents still sliced through his heart, making an open wound that just never completely healed.

"That explains a lot about Oz. I thought he was unreasonably overprotective, but he really has been your papa bear."

"Don't say it like that." Tate swatted Pilot's arm. "But, yeah. He's been more than just a manager to me. So, yeah, I listen to him. Most of the time. He took me in at sixteen. Who wants to take in a hormonal teenager? That's like saying you enjoy hemorrhoids or screws being drilled into your head." Tate laughed for real this time. He'd had plenty of good times with Oz, good memories, and a new appreciation for what he'd put the man through. "I haven't been easy on him, that's for sure."

"He's been good for you."

"I don't know. We made the best of a bad situation. He's pretty cool though. He lets me make mistakes and he's always there when I fall. He's the only one who's ever really been there."

Pilot tightened his grip and kissed Tate on the top of the head. "I'm here now. I'm not going anywhere."

"Thank you."

"No need to thank me. Just keep loving me and we'll make everything work out. I love you, Tate."

Chapter 26 - Back in Anaheim for Round 3

The day started off way too early, and Pilot stayed in bed too long. Finally hauling himself out, he made his way to the shower and turned the water on cold. He did a quick jump in and out to wake himself up a bit before getting dressed and strapping on his gun. Coffee in hand, he headed to the track.

People already mingled around the pit area, hoping to get a glimpse of their favorite racers, or maybe more, like an autograph or picture. Pilot felt content to stay in the background. He didn't know how Davey dealt with all of the attention. Tyler had attention, too and was less poised about it. He grumbled sometimes that he'd never meant to be in the spotlight as a mechanic, but Apex kept thrusting him there, like it or not.

Lost in his thoughts, he bumped into someone, almost spilling his coffee. "Oh, shit. Sorry, man."

He looked down to see Bryce. "It's okay, no harm." His voice seemed soft as he stepped back.

"You sure you're okay, Bryce?"

"Uh, yeah. It's cool." Bryce started to back away from him.

Pilot's mouth went dry. He didn't want Bryce to just walk away. "You, uh, racing today?"

"Uh, yeah." He lifted a hand, as if to say, we are at a Supercross track. Pilot suddenly felt stupid.

"Right. Well, hope you do well, then."

The kid looked up at him with huge blue eyes. Pilot was taller by a good foot and a half for sure. Bryce had the cutest freckles splattered across his nose and cheeks. They made him look young, but Pilot knew he was older...old enough. "Thanks, Pilot."

Pilot nodded, amazed at how much he liked Bryce. He had enjoyed hanging out with him after the last race, and he knew Tate had a crush on the kid. He could certainly see why.

Pilot's stomach flipped, and he felt a bit guilty for it. He wanted to take Bryce back to his hotel room with him, but how could he even be thinking about that? Tate already had his heart. Pilot had asked Tate about the kid before to see where Tate's head was about him, but Pilot wasn't sure where his own head was. He loved Tate and he'd never act on any other attractions, not that he had any. He didn't really. Except, all of a sudden looking at Bryce. The kid was getting under his skin and he didn't know what to do about it—except ignore it. It was obvious he needed support, friends, and Tate needed to be there for him, so Pilot would be there too. "Hey. I know Tate's your friend..."

"So? We're just friends. I swear." Bryce put his hands up and took another half step back. The apprehension in his eyes had Pilot chuckling.

"It's okay, Bryce. I'm cool with that. I just wanted, uh...I guess, uh. I just wanted to say that I'd like to be friends, too." He stuck out a hand, hoping to shake on it and put the kid at ease. He never wanted Bryce to be afraid of him.

Bryce's eyes widened, looking even darker blue than earlier. He was very adorable. He stuck his smaller hand out, gripping Pilot's. Without thought, Pilot used that hand to pull Bryce into a hug. It felt natural, comfortable. He rubbed a hand down Bryce's back, wanting to comfort him. Pilot's protective streak reared its head.

When Bryce pulled back, Pilot let him go. His cock had started waking up and taking notice of the attractive young man, and he didn't want to cause any tension between them by rubbing it up against the kid. "So, yeah. Friends."

"Thanks."

"Good luck today."

"Yeah, you said that." Bryce nodded and stepped farther away, walking slowly backwards away from Pilot with a confused look on his face.

Pilot waved goodbye and hurried on to the Apex pit. He still had a job to do and even though he'd rather stand around gawking at the kid, he had to get on with it.

He tried to puzzle out how he was going to bring this up with Tate and wondered what Tate would think about it. He didn't really know, but he knew he had to tell him, or things could get very awkward between them. Yeah, Bryce was fucking adorable, but he loved Tate, and that was that.

Tate watched Andrew tapping on his laptop that he'd plugged into the bike. He had finished third and made the transfer in the first heat race, but the bike needed some fine tuning. Andrew would damn sure make that happen. Tate enjoyed looking over his shoulder and learning what he could and Andrew was really patient with him. They needed to work together to get the bike running the best it could. Top performance. Tate got up and worked out every damn day and watched what he ate to be at his best, and his bike had to be the best also, especially if he ever wanted to beat Davey.

"Tate!"

He looked up to see his coach, Joey, dashing into the pit with a worried look on his face.

"That kid, Bryce. Isn't he your friend? He just wrecked."

"What?"

"He'd missed the transfer in his heat and was racing LCQ and some dick bumped him. That would have been okay, but then someone else ran over him. Not sure who that was." He shook his head and stared at Tate with wide eyes.

Tate's heart leapt into his throat. It sounded like Bryce might be hurt and he would be out of the Main Event. Knowing how he felt about that kind of thing himself, he could imagine how Bryce felt. Plus, his parents hadn't come to the races. They were actually giving him the space he'd asked them for and now this. Tate grabbed his phone and texted him, but worried that Bryce wouldn't be able to get to his phone.

"Shit. I have to go. I have to see if he's okay."

"Go," both Andrew and Joey said at the same time. Tate couldn't argue. He took off toward the medic area and texted Pilot as he went.

When Tate arrived, he pushed his way through the crowd that had gathered. It seemed like mostly fans and onlookers with security holding them back. There were also people that Tate recognized from Bryce's team and sponsors, but he didn't really know any of them. They let Tate in though, so he figured they at least knew who he was, or maybe it was just because he was in his racing gear. He still had his goggles looped around his neck.

Bryce was stretched out on a board and a medic wrapped his leg. Tate could see his chest and stomach jumping as he tried not to cry. Tate wanted to fix it. He couldn't stand seeing this guy hurt. "Hey, Bryce," he said softly squatting down next to his head.

"Tate?" Bryce seemed so young in that moment, his eyes all red and puffy from crying...innocent and in pain, he tugged at Tate's heart, making his throat close up.

Tate rubbed his fingers across Bryce's forehead and cleared his throat. "Yeah. It's me. You okay?"

He shook his head and squeezed his eyes shut tightly, creating wrinkles around the corners. His, "no," sounded like half answer and half sob. "I have to go for x-rays."

"Okay. I wish I could go with you. You have your phone? I want you to keep me posted."

Just then Pilot pushed his way forward with Tyler in tow. "Hey. What's going on?"

"He has to go to the hospital," Tate said, his voice cracked a little as if he might cry.

Pilot nodded. "I'll go with you."

"Uh, what about Tyler?" Tate knew Pilot couldn't just blow off his job. He really wanted Pilot to go with Bryce, though. He looked over at Tyler, begging with his eyes.

"I'm fine," Tyler huffed. "You can walk me back to the pit and I'll stick with Tony. It'll be fine. Hell, I haven't even received any death threats this week. Oh, except from some chick that wanted Davey to be her future husband." He rolled his eyes.

That got Bryce laughing a little, and that pleased Tate. "Okay. If it's good with you. Keep in touch." He leaned into Pilot and gave him a peck on the lips.

It took everything he had to leave Bryce alone, but he had to race. He lingered as long as he could, then left with Tyler. He felt better knowing Pilot would be with Bryce. He trusted Pilot and knew that he'd make sure Bryce was taken care of.

At the starting gate, Tate situated himself over the bike, preparing for the race. Emotion and worry bubbled up inside him. He knew he'd have to leave it in the dirt. He pulled out his phone to check for any messages one more time, before handing his phone off to his team and putting his helmet on. The mechanic assistant on duty handed over his goggles and he pulled them over his helmet. They were stacked with tear off sheets that he could pull off as they got dirty along the way, and he'd need that on this track. It would be messy.

"Tate!" Davey called out to him.

He turned toward Davey who came up behind him. "What?"

"He's going to be fine. Focus on the race."

Tate exhaled and gave Davey a quick smile and a thumbs up. "I got this." A strange swell of happy exploded from his gut and drowned his heart. He had friends. Real friends. Not just people you joked around with or rode with, but people that knew him and wanted him in their lives. Davey, Tyler, and Mickey all had check marks by their name in the friend column. Oz, hell, he was family if anyone was. That left Pilot in the love department. He wasn't sure about Bryce. He knew Bryce was a friend, but that wasn't enough. Not anymore. He also knew he wasn't going to figure it out with the gates about to drop.

His mechanic checked with him one more time and Tate was ready. He didn't have to wait long before the track girl in her fake leather halter and miniskirt held up the 30 second board. Then, as she skipped off the track, Tate's heart took off before the gates even dropped. When they did go down, everything else in the world disintegrated into the red and brown dirt.

Tate jumped off the start like his ass was on fire and leapt to the front. It was a monumental holeshot and the first he'd ever taken in a 450 main event. He scrubbed the first jump taking it low and hard. The course was wet and rutted out all over the place, but Tate's concentration was dead on. The bike moved with him like just another part of his body—and his body was fit. He took a triple and spun through the first 90 degree turn. He felt the track in his soul and knew this was his race to win.

Tate whipped his bike over the jumps, taking advantage of being out front and putting his bike exactly where he wanted it. He could tell by sound and instinct that the other racers trailed behind him, but he kept the throttle pinned, determined to stay in front. He rode the track like a dream, using all the techniques he knew and practiced to gain as much time as possible ahead of anyone else. He didn't want anyone, especially Davey, catching up to him.

Andrew held up his white board as Tate passed him from the mechanic's area. It said, *Half Way!* and had a face with crossed eyes on it. Tate had no idea what that meant and he didn't care. He had 10 laps left. He could do it. He could finally beat Davey and win a 450 race. He stuffed down the excitement and scrubbed low over the next jump, forcing his mind to stay where it belonged, just like he shoved his bike around.

A few more laps, and Tate popped over the whoops and got up behind a lapper who roosted him good. He pulled the tear away off and passed the guy, giving back what he got. Mud flew everywhere, but at least there didn't seem to be a lot of rocks in it. It slowed him down a bit and he could sense another bike approaching, but he wouldn't let that bother him. Tate's bike ate up the next few laps with ease.

When he passed the mechanics again, Andrew's pit board had his lap time and a two to go reminder, but also said, *D's coming.* That meant Davey.

Tate took a deep breath and concentrated on riding his own race. He couldn't afford to make any mistakes. He had the advantage of being in the lead, and he knew Davey—knew how he rode. He wouldn't be pulling a block pass on him like some others would. Regal would knock him down in a heartbeat and so would Cole, but not Davey. At least not with Tate.

He could sense Davey's bike behind him, closing in.

Final lap.

Tate knew better than to try too hard at blocking Davey. It would only slow them both down and maybe allow someone else to sneak in. He wanted to have some kind of feel for where Davey was, but had to find his own course. He knew the track now and knew when to pull inside, which ruts to follow and which to avoid, when to take a triple with plenty of air, and when to stay low.

He could see the finish line with the Giant Energy Drink sign looming over it. Davey's front wheel rode near his back tire, just to the side. Close. Tate kept the throttle pinned, going all out. It was now or never. He purposefully swerved toward Davey when he knew he had a safe edge, throwing him off his path and slowing him a little, but the little nudge didn't slow Tate down a bit. It gave him the distance he needed.

He approached the last jump, racing forward. He got a ton of air and flipped his bike horizontal as he sailed over the finish like those superheroes Davey always prattled on about. *Yeah! Super Tate!* After he landed, he pumped his fist in the air. Somewhere along the way his heart landed in his throat, making a tight fit. His first thought was for Bryce who would have a DNF next to his name in the LCQ; did not finish in the last chance qualifier. He would be upset about not making the main event, but maybe he would be happy that Tate won.

Andrew came up behind him, jumping with excitement. He leapt forward and hugged Tate before slinging his leg over the back of the bike behind him. Tate rode him double off the track. When they got to the press area, he let Andrew take the bike, seconds before a network news staff member popped a headset on him and shoved him up to the podium.

They asked about the race, the holeshot, how he'd kept Davey at bay, and then they asked something he hadn't expected. A woman with a ponytail hollered out, "Is Bryce Nickel your boyfriend?"

Tate chuckled. Easy question, but sometimes questions like that would haunt you. "No, he's a friend. And he was hurt on the track. I'm concerned about him."

"So, who is your boyfriend?" This came from someone else, but Tate wasn't sure who, not that it mattered.

"My boyfriend is that two-wheeled 450 that I just rode hard to win. I named him Brad."

That got a lot of laughs which was the reaction Tate was used to. The reporters kept firing questions at him, but his mind was now on Bryce and Pilot and he had to get the hell out of there.

"Excuse me folks, gotta go see about Brad!" He pulled the headset off and shoved it at the staff member who had put it on him and walked off the podium. As he made his way toward his pit, he realized that he hadn't thanked his sponsors or anyone. MSR management would probably be pissed, but fuck them anyway. They didn't think he could win, didn't think he'd ever beat Davey. Oz hadn't thought he'd pull it off either, but Joey knew. Joey constantly pushed him for more. Well, what do you know? Tate put another check mark in the friend's column. He was starting to rack them up faster than trophies.

Chapter 27 - The Hospital, Anaheim

They took Bryce out of the room to get an MRI of his knee, leaving Pilot to sit and wait. He couldn't make himself leave, even to check in with people in the waiting area who would want to know what was going on. He didn't have anything to tell them anyway and the thought of Bryce returning to an empty room crushed his heart. So, he waited, checking his phone for any news from Tate or the Apex team.

Eventually, a nurse wheeled Bryce back into the room and situated him on the bed with another icepack on his knee. Pilot let out a huge sigh; he needed Bryce to be better. That mattered. He could examine the why of it later. But, under the surface, a lot more concern for Bryce rolled around than should be there.

Reasonably, he knew that Tate favored the kid, and he suspected that Tate's feelings ran deeper than he let on. Yet, that didn't bother Pilot at all. He wasn't jealous or envious. Pilot knew Tate loved him and that was enough, but he suspected something more going on with Bryce and not just from Tate's side. Pilot did not want to keep picking at it like a sore, only to make it bleed.

He stood by the bed, looking down at Bryce. His purple streaked hair flopped over his eyes, making Pilot want to move it. The kid's eyes practically jumped out at him, bright blue, dazzling in the harsh hospital light. "How you doing, kid?"

Bryce gave him a halfhearted shrug and frowned, making Pilot want to change his facial expression. He needed Bryce smiling and laughing like he had been at the bar. This sullen, hurt Bryce had his heart cracking. He didn't know what to say to make it better, and really? What words could make this better?

He rested his hand on Bryce's good leg. He hoped Bryce would appreciate the affection, but even if he didn't, Pilot needed the contact. Since starting this relationship with Tate, he was becoming a much more

156

tactile person.

Bryce exhaled loudly. "I just want them to hurry the hell up and tell me what's wrong so I can get the hell out of here."

"Yeah, it sucks. Waiting is the worst."

Tate stormed into the ER and charged over to the waiting room where several people from the track stood around. He recognized a few from Bryce's team like his manager, George, his coach, Reuben, and a few others from the TopSport crew. Angel sat in a chair with her legs crossed and phone to her head. He waved to her and then headed for the desk. He could check in with the others later, but Tate couldn't wait to see Bryce. Thankfully, they let him back without much fuss. He didn't have to throw a tantrum or anything, just stick a name tag on and head on down the hall.

When he found the room, he rushed in and made a beeline for the bed. "Bryce. What's going on?"

"Hey." He seemed kind of out of it, so Tate turned to Pilot.

"He's had some pain killers. They took him for an MRI a while back." Pilot shrugged, and Tate followed the line of his shoulders down his arms to watch his hands caressing Bryce's leg.

Bryce stared up at him with huge blue eyes, that even drugged seemed to look into Tate's soul. "Tate? How'd you do in the Main Event? We couldn't get the race on this stupid TV."

"First. I was in such a hurry to get here, I just left them all behind."

Bryce hollered out and raised a fist in the air. "Yeah. Really? First? That rocks."

"Congrats, baby." Pilot stood up and walked around the hospital bed with arms open.

Tate fell into them, loving the warm hug.

"I kicked ass. Davey tried to make a comeback at the end, but I wasn't letting that happen. Not tonight." They sat down again, on either side of the bed. Tate rubbed Bryce's arm, while Pilot went back to fondling his good leg. Tate watched the touches from Pilot with interest. He kept waiting for that jealous streak to show up, but it didn't—at all. In fact, it made Tate horny. Thinking about where those gentle touches could lead, turned him on. He'd changed quickly in the pit, and now his dick was pressing hard against the zipper of his jeans. He tried to adjust himself, discreetly. He didn't know what to think about it all, but he wanted to see Pilot doing more to Bryce than rub his leg.

A knock on the door got everyone's attention, and a tall, dark skinned man with dark hair entered the room. "I'm Doctor Patel. Orthopedics. Your team called me in for this." He circled the small room, and came up beside the bed, reaching his hand out to Bryce to shake.

"I'm Bryce." He shook the doctor's hand. "You have results? How bad is it?"

"I do." He looked around the room, taking in Tate and Pilot.

"They're good. Go ahead."

The doctor nodded. Tate sucked his bottom lip in, biting it, wanting the news to be good and fearing the worst. He grabbed Bryce's hand and squeezed a little.

"I looked at the MRI. I don't think you tore anything. May I?" He pointed to Bryce's knee.

"Sure."

The doctor removed the ice pack and prodded the knee. Tate could see where Bryce's race pants had been cut at his thigh, and pale white skin peeked out. His knee was red and obviously swollen. The doctor made a humming noise and moved Bryce's leg, which made Bryce cry out. "Hurts there, huh?"

Bryce's voice broke, holding back evidence of his pain. "Fuck yeah. Sorry. Yes, sir."

"Uh-huh. Okay." The doctor patted his thigh and turned to face Bryce. "You've injured your posterior cruciate ligament or PCL. It doesn't seem to be torn, maybe pulled a little. It's not from twisting, you see, but it was hit. Probably your bike or your competitor's bike. Maybe? What happened when you wrecked exactly?"

"Right." Bryce took a deep breath, his eyes flashing. "That dick blocked me and I went down, but that was okay, but I went down in the middle of the track, so when I got up, someone came over the jump and landed on me, pinning me between our bikes." He used the hand Tate wasn't holding to demonstrate the bike flying through the air, and crashing into his lap, as if it were the track.

"That would do it."

"Fuck!" Bryce called out again. "How bad?"

"I don't think you'll need surgery. That's good, yes? Stay off of it for a few days. Then, physical therapy. I'll have you out of here in a few minutes. Keep icing." The doctor put the ice pack back on Bryce's leg. "You need to get the swelling down before therapy. Before you even try to walk on it. Yes? Okay. Discharge papers and you'll be out of here." He shook Bryce's hand again, nodding to Tate and Pilot.

The doctor's words relieved Tate. It could have been so much worse.

Surgery could have knocked him out for the rest of the season. "You'll be back on the bike in a month, maybe two. You'll see." He gripped Bryce's shoulder.

"Right." Bryce rubbed his face, as if he could rub his expressions away, but Tate could still see the pain.

He could understand. If he was the one in the bed, he'd be bawling like a baby and not just from the physical pain of the injury. Not being on a bike for months? *Hell-to-the-no.*

"You want to stay with us?" Tate blurted out. "Can he?" He looked over at Pilot. The expression fell off of Pilot's face as if he'd dropped a painted mask, melting off to show nothing beneath, and Tate couldn't read him. "What? Please?"

Bryce moaned loudly. "You don't have to do that. Really."

"No, I want you." Pilot's blush rushed over his face. "I mean. I want you to come. Fuck! I mean I want to know you're okay and your parents aren't here, right? So, come with us to our hotel room."

"Yeah. Okay. I need to get stuff from my room." Bryce looked down at his hands. Tate couldn't help wondering what he was really thinking. He was about to ask, but Pilot nudged him.

"Let's go tell everyone what's going on. We'll be back in a minute, okay?" He squeezed Bryce's leg, but he might have been squeezing Tate's heart.

"Okay." Bryce gave them a fake smile. Tate didn't like it, but he knew he needed to talk to Pilot. He wasn't sure Pilot was as happy about Bryce staying with them as he was.

He followed Pilot out of the room, holding his breath. When they were a few steps down the hallway, he couldn't take it. "I know, I know. Pilot, please? I can't stand the thought of him being alone tonight."

Pilot stopped, standing still for a minute, before turning to face Tate. His expression was a mix of uncertainty, pain, and love. "Me either. Tate, man?" He shook his head and held his hands out to the side in resignation. "I don't know what we're doing here. You and I are so new, but...I don't. It feels right, Bryce feels right. You know what I'm saying? I know you care for him. I do too."

"Okay. Yeah. I like him. More than I've said. I can't help it. That doesn't mean I don't love you. Damn, Sean." Tate stepped closer, hoping Pilot would pull him into his arms. He waited a minute, unsure of what would happen, but then Pilot reached out. "Thank you."

"Tate. I love you. I care about Bryce. I ran into him earlier today at the track. He just, I hugged him and...just damn, he's so fucking cute."

"He is isn't he?" Tate tilted his face up and Pilot kissed his forehead and then his lips.

"This is crazy. What are we doing?"

Tate stepped back away from Pilot, trying to find some balance. "I don't know. I—" He held up his hands. He didn't have the words. He had an idea of where this was going and what he wanted, but he didn't know what Pilot thought about it and he was afraid of saying it out loud.

Pilot slid his hand down Tate's arm and laced their fingers together. "This is the strangest thing that's ever happened to me."

"What?" Tate wanted Pilot to tell him what he wanted to hear. He wanted Pilot to fix it—make this thing growing between them right.

"I love you, Tate. I'd probably do anything you asked me to." His eyebrows dipped over his dark eyes. If Tate had to describe Pilot, he wouldn't necessarily start at his face. He was sexy enough with brown hair and dark, bedroom eyes and a nice symmetrical face. Attractive, hell yes. But he wouldn't necessarily stand out in a crowd, not like Bryce's lightning blue eyes and freckled cheeks and nose. It was Pilot's body that made him really stand out. Tall and muscular and built like a god, like Thor without the long blond hair. Beyond all of that though, Pilot had a good heart and Tate couldn't help hoping that it was big enough for both him *and* Bryce.

He needed to hear Pilot say it, but the thought of asking such a thing had him sweating. "What do you, uh? What?"

"Don't look at me like that, Tate."

"Like what?"

"With those big eyes. Shut your mouth. You know what I'm saying."

Tate dropped his head, faking interest in the top of his sneaker. He was happy he'd stashed clothes in the pit or he'd be standing there in his race boots or barefoot.

"Tate?"

"I don't know." He hesitated, afraid to take that last leap. "It's just that it'd be a hard choice to make. If Bryce were, you know, more. Then, I wouldn't want to pick."

"Between us?"

"Yeah."

Pilot's boots tapped the floor as he started walking. "Come on."

Tate followed him into the waiting room. He had more to say and he needed to hear more from Pilot, but maybe it could wait a little longer. There were still a lot of people waiting on news.

Pilot stopped at the door and turned around fast, almost knocking Tate over. Pilot grabbed him, pulling him close. His face was fierce with want and need. "I don't understand this. I'm not going to pretend I do, but Tate. Thinking of the two of you. Together. With me." His face softened as he spoke. Tate felt Pilot's cock hardening against his leg, and his own dick responded in kind.

"Me, too." Tate's words were breathy.

"Then, we're doing this?"

"What? Say it."

"You want him in, with us, together. For more than sex."

Tate stared into Pilot's dark eyes, seeing nothing but love. Reassured, he breathed out slowly. "Yes." Because he knew for Pilot, there really couldn't be anything just about sex. Not now.

"Okay. A relationship."

"With all three of us."

"Can we do it?"

Pilot finally let Tate go, but he wasn't sure that he wanted to leave Pilot's strong arms. "It's up to him now. You know? If he wants it. I'm not pushing him into it. We can't."

Pilot gave him a quick nod. "Agreed. Okay. Let's do this." He pushed through the doors to the waiting room, to let everyone know about Bryce's injury

Chapter 28 - Released from hospital, Anaheim

"Okay! Get me the hell out of here." Bryce had endured enough of being stuck in the hospital. He dropped his ass in the wheelchair that Pilot rolled in. He wasn't even going to argue about it. The pain meds had him feeling a little high, but his knee still ached some. He wanted to go somewhere he felt safe so he could just crash.

He rubbed at his eyes with the back of his hand. He wasn't sure how he felt about Pilot and Tate jumping in to take care of him, but he was going to let them. They were acting a little strange. Pilot obviously had protective instincts kicking in. That was fine, but he didn't want him thinking Bryce was a kid. His desires were anything but childish.

Tate's fidgeting seriously wigged him out, though. He didn't know why Tate was suddenly so uncomfortable with him. They'd been fine until he asked Bryce to stay with them. Tate probably thought Bryce wanted more than just hanging out with them, and he did, but maybe Tate wanted that too. Maybe that was the problem. He must have been fighting with Pilot over it. Or Bryce could be making it all up in his head. He didn't know them that well. Maybe Tate was just tired. It'd been a long night.

"Hey, I don't have to stay with you guys. You could just drop me off at my room."

"Don't be stupid," Pilot answered from behind him as he pushed Bryce through the halls. "Here. Push him, Tate. I'm going to go get the car."

"Okay."

Pilot walked away and Bryce felt guilt hit him like a punch in the chest. He didn't want them to split up. "I'm sorry, Tate. Don't let me get between you two."

"It's not like that, wonder-boy." Tate pushed the wheel chair through the sliding front doors and stopped by the curb. He ran his fingers through Bryce's hair.

"What's it like then?" He tilted his head back so he could see Tate behind him. They stared at each other for a minute and Bryce could feel the energy tingling between them. Tate leaned forward and pushed his lips against Bryce's. It felt odd with Tate being upside down, or maybe he was upside down. Either way, the kiss happened, even though it wasn't supposed to. When Tate straightened up, Bryce saw that Pilot had already pulled up to the curb. He had to have seen them kiss, but when he got out of the car, he smiled like it was his birthday or something.

He came around the car and stopped in front of Bryce. He gave Tate a silly look and then leaned forward, putting his hands on the armrests and getting in Bryce's face.

"What?" Bryce snapped, expecting a fight and already on the defensive.

Pilot chuckled and pressed his own lips against Bryce's. The kiss was probing and asking for more and Bryce couldn't help himself. He opened his mouth and let Pilot take it. His tongue tasted like stale coffee, but Bryce didn't give a damn. His tongue slid against Pilot's and licked into his mouth. His stomach fluttered with excitement. Tate's fingers tickled the hair at the back of Bryce's neck before sliding across his shoulders.

Holy hot hell! Bryce wanted both of these men. He reached down and shoved his junk around under his track pants, happy he'd been able to get his cup and jock strap off earlier. He still had on compression shorts under his pants, just enough to keep his dick from poking up at a funny angle if he wasn't settled in right. Why it mattered, he didn't know. No one else would see him, but he didn't want to feel embarrassed in front of Tate and Pilot.

Pilot pulled back and looked at him with lust-filled eyes that made even more blood rush to his cock. The surprise of it, overwhelmed him just a little. "I don't know if I can do this," he blurted out. He wanted it, but he wanted their friendship more.

Tate had his hands in Bryce's hair again. They felt like they belonged there. "We're not going to push you into something you don't want. No matter what, we're here for you. Friends. Like I said before."

"But? You want more?"

Pilot squatted in front of him so they faced each other, eye-to-eye. "We do, but what you want is important to us and we care about you. If you say no, it's no. Okay? Come on. Let's get out of here. We'll talk later."

Pilot helped Bryce into the car. This day had been crazy. First the horrible race day and wreck. He didn't even get to the Main Event. Hours in the hospital and now Tate and Pilot were making moves on him. Thinking about all of it made him a little dizzy, or maybe it was the pain meds. The latter was probably more likely since he fell asleep against the car window on the way to the hotel.

They had been booked in the same hotel where most of the other

Supercross teams had rooms. He was on the second floor, so Tate and Pilot insisted that he stay in the car and off his leg while they packed up his stuff for him. Bryce couldn't remember if he'd already packed his clothes, or what clothes he had out and he was afraid they were going to see it. He needed them, but he wasn't a stupid kid and he didn't want them to think he was. His face flushed, knowing they'd see what he had in his room. Would it ruin everything with them?

They dropped his stuff in the trunk and got in the car without a word. Bryce chewed the inside of his mouth, worried about what they weren't saying. They drove around to the back of the building where their room was. Thankfully, they were on the ground floor and he didn't have to fuck with stairs. He swung his legs out of the car and pushed himself up on his good leg, holding on to the car door.

Pilot came around the car and scooped Bryce up, hard arms wrapped around him. Tate opened the door and carried his luggage inside while Pilot carried him. He felt a flush crawl over his face. Once inside, Pilot put Bryce down on the bed. One bed. King sized, but still only one bed. Bryce hadn't asked; he'd assumed they had a double. His anxiety over it made him feel like a big baby, and that's exactly what Tate and Pilot would think about him, too.

"Hey, man," Tate said scooting in beside him on the bed. "Why don't you take a bath, clean up, and put on some clean clothes. It'll make you feel better." He winked.

Damn.

Tate winked at him.

He wanted them. Wanted to go along with them. He was afraid, though, and he figured if he was this scared, then he wasn't ready. He had to trust that above all else. But, close friends. Maybe they could start there. Tate helped him into the bathroom and started the water in the tub.

Tate pulled Bryce's shirt up over his head. He'd already taken off his gear and folks from the team had collected all the pads and chest plate and boots at the hospital. He pulled at the buckle of his pants, frustrated that he'd have to throw this pair away since the EMTs ruined them by cutting them instead of just letting him take them off. He dropped them to the floor and started pulling his compression shorts off. They were tight and getting them down his thighs without putting weight on this bad leg proved difficult. Tate hurried to help and ended up sitting on the floor in front of him, looking at his cock. Bryce couldn't stop it from getting hard as Tate watched him.

Tate opened his mouth like he wanted to say something, or maybe he wanted to suck Bryce's cock. Bryce started shaking. He wasn't sure if it was nerves, excitement, or an overload of the pain meds, but it made Tate shut his mouth and stand up. "Here. Let me help." He wrapped his arm around

Bryce's naked waist.

Bryce wanted to feel him skin on skin, but Tate had on a long sleeved t-shirt. Tate took his weight and helped him get settled in the tub. The water was on the hot side, but it felt good as he eased down into it. Once he settled, Tate stood up and looked down at him, focusing on his face. Bryce started to thank him, but what came out was, "I'm not a kid."

"I know you're not."

"Okay then."

Tate smirked and then left him alone in the bathroom. He didn't know if he wanted Tate to come back in or not. He was torn in half by wanting and fear. He sighed and grabbed the soap.

By the time he finished washing up, the tub water turned dark with dirt from the track. He tried to stand up and slipped. "Tate!"

The door opened. "You okay?"

"Yeah, but I need to rinse off. Help me stand up."

Tate didn't even laugh at him, just stepped in and helped him up and turned on the water. He rinsed off and Tate helped him out of the tub, throwing a towel on his head and handing him another. Bryce dried off and wrapped the towel around his waist. Tate helped him into the main room and sat him on the edge of the bed. He scrubbed at his hair with the towel.

"What do you want to wear?" Tate asked, pulling one of his bags up.

Pilot had stretched out on the bed with pillows behind his back, against the headboard, and was flipping through the channels. "Need help?" he asked.

Bryce froze. He didn't want them going through his clothes. Didn't want them to see it.

"Look," Tate said, unzipping his big duffle with the double zipped top and flinging it open. "You've had a shit day and you should just be comfortable. Be yourself. We're not going to pressure you or judge you or anything. Okay? We—"

"What?"

Tate huffed and pulled out the one thing Bryce didn't want them to see. "We care about you. We don't think you're a kid. We're both *extremely* attracted to you. Just be yourself." He handed Bryce the pajamas.

Maybe it would be okay.

"Davey McAllister has a superhero fetish. Do you think he's less than manly?" Pilot asked. "Tyler says he has underwear in almost every variety. Superman, Batman, Green Lantern, Spiderman."

Tate laughed. "Nothing manly about him."

He really wanted to wear his tiger pajamas, but he cared about what they thought more than anyone else. He glanced at Tate, expecting to see some kind of judgment, but that's not what he saw. Tate might not understand, but he cared enough that he wouldn't laugh and he didn't seem to think Bryce was stupid. "Okay."

He pulled the soft hoodie top over his head. That was the worst of it with the tiger ears on the hood. The pants were just tiger stripped pajama bottoms. He pulled them on under his towel with Tate's help. Then Tate looked at him with more compassion in his eyes.

"That's damn cute, wonder-boy." Tate leaned forward and kissed Bryce. Just a peck on the lips, but it was enough to make Bryce smile.

Pilot stood up. "Into bed with you. Do you need more ice?"

"Probably."

Pilot helped him into the bed and Tate put some ice in a plastic bag the hotel supplied and tied it off. They wrapped a hand towel around the ice and situated it on Bryce's knee.

"It's late. Let's get some sleep and then food and then we'll figure out what to do next." Pilot seemed to be really good at directing things, taking charge. Bryce was happy to let him do it. In a few minutes, they were all snuggled in together with him in his tiger pajamas. Tate wore tight briefs and an oversized t-shirt that probably belonged to Pilot, while Pilot wore just a pair of red boxers. They looked nice against his tanned skin. They both seemed relaxed, and Bryce wasn't uncomfortable at all. It felt right being with them. It was enough for the moment.

Chapter 29 - Between Races, Denver

Tate could not deal with his frustration. They had to change their flights and book one for Bryce, leaving Anaheim, so they could be on the plane with him. They didn't want Bryce flying alone, and they'd agreed he would come stay with them for a while. The worst part of all that had to be losing a day at the track. They didn't get home until late Monday night and then he'd slept in Tuesday, just because the exhaustion overwhelmed him. Plus, he still had to deal with the frustration—of the sexual nature.

Tate and Pilot stuck to the plan and weren't pushing Bryce, but he was sleeping in their bed, even though they weren't having sex. He wanted Pilot desperately and he wanted Bryce even more.

Pilot seemed to be dealing with his own issues. Tate had been hoping Pilot would join him in the shower, but Pilot had been too worried about making breakfast for Bryce. Tate thought he would be jealous over something like that, but no; he was just horny.

At the track on Wednesday, he couldn't concentrate, thinking about Pilot taking Bryce to the first physical therapy appointment. Joey had to yell at him to concentrate several times.

"Are you going to follow up your win at Anaheim with a crappy performance in San Diego? What the hell, Tate?"

"I'm worried about Bryce. Sorry."

"Bryce? The kid with the purple hair? That Bryce?"

"Yes. That Bryce."

Joey popped Tate upside his helmet. "What are you doing messing with that kid? I thought you were living with that bodyguard dude? I can't freaking keep up with you."

Tate held up his hand. "I'm living with Pilot. He's my boyfriend. That's why we're in Denver."

"So, what is Bryce?"

"Right now, he's a close friend."

Joey threw his hands in the air. "Right now? What's that mean?"

"We want him to be more than that. He's staying with us, but..."

"We? You and Pilot? Is the kid even legal?" Joey's eyes grew wide.

"Yes. He's eighteen. In Supercross years, that's like twenty-five. And *we* means both of us. Me and Pilot."

Joey shook his head. He seemed more confused than judging, not that Tate cared. It only mattered what Pilot and Bryce thought about their relationship, ultimately. Everyone else would just have to accept it. He was pretty sure they would, if they could get it worked out.

He started his bike back up and took off, pinning the throttle. He didn't want to talk anymore; the dirt called.

Newly invigorated, Tate drove the truck back to the house. His excitement to see both Pilot and Bryce grew higher and higher the closer he got to home. He hoped they'd be able to talk a little more and iron some things out. He couldn't possibly be any freaking hornier and didn't know what to do about it. He had two hot guys living with him, sharing his bed, and he couldn't have sex with either of them. Not yet. Hopefully soon. But that wasn't the most important thing. He knew the no sex had to be driving the other two crazy, too.

They could tell Bryce wasn't ready. They had to earn his trust. Their dynamic seemed to be working, though, if Tate could just hold out a little longer. They got along fabulous, but a three-way boyfriend-type relationship was not normal or expected. They had to prove to Bryce that they were serious—that they meant it. Tate and Pilot were both playing for keeps, and they had to show that to Bryce.

Tate wanted to make Bryce happy. He passed a shopping center that had a beauty supply store in it and he got a fabulous idea. He flipped his blinker on and changed lanes to do a U-turn. Then, he pulled into the shopping center and parked.

The lady in the beauty supply store helped him out and in a few minutes, he was back in the truck and headed home.

Home.

He smiled ear to ear. Yes, it was home and he hoped it would be home for Bryce, too.

Bryce sat on the couch, icing his knee and listening to Pilot puttering around in the kitchen. He came back into the living room and handed Bryce a tall glass. "Water. You need it."

"Yes, Nurse Pilot."

Pilot chuckled and sat down on the edge of the couch beside him, leaning over him, supported by the back of the couch. "Hey, kid. I want to tell you something."

"I'm not a kid, but okay? What?" He took a sip of the water and waited.

Pilot leaned in and kissed him on the forehead. "My name's Sean. Sean Mahan."

"Okay."

"I figured if we're going to do this at all, you need to know that. Very few people do. Very few people call me Sean. But you can...if you want."

"Why would everyone call you Pilot? Sean's nice."

Pilot chuckled. Bryce loved the low sound. He was beginning to love an awful lot about Pilot.

Pilot leaned back, getting comfortable. "Well, uh, I joined the Army right out of high school and, uh, I wanted to be an Aviation Specialist to start out. I love planes, like since I was a kid, you know? So, uh, my class at Basic teased me that I'd be rubbing elbows with the pilots and I guess that's how it started. But as we went on, I was always the go-to guy for everything. Very much a leader, so it really stuck. Then it didn't turn out that way. I mean, I didn't do Aviation. I went a different route. Because of the security company, Johnny's Uncle's company. You'll meet them soon. Anyway, I knew I'd have a place here if I went with security, so I became an MP. But the name was already stuck to me and I've been Pilot ever since. Johnny and his uncle are the only other people that don't call me Pilot and get away with it. Well, Johnny will sometimes, but, uh, I guess that's a different story."

"Does Tate?"

"Sometimes. Mostly when we're, uh, you know, intimate."

"Having sex?"

Pilot nodded and a little blush crept over his cheeks. It melted Bryce's heart a little. He figured they were going to talk about sex soon enough, though, so he better just get over it. All three of them were developing blue balls from being so close to each other the last few days with zero action.

Bryce pushed the tiger hoodie off his head, wanting to be serious and having a hard time with that while wearing tiger ears. Pilot must have noticed, since he lifted one eyebrow. Damn, sexy man. "Listen. I know y'all haven't had sex since I've been around. It's okay. I know you're a couple. I can like, sleep on the couch." He held his breath hoping Pilot wouldn't let him do that.

"Not happening. Bryce. Right now. We need to be together—even if we aren't having sex. We're not a couple any more. We're a, uh...triple? Tri-pule? Tri-pod? I don't know...something like that."

Bryce laughed for the first time in what felt like weeks. "I think you're both crazy. Tri-pod." He giggled. "That's an accurate picture of how all three of us look around here."

The front door opened. "Tate!" Pilot called out at the same time Bryce did.

"Hey guys!" he answered. "Got something for you." He handed Bryce a plastic bag. "I gotta get a shower. Give me five."

Bryce watched Tate strut down the hall to the bathroom. His ass looked tight and sexy in his track pants. Bryce thought he'd never get tired of seeing that. He looked down at the plastic bag. A gift? He opened it up and saw the hair color in it. Purple and black.

"Guess he likes your look."

"I guess." Bryce's heart thumped in his chest. No one had ever cared about him like this. These guys were chipping away at his walls with a jackhammer.

Chapter 30 – After the Race, Oakland

Tate finished the Main Event in second place. Davey beat him again. He should have been a little happier about it—at least he made the podium. Oddly, he didn't care. He didn't think he'd even care if he would have beat Davey. He gave it his best run and it left him refreshed and a bit tired. He only wanted to get back to the hotel room where Pilot and Bryce would be waiting for him.

They had both been at the race, of course. Pilot keeping watch over Tyler, but also keeping his eye on Bryce who had insisted on being there. Bryce wanting to watch him race gave him a completely ridiculous thrill, but he also felt bad because Bryce couldn't race. He wouldn't be back on the track any time soon and Tate knew if it were him, he'd be going crazy. He had to have a bike on the track almost every day. He didn't want to think about not being able to ride. A cold chill shivered down his spine just trying not to think about it. For Tate, it went beyond racing and Supercross; it was a fundamental need. He ate jumps for breakfast and drank the dirt like water.

He pulled off his jersey and unfastened his armor. He couldn't get his gear off fast enough. He quickly changed into a pair of Ralph Loren, destructed jeans that looked and felt old and beat up and loose t-shirt with the Thor logo on the front. He stuffed his feet into his Chucks and dashed off. He left the team to take care of the bike; he couldn't be bothered. He'd texted for an Uber to pick him up at the front of the venue before making his way through the lingering crowds. He needed to feel Pilot's arms around him and his arms around Bryce, or some other combination of that.

The Uber guy had been cool and Tate signed the back of an envelope for the guy before getting out at the hotel. He was anxious about getting to the guys, but he was never short with fans.

The Uber drove away and Tate headed for the stairs.

"Hey man! Aren't you Tate Jordan?"

Tate stopped and stepped off the stairs, turning to face whoever had called him. "Yeah? What's up?"

A shadow fell across the sidewalk under the yellow hotel lights, then a bulky figure stepped forward. He moved fast, grabbing Tate and yanking him into the dark recess behind the stairs. Tate screamed.

His heart stopped. He just knew he'd never see Pilot and Bryce again. He tried to fight back, but his head hurt and his cheek slid across the sidewalk.

The world disappeared.

Pain and darkness and screaming; a loud wailing pierced his ears. Tate wanted to scream, wanted to fade back into the dark where the pain would leave him.

Pilot's voice called out his name. He'd know Pilot's voice anywhere. Beyond that, he heard sobbing and screaming—Bryce? His guys. He had to open his eyes.

"Tate? Baby? Stay with me. Stay with me." Where the hell did Pilot think he was going to go? His arms and legs weighed a million pounds. His face stung worse than getting roosted with rocks on the track. Where were his goggles?

He stuck his tongue out, tasting blood. "Bit my tongue." He thought he'd spoken, but Pilot was still begging him to stay.

He needed to pull the tear away off his goggles. He must have ate some serious dirt; he couldn't see in front of him.

"What's he doing?" Bryce had stopped crying.

"Don't know. Tate? Can you hear me?"

He had to get the blood out of his mouth. He started coughing. Other voices crowded in once that loud wailing noise had stopped.

"Okay. Here. Don't try to talk. No, he's all right. We'll take care of him." Someone stuffed something in his mouth and a warmth flooded over him.

He was moving.

"Only one. No, one. We have to go."

Tate finally opened his eyes. The world swam away, blurring into the distance. Where was Pilot?

"Relax, Mr. Jordan. We're taking you to the hospital. Okay?"

"P-P—"

"They're going to meet us there, okay. Just relax. We'll take good care of you."

Someone patted his arm gently. They said everything would be fine. He closed his eyes and let go.

Pilot paced the floor in the ER waiting room. Bryce sat in one of the chairs with one long leg pulled up in front of him, arms wrapped around it and the leg with the brace stretched out in front of him. At least he'd stopped crying. He'd been sobbing most of the way over to the hospital. Every tear shattered off another piece of Pilot's heart. He secretly vowed to make sure Bryce never cried again after this.

The paramedics would only let one of them come and Pilot couldn't leave Bryce behind. The ambulance drove off and Bryce started saying sorry over and over until Pilot pulled him into his arms and kissed his head before telling him to shut up. Before they could go to the hospital, the police had come and questioned them. They were searching for the attacker, but Bryce had only seen him from behind, so finding him would be unlikely. Pilot had chased after the bastard, but he'd had a head start. Fucker, better hope the cops found him first. How dare anyone lay a finger on *his* Tate?

He stopped pacing and looked at Bryce. "It's not your fault. You didn't do anything."

Bryce sniffled and Pilot couldn't take it anymore. He strode across the floor in two long strides and reached for Bryce. He pulled him to standing and wrapped his arms around him, holding all his weight. "It's not your fault, Bryce."

"If I hadn't been here—"

"Stop it. You don't know that."

"There's more. Pilot?" He spoke into Pilot's chest.

"What?"

"Someone's been sending me nasty emails and texts. I've just ignored it, but I'm pretty sure who it is. He-He..." Bryce started sobbing again, and Pilot's heart wrenched.

"Why didn't you tell me? You know security is my business, Bryce. I could have done something. Hell, I still can."

Bryce pulled away and turned his back on Pilot, pivoting on his good leg. "What? What could you have done? It doesn't matter."

Pilot could tell he was pulling away, internalizing his pain. "Bryce. Stop."

Bryce turned around and the death-gaze of his blue eyes pierced Pilot's soul. "I bet it's him. Warren Fucking Tanner. He's been—" Bryce shook his head, knocking the anger off, only to replace it with fear.

"I'm not going to let anything happen to you." Pilot rushed forward, wanting nothing more than to pull Bryce into his arms and comfort him, protect him.

He pulled away, grabbed his crutches and hopped off, leaving Pilot standing there wondering what the hell he was going to tell Tate if Bryce left them. He followed Bryce and watched him through the glass door as he hobled out to the curb. He'd pulled his cell phone out and was talking on it, balancing himself on his crutches. After about fifteen minutes, a car stopped and Bryce got in it.

Pilot rushed out the doors. Everything in him told him not to let Bryce go, but he couldn't do anything as the car pulled away. He should have stopped him sooner. He'd stood there like a fool and just watched him leave.

He pulled his phone out of his pocket and tapped the screen until Bryce's number rang. It rolled to the voicemail and Pilot hung up. He texted instead. *Please don't run from us. We need you.*

After a minute. A text came back. *No you don't. Tell Tate I'm sorry.*

Pilot scrubbed at his eyes with his free hand. He would not cry. This thing with Bryce ended before it had even really got started, leaving a giant gaping hole in his chest. And worse, he worried Tate would be angry and blame him.

He went back into the hospital. He needed to see Tate, needed Tate to be okay.

Chapter 31 - February, South Carolina

His parents drove him batty and he missed the hell out of Tate and Pilot. If he could, he would be with them, but he had to put all this shit first. He hadn't been honest with them, hadn't told them about Tanner stalking him. He thought he'd be safe with them and hopefully out of sight, out of mind with Tanner. He hoped it would blow over. He'd been so wrong and being there with them put Tate in danger.

Pilot had texted Bryce over the last few days, letting him know Tate was okay. He had a concussion and a banged up face, bruises everywhere, but nothing broken or serious. Thankfully. Bryce knew how hard it was to deal with injuries firsthand.

He thumped his fingernails against the brace on his leg. He had an appointment in just a few hours to find out when he could ditch the contraption. He couldn't wait, but he didn't want to leave the house either. Facing the world seemed a dreadful plan at the moment.

He'd had to tell his parents about everything, not only Tanner, but Tate and Pilot, too. They weren't happy about any of it. His mom swore it wasn't because he was gay, but she didn't like Tate. She didn't like his reputation, how much older he was, or that he'd bring Bryce into a relationship with another guy. She thought it was twisted, perverted, but Bryce didn't. He had strong feelings for both of them, equally, and he'd been pretty damn sure they felt the same. If things had been different, it might have worked out. If he hadn't screwed it all up, letting his emotions overwhelm him like that. Again.

Why the hell had he run away? He'd never be able to face Tate now.

At least his mom helped Bryce get a restraining order out on Tanner, the psycho. She also insisted that he send all the information to Pilot. That had surprised him, but his mom said they should know—that they had a right to know, especially since he'd physically attacked Tate. At least Bryce *thought* he had. Plus, Pilot might be able to help catch him. Bryce didn't know about that. Pilot wasn't a private detective. He'd listened to her though and sent the emails and texts.

Bryce waited in the living room for his dad to get home to take him to the doctor's office for his follow up appointment. He wanted to go by himself but his parents wouldn't allow it, and a part of him was scared to go anywhere alone, so he didn't fight them on it.

His phone beeped, *signaling a text. He looked at the screen, seeing Tate's beautiful smile and feeling a deep pain burned inside him. He swallowed it back and tapped the screen to read the text. *Miss you. I'm flying home in about an hour. I'm missing next week's race. That sucks worse without you here. Please come home.*

No way could he put Tate in danger like that again. Plus, his parents wouldn't understand how he could just go back after what had happened.

He didn't answer Tate's text. He couldn't bring himself to answer, because then he'd cave in and call him, and then he'd talk Bryce into going home. It wouldn't even be hard because Bryce knew the truth was that he'd felt more at home between Tate and Pilot than here, in his little single bed, in his room at his parent's house where he'd grown up. It wasn't home anymore. Not after being with Tate and Pilot. No, it wasn't a normal relationship, but when had anything ever been normal in his life?

Normal? He didn't know what that looked like. He spent his childhood on the track. Homeschooling provided his education. His friends? Other racers. They couldn't even be called friends, really. They were competitors. There had never been time for doing normal things either, like going to the movies or just hanging out. Bryce didn't really care about that, though. He wouldn't trade motocross for anything, especially now that he could race in the Supercross 250 series. Other kids, normal kids, didn't get dreams like that to come true. So, he could hardly be angry at his parents for it.

On the other hand, Tate and Pilot gave him something his parents never could. They balanced out his life. They cared about him in a romantic way. He'd never known what that could be like before. He'd never had that kind of relationship, but he wanted it.

He heard his dad's car pull up in the driveway and let out a sigh.

"Bryce!"

"Yeah, I'm ready, Dad." He grabbed his crutches and stood up.

His mom rushed into the room and kissed his forehead. He knew she loved him, but she also made him feel like he was twelve. He pulled away and hobbled out to the car. After a few minutes his dad came out and started the car. "You know, Bryce. Your mother cares about you. We both love you. You don't have to be so cold."

"I know. I'm just frustrated." He looked out the window. "Sorry."

His dad drove quietly for a few minutes, until they reached the stop light to turn down the main road that ran through town. "None of this is our fault you know. We just want what's best for you. We know you don't tell us everything, and you don't have to. But, if you'd listen—"

"I'd never leave home. I'd live with y'all forever. Geez, Dad. I have a career. I'm way ahead of most guys my age. I've even got a plan for when I stop racing. I'm not stupid."

"Oh? Plan? Let's hear this plan of yours."

Fuck his parents and their judging him. He knew that they thought, because he dyed his hair black and purple and wore gauges in his ears and listened to hard rock, that he couldn't run his own life—wasn't mature enough. They had no clue, didn't know him at all. He may be a little immature about some things, but that might have come from missing out on so much of that *normal* kid stuff. Yet, where the big stuff was concerned, he knew what he wanted and how to get it. "I'm going to learn to work on the bikes. When I'm finished racing I can work on someone else's team. Motocross is all I know."

"You could go to college. You're right. You're not stupid. At all, Bryce."

"I'm not going to college."

"Bryce—"

"Dad! No! You don't get to tell me what to do. I'm grown."

"You still—"

"Stop. We both know that I don't have to be here. I appreciate your help and I know I sound like a brat and I'm sorry. You just don't understand. You don't know how I feel." He didn't have to stay with them, even if he didn't go back to Tate and Pilot. He made enough money to afford an apartment. Or something.

"Help me understand."

They pulled into the doctor's office and Bryce didn't want to talk about it anymore. He knew he didn't have to take their shit. They loved him, but love didn't mean controlling someone. Pilot and Tate had helped him realize that he was really an adult and could do what he wanted. He had a career that came with a nice bank account. He could get a hotel or have his team help him get a rental somewhere, if he didn't want to go back to Pilot and Tate. The truth was that he did want to go back to them. Bryce had always been the kind of guy to be honest with himself, even if he wasn't honest with anyone else. He was angry and tired and lonely. He didn't know how long he'd be able to hold out.

The next few days, Bryce hid out in his room. He was supposed to go to physical therapy. He didn't want to do it. He felt freer since he didn't have to wear the brace any more, but his heart didn't agree. He wanted to be that fun loving guy that made his boyfriends laugh and kiss him. He hated living in fear, hated what he was becoming or rather what he was letting himself become because of Tanner. Between that dick stalking him and his parents smothering him, he felt like a scared little kid hiding behind his mommy. He hated that.

Pilot had sent him an email saying that they were pressing charges against Tanner and the police had evidence that he'd been in town, but no one could find the asshole. That only made him feel marginally better.

"Bryce!" His mother tapped on his door. "Come eat."

"I don't want to."

"I don't care. Come on."

He still had to use his crutches, but he was supposed to slowly start putting more weight on his foot. He didn't know what *slowly* meant, so he just used his crutches to make his way to the table. His mom had set out a comfort food smorgasbord with fried chicken, mashed potatoes and gravy, coleslaw, and homemade biscuits. "Damn, Mom. I can't eat all of this. I haven't even been working out."

"That's crazy. One good meal is not going to kill you."

"Did you call my trainer? 'Cause as soon as I'm cleared I need to be back on a bike and ohmygod I cannot weigh two hundred pounds."

"You can start going to physical therapy and work it off." She put her hands on her hips and scowled at him.

"Tate would never eat this," he grumbled under his breath, pulling his chair up to the table. He scooped out coleslaw and grabbed a chicken breast. He pulled the breading off of it.

His mother huffed. "Sorry, Bryce. It's just that you've been really down and I thought you could use a good meal."

"I could, but I can't. I appreciate it."

His dad came in and gave the appropriate ohs and ahs over the meal while Bryce picked at it.

"Bryce, honey." She put her hands in her lap. "We understand what you're going through."

"No, you don't."

"You need to get over it. They'll catch that boy soon enough. You'll be back on the track and Tate Jordan will be a memory."

"No, he won't. Neither will Pilot."

His dad scooted his chair back with a screech as it shifted across the floor. "Tate Jordan is not the kind of guy you should associate with. Surely, you can find someone better. A nice boy?" He gave his father credit for not choking on the word *boy*, but he still didn't get it.

"You don't know him."

"I know enough." His dad's eyebrows lowered over his eyes that were so much like his own, a deep infinite blue that you could lose yourself in.

Bryce dropped his fork on his plate. He couldn't eat any of this food anyway. "No, you don't. Tate is the sweetest most caring man. He'd do anything for me. He has. He's proved that."

His mom stood up. "By dragging you into that perverted relationship?"

"Mom. Why do you think it's perverted? Jeez. Just because it's different? Love is love."

"Two people is love. Three is...I don't know what it could be. Perverted." She held her hands up as if that was the end of it, but for Bryce it was far from over.

"No. You don't get it." He breathed deeply, not wanting to get upset and raise his voice because that would only prove his immaturity. "We haven't even done anything except kiss. They haven't pressured me into anything. They just love me. That's all. And you know what? I love them." He did. That much he knew. He might have screwed up the rest, but he loved them both deeply.

"How can you love two people?" Was she trying to understand or giving him more arguments?

"It's easy. My heart is that big. You taught me how to do that. How to love unconditionally. Are you going to take it back now?"

His parents didn't say anything after that. They didn't have to. Bryce knew what he had to do. He smiled as he pushed himself away from the table. His parents didn't understand, but they'd taught him all he needed to know: how to love and how to be brave. He had to fix this mess.

Later that night, he booted up his laptop, convinced he needed to send

Tate an email and try to get his feelings out. He tapped his fingers to the off-beats of the Ska music playing in his room. It was a bit on the loud side, but he hoped that would give his mom the hint to just leave him alone.

Once the laptop was up and he opened his email, he saw he had several unopened emails from at least two different addresses that he didn't recognize. The subject line caught his attention, though...

Open this now, Bryce, or Tate's going to get it!

Warren Tanner. Again.

Or rather, still. He'd been deleting some of the emails, but then he started just saving them in a folder without opening them. This one he opened and glanced over. It talked about getting sexual favors in exchange for him leaving Tate alone.

Nope. He couldn't deal with this. Tanner had spread his lies around the camp and it had given Bryce some trouble with his parents, but hadn't touched Tate and his reputation. It seemed like Tate could blow off anything. There had been some social media rumors going around about him beating up his last boyfriend, and God knew his mom had a field day with that one. Bryce knew better, though. Tate wouldn't beat up anyone. He was gentle to a fault. So he wasn't too afraid of threats against Tate. Not from Tanner.

But Tanner could spread rumors about Bryce and end up getting him kicked off of his team.

With a sigh, Bryce drug the emails into the folder he'd set up for the ones he hadn't even looked at and then forwarded them to Pilot. Maybe he could help. He opened another message box to try and get an email for Tate together, when his phone rang.

Pilot's picture popped up on the screen. It had only been a second since he'd sent that email. Had something already happened to Tate? He answered quickly. "Pilot? Is everything Okay? Is Tate okay?"

"Yes, we're okay. Tate's fine. Are you?"

Bryce blew out a breath with a huff. Now that he'd heard Tate was okay, relief washed over him, as well as all the other conflicting emotions that had just stopped when he worried about Tate. "I don't know..."

"Hey. We're worried about you. We just want the best for you. Whatever that is."

"Yeah? Even if I don't come back?"

Pilot chuckled. "Of course. Didn't we say that to start with? We care about you and that doesn't just turn off. We get it. Your struggles. You have to know Tate gets this, right? He knows the same pressures you do, being in Supercross. You can talk to him and he will listen. Promise."

"I know." He hated that he sounded like a petulant child when Pilot was speaking to him like an adult—how he wanted to be treated. He cleared his throat and tried again. "I miss y'all. I'm hurting with my leg. I'm worried my team is gonna drop me and now I'm getting more of these threats from Warren Tanner. So, I'm not myself. I'm, uh, scared...honestly. I'm scared of everything and I hate that."

"Okay. I get it."

"Do you? Really?"

"Babe...I was in the military. I've been to Iraq where I patrolled convoy routes. I know fear. We had no clue who the enemy was, what they looked like. Attacks could come from anywhere and I had to keep our guys safe."

"You're good at that."

"It's a lot easier here, but that's not the point." He sounded frustrated.

"Sorry."

"Don't be sorry, just understand that everyone faces fear. I'm scared now. I'm scared that Tanner or some other asshole is going to try and hurt you or Tate, and I won't be able to do a damned thing about it."

"Yes, you will." Bryce was confident in Pilot's abilities, even more so now, knowing his background.

"Thanks, Bryce. That means a lot." He paused and for a moment neither of them spoke. "We miss you, too, by the way. I miss you, uh...more than I thought I would, to be honest."

Bryce pushed away from his desk with a grunt and flopped down on his unmade bed. "What do you mean?"

"Bryce," he said with a sigh. "When we first brought you in with us, I thought, I don't know...you and Tate had something. Chemistry, but maybe more than that. You had a connection that I didn't have with either of you and I was afraid that if I didn't let y'all explore that, I'd end up losing Tate. Or he'd regret being with me or something..."

"So, you don't really like me?" He pulled his pillow over his head with his free arm.

"I didn't say that."

"You implied it."

"No. I didn't. I liked you enough, Bryce. I figured that at a minimum, it'd be some good sex. You know. I think you're sexy and smart. I always have. So..."

"I'm still not sure what you're trying to say, Pilot." Did he like Bryce or not?

"I'm saying that yes, I was attracted to you, and despite my reasons for bringing you in our relationship, I'm still attracted to you and I really like you. And like I said, I miss you."

Bryce's mouth twitched, but he held back his smile. "I've had my doubts about us. You and me. Not Tate. He's...well, you know."

"He's a boy-crazy shit." Pilot chuckled. "Seriously, I know what you mean. You have a lot more in common with him. I probably seem like

181

some old dude."

Now, Bryce laughed. "No. It's just that you're right. About Tate and me, I mean. We have Supercross and we're closer in age, but you're not fucking old, man."

Bryce sat up and his pillow fell to the floor. It had a red and blue *Motocross University* logo on it. "Pilot?"

"Yeah?"

"I want to come back. I do miss you. Both of you. I want to see where this can go and I don't know, like get to know you better. I just want to be sure that you aren't asking me back just because of your protective streak or that you think that's what Tate wants. I want you to want it because you want me, and uh...you know...more than just sex."

"That's a pretty grown up attitude for someone that's been hiding away like a brat."

"Hey!"

"I'm gonna pick on you. That's what I do." Pilot chuckled again, and Bryce decided two things. First, that he loved hearing that deep rumbling laugh from Pilot, and second, that his words were fair enough. He had been acting bratty.

"Okay. So?"

"I don't normally open up so easily, Bryce." His words were soft and serious, his earlier joking tone gone. "But, I do want you back here. I know Tate does too, but I want you for my own reasons, not just because of what Tate wants."

"And?"

"And what?"

"Spit it out. What are your reasons." He waited for a second, taking in his room. Motocross pictures on the wall along with parts magazines stacked on his desk. A poster of *The Mighty Boss Tones* hung over his bed. He thought that this time, maybe he could pack all of that up and bring it with him, if he went back to them, but first things first...

"Tell me."

"I really like you. I want to spend more time with you. Get to know you. See you succeed. Is that enough?"

"I don't know. It's a start."

"It's not going to happen overnight, Bryce. It's a process. We have to work on it. Every day."

"I know that."

"Then, what's stopping you?"

"I don't want to see Tate hurt. I don't want to bring this Tanner shit with me. I want...I don't know...closure. Or something like that."

"The world doesn't always work that way. Doesn't work how we want it to. You make things happen. You don't stand around waiting. I didn't think I'd have to tell *you* that."

Bryce shrugged, though he knew Pilot couldn't see him. "I don't know."

"Think about it. All of it."

"Okay." That's exactly what he needed to do, but Pilot made it sound a lot easier than it actually was.

Chapter 32 – February, Glendale

Arizona weather was perfect in February. Shannon couldn't be happier to be there while the temperatures were lower, cooler. If they raced there in May, it would be like death. Sweat poured off of him already, and he'd only managed to get through the track walk. He still had to do a few practice runs, qualify, and then place in his heat, and then, the Main Event. If he didn't place in his heat, he'd have more races. Shannon couldn't worry about that. He aimed to win his heat and move easily to the Main Event.

He turned up his water bottle, not watching where he was walking, as he headed back to his pit. He bumped into someone. "Hey, watch it."

"Fuck. You? Watch where you're going, Parker." The nasty words fell from none other than his prior teammate Cole Lindt's mouth. Cole shoved him with a dare.

"Come on, man. We used to be buds, bro—"

"I was never your *bro*." Cole crossed his arms over his chest.

Shannon flung his arm out, splashing the water. "Seriously. You know what I mean. We were friends until you turned into a pussy."

"You know what? Just fuck off, Parker." Cole turned to walk back the way he came, but Shannon didn't want to let it go that easily.

"Nah, nah, man. Come on Cole. What the hell? You never even said why you backed down last season. We could have been a good team."

Cole stopped and put his hands on his hips, and just stood there. Shannon thought he was thinking about whether he wanted to keep acting like a pussy or not. He was about to give up on the fucker, when Cole turned around. Shannon couldn't read the expression on his face. Was he frustrated? Constipated? What? "Cole?"

"Yeah. The thing is...I thought you were cool. I didn't want to have anything to do with them. I thought being gay meant they were, I don't know, less than us? Less than men?"

"Right. That's true. They're pussies and if you want to hang out with them, you're a pussy too." He pointed a finger at Cole and gestured with his water bottle.

"Nope. You're wrong. They're just people. No different than you or me and they didn't ask to be harassed—"

"The hell they did? Hanging out in back alleys with their pants down, groping each other. In fucking public. That's asking for it."

"Did you? Was that you?"

"Was what me?"

Cole shook his head. "I always wondered. I suspected it was, but I was never sure. Did you take that picture, Parker? Did you spread it all over?"

"What? That picture with McAllister's hand down your boy's pants."

"He's not my boy. Not then, not now."

"See. You know. You get it."

"The picture?"

Shannon couldn't help his chest bowing up. He'd snapped that picture and he was damn proud of it. Proud of exposing their homo-asses. He had debated what to do that night. He'd walked out the back door to take a leak, when the bathroom was full, and there they were. All mackin' on each other and shit, and feeling each other up. Made him sick. Shannon had thought he would puke. He'd wanted to beat the hell out of them, but then he thought that if they were exposed, it would run them out of Supercross, and that would be worse, especially for McAllister. "Yeah. I did what I had to do. You know?"

"No. I don't. That pretty much makes you the asshole of the year."

"Dude?"

"No, *dude*...I don't want to see that shit either, but what they do in private has got nothing to do with me. I don't give a fuck. I want to beat McAllister on the track. Just like every other Supercross racer. On the track. Not with fists and violence. Not with low down dirty tricks—"

"You miserable shit. You just back-pedal your way out of it. You were in. You did just as much as I did." He took an angry step toward Cole.

"No. I didn't. And when I figured out how far you were willing to go, I backed the fuck off. Because that's crazy and it's criminal. And I'm not blowing my ride for you or anyone."

Shannon took another step closer. Cole didn't back down. "That's bullshit. You're bullshit." Shannon shoved Cole's shoulder. He wanted to beat his ass, make him pay. He wanted to shove his homo-loving face in the dirt.

Cole rolled with the shove and shook his head. "You're so not even worth it, Parker. Just piss off and leave me the fuck alone." He turned then, and started walking away.

Shannon flinched. He wanted to jump on Cole and beat his face in, but he couldn't. He needed a win. He needed to stay out of the media. No drama. He'd placed in the top ten in the last race and he'd signed a contract. If he wanted more money, he'd have to stay out of trouble. Cole Lindt just wasn't worth it. He needed that money, so he sucked it up and stormed off.

Chapter 33 – February, Denver

"This is not my fault!" Tate screamed.

Pilot's eyes widened, but he didn't yell back. That was worse. It made Tate feel like a three year old throwing a temper tantrum, and that just pissed him off more.

He flicked his fingers at the computer Pilot had set up on the breakfast bar. "Figure this out. If it's not Warren Tanner, who the fuck is it?" Tate couldn't even believe the letters that Bryce had forwarded from the dickwad, but they didn't prove anything and there were other threats as well from more anonymous sources.

"Tate. I'm not a private detective."

Tate scowled and cursed under his breath. He knew that, but it didn't help. Warren obviously had been stalking Bryce and he'd been in the area when someone attacked Tate. The police insisted that Warren had an alibi, though. What fucking alibi? "Why can't you just figure the shit out?"

"Tate? You're being irrational."

"No. Irrational is Bryce leaving and you letting him."

"What was I supposed to do? Kidnap him?"

Tate glared at Pilot.

"Tate. Come on. You said yourself we can't force him."

Tate knew Pilot was right, but he didn't want him to be right and he didn't want to give in. The world around him had started to crumble to pieces and he couldn't stop it.

"Tate? I tried to talk to him. Don't—I'm still here, Tate."

"Fuck this!" He wanted to stay mad. Staying mad would keep him from crying over his broken life.

"Seriously? Stop being so melodramatic."

"Melodramatic? I've got your melodramatic." Tate grabbed his crotch in an obscene gesture.

The dam holding back his emotion creaked with the pressure building.

He didn't really want to explode all over Pilot. He'd already said too much that he couldn't take back. He just needed to get the hell out of there. He grabbed the truck keys, sliding them across the counter and stomped through the living room to the door. He didn't slam it behind him, though. He just left it wide open, swinging a little from the force of shoving it open.

He heard Pilot calling out to him, but Tate couldn't listen. He climbed up in the truck and shoved the stick in reverse. He had to get the hell out of there.

Earlier, Tate had arrived home after practice, but hadn't even pulled the bike out of the back of the truck when Pilot got his attention to tell him the cops had dropped the charges against Tanner. That had started the screaming on Tate's part. Pilot didn't so much as raise his voice, but that only made Tate's actions worse.

Tate needed to be on the track.

He drove north heading back to the practice track. They would be closed by the time he got there, but hopefully he could find somewhere to stay overnight. He thought he remembered a few hotels around that area. He just needed some time alone. Breathing room.

Tate hated that the track was so far away from Pilot's house. He drove by the entrance, and like he thought, it was closed. He circled around and headed back toward town. At least the long drive had calmed him down, and his heart had finally stopped running that six minute mile.

Tate pulled the truck to a stop at a red light. He wondered why he left. What the hell he was doing? Why was he doing this? He couldn't go back now, not after the way he stormed out. He fucked it up—all of it.

Why had he thought adding Bryce to their relationship would be a good thing? He was too young. Bryce hadn't even really come out of the closet or even had a boyfriend before. Tate pushed the issue because...why? He wanted Bryce that much? Worse, Pilot went along with it, but was it what Pilot really wanted or did he think he had to in order to keep Tate? Things had been fine with Pilot. They got along, cared for each other, loved each other. The sex was great. Bryce hadn't even been kissed before. Or rather, he'd just been kissed, and so far in their relationship, that's all they'd done. Relationship? A relationship between all three of them? How could that even happen?

But it had, and until Tate got jumped, it had been working. They clicked together, didn't they? Balanced each other out somehow? Pilot was the grumpy one, always so serious and he needed Tate and Bryce to lighten things up, and he needed more people to love and take care of. Who didn't need that? Pilot needed it more than most. Pilot seemed happy with that. And Tate? He never took anything serious before—except racing. Pilot and Bryce gave him something serious in his life, grounded him. Then, Bryce, well he was just adorable, if a little cocky. But you had to be cocky to race motocross and even his sarcasm was adorable.

If Pilot was the head in the relationship, Tate was the heart, and Bryce? He was the soul. No doubt. The kid was deep. Tate really needed to stop thinking of him as a kid. Even at eighteen, Bryce had a maturity about him that rivaled anyone Tate knew, including himself. There had to be some way to get them all back together. It had to start with reassuring Bryce and that meant figuring out who had jumped Tate. That was why Tate became so angry. He couldn't fix it by himself and it hadn't been fair to blame Pilot.

They needed help.

Pilot stared at the open door and watched as Tate drove away. His heart had been ripped into thirds. First Bryce, now Tate. How could he live without them? How could he go back to his lonely existence? He hadn't known just how gray his life had become. The only spark of color had been from fighting and that color had been all red. Now he had blond and purple and neon yellow. How could you let that go and slide back into a monochromatic life?

He shut the door and went back into the living room. He had to get his guys back. He had to figure out who had jumped Tate and why. He sat there thinking about it for a long time, but he hadn't realized how long until someone knocked on his door.

His heart leapt, but he stopped it from getting too excited. Tate or Bryce would just walk in and he didn't want to see anyone else.

The knock became incessant and Johnny yelled for him to open the fucking door, so he got up and forced his body to walk over and open it.

Johnny barged in and crossed his arms, staring daggers at Pilot. "You've been ignoring me. Not answering texts—"

"What?"

"What happened? What's going on? You never talk to me anymore and that's fine Pilot, but I can tell something is wrong just looking at your face. Where's Tate?"

"Gone."

"Gone like gone, gone? He left you?"

Pilot shrugged. "He didn't take anything, but he was pissed when he left. So, yeah. Gone."

"How could you let him leave like that?"

Pilot's raised an eyebrow and glared at Johnny. "Let?"

"Yeah, I didn't get you guys at first, but you've never been happier. That's what the hell I care about. And what now? You're fucking it up? Let him just leave? I thought we'd been over this...what the hell good is having our dream? Our company? What good is it if you don't have someone? Fix this." He waved his hand around as if the entire world could realign at his whim.

"You're as bad as Tate. How the hell am I supposed to fix it?"

"You're not just Pilot. You're *the* Pilot. You drive. You command the fucking ship. So, take the reins."

"You're kind of mixing your metaphors."

"Fuck you."

"I thought you were pissed about me being in a relationship. Now you're happy? Pissed that he left?"

"I wasn't pissed. Never pissed. Just, God...jealous, okay. I can't find anyone and you just slide right into this thing with Tate? It's like you've been together forever."

Pilot chuckled. He wondered just how pissed Johnny would be if he knew about them trying to add Bryce to their relationship. "Nothing perfect about either of us. But, I lo——" He stopped himself from saying it. He didn't want to tell Johnny before he told them. He'd told Tate, but not Bryce. He needed both of them home first. "Fuck."

"You love him. You don't have to say it, brother. I know. I see it in how you look at him."

"Yeah." Something thick caught in his throat. His brain stopped and shifted gears, running in reverse. "What do I do?"

"I'm the last person to give you relationship advice." Johnny plopped down on the couch.

Even Johnny looked to Pilot to make things right. He had to make things right. He just wasn't sure how. He had to do something, though. They had to figure this shit out somehow and they had decent connections and access others wouldn't have. No, they weren't detectives, but they were smart.

Pilot let Johnny in on what had happened with Tate's attack, but still didn't mention Bryce being with them in a relationship. He didn't know how to open that can of worms, so he let Johnny go on thinking Bryce was just a good friend being stalked by a mutual asshole from the race camp.

Hours later, Johnny finally left and the house fell silent, except for the ticking clock. Pilot checked his phone, but he didn't find any messages from Tate. Worry weighed him down as he tapped his screen to send a quick text. *T? you ok? You coming home?*

Pilot only waited a few seconds before Tate texted back. *IDK. Y?*

"Fuck this." Pilot tapped his screen again, probably poking it harder than he should, but it got the phone dialing. Pilot had enough of Tate's tantrum.

It rang twice before Tate's soft voice answered. "Hey."

"Hey. What do you mean you don't know? Are you okay?"

He heard a long exhale. Pilot was about to give up when Tate finally spoke up. "I just wanted to ride."

"The track's closed."

"I know. So, I'm just gonna crash at this hotel and get up first thing in the morning."

"Are you serious?"

"Yeah, but, well, now..."

Pilot started pacing. He didn't want to say the wrong thing and set Tate off again. "Well, what?"

"I don't know. I guess I figured you wouldn't want me around after that tantrum, but I, uh, I miss you."

"Fuck, Tate. I miss you, too, of course I want you around. Why the hell'd you get so mad?"

"I just, it's just, damn. This just means so much to me. More than anything."

"I understand, but Tate? No matter what happens with Bryce, you and I have to be good. Right? We're okay. We'll be okay."

"I know, but I want him to come home."

Pilot growled a bit. "I want you to come home, too."

Tate didn't answer.

Pilot was not going to leave things hanging with Tate. That could not even happen. "Have you already checked in to the hotel?"

"Yes." His voice was soft and timid as if afraid Pilot would be mad.

"Okay. Text me the address."

"Why?"

"I'm not letting you stay there alone. I'm coming up there. And Tate?"

"Yeah?"

"You better be naked when I get there."

Tate disconnected the call and quickly texted the hotel information to Pilot. Then he stood there, staring at his phone, wondering what had just happened. The highs and lows of the day exhausted him and he wanted to crash, but Pilot was on his way. He would be there soon enough.

He dashed for the shower and prepped himself. He wanted to be ready for Pilot. Every second that passed had his body humming with anticipation. He leaned over the bathroom counter and fingered himself, using long lubed strokes. His cock slapped hard against his stomach. He needed Pilot. Hell, Pilot would have already been pounding his ass if he hadn't acted like such a brat.

A long, low groan involuntarily left his mouth. It felt so good, but not as good as Pilot's cock would feel. He slowed down and went back to the main room. He pulled the bedspread and top sheet off the bed and stretched out on his stomach. He'd have to get up for Pilot, but he had a few more minutes.

Tate closed his eyes and thought about Bryce. He hoped they could work things out with him, but even if they didn't, he'd still be there for him as a friend if nothing else, and Pilot was right, their relationship would be okay either way. Well, as long as Tate stopped acting like a little bitch about things.

Pounding on the door had Tate leaping up and sprinting across the room. He looked out the peephole and saw Pilot's broad chest. He opened the door, standing behind it so Pilot could come in without the entire world seeing Tate's naked ass.

Pilot slammed the door behind him and threw the metal latch closed to keep anyone else out. "I really don't like the tantrums, Tate. You're better than that. You're not a child."

"I know. I'm sorry."

"When you're upset, we can talk about it. You can tell me anything. I *expect* you to."

Tate nodded and sucked his top lip into his mouth.

Pilot touched his mouth with his fingers, and pulled the lip back out. "That's mine."

"Okay."

"I'm glad you listened to me." Pilot wiggled his eyebrows and grabbed Tate's waist, pulling him closer. He kissed Tate, gently, and then sucked that top lip into *his* mouth. "Yeah, good. Get on the bed."

Tate rushed to comply with Pilot's commands, and crawled up on the bed on his hands and knees. He could hear the clang of Pilot's belt as he unfastened it then pulled it from the loops. Tate's breath came in shallow pants as his heart rate sped up. "Hurry up."

"No. Turn around and face the wall. And wait."

Tate did as Pilot commanded. He kind of liked Pilot bossing him around, liked the pounding of his heart as he waited. He could hear the blood rushing in his ears. He waited.

Smack! Pilot's belt came down hard across his ass. It didn't really hurt, just stung a bit and sounded worse than it felt. Pilot did it again, the loop of leather ringing out as it hit flesh. The third time, Tate grunted. "I have to ride tomorrow. Please, enough." The sting on his ass made his dick extremely hard and his balls pulled up tight.

"Then I'll pound your ass another way."

As soon as he slid inside Tate's hole, the burn and stretch took all of Tate's concentration. His world narrowed down to this one moment, feeling and needing and gasping for air. Pilot overwhelmed him with muscle and skin and sweat. Pilot's earthy aftershave combined with the heady scent of sex and want swept over him, engulfed him. He cried out, a noise that had no words, yet carried a ton of meaning.

Pilot draped his big body over Tate's and nuzzled under his ear. He whispered, "I've got you." The softness and caring of his voice contrasted with the aggressive thrusts of his hips and pelvis. Pilot used his powerful legs to rock into Tate and his strong arms to wrap abound Tate's body.

The angle changed as Pilot shifted his hips and fucked rhythmically into Tate. His cock brushed across Tate's spot with each stroke, sending him higher, Tate's moaning rising in octave along with the added pressure. The promise of an orgasm had just started tingling through him when Pilot stopped, pulled out and flipped Tate over.

They stared at each other for a moment. Tate lost himself in the depths of Pilot's dark eyes, and for that one moment, nothing else existed but his love and want reflected in Pilot's intense gaze. Pilot looked away first, but his eyes lowered just enough to watch his cock sliding back into Tate's hole, before returning to his face. "I love you. So much, Tate." Pilot laced their fingers together and pulled them above Tate's head.

Barely moving, Pilot rolled his hips in a subtle wave. Tate couldn't breathe, couldn't think. Every nerve ending fired. "Sean!" He came hard, shaking and trembling, his load squishing between their sweaty bodies.

Pilot grunted and jabbed in with quick bursts, until his body froze up and Tate could see the cords in his throat straining. "Gah! Tate."

He collapsed on top of Tate, and for once, Tate didn't mind his weight at all. He welcomed it, feeling safe and loved and cherished, but he wanted that same feeling for Bryce too, and his absence still felt like a gaping hole between them.

"I'll fix it. I promise." Pilot seemed to know exactly what Tate had been thinking.

The next morning, Tate had Pilot up at the crack of dawn. He needed to practice, but wanted Pilot to stay with him, so he made a few quick arrangements and just after eight a.m., he and Pilot headed to the track. Pilot helped get the bike off the truck and on the track, but Tate had the staff bring out another bike. It wasn't race quality, but it would do.

"What the hell's this?" Pilot growled.

"Ha. A bike, you know what a bike is? Right, Pilot?"

"Okay, sass-mouth, who is the extra bike for? You don't think I'm getting on that death-stick?"

Tate pushed the bike over to him. "Yes. You're getting on this fine machine." He added with a whisper, "Don't talk about her that way. She might be touchy."

Pilot shook his head, but grabbed the handle bars of the bike. "You're crazy. You know that?"

"Ha! You love me, anyway."

Pilot leaned in and kissed Tate's forehead. "Yeah, yeah. I love you. Now, show me how to work this thing."

After spending a few minutes talking about the bike and giving Pilot a decent tutorial on riding, Pilot felt ready to ride.

"Wait." Tate pointed over to the small trailer that stood near the track and posed as an office of some sort. "Go in there and get some gear on. You can't ride like that."

Pilot picked up his booted foot to say that he had protection, but Tate shook his head. "Not good enough. Jeans aren't good enough and you need under armor and a helmet and goggles. They'll have shit in there." He waved Pilot over to the trailer. He couldn't wait to see Pilot decked out in riding gear, but he worried they might not have pants big enough for him. If they didn't, he'd have to order some special, because he really wanted to see that ass in a pair of riding pants.

A few minutes later, Pilot came back out. He wore the boots and a jersey over some chest armor, and he had a helmet under one arm. He flicked goggles back and forth in his other hand. He wore his own jeans. "They didn't have pants to fit me."

"Well, you can't jump. You'll have to take it kinda slow. I'll let you get the hang of it, but then I need to practice. We'll order you some pants."

Pilot lifted one eyebrow.

"If you like it. Come on."

After a little bit of riding back and forth and going slowly over a few bumps, Pilot seemed to have the hang of the basics, so Tate stopped him. "I have to ride now. Did you like it?"

"It's cool. Maybe, uh, maybe we can order some pants and other gear." He pulled off his goggles and helmet and smiled up at Tate. "That was pretty fun. I want to go faster."

"I'd love to be able to ride with you and Bryce. You know, just for fun." Tate looked down at the dirt and dug his toe in. "Do you think we'll get him back, Pilot?" He started to tear up, and swallowed it back, choking on the emotion.

Pilot laid the bike down in the dirt and put his helmet and goggles down beside it, before walking over to Tate and pulling him into his arms. Their chest protectors bumped against each other. It didn't matter, because Pilot's arms still reached around him and his lips still kissed Tate's forehead and his cheek and his lips. "We'll do whatever we have to. We'll try. That's all we can do."

"Love you, Pilot."

"Love you, too. Now go. Put it out there on the track like you do, then when we get home, we'll have ice cream."

Chapter 34 - In the Rain, Atlanta

Bryce got out of the cab and stared up at the hotel. He didn't even know what room they were in but he knew they'd be at this hotel with most of the other Supercross folks. He turned off his MP3 player and let his earbuds hang over his hoodie.

Just a few hours earlier, from the window of the plane, he'd watched the sun setting, casting pink and purple streaks through orange clouds. It had taken him a long time to get from the plane to pick up his luggage, just one large suitcase. Then he had to wait for a cab, the old fashioned kind. His parents didn't trust Uber and he'd promised them that much.

As he stood in the hotel parking lot, the dark sky loomed overhead, vast without a single star, making him feel insignificant. Lightning flashed and Bryce jumped. The rain threatened. He could smell the charged ozone like grapefruit and cut grass. He shifted his weight from foot to foot, unsure of what to do. His suitcase sat on the curb beside him looking gray and hard and final.

He wasn't sure if he could ever go back to his parents after the fight they'd had. It had started out as opinions and discussions and just when he had thought they were coming around to his way of thinking, it turned from bad to worse and both sides said things they couldn't take back. The worst, was what they'd said about Tate. How could they? Tate and Pilot both had been there for him through everything. Tate understood what it meant and what it felt like to be unable to race. His parents didn't get that. Not in a million years would they understand. They thought he was just acting like some horny teenager. He was neither of those things, but they couldn't see that.

No, Bryce's interest in Tate went deeper than his cock. Hell, they hadn't even had sex yet. Bryce groaned thinking about cock, his and theirs, and wondered what it would really be like. Could he really have both Tate and Pilot? Did he want that? A part of him, besides his dick, wanted that very much. Two loving caring men that wanted him, cherished him. That was how they'd made him feel. Yet, he still hesitated. Afraid.

Lightning flashed again, followed by a boom of thunder, so close together that the storm had to be near. He waited in the calm night air, feeling the charge of the ozone against his face and in his chest. Then the sky ripped open and poured down cold water, soaking through Bryce's clothes, through his jacket and t-shirt in seconds. His hair flopped in his face, wet and cold and plastered to his forehead. Now he was really a mess. He started to cry. Not sobbing, just tears trickling down his cheeks, joining the rain. He nudged them off his cheeks with his shoulder and took a deep breath. He couldn't stand out in the rain forever.

Hoisting up his suitcase, he trudged across the parking lot and under the awning of the second floor. His injured knee ached from the trip. He'd probably pushed too hard, but he didn't know how to go slower. He wasn't made that way; he took everything head on, at full speed. He took a deep breath, preparing to jump in, and then pulled out his phone, hoping it had stayed dry in the pocket of his jeans. He flipped to his messages and shot a quick text to Tate, asking what room he was in.

216

It *would* be on the second floor. *Figures.*

Bryce practically dragged his suitcase up the stairs and down the walkway. There was no awning over the second floor and rain beat down on him harder. Lightning lit the sky along with another round of rolling thunder that made Bryce jump and drop his suitcase. He swore under his breath.

Up ahead, a door opened and Tate's blond head peeked out. "Bryce!"

He couldn't move. He tried to pick up his suitcase, but suddenly it had doubled in weight along with his feet. Tate looked like an angel, hanging out the door. Did he still want Bryce? He didn't know what to say or do, frozen there in the rain.

In a second, hands were on him, on his luggage, hauling him into the room.

"You're gonna get sick standing in the rain like this. What're you thinking?" Tate asked.

Bryce shrugged and let Tate pull off his jacket and yank his wet t-shirt over his head.

"Get out of those wet jeans," Pilot commanded him, but softly.

Bryce obeyed, yanking the denim down his legs. He toed off his sneakers and dropped his jeans, leaving him standing there in wet socks and underwear. Tate put a towel over his head and scrubbed to dry his soaking wet hair. Pilot rubbed another towel over Bryce's body. They worked together, drying him, and then gently pushed him down on the bed and peeled off his socks. Tate knelt on the floor in front of him. He looked into

Tate's sea-green eyes. A storm swirled with unasked questions.

"I don't want to push you, Bryce. Whatever you want is okay. But you need to get your boxers off and get under the blankets."

Bryce nodded, but instead of reaching for his undies, he reached for Tate, needing to hold him. Tate leaned into him, pushed his still damp hair out of his eyes. Bryce couldn't take it anymore. The look of concern and love pushed him over that metaphorical edge. He pounced, throwing his arms around Tate's neck and rubbing his cold face into his chest.

Tate pushed Bryce's head back with warm hands and looked at him again. "Is this what you want?"

Bryce nodded and bit his bottom lip.

Pilot's low baritone broke the mood from beside them. "You need to say it, baby."

"Yes," Bryce gasped, the word and its forcefulness surprising himself. Then, just the corner of his mouth flinched up in a smile he couldn't contain. "Yes," he said again. "Please. Pilot, Tate."

"I've got you," Tate whispered, pulling Bryce in closer. Hands touched the waistband and pulled his underwear down and he let them. Tate kissed his face, cheeks, forehead, nose, and finally his mouth. Bryce wanted more and opened up, jutting his tongue out for Tate to slide his own against, like rubbing velvet the wrong way.

Pilot leaned between them, and Bryce held his breath. For a second, he thought Pilot was going to be jealous and push them apart, but he didn't. He just leaned in to get his own kiss. The first was a tentative peck, then Bryce turned his head and Pilot owned the kiss, owned him. His tongue and lips were on Bryce, demanding, pushing in, as if he'd waited a lifetime for the kiss. Pilot had been holding back after all, but that time was over.

He picked Bryce up, pulling him into the strongest arms that had ever held him. His feet left the floor, so he wrapped them around Pilot's waist and hips. His naked cock rubbed against the soft sweatpants Pilot wore. Tate pushed against him from behind. At some point, Tate had pulled his own shirt off, but Bryce couldn't remember it happening. He only knew that he'd been sandwiched between two hard chests, skin to skin to skin.

"Bed," Tate said, and Pilot slid them all down on the king sized bed that dominated the hotel room. The comforter had been pulled back, and cool sheets met Bryce's shoulder and hips. He slid his legs down, only to have Tate's legs wrap around them. Pilot's hand slid down his arm, his ribs, to his hip, where it stopped, resting there like it held the warmth of the sun.

Tate's nose nestled under his ear, in his hair. He could hear Tate's hard breathing. "What do you want Bryce?" he whispered, and the feel of it had his cock twitching.

"You. Tate. Pilot. You both. Can I?"

"Please..." The word rolled off Pilot's tongue like a request for air.

Bryce needed to show them that he was in—all in.

He leaned into Pilot, begging for more kisses with his tongue across thick lips. He ground his ass backwards into Tate's crotch. Both men moaned around him. Their hands on him seared, insistent and demanding. Tate mouthed along his neck and licked his collarbone. Pilot kissed his lips. They leaned in and kissed each other over him, and the sight of these two together had his cock dripping. "More," he groaned out and stuck his tongue between their lips in a wet three-way caress.

Tate chuckled and pushed Bryce onto his back. He got out of the bed, but only long enough to pull his fancy, designer track pants off. He was naked underneath and his cock popped out, cut and pink and perfect, as he pushed them off. While he watched Tate crawling back into the bed, Pilot shuffled on the other side, to pull his off own sweats.

Bryce glanced between them both. How had he ended up here, between two naked men that he wanted so desperately?

"Bryce?" Pilot asked. "Have you ever? What do you want?" His dark eyes roamed over Bryce's body like sweet caresses.

"No," Bryce could feel the blush creeping over his face. "I've never done anything but kiss."

"Okay. Slow then." Pilot's smile was like an old friend, comforting and inviting. "It's okay. Just tell us what you want. When to stop."

"I want it all."

Pilot looked over at Tate. "What does all mean, exactly?" he asked.

Bryce tugged at his arm, wanting them both closer, as close as he could get them. "It means everything. This isn't just sex for me. It never was. I want that, but I want you more. Both of you. Like you said. I want to try a relationship."

Tate exhaled loudly, as if he'd been holding his breath the whole time. Maybe he had, but he didn't give Bryce time to think about it. His mouth was on Bryce, nibbling his chin, and licking down to his chest. He flicked his tongue across Bryce's nipple. Pilot joined him, his hands rubbing his thigh and hip. The room lit up accompanied by a boom of thunder, punctuating Bryce's need.

Then someone touched his balls, kneading them. "God more," Bryce groaned out. He'd never felt anything so erotic in his life. He glanced down to see Pilot's hand engulfing his sack while Tate grabbed his cock and started stroking. "Oh, God! I'm gonna come."

"Go ahead," Pilot whispered. "We want you to feel good."

"Don't." They stopped moving, but didn't release him. "Don't want it to be over that quickly," he spit out fast before they misunderstood. Both hands started moving again.

Pilot chuckled low in his throat, but it was Tate that said, "It won't be over yet, wonder-boy. Don't worry about that." Then, he leaned in and sucked the skin of Bryce's neck between his teeth. Pilot's tongue flicked across his nipple.

Bryce had never imagined it could be like this. Tate used Bryce's precum to get things sliding along, but it only took a few strokes before Bryce shot off like a rocket. Cum flew in the air landing on Tate and on Bryce's chest. Pilot licked at it with that low chuckle rumbling through his chest again, like some large cat purring.

He lay there in awe of the two men petting him, touching him—his thigh, his hip, his ribs, arms. Bryce couldn't believe his first experience with someone else sexually was actually with two someones, but it felt right—good. He wanted more. No, he needed to make them feel just as good as they'd made him feel. He needed them to come, too.

He shoved Tate back and slid down over his body, until Tate's hard cock jutted out in front of his face. Clear fluid beaded up at the pink tip. He stuck out his tongue and touched it, licking up the precome.

"You don't have to, Bryce," Tate said, his voice low and husky.

"Oh, I want to." He licked at his cockhead with his tongue flat, loving the way it felt, so rigid yet soft. He let the crown slide between his lips. Every move had Tate moaning, coming unglued, bit by bit. Bryce's heart stuttered.

The palm of Pilot's hand caressed Bryce's ass, as he slowly went down on Tate. He lifted his hips, silently begging for more, even though he wasn't sure what he was begging for...just more Pilot touching him.

He sucked Tate's cock into his mouth as far as he could get it, impressed with himself that he could take so much. Tate carded his fingers through Bryce's hair. He could hear the patter of the rain on the roof accompanying Tate's panting and his own heart beating in syncopation.

Bryce knelt up on his knees, leaning over Tate, as he worked. He knew he'd wanted to do this, suck Tate's cock, since the very first second he'd met him, but he had no idea it'd be like this. He loved the feel of Tate in his mouth, sliding against his tongue and tasting like...Tate. He didn't want it to end, but his jaw was starting to ache with just a few sucks, up and down.

Pilot's hands gripped his hips then. He felt a hot rod sliding across his crack. Pilot was going to use his butt crack to get off while he sucked Tate. The thought of it, the image in his head, had his own cock stirring back to life. He pulled off of Tate just long enough to moan out, "Yes, Pilot. Do it." Then he sucked back down farther than he had before. He could feel Tate's cock knock the back of his throat. For a second he froze there, but when he realized he wasn't gagging, he swallowed.

"Oh, God!" Tate let out a little growl and shivered. Bryce figured he liked that very much, so he did it again before pulling back and increasing his suction. Lightning flashed, lighting up the room like a strobe light, then vanquishing them back into near darkness.

Pilot added some lube with a cold squirt, then rubbed his cock through the sticky mess, up and down Bryce's crack. But Bryce didn't care. The deep sounds Pilot added to the room were incredibly sexy and rumbled in time with the thunder.

Despite the ache in his jaw, Bryce kept sucking Tate. He was hard again from the feel of it all and the sounds. *God the sounds!* His mouth slurped and Pilot groaned while Tate gasped. Bryce grabbed his own cock and pulled it in the same rhythm he sucked Tate, which matched the pace that Pilot set against his ass. The three moved like one machine, three pistons working in time. It felt incredible, and Bryce ached to come, but he'd already come once and didn't think he'd be the first to go off.

He stole a glance up to Tate who watched Pilot over Bryce's shoulder. Bryce would have thought he'd be jealous if his man was looking at someone else while he was giving him head, but no. None of that. It brought a strange joy to Bryce's heart. They were bringing each other pleasure in a strange triangular way that just seemed to work.

Bryce increased his suction and tried using his tongue along Tate's shaft as his mouth slid up and down. In a moment, Tate called out, making a high pitched noise, then he grunted. His cock swelled seconds before he came, shooting into Bryce's mouth and throat. Surprised by the sensation, Bryce pulled back and half of it spurted out over his mouth and chin and down Tate's dick. Some of it he swallowed. He'd been afraid he wouldn't like the taste, but while it wasn't anything like chocolate, it wasn't disgusting either, just a little sour.

Before he could even wipe up the mess, Pilot grabbed his hips harder and lunged forward, shooting his own load, hot across Bryce's back. That was the last bit to throw Bryce over the edge. He jerked his cock as he added his own spunk to the party, making the room reek of sex and sweat.

They were amazing.

Lightning flashed again, as if in agreement.

Bryce collapsed onto Tate, his arm stretched over his hip and his head rested on Tate's lower abs. Pilot slid down, spooning Bryce's side and resting his head on his arm near Tate's head. They lay that way for a few breaths, then when thunder rolled through again, Tate started laughing. His stomach jerked and rolled, dislodging Bryce's head, which only made Tate laugh more.

"Shut up, you," Pilot groaned playfully.

"Come here guys. Cuddle fest is on!" Tate said. "Let's clean up first." Tate rolled Bryce to his stomach and stared at the mess Pilot had made between them. "God, Pilot. You're like...volcano man or something! Look at this mess."

Pilot laughed, getting up to go to the bathroom and grab towels to clean them up. Bryce had the worst of it, having come twice. Tate tickled him as he wiped it up.

When they'd finished, they cuddled in together. Pilot pulled the top sheet up over their shoulders. Bryce ended up in the middle again and decided he enjoyed it there. It felt like where he belonged with their legs tangled and arms circling and noses snuggling. The storm continued to beat down outside, but inside Bryce was warm and loved.

A bang at the door lifted Pilot's head off the pillow. He didn't want to get up, reluctant to leave the warm bed. Bryce lay in the middle with his face smashed against Pilot's chest, and Tate's calloused fingers rested on Pilot's hip, arm stretched across Bryce. The knocking came again and louder this time. He got up and grabbed a pair of sweats out of his suitcase and made his way to the door. He peered out the curtain to see who was there, expecting housekeeping, but no. "Shit."

He opened the door.

"Good morning, Pilot. Get your ass outta bed already."

"What're you doing here, Johnny?"

"I came to watch your boy race. Shouldn't you guys be up by now?" Johnny pushed his way into the room.

Tate and Bryce sat up in the bed. Bryce's eyes went wide.

Johnny's went wider, and his jaw dropped open. "Shit! What the hell? Two guys? Is he even legal?" Johnny pointed at Bryce.

Tate's eyes narrowed. "Yes. Nice to see you too, Johnny."

Johnny didn't reply, he turned and gave Pilot the evil eye. "This...this is...fuck! I don't even know what this is." He threw a hand in the air.

"Let's step outside." Pilot looked at his watch. They still had plenty of time to get to the track. It wasn't race day, but Tate needed to do a track walk and Pilot had to check in with Tyler and the Apex crew. He needed to take care of Johnny's temper first, though. He really didn't want to deal with his friend. He'd rather get back in bed.

He shoved Johnny out the door and shut it behind him. The concrete walkway tingled cold and wet under his bare feet. "What are you so pissed about?"

"This isn't you Pilot. My God! Is this Supercross shit turning you into some kind of perv? Suddenly, you have to be sexing it up with two hot young guys? Since when has that been you?"

"Johnny, I'm not like that. *This* is not like that." Pilot gestured to the hotel room.

"It looks like, just like, *that.*"

Pilot looked down at his feet and curled his big toe, scraping it across the cement. "You don't know what you're talking about."

"No? Well, you've shut me out, so how could I know? I'm here trying to support you. And Tate. And I walk into the Great American Fuck-fest."

Pilot tried to calm things down. He didn't want Johnny mad; he wanted him to understand. "I appreciate that you came out. I know Tate will, too."

"Whatever." Johnny crossed his arms over his chest.

"Look. I don't know what to tell you. We're both in love with him. Bryce."

"Both?"

"Yes. Tate and me and Bryce. All three of us are in a relationship. This isn't just fucking, Johnny. I need you to understand that."

There was hurt on Johnny's face, but Pilot wasn't sure why, except that he hadn't shared any of this with him. Johnny turned away and took a few steps.

"Johnny?"

He whirled around. "No. This is bullshit. I'm your best friend. More of a brother to you than your real brother, the dickhead. And there's shit going down in your life and you shut me out. How am I supposed to understand? You've never had more than a one night stand and now you're shacking up with two guys?" He held up two fingers.

Pilot shrugged. "I'm still not sure how it happened."

"You know what? I don't care. Just fuck you, Sean."

This time when he stormed off, Pilot let him go. They'd talk again after Johnny cooled off. This wasn't really about Pilot being in a relationship with two guys. It was about their relationship and how they weren't nearly as close as they had been. Pilot blamed himself, but how could they be that close when Pilot's free time was now all about Tate...and now Bryce, too. He'd have to make an effort to make sure Johnny got included in things. He needed Johnny in his life, because, yeah, he was more of a brother than Colin had ever been. He couldn't lose that.

Chapter 35 - Next Race, Daytona Beach

The track had been set up on one corner of the field between the bleachers and the infield of Daytona International Speedway. Trucks and RVs caravanned on the far side, behind where they'd set up the long line of pits along the track. The Florida sun pounded down on them relentlessly, but Pilot didn't give a fuck about the heat. Bryce had come back to them and Tate was happy and they were going to make this three-way relationship work out. Pilot could almost be happy as well. Only one thing still stood in the way and that was whoever had attacked Tate. That mother-fucker had to go down. Until then, Pilot couldn't relax and enjoy his life.

Pilot followed Tyler from their RV down to the Apex pit. They were meeting with both the Apex and the MSR teams to talk about what had happened, what evidence there was, what little information Pilot had found on the internet, and what they could do about it. Pilot didn't think they could do anything. This threat had been plaguing them since that photo of Davey and Tyler had been leaked the previous season. It had quieted down when that Shannon Parker dude wasn't racing, but he was back and so were the threats.

"It's getting worse." Angel's voice traveled out from their area as they approached. She sat in Stewart's lap. Davey leaned against the semi-truck beside the couple and he glanced at them as Tyler and Pilot walked up. His whole face lit up like it was the first time he'd ever seen his husband. Pilot smirked a little, but knew Tate's face did the same thing when either he or Bryce walked up.

Pilot dropped his own face into a scowl, realizing that his lovers were not present. "Where's Tate and Bryce and what's getting worse?" Pilot practically growled. He had enough of this one thing gunking up his works and he wanted the clog in the drain cleared—fast.

Angel stood up. "They'll be here in a minute. First, I'll show you what's getting worse. Here." She crossed over to the tool boxes and flipped her laptop around to show Pilot the emails she'd been getting. He started glancing over them. "We also have real letters, mail. We turned them over to the police. The Supercross authorities are aware of this. They're not only threatening Davey and Tyler, but they've added Tate and Bryce to their list."

"Think it's Parker again?" Pilot wanted that fucker dead. Threatening his family, that's what they were doing.

"Uh, maybe. He had help last time and we think he does this time too, if it's him. He didn't attack Tate directly. We know that much."

"How do we know that?"

"Because he has an iron clad alibi with time stamped video to prove he wasn't anywhere near the hotel when the attack went down."

Davey leaned against the tool box. "That sounds a little contrived...too convenient, if you ask me." He'd obviously paid someone or somehow convinced someone to do the deed while he was tucked away safe. "I agree. That doesn't mean he can't be taken down. If he hired someone..."

Angel answered that one. "If we get proof, we'll nail him."

Broady finally spoke up from where he stood off in the far corner, scoping out the area. "That's the thing, isn't it? We aren't cops or detectives. We need to just let them do their job while we remain vigilant. Maybe Tate and Bryce need extra bodyguards for a while."

"Good point, Broady." He had to admit the truth of it, even if he didn't want to. He'd definitely talk to the guys about extra protection. He'd lose it if either of them were hurt again. It'd been too much already. He shut the laptop, unable to keep looking at the disgusting letters. He wanted nothing to do with that. "I'm wondering if Bryce's stalker has anything to do with this. I've been looking for a connection, but honestly, I've got nothing."

After a few minutes, Tate and Bryce showed up with Tate's manager Oz, his coach, Joey, and Bryce's manager, who Pilot didn't really know, except his name was George. Everyone exchanged hello's and small talk. Then, Bryce said something that got Pilot's attention. "So, maybe we should hire a private detective."

"Yes. Angel? You hear this?"

"What?"

The idea excited Pilot. This could be the answer to bringing the mess to a quick end. "Bryce said we should hire a private detective. We're only security, but we can hire a detective." He pointed to himself and Broady.

"Great idea. Yes." She pulled a small cellphone out of the front of her shirt. Where had she hid the thing? In her bra? She moved out of range while she talked.

Oz came up and patted Pilot on the arm. "Maybe that will help, but I want Tate protected in the meantime. I can't have him missing any more races."

"I can't have him hurt."

"Same thing." Oz nodded. Pilot understood better than the man probably realized. He knew what Oz meant, even if he couldn't say it.

"I don't want me hurt, either. Or Bryce." Tate wrapped an arm around Bryce's shoulder.

Bryce's manager didn't say anything, but he nodded, looking worried, and crossed his arms over his chest.

Bryce had started physical therapy and was walking on his bad leg again, but he still wasn't ready to get back on a bike. During the week, they'd made their way out to the track and Pilot had rode the bike a little and Tate showed off, but then Pilot sat with Bryce while Tate practiced with Joey. It had been fun, but he could tell that not riding was killing Bryce. Pilot put his arm around both of them. "I don't want either of you hurt." He kissed the top of Bryce's head.

Angel came back over and looked at Oz. "We're getting a private investigator. Apex is fitting the bill, but if you want to hire someone too, we can get them working together."

Oz held up his hands. "This is so outside of my circle. I'll let you handle it, but I'd like to be updated regularly."

George added, "Me, too."

"Deal." Angel stuck her hand out and Oz shook it, then she shook with George.

Pilot pulled Bryce a little closer and put his hand on Tate's shoulder, needing to touch both of them and reassure himself of their well-being. "We need to get to the bottom of this."

Tyler bumped his shoulder into Davey then addressed the teams. "I think Shannon Parker is our number one suspect. Everything is just too coincidental with this guy. We should have the PI on him first."

"Yeah," Angel agreed. "That almost goes without saying. If that dickwad is behind all of this, I want the troll put down."

Stewart wrapped his arms around her waist. "I love it when you're so fierce."

Everyone laughed, but Pilot understood how she felt. Maybe Tate understood how Stewart felt, too, because he looked up at Pilot with that same expression of awe and heat that did such strange and wonderful things to his insides.

Despite the distractions, Tate finished in second in the Main Event. He rode like he had something to prove and maybe he did, but Pilot really didn't care, except that Tate was happy when they ended the day in the hotel room.

Bryce's leg started bothering him and Tate made him get in bed, which was cute. He liked watching Tate boss Bryce around a little, especially when Bryce pouted. It made Pilot want to bite his bottom lip. Before he could crawl across the bed to indulge himself, his cellphone rang.

Pilot would have ignored it, but it was Johnny and he'd been ignoring him for too long. He tapped the screen. "What's up, J-man!"

"Hey! I watched the race. Give Tate my condolences on second, man."

"Har-har. Second is great any day, but even better after his injuries." Pilot sat on the edge of the bed and rested his hand on Bryce's leg.

"I know. I'm just giving you shit, man. So, when are you coming home? Uncle Gary and I want to do dinner with you and your guys." It was a major capitulation and the change relieved him, which made him feel bad about his plans.

"I'm, uh, not. Not any time soon."

"Uh, aren't you on break? Aren't you off a week?"

Pilot rubbed his forehead. "Yes, but we need to spend time together and Bryce needs to get back on a bike, so I need to be there for him."

Bryce leaned forward. "No, we don't."

Pilot shushed him.

"Listen, Sean. I get these guys mean a lot to you, but come on. We're family. And I'm trying to include them. Both of them..."

"Yeah, so you should understand. Or at least try to. When the season is over, you're gonna get sick of us being in your face."

Tate stepped out of the shower, pulling on a pair of sweat pants. "Hey invite them to the end of season party."

"What's that?" Johnny asked.

"Right. Good idea. So, Davey and Tyler are having a big end of season party and they said bring who we want. It'll be fun, so you and Uncle can come. There's a pool and a dirt bike track and shit." He looked up to get Tate's confirming nod. He hadn't been there himself, but Tate had.

"Okay. I'll ask Uncle." Johnny didn't sound thrilled, but he'd get over it. "I'll try to come out to another race or two, okay? Is that okay?"

"Of course, man."

After they shared small talk and hung up, Tate slid in behind him, rubbing his shoulders. "I like Johnny. He's just concerned about you."

"I know."

His shoulder rub included neck kisses and then a hand slid down and snuck under his shirt. Pilot twisted around to look at Tate. He still loved his sea green eyes and luscious mouth and he had to kiss Tate right then. He reached around and pulled Tate in, kissing him and wanting to get as close as he could. In a heartbeat, Tate had scooted around and let Pilot pull him into his lap.

"Hey!" Bryce gripped Pilot's waistband with his toes, making him laugh.

Pilot leaned back on the bed with Tate stretched out on top of him. "Come here, Bryce."

Bryce crawled down the bed and leaned in to kiss Pilot. Tate stuck his tongue between their lips, and suddenly they had that weird three-way kiss going again, but Pilot liked it. Tasting both Tate and Bryce at the same time was incredible and made his cock plump up hard.

"Mm..." Tate wiggled, rubbing against Pilot's dick. "Gah! I want both of you. Right now."

Pilot shifted, dumping Tate onto the bed. "I like that idea. What about you, Bryce?"

Bryce was up on his hands and knees, leaning over Tate and licking at his lips. "Yes, yes, please."

"Scoot up, Tate." Pilot started directing. It worked better that way. He pulled at Tate's sweat pants, as he scooted farther back on the bed. Tate hadn't bothered with a shirt, so making him naked was quick work.

Bryce stood up and pulled off his shirt and jeans while Pilot pulled Tate's clothes off. Both of them were naked on the bed rather quickly. He watched them rub against each other.

For a moment, his prior conversations with Johnny crept back into his head. He'd acted like he thought Pilot was trying to live out some perverted fantasy with two young, hot guys, and he needed to grow up. Life was about so much more than sex. But, Johnny was wrong. Oh, they were hot, young guys, but Pilot wanted so much more from them than just some sexy fantasy.

Tate stopped kissing Bryce and looked at him. Pilot could swear he saw love in those stormy eyes, along with want and need. "What are you waiting for?" he asked.

Pilot shook his head and slid out of his jeans. "Not a thing. Not a damn thing."

"Good." Tate winked at him before turning back to Bryce, who had been kissing Tate's neck while he waited for more attention. Tate ran his hands into Bryce's black and purple hair, tugging just a little to get him to look up. "I love you, Bryce."

Bryce's face lit up; his smile filling the room with joy. "God, I love you, too. Both of y'all, so much." He turned to Pilot who climbed over them.

With both of their bodies underneath him, Pilot couldn't think of anything else except touching them. He needed to feel their skin, their hair, their hearts, and their souls. He couldn't get close enough, couldn't taste enough.

Bryce giggled. Pilot's hand was on his ass, and the other around Tate's shoulders and his lips were on Tate's neck, but Tate's mouth and hands were on Bryce. Pilot shifted to help tickle Bryce because his laughter sounded like heaven. Bryce squirmed around, shoving at them until Pilot caught his mouth with his own, their tongues dancing to music only the three of them could hear.

Tate knelt up on his knees, one hand on Bryce's arm and one on Pilot's shoulder. "You two are so hot."

Pilot leaned back and looked at his lovers. "Spread your legs, Bryce."

He did.

"You are so beautiful." Pilot couldn't get over how lucky he was. Bryce was beautiful both inside and out, and full of such delight. His dark hair was trimmed up around his cock. Pilot leaned in and nuzzled his balls. He smelled like hotel soap and salty sweat. Pilot needed to taste him, lick him like a treat. His tongue lathed over Bryce's sack. Pilot lifted his gaze up Bryce's body to see him kissing Tate.

"I want your mouth," Tate said, his voice husky and so turned on.

"Yes," Bryce moaned and Tate moved to straddle his shoulders. Pilot could see Tate's ass shift back and forth as Bryce took him.

Inspired by their actions, Pilot shifted and sucked Bryce's cock down. The feel of his tongue rubbing against that soft skin made him want. His abs flinched and he rolled his hips against the mattress almost involuntarily. He pushed Bryce's legs higher and lifted his ass, letting his mouth trail down, hot and wet, behind Bryce's balls and down his taint. He flicked the tip of his tongue against Bryce's hole. He wiggled and made a soft, needy sound around Tate's dick.

Neither of them had taken Bryce's hole yet. They had been going slow. Hand jobs and blow jobs and rubbing off had been enough. It wasn't enough anymore. "Please, Bryce."

For a minute he heard the slurping sounds of Bryce working Tate's cock, while Pilot kept working his tongue into Bryce's hole. He pushed in and out, licking around the edges and plunging back in. Finally, Bryce shuttered, his legs trembling under Pilot's hands. "Yes. Please, Pilot. Fuck me." His voice wavered.

Pilot smiled and sat up. He moved off the bed and dug through his bathroom kit, digging out the condom and lube, wondering why he hadn't grabbed the stuff before they'd started. He turned around just in time to see Tate come. He pulled off and shot some of his come over Bryce's face and Bryce flinched and laughed. "Damn, Tate!"

Pilot grabbed a towel from the rack by the sink and headed back across the room. He wiped Bryce's face. "You still want me?"

Bryce licked his lips, whether he was just hungry for more, trying to get every last bit of Tate, or trying to get his lips to stop tingling, Pilot didn't know, but he nodded and there was heat in his shiny blue eyes.

"Good." Pilot tossed the supplies on the bed and grabbed Bryce's calves and yanked him down the bed. Bryce giggled as Pilot manhandled him. Once he flipped Bryce and had him up on his hands and knees, Tate lay across the bed in front of him, so his face was under Bryce's and they could kiss.

Pilot took time to lick his ass some more, then stretch him well with lubed fingers. Tate kissed him and rubbed his back. They worked together to relax him, knowing he'd be nervous. Pilot had to make this good for him. When he seemed stretched enough, Pilot knelt up to work the condom, but Tate was right there, opening it and rolling it down Pilot's cock. He rubbed a slick hand up and down, coating it thoroughly. Pilot leaned in and kissed Tate, tongues rubbing against each other, hot and wet. Tate's smile was his reward. It made his heart flutter and everything felt lighter.

"Hurry up." Bryce's voice was needy and hoarse, and he wiggled his ass to accentuate his demand.

Tate laughed and smacked his ass with the flat of his hand. "Bossy!"

"Yes." Bryce laughed again. Pilot loved how happy these two were, and that he had any part of that happiness made it even better.

He position himself behind Bryce and pushed the head of his cock against Bryce's hole. Bryce trembled again, and Tate rubbed his back, making shushing sounds.

Pilot pushed until his head popped through the ring of muscles. "You okay?"

"Yes, ugh! Get it over with. Push in."

Tate chuckled and kissed down the back of Bryce's neck, licking at the sweat that had started building.

Pilot pushed in slowly, stretching him steadily until he was seated and Bryce had taken all of his length. "Bryce? Okay?"

Bryce's head jerked up and down. "Do it." His voice was strained.

Pilot pulled back and rolled his hips in slowly. When he didn't get the reaction he wanted, he canted to the side and fucked out and in again. He did it a few more times, adjusting his position until finally Bryce cried out and his body relaxed. Pilot held that position and fucked faster and harder.

He watched Tate crawl under Bryce, his head close enough to lick at Bryce's cock. Pilot reached forward, kissed between Bryce's shoulder blades, then wrapped his arms around his chest and lifted him up, giving Tate more room.

Pilot fucked him with a nice steady pace while Tate sucked his cock. They loved each other in perfect harmony and Pilot had never seen anything as glorious in his entire life. He wanted to see Bryce come undone, though. He needed to see his face. "Stop. Tate, stop."

He sat up, his hair sticking up in every direction and eyes delirious. "What's wrong?"

"Nothing. I want to see Bryce." Pilot flipped him over on his back. Bryce spread his legs and lifted, showing Pilot his hole. It was red and still stretched from having been fucked. Pilot slid his cock back in and Tate lay beside them, so that he could get his mouth back on Bryce's cock. Pilot controlled the rhythm working in time with Tate.

He watched Bryce's face. His eyes closed and the tip of his tongue poked up out of his mouth, touching his upper lip. His dark brows dipped down over his eyes in concentration. Pilot's own orgasm grew in his stomach and the small of his back. He could feel it tingling and he needed to chase it. He snapped his hips, his thighs and ass working hard.

Bryce called out, his eyes flying open and ecstasy molding his expression into something entirely new. His ass clamped down hard as he came, jerking into Tate's mouth. Pilot didn't have to chase anything then. His orgasm barreled over him. He exploded into the condom. His arms shook and he lowered himself down onto Bryce, who promptly wrapped his legs around Pilot's waist.

Both Tate and Bryce kissed his face and sweaty hair. "God, turn the air on."

He could feel Bryce laughing under him and Tate joined in, pushing at Pilot's shoulder. "Don't squish my boy, bunny."

Then, they were wrestling, Tate and Bryce ganging up on Pilot. He let them pin him to the bed. His reward for that was more kisses, pecks all over his face and two tongues licking into his mouth. His arms circled them both, one on the left and one on the right—where they belonged.

When the laughter and kisses subsided and breathing returned to normal, Pilot could feel their hearts beating against his side. "This is it for me. You two. We share each other, but only us. No one else."

"Of course," Tate scoffed.

Pilot felt Bryce's eyelashes brushing quickly against his shoulder. "Only you, Sean, Tate. I could never want anything else. I don't know why, but this is perfect. Thank you."

Chapter 36 – March, New Jersey

Pilot crossed his arms over his chest. He was hot in combat boots, loose jeans, and long sleeve t-shirt, but he couldn't complain because Tate and Davey were decked out in their race gear and they had to be hotter than him, yet they never complained. He wiped his forehead and searched the immediate area.

Tyler and Mickey bantered back and forth while working on the bikes, Davey's and their 250 racer's. Bryce watched them, interested, his blue eyes taking in every move they made and asking questions about shit Pilot was clueless about.

Bryce wouldn't be racing, since this wasn't his division. The 250 East racers were on the track and they didn't race both East and West at the same time. That gave Bryce extra time to heal, but Pilot could easily see his frustration at not being on the track. Bryce needed to be on the back of a bike, just like Tate and Davey. Maybe that need, that drive, made them different than others that rode dirt bikes, but never made it to this level of competition. That need had them living and breathing bikes, and when they weren't on the track, more often than not, they were working out.

Bryce had started practicing on their off time and that helped his mood a lot. Watching the Apex mechanics seemed to help him, too.

Pilot made a mental note to buy him some tools so he could work on bikes during the off season. *Oh!* And a bike to work on. He figured he could afford a cheap, used one for him to practice on. Why not? Hell, Johnny was right about having people in his life that made him happy. Otherwise, saving all that money wasn't really worth it. His dream wouldn't mean half as much, and making Bryce and Tate happy meant everything to him, so buying something for Bryce to work on would be a small but important thing to do. Maybe it would help that dynamic of their relationship. He still didn't always feel close enough to Bryce.

In the glow of his crazy three-way relationship, he realized how lonely he'd been before. Working at the gym, fighting, and his security job really didn't fulfill him like these two young men did. He felt more relaxed and that ever present need to rip someone's head in had left him. He'd felt that tense aggression since leaving the service. It was like no matter what he did, he wasn't doing enough. He felt like he had to fight every second of every day to stay in control, or his whole world would come crashing down around him. The fighting had helped with that, but not nearly as much as being with Tate and Bryce had. He couldn't regret leaving the underground fighting.

"What are you smiling about, big-guy?" Mickey asked, pointing a greasy wrench at him.

Pilot let his smile morph into a smirk. "Wouldn't you like to know?" He winked. Mickey was fun to flirt with. He was straight and that made him safe, but he was also up for it—a real joker.

"Uh, no. Maybe I wouldn't." He looked over at Bryce who shared Pilot's smirk.

Tyler laughed. "I can just imagine! Sure you don't want details, Mick?" He wiggled his eyebrows, playfully.

For once, Mickey didn't seem to have a smart come back. "Uh..."

"It's pretty hot!" Pilot laughed, as Mickey's face turned pink.

He held up his wrench. "No. Uh, I'll take a pass on that one. You dirty dog."

"Very dirty," Bryce commented.

Mickey shook his head. "Fuck this. I'm getting back to work."

Tyler burst out laughing. "Now I know the secret."

"What secret?" Mickey asked, scowling.

"The secret to get you to shut up and work. Just start talking about gay sex."

Mickey's face flushed with pink again, darker this time. "Oh, God! Shut up."

Tyler and Bryce laughed even harder and Pilot couldn't help but laugh too.

"What's so funny over here?" Angel asked walking up with Stewart at her side.

Pilot shook his head, sure the blush had spread all over his face for them all to see. He didn't want to share the joke with Angel. She was his boss on this job.

Tyler piped up. "Nothing. Inside joke." He waved his wrench, as if to tell them to ignore their shenanigans. Pilot felt grateful to Tyler for that and relieved that they backed him on it, keeping it to themselves.

"Okay, fine." Angel scowled, but Stewart just chuckled. He probably figured it was a guy thing, and it was, but probably not like he was thinking. Pilot bit his bottom lip to stop himself from laughing more.

Before they could dig into it further, Angel's cell phone chimed. She scowled again and answered it. "Angel."

Pause.

"Yeah? Fuck. Send it over." Pilot had never known a woman to have such foul language. Angel dropped the f-bomb like it was her favorite word. "That fucker!" Maybe it was.

"What's up?" Tyler asked, setting down his tools and picking up a rag to wipe his hands.

"So, our private eye guy...wait." She tapped at her phone and swore under her breath. "He caught our good friend Shannon Parker paying off one of the 250 riders."

"Paying them for what?" Pilot asked.

She kept flipping through her phone. "Well, the PI, Slaughter, followed the rider. He spray painted your hotel door, Pilot, sorry. But, what else he's supposed to do, we don't know, nor do we want to find out. At least not by just watching him."

"So what now?" Bryce asked, his face darkened with anger. Pilot understood how he felt. These attacks were personal.

"Yeah, good question." Pilot tucked his hands in his pockets, gaining control, before they hit something solid like a toolbox or the side of the rig.

Angel finally looked up from her phone. "I forwarded the pics. Evidence." She grinned like she'd just got away with something she wasn't supposed to do. "Sent them to the race officials and Slaughter took the information to the cops. They're arresting the 250 guy now."

"Okay, what about Parker?" Pilot wanted to go beat the shit out of the fucker.

"He's on the track right now."

That didn't make Pilot happy. Tate was also in that heat. Pilot couldn't hold back a snarl.

"Come on." Tyler said. "We need to go watch the race. It should be starting, like now. Davey's bike is good to go. He'll be here..." Tyler looked at his watch. "In about twenty minutes, Mick. You can handle it."

Mickey nodded, nothing but serious now, while the rest of them headed for the track. If Shannon Parker fucked with Tate, he was going to be sorry.

The race went smoothly. Tate won and Parker couldn't even keep up. Tyler gave Pilot and Bryce high-fives and they greeted Tate and his mechanic, Andrew, when they rode toward the press station. When he finished talking to the press, Tyler filled him in on what was happening.

"What did he spray on our door?"

Angel pursed her lips like she didn't want to say. Stewart bumped his shoulder into hers. "Fine," she gave in with a heavy sigh. "Die faggots."

Pilot growled. "I'm gonna—"

"Nothing. You're going to do nothing." Tate glared at him. "You don't put yourself in danger." He pointed his gloved finger at Pilot. He was right.

Pilot held up his hands.

"Stop it. We're letting the officials handle it. Look." She pointed and they all turned to look just in time to see track security, escorting Parker off the track. His mechanic took his bike, so he could go with them.

"This is going to make his sponsors happy." Tyler's smile almost looked evil. "And *that* should keep his ass off the track. Hopefully. This time."

"Come on." Angel pulled at Stewart's jersey, but she indicated all of them with her head nod. They followed her back to the pit. She checked her phone again. "The 250 kid squealed."

"Who was that?" Tate asked.

Angel looked down at her phone again. "Uh...Ethan Bowers."

Tate made growling noise. "Fucker."

"You think that pisses you off? Listen." Angel flipped through her phone and started reading. "He said Parker paid him three grand to spray paint the door and then wait until they showed up. Then, he was supposed to attack Tate again. But, he wasn't the guy that did it the first time. They arrested a second person with him. This other guy, uh, Tanner, Warren Tanner, was supposed to hold Bryce back." She looked up with a quizzical expression. "I don't think they realized you'd be with them, Pilot. That would have been something to see."

Pilot wasn't listening to her anymore. He was looking at Bryce. His face had paled and he looked like he was going to puke. Tanner was the guy that had been stalking him. Pilot pushed passed Tate and Tyler and pulled Bryce into his arms, hugging him tight to his chest. If anything happened to him...

He kissed the top of Bryce's head, not wanting to even think about anything happening to him.

Tate filled the others in on the guy and Angel started clicking away at her phone again. "Shit! They let him go. They didn't connect the dots fast enough. I'm filling them in."

Bryce started shaking in Pilot's arms. "It's okay, baby. They'll get him."

"I'm so sorry," Bryce cried into Pilot's chest.

Tate came up beside them, rubbing Bryce's back. "Uh-uh. We talked about this. None of this is your fault. It's all on Tanner. And Parker."

Pilot swallowed his rage back. He wanted to kill both of the motherfuckers. He'd take apart anyone who threatened Tate and Bryce.

"Relax, Pilot," Tyler said, grabbing his attention.

Tyler was right. Pilot had bared his teeth and clenched his jaw, but he couldn't lose it. He had to be there for Bryce.

Chapter 37 – New Jersey

Shannon Parker was so angry, he felt like a rabid dog. He wanted to bite and scratch and punch and kick. Anything to get these fuckers to listen to him. He railed at them to no avail. They glared and shrugged and acted like Parker had done something wrong. He hadn't done anything wrong...those faggot-bastards deserved worse than what he'd dished out. "It's your responsibility to keep this sport clean. How can we race with these...these abominations on the track?" He poked the desk in front of him with his index finger.

"Sir, I think you need to keep quiet until your team arrives." The asshole looked at him over the edge of his glasses that he'd slipped on when they'd entered the trailer. To hell with them. He sat back to wait for his team. They would set these assholes straight.

The next time the door opened, it was Mr. Wolfe and his agent, Peri. They scowled at him just like the other Supercross officials. What the hell? They were supposed to be on his side. "Peri? Tell them this is bullshit."

Peri crossed his arms over his chest, looking very unhappy, but it was Mr. Wolfe who spoke up. "We've reviewed the charges, Parker."

"So?"

"Are they lying?"

"No, but that hardly matters." Shannon stood up.

"You little prick." Jack Wolfe snarled his words at him, taking him off-guard. "You think you get to decide who can race? Didn't I ask you to knock this shit off and just race? You couldn't do that. Is it really that you're the biggest homophobe on earth or are you just hiding behind that front because you can't beat them on the track?"

"Jack..." For a moment Peri seemed like he would come to Shannon's defense. "This fucker is not even worth it. Let's go."

"What? You're abandoning me? I thought we had a deal?"

Mr. Wolf shook his head. "You broke the deal when you started paying people to hurt other racers. By the way...I'm gay." He pointed at Shannon and narrowed his eyes. "And you're finished in this business. I hope you rot in jail."

The two men turned to go. "Oh, that fuckin' figures." He followed them outside the trailer and made it to the bottom of the stairs before the Apex team walked up with two police officers. "Oh, bullshit."

That Apex bitch smirked at him like she'd managed to pull this shit off by herself. "You cunt. This shit is not going stick. This is all bullshit."

"You don't deserve to race with these guys, Parker." The big guy with her, pulled her out of the way while the cops stepped forward and started reading off his rights.

"Fucking whatever." Shannon held his hands out. He wasn't going to fight the police. He'd just call...who the hell would he call? He'd spent most of the money he'd made on hiring that punk-snitch to do the dirty work. The only people to call were Wolfe and Peri. Fuck that shit.

The cops started walking him off and he heard Wolfe apologize to the Apex bitch. Go figure. Those assholes just didn't get it. The world was going to hell.

Chapter 38 – Between Races, Denver

Pilot let himself in the house and pulled off his tie. He hated wearing the damn thing, but sometimes the job required it. He'd spent the day with their forensics team doing a threat assessment for a new high-rise office building that was soon to open its doors. He needed to meet with the CEO several times to go over, not only the electronic aspects of security, but the overall building as well. He had to review the parking garage and reception area, the elevators, the roof, and the penthouse where the CEO wanted to keep an apartment. That made things trickier, but he'd been thorough and so had the rest of the team. They'd agreed to setting up a few more cameras and a 24/7 staff of at least two men to maintain it all and work with the companies own IT staff to ensure it all tied in together. Intricate, complicated, brain work, and it made Pilot a hell of a lot more tired than just simply shadowing someone.

He stripped his button up shirt off and tossed it over the couch. It was Spring and Pilot was thankful for the warmer weather, but that also meant his guys weren't home yet. They'd be trying to get extra time in at the track where they practiced.

Tate's coach, Joey, and Bryce's coach Reuben, would be in town to work with them the following day, but that didn't mean they'd slack off at all. The guys only had a few days in between races to get practice time in, and Pilot just had to get used to both Tate and Bryce and their determination. He admired it, even if he missed them when they were gone to the track without him.

He flipped the light on in the kitchen and opened the fridge. It was empty. They'd have to do take out again and he knew the guys hated that. It was hard to find food that met their requirements. Everything had to be ordered with the sauce on the side, and heaven help them all if the place got the order wrong. It was never just as simply as take out order or pizza. Hell, living with two supreme athletes had put Pilot on the same diet, and he'd kill a bitch for a slice of pizza or a greasy burger. He grabbed a bottle of water and shut the fridge. They really needed to break down and get some groceries.

Before he could think much more about it, the front door flew open, accompanied by raucous laughter and the sound of equipment hitting the floor. Pilot circled back to the front room. "Hey, guys."

"Pilot, hey!" Tate pulled off his boots, dropping them right next to a pile of shin guards and helmets and gloves.

"This isn't an equipment room." Pilot could feel the frustration boiling over. "You're gonna kill someone if you leave that shit there."

Tate had the decency to look down at it, but it was Bryce that started picking it up.

"Put it in the garage or just leave it in the truck."

Bryce nudged the door open. "I'll just put it in the truck. We've got an early start tomorrow anyway." He carried a load out the door.

"Damn," Tate said crossing his arms and kicking off his other boot. "Did ya have a bad day?"

"No, not really. But, I'm tired and this is just..."

"Sorry. You don't have to yell at us though. We aren't children."

Pilot waved his water bottle at the remaining equipment on the floor. "You act like it, though."

"Seriously, what's bothering you? Really." Tate raised an eyebrow at him.

"Fuck. This just isn't how I imagined things would be."

"What'd you think. We'd be fucking all the time? Running around half naked, playing grab ass."

"No, but—"

"We may have unconventional jobs, but we still have a life. We still have to work. Shit, it's fun, but it's still work. We get paid to be in top condition, not to be Pilot's personal harem."

"I know. I didn't mean it like that. It's just that we need some rules around here."

"Rules?"

Bryce came back in and glanced between them quickly, before grabbing the rest of the gear and heading back outside.

"You just let him do all that work, Tate."

"I didn't tell him to do it. You did." For a second Tate stared him down, the brave fucker. "I don't know why you think we need rules. I thought things were fine. What the hell kinda rules do you want, Pilot?"

"I don't know. Just. This all feels out of control. You need to eat right, but there's no food in the house. When we do eat, someone needs to clean up and not leave the dishes. Hell, Tate, you leave your shit everywhere."

"Oh. So you want a chore list?"

Bryce walked in and shoved the door shut. "I don't mind a chore list."

Tate stepped forward to give Bryce room to take off his boots. "Why don't we just make the youngest do everything then."

"What?" Pilot asked at the same time Bryce said, "That's bullshit."

Pilot was glad he was sticking up for himself a little. Bryce had been the odd factor in all of this and the kid was sweet, but it changed everything. "Look. We're not making anyone do anything, but with three adults in the house now, we're gonna be stepping on each other and shit. We just need to make things go smoother. That's all I'm saying."

"You want me to leave?" Bryce dropped one boot to the floor, his other foot stalled in the air, boot still on.

"No. No way. That's not what I'm saying. Come on, guys."

A smarmy grin crossed Tate's face. "You think we're ganging up on you. Don't you? Are you feelin' left out, boss?"

"No. Seriously, Tate. I'm just aggravated at how things have been going."

Bryce's second boot finally dropped. "How things have been going how? With our schedules? Cleaning the house? In the bedroom?"

Pilot groaned. "Not in the bedroom. This isn't about sex."

"Then, what's it about?" Bryce leaned up against Tate. He was almost as tall and just as thin. What had Pilot done to end up with not one, but two sassy-mouthed riders? His life would never be the same, but he didn't care. He was willing to compromise, but most of the concessions had been his deferral to their needs for their careers. He was okay with that, but he still needed order in the house.

"Okay, just listen. I'm not talking about writing up a bunch of do's and don'ts or making a chore list. I just think we need some guidelines. For all of us. Because I need things to go smoother, but it should benefit you two, too..."

"How so?" Tate asked.

"Well, for starters...we never bothered to pick up groceries, so..."

"Ugh," Bryce groaned. "Take out again." He shoved past Tate and Pilot, and started rooting around the papers on the breakfast bar. "I'm starving. Where's the menus?"

Pilot pointed at him. "That's another thing. If we were more organized, we'd know where they are and we'd know what we wanted from where and could place an order quickly."

"Fine," Tate grumbled. "We can get organized and have guidelines, but I think Bryce and I need to gang up on you a few times a week. Put that in your guidelines."

"What?" Pilot didn't have a clue what he meant, but obviously Bryce did.

"Yeah! Gang up on Pilot day. Starts now." He abandoned his search for the menu and lunged at Pilot, grabbing him around the waist. Simultaneously, Tate jumped at him, grabbing his shoulders.

They really meant gang up on him. "Fine, Fine. But, it also means, we get tickle Bryce day." He leaned forward and started tickling Bryce under the arms. Tate was slumped over Pilot's shoulders, and hanging on for life as they all started bucking around.

Bryce squealed and Tate laughed and they all fell over the arm of the couch. "Not so easy ganging up on me is it?"

"No, but it's fun," Tate breathed out.

Bryce caught his breath and leaned forward. Pilot's leg was wrapped around his hip. "Pilot?" he asked with a new seriousness in his deep, blue eyes. "What about everything else? The important stuff?"

Tate shoved Pilot's head off his lap. "What do you mean?"

"Well. Not this running the house bullshit. Not the sex, I know that's awesome. I mean...you know. The relationship stuff. The feelings. I know how I feel about y'all, but..."

"Do you think we don't like you?" Tate asked.

"Do you still want me here?" Bryce countered.

Pilot bit his lip. Things weren't how he'd thought, but he'd grown attached to Bryce despite everything. He sometimes felt jealous of the way they had a connection that he didn't seem to share, at least his connection with Bryce wasn't as strong as Tate's was with Bryce. Yet, he didn't want to go back to living without him either. "I want you here. I want both of you."

Bryce rewarded him with a shy smile and Tate beamed with happiness. Then, he tackled Bryce. Despite a few tummies rumbling, they seemed to be more interested in playing around. The wrestling turned serious and quickly morphed to kissing and taking clothes off.

Pilot grabbed one hand from each of them and tugged them into the bedroom where they'd be more comfortable. He was never more pleased that he had a huge California King sized bed, perfect for skin on skin on skin contact.

Chapter 39 – March, Indianapolis

Bryce had been having a super day hanging out with the Apex team and Pilot. He loved watching Tate race, too. They'd practiced some during their off time and Tate was quick to give him all kinds of pointers that would help him. Bryce couldn't wait to get back on the bike, on the dirt, for race day. He still had a few races on the East Coast to wait out, but when they were back in the West, he'd be ready. His team had sent him a new bike that he'd been practicing on, so he knew he was good to go, and beyond ready to be racing. He had worried about his team a little, afraid they'd drop him after the injury, but Tate had been right. They wanted him to keep racing.

Now that Parker had been arrested, they could relax some, but until they found Tanner, he felt like their life was still set at Defcon 1. Pilot seemed on edge because of it.

"Hey, you ready to go? The Main Event is about to start." Pilot grabbed Bryce, holding him tight, but leaving him unsure if Pilot was just loving him or accidentally strangling him. But, no. He was angry that Tanner had threatened him and was still loose. He acted like he couldn't stand letting Bryce out of his sight, and he'd been doing that tight hug thing a lot the last few days.

"Yeah."

Almost everyone in the pit was getting ready to go down to the track to watch both Tate and Davey race. They were amazing to watch together, like they were born to ride with each other. Some of that probably came from training together, but part of it was just that they were both so talented and driven.

Pilot grabbed Bryce's hand and laced their fingers together. This was a side of Pilot that Bryce hadn't seen much of, and his face must have shown his surprise. "Don't look at me like that. I'm sweet."

"I guess, when you want to be."

Pilot leaned over and kissed the side of Bryce's head. "I want to be." He led Bryce out of the pit area set up in the parking lot and into the main stadium. They'd be able to watch from the edges of the stadium seating, close to the track.

"I'm glad and I get it, but I'm not going to just disappear on you."

"I know. Humor me."

Tyler walked up beside them and nudged Pilot's arm. "Protective much?"

Pilot just growled at him and Angel busted out laughing.

Bryce shook his head. He would put up with the behavior until they caught Tanner. It made him feel better anyway. Made him feel protected, but more than that, it made him feel like he meant something to Pilot. He meant more than just a sexy fuck to share with Tate. Since he'd been back, both Pilot and Tate had gone out of their way to make him feel included. He hoped they'd get to the point where he just felt included without trying, though.

When they got to the track, he stood close to Pilot, but let go of his hand. He was too excited when the gates dropped and Davey and Tate raced neck and neck, but Bryce knew something that probably no one else did. The stress of the situation and the issues that Tate faced made him race better. There was no way in hell Tate could lose this one, despite Davey's best efforts. Tate put all his shit—stress, fears, worry, all of it—on the dirt. Bryce had seen it when they practiced. He understood it. Tate became a better racer because the dirt flowed in his veins, was a part of him, and he sacrificed all his problems, all his love, all his fears to the track.

"Damn! Look at that. I don't know who to root for." Angel hollered and put her arm around Bryce, shaking him a little. "Tate is kicking serious ass out there. Come on, Davey!"

Bryce relaxed in her grip. He really liked the Apex team. They felt more like a family than a race team. His team was good, professional, and he liked everyone and got along with everyone—even after they found out he was gay, which was inevitable after Tate had been attacked. But, they weren't like this. Here with Apex there was more than just getting along professionally. They shared a genuine fondness for each other. Even the girl they had racing 250s, Bolster. She was quiet and didn't hang out as much, but they all treated her like a sister when she did get to hang around. She was younger, still a minor, so her parents were with her a lot. Bryce knew what that was like. He'd only just left his own parents. That connection helped them get along, and they were starting to become friends.

He basked in the glow, enjoying the race, thinking of how his life had gotten so much better, even with the Tanner issue still hanging over their heads. Tate and Pilot were awesome boyfriends and they were just getting started.

The race wound down to the final two laps. Excitement joined the warm feeling in his gut and Bryce stretched up on his toes. "Go, Tate!" he screamed, even though he knew Tate couldn't hear him.

The crowd cheered wildly. Everyone loved Davey. He was like the boy next door, but Tate had been proving himself on the track this season, and it was exciting to watch these two go head to head. Tate played the underdog, giving it his all. Davey was the golden boy champion, determined to hold on to that red "one" plate. The press and the fans ate it up. This race was no different. In fact, they proved their prowess on the track with each turn and jump.

They ripped through the final rhythm section and onto the main straight that led to the finish line. Tate out maneuvered Davey, pulling ahead. He stayed on the throttle hard and in the next set of jumps, he scrubbed a triple, but Davey didn't and that put him another half second behind. Tate could to do it. Bryce knew it. He was totally focused on the race, when someone grabbed his arm and spun him around.

"I'm gonna kill you for what you've done to me. Faggot!"

Warren Tanner.

Bryce's eyes went wide and his heart lurched. He couldn't breathe. He took a step back, bumping into Pilot. Then Tanner's eyes went wide and he took off, pushing through the crowd. Pilot trailed right behind him.

"Shit! Shit!" Bryce grabbed Angel by the arm. "He's gone after Tanner!" He pointed in the direction they'd run. Angel stretched up to look and started cussing under her breath, then tapped on her phone.

Bryce's heart thumped wildly in his chest. "What do I do?"

"Stay here with Tony. I mean it." She pointed at him and then at Tony, who was Davey's personal driver. He was always around and he was a big guy, though not as big as Pilot.

Davey's bodyguard, Broady, stayed posted closer to the track in case either Davey or Tyler needed him there. Tyler was in the mechanic area with his whiteboard, helping Davey through the race. Stewart was up in the tower. Bryce knew he would be safe with Tony, but he suddenly felt alone. His hands trembled, so he shoved them in his pockets.

"It's going to be fine. Relax. Angel can handle her shit. Okay." Tony put his hand on Bryce's shoulder.

Bryce nodded and sucked his bottom lip in between his teeth. He tried to focus back on the race, but it was over. "Shit. Who won?"

A stranger leaned over. "Tate by seconds. How'd you miss that? It was incredible!"

Bryce didn't bother answering. "Come on." He nodded for Tony to follow him. They were going to see Tate and Davey and fill them in. He had to do something, or he'd be going after Pilot.

By the time they got to the press area, Tony had a text from Angel.

"They got him. Pilot held the fucker down until the cops came. I don't know how he held himself back, but he didn't beat the fucker's head in or anything. Just held him down."

Bryce nodded and pushed through to where Tate stood with a headset on, talking to the press. Bryce didn't care about any of that. He needed comfort from his boyfriend. He pushed between two camera men and their crew and launched himself at Tate.

"What is it?" Tate asked, wrapping his arms around Bryce without any hesitation. He could hear the reporters in the background going nuts, asking if they were boyfriends. Tate ignored them and cupped Bryce's cheek. Tears had leaked out. "God what?"

"They caught him. Tanner. Pilot caught him."

Tate pulled him in tighter. "Thank, God."

The reporters screamed out their names and questions all at the same time. Tate must have realized the chaos was building around them. "Sorry. This is personal. You'll have to talk to the Apex team for an official statement. We have to go." He pulled the headset off and thrust it at some guy, probably an assistant, not looking to see if he caught it. Then they left, Davey, Tyler, Broady and Tony right behind them.

Pilot's heart hammered more from the anger boiling through his veins than from the effort it took to chase after the ass wipe. Tanner was not getting away if Pilot had anything to do with it. He pushed through the crowd, watching as Tanner shoved people out of the way. He closed the gap between them with every long stride.

Near the end of the row of race pits, he could see Tanner only a few feet in front of him, and the crowd broke. Before he could sprint away, Pilot turned on the speed and lunged for him as soon as he was close enough. He grabbed at Tanner's shoulders, throwing his force into his back. He used his signature move from fighting to tangle their feet and legs, tumbling them both to the ground with Pilot on top.

Tanner twisted and fought to get loose, but Pilot shoved his face into the ground. He wanted to really hurt the bastard, but he knew he wouldn't get away with it. Angel had no doubt already called security. Pilot put his knee in the small of his back and grabbed his arms, pulling them just enough to get Tanner's attention.

"Get off of me fucker!"

"I don't think so. You're lucky this happened here. I really want to take you apart limb from limb. Very slowly and with a lot of pain."

Tanner said something else, but it was muffled, his face still pretty much in the dirt.

He shook his arms. "What was that dick face?"

"Said I didn't do anything to you. Didn't do anything to McAllister, either."

"Hmm...you must know who I am then."

"Fucking Apex bodyguard. Yeah, I know."

"Well, smartass, do you know that Bryce and Tate are my boyfriends? Mine. When you fuck with them, you fuck with me."

"Oh, shit...perverts...all of you."

Pilot pulled his arms tighter, making Tanner squeal. "You are sick, dude. The only thing perverted is how you've been obsessing over Bryce and Tate. That is not fucking normal. And guess what...you're going to jail now."

Tanner started struggling again, jerking his shoulders and hips.

"Oh, no. Stay the fuck down, Tanner, or I will hurt you." Pilot gave a little more pressure with his weight on his knee and Tanner stilled. "Please, give me a reason."

"This is Tate's fault," he complained. "He made me like this. He made me fuck him. Then I couldn't stop thinking about him. Fucking Tate Jordan."

Furious did not even begin to name the rage flowing through Pilot. He didn't want to believe Tate had ever had anything to do with his creep, didn't want to even think about his hands on Tate, much less any other part of his anatomy. He leaned forward and gripped Tanner's arms harder. Pilot's finger wrapped almost completely around his skinny biceps. He wanted to rip them out of the sockets.

"We've got it from here, Mr. Mahan. Stand down."

"Mission fucking accomplished." Pilot let Tanner go so the security team could slap him into handcuffs, but he wasn't happy about any of it.

Later that evening, Pilot met the guys back at the hotel room. He came in carrying ice cream and paper bowls he'd picked up at the grocery store.

"It's ice cream time!" he called out. Bryce and Tate helped dish out the treat and Pilot sprinkled extra marshmallows over the top. "Rocky-fucking-road for everybody."

They sat on the bed, cross-legged, eating their treat. Neither of the guys complained about it either, which was a first. He guessed after the day they'd had, all of them needed something, but Pilot couldn't get his mind off of what Tanner had said. "Can I ask you something, Tate?"

"Of course." He spooned another bite in his mouth.

He watched Tate lick the ice cream from the spoon. He didn't want to bring it up, but he couldn't let it go. "I have to ask you. I have to get it out in the open. It's driving me nuts."

Tate's brows pinched together. "What is it? Just say it."

"Tanner said—"

"Oh." Tate put his spoon in his bowl and studied it like it was the only thing in the room. He clenched his jaw so tightly, Pilot was afraid he'd bust a tooth.

Bryce stretched his foot out, tapping Pilot's thigh. "What?"

Pilot pursed his lips together. He knew what Tate was going to say and it had to be true by the look on Tate's face. He looked like he wanted to puke or punch someone—like he was guilty. It still had to be said. "Did you fuck him?" he finally blurted out.

Tate sighed. His shoulders slumped, as if all the fight just left him. "If you want to call it that. It was more like he used me to get off and I was in a really dark place, so I didn't fight it."

Bryce's eyes grew wide. "You let him..."

Tate stood up with a huff and put his bowl in the hotel sink. "I wouldn't say let him. Wasn't really like that."

Pilot could feel the heat creeping over his face. "If he raped you—"

"I wouldn't call it that either. It was more that it didn't turn out how I thought it would and by the time things got rolling, I couldn't stop it."

Fury buzzed through Pilot. "That sounds like date rape, Tate. You should have told someone."

"Told them what? That I let that ass-hat fuck me? That I took it up the ass? Willingly. Then, changed my mind when I realized what an ass he was and that the only thing he cared about was getting his fucking rocks off? No. I wasn't about to tell anyone that I let him use me like that. Fuck that."

Bryce put his ice cream on the bedside table and stood up to wrap his arms around Tate. At first, Tate tried to push him away. He was obviously mad, but he gave in quickly and Bryce wrapped himself around Tate, kissing his cheek and neck with little soft pecks. "It's okay, Tate," he murmured softly.

Watching Bryce and his gentle, loving way, dispelled all the anger he'd been holding onto. It just fell away like the bottom falling out of a bucket of water. Pilot crossed the room and added his arms to the hug, surrounding both of them. "I'm sorry, Tate."

Tate shrugged them off. "I'm sorry. About all of it. It's my fault. All of it."

Bryce's blue eyes were wet with unshed tears. "No. It's Tanner's fault. We love you, Tate. This doesn't change that. At all."

Tate looked up at Pilot for that same confirmation with need shining so brightly, even a jackass like Pilot couldn't miss it. "He's right, Tate. Doesn't change anything. Maybe it makes me love you more. I love you both."

"I love you guys, too. Thank you." Tate's voice was soft and serious and still hurting. Pilot, determined to remove that hurt, bent his head and kissed Tate, gentle at first, but quickly turning it into passion.

Bryce's tongue snaked in between them, bold and demanding. It made Pilot's cock hard. He wanted both of them naked. "Let's go to bed."

Chapter 40 – April, Between Races, Denver

Tate unlocked the door and they dumped their gear on the floor, even though they knew it irritated Pilot. The area had still ended up as a mud room slash storage area for motocross crap. "Damn. I'll clean that up later."

"I'll help. Guess Pilot's not home yet?"

Tate shook his head. "Let's get cleaned up while we wait." He took Bryce's hand and led him into the bathroom where they stripped out of the rest of their gear, pants, shirts, and shoes. Tate turned the water on.

"I had fun today." Bryce stepped in the shower, while Tate watched his sexy ass.

It had been a good day. Tate liked practicing with Bryce and watching him improve on the track, but he liked watching his naked body in the shower even better. He got in and grabbed the soap bar, lathering it between his hands. He couldn't wait to get them on Bryce. "You looked good out there today. Come here."

Bryce stepped a little closer and Tate rubbed his shoulders and down his chest with soap. Bryce smirked at him, as if he knew something Tate didn't, but Tate knew. "Watching me ride or watching my ass?"

"Both," he laughed and continued lathering Bryce's body, his hips, and around to his ass, pointedly ignoring his cock and balls. The suds sluiced down his legs. Bryce had a similar build to Tate, all long, lean muscle. His abs and legs were well-defined with no fat at all. He thought Bryce might look better with just a little cushion, but that wasn't going to happen any time soon with Bryce on the same type of diet and workout schedule that Tate had. They had to keep in top shape. Had to stay away from Pilot's ice cream fests for sure!

Tate nudged Bryce's shoulders, turning him around to face the tiles, and finally slid his hands around to glide over Bryce's balls, then up and down his already hard shaft. Tate nudged his nose under Bryce's ear. "I'm hungry now," he whispered, making Bryce shiver.

"I'm not stopping you."

Tate couldn't help the snort of laughter that came out. He loved how brazen Bryce could be at times. He looked like the sweetest fruit in the bowl, but he could be tart. "You're like a kiwi."

Bryce giggled. "What?"

"Never mind. Turn around." Tate shoved Bryce toward the tile, so his shoulders pressed against the cold wall, then Tate sank to the floor. He sat on his ass, saving his knees, and leaned up, licking under Bryce's balls and the base of his cock. "Do you like that?" he asked when Bryce moaned.

Tate looked up at Bryce. His eyes fluttered, half lidded and his pink lips parted. He didn't answer in words, just thrust his hips a little, encouraging Tate to do more. He licked at the mushroom shaped head. It was peachy and tasty, hot on Tate's tongue. He wanted to do more, but the shower floor would kill his knees, if he got up on them. "Fuck it. Rinse off."

"What?" Bryce looked at him, confused.

"The floor is just too hard." Tate soaped his own shoulders, until Bryce grabbed the bar from him.

"I've got this. My turn." Bryce proceeded to wash Tate, just as he'd done. His touch was just heavy enough to get the dirt off, but his fingers skimmed lightly over Tate's belly and down to his own hard dick. "I like this." He stroked Tate's cock with soapy fingers. His calloused hands rubbed over his body with nimble fingers, not overly long, but proportioned perfectly, and they felt wonderful on Tate's body.

Neither of them got off in the shower. They rinsed and grabbed a few towels to dry. Bryce padded into the bedroom and rummaged through the drawer of the big dresser that Pilot had designated for him. "Hey! Where're my jammies?"

"Uh...the dryer maybe?"

Tate watched Bryce dash out of the bedroom naked, heading for the laundry room. He chuckled to himself and pulled on a pair of loose sweat pants. He scrubbed at his hair with a towel and walked out to meet Bryce in the living room.

Bryce came in wearing the orange and black striped pajamas, complete with hoodie on and tiger ears up.

"You're so fucking adorable." Tate couldn't help but smile.

"Shut up. You still hungry? I can give you a hot dog." He grabbed his crotch and Tate lunged for him, but Bryce took off around the couch. Tate chased him for a minute or two, noticing how evenly matched they were physically. On the bikes, Tate had the advantage, but around the living room, Bryce moved just as fast as he did, if not faster.

Finally giving up, Tate plopped down on the couch. "Want to watch a movie?"

"As long as there's snuggling."

"Oh, there's snuggling, wonder-boy."

They put *Fast Seven* in and cuddled up on the couch. Tate watched Bryce as much as the movie, still surprised that they had worked him into their lives so easily. He fit like the piece of the puzzle that had been missing. The three of them were perfect together.

"Hey, Tate? Who's hotter? The Rock or Vin Diesel?"

"Hmm...they're both pretty hot with their bad boy attitudes and all those muscles. The Rock is bigger though. I like his eyebrow thing."

"Yeah." Bryce wiggled around, getting comfortable in Tate's arms. "Who's hotter The Rock or Pilot?"

Tate almost burst out laughing, but held it back when Bryce glared at him. He was serious, at least somewhat serious. "Pilot's hotter. I can put my hands on him."

"And your mouth."

"Yep." Tate put his mouth on the side of Bryce's neck, making him wiggle a little more.

When he settled down, Bryce said, "Seriously, though. I've always liked big guys like that. You know, all that muscle is so sexy, but I never thought I'd end up with someone so big in real life."

"He is big. His biceps are bigger than my head."

"Totally." They both laughed softly.

Bryce sighed. "Seriously, I thought he was going to tear my asshole up. But, uh...he didn't. He was so gentle. You know?"

"Yes. He's like the gentle-fucking-giant." Tate chuckled at his own joke, though it wasn't very funny. Bryce looked up at him with heat in his blue eyes, making them darker. "I wouldn't hurt you either. Do you want it? How do you want me to fuck you Bryce?"

Bryce pulled away, half sitting on the edge of the couch. He bit his bottom lip, and it was too much for Tate. He tackled Bryce, pushing him down into the sofa and covering Bryce's mouth with his lips. His tongue plunged into wet heat. Bryce tasted like granola and passion and home. His hands dug into Bryce's black hair, pushing his hoodie off his head. He ground his hips into Bryce and Bryce ground back, thrusting their cocks together with just enough friction to make him crazy. "God, I want you. All the time."

"I want you, too. Now...that's how I want it, Tate."

Tate could see the passion in Bryce's eyes, so deep blue, begging him for more. He leaned back in to take another kiss. He stood up and worked his sweat pants off, before helping Bryce pull his pajama top over his head. His tiger stripes hit the floor, leaving Bryce naked in front of him. Tate trailed his finger down the center of Bryce's chest. "Ready?"

"Yeah..."

There was lube in the entertainment consul that Pilot had stashed before, so he grabbed it and Bryce eased down into the couch, spreading his long, lean thighs and sexy as hell. He knelt beside the couch and sucked Bryce's cock. He could be happy doing that all day, but his own cock wanted more than that. He stopped and looked up at Bryce. His eyes were closed, and his mouth hung open.

Tate chuckled and squirted lube in his hand. He wanted to spend some time working Bryce open. He knew Bryce could take Pilot, and he was bigger than Tate, but he still wanted to make sure he was good and ready. Plus, it was just fun and sexy. His fingers worked their way in and out, plying and stretching his hole, and making him moan and writhe. "You're so sexy, Bryce."

"Mmm...more...come on...fuck!"

Tate took his reaction, and the thrust of his hips, as a sign to get a move on. He slicked up his cock and lined it up at Bryce's hole. Bryce put one leg up on the back of the couch and the other foot on the edge of the cushion. He lifted his ass as Tate pushed forward.

The tight heat clamped down on his cock as Tate waited for Bryce's body to get used to him. He wanted to explode with how hot he felt. He repositioned himself to his knees, holding Bryce up, but it was sort of difficult. He needed to spread his own legs wider for leverage and couldn't because of the couch. "God damn it!"

"Uh...you're not supposed to say that." Bryce laughed.

"Shut up. Turn over." He shoved Bryce's legs and moved back to let him get situated. When he had his face and shoulders down by the arm of the couch and his ass in the air, Tate smacked his ass. "Don't laugh at me, brat."

"Ah...I'm not. Come on."

Tate leaned over and kissed where he'd left a pink hand print. "Better?"

"Yeah...now fuck me."

Tate slid his cock back into Bryce's hole. This time he had enough leverage to move. He tilted his pelvis just a bit before thrusting long and hard, hands gripping Bryce's hip.

Bryce's moans sent a tingle down Tate's spine. He did that, made Bryce make that sound, and he wanted to hear it again and again. He fucked hard into his ass, and was rewarded with more groans of pleasure. He kept his control, barely, until Bryce completely came undone, making noises that Tate couldn't even name. He shuttered and his ass clenched up tight, making Tate moan in return.

The tingling spread from his cock to the small of his back and before he knew it, lighting sparked behind his eyes, as his body seized up. "Uh...Gah..." As he started to relax, he leaned over Bryce's back, and Bryce slid his legs down the couch, until Tate was lying on top of him, skin touching, chest to back, crotch to ass, legs on legs. "I swear my whole body was paralyzed for a minute."

"I feel your cum dripping..." Bryce giggled. "Down my butt cheek."

Tate giggled, too. "I like that. Mmm...entirely too much." He nuzzled the back of Bryce's dark hair.

"That tickles." Bryce wiggled around until they lay on their sides facing each other. After a few lingering kisses, Bryce tucked his head against Tate's chest.

They lay there together for a few minutes until the front door opened, and both of them jumped up to look over the couch to see Pilot come in. "What're y'all doing?"

Tate wasn't sure if Pilot would be mad or not. He raised his eyebrows, silently questioning, while Bryce stuttered something, but didn't really say anything at all. Pilot seemed stunned. He didn't say anything, but it seemed clear what they'd been doing.

"Uh, sorry, Pilot. We couldn't wait for you. I had to have him."

Bryce giggled a little. "Are we in trouble?"

Pilot laughed, his low voice booming through the room. "No...I'm not mad. You two are so fucking sexy and thinking about you together makes me hard."

Tate wiggled his eyebrows. "Well, join us then."

"I would, but then we'd never get anything done."

"How's Johnny?" Tate asked instead of acknowledging Pilot's comment. He knew he needed to change the subject before Pilot changed his mind and they all did get hot and heavy all over again.

"Good. We're good." He winked. Tate knew that their day together was about more than just hanging out, but he wasn't saying anything.

"Come out to the garage, guys." Pilot obviously couldn't wait to show Bryce what he'd done. That was fine with Tate.

Tate pulled on his sweats and chuckled as Bryce yanked on his pajama pants. He felt excitement building in his stomach and chest. He couldn't wait either and practically bounced his way through the kitchen to the interior door to the garage. "Easter Bunny! Woo-hoo! Hurry up, wonder-boy." He shoved Bryce's shoulder to get him to move faster.

Pilot flipped on the light and stepped out of the way to give Bryce the perfect view as he stepped barefoot onto the concrete floor of the garage. Tate followed right behind him.

"OhmyGod! What? What is this?"

A beat up old bike that had seen way too many better days was up on a stand next to a brand new, shiny, black and red tool box.

Pilot rubbed Bryce's shoulder. It seemed like he always wanted at least one hand on Bryce if they were in the same room together. That gave Tate a warm, happy feeling in his stomach. It meant that Pilot cared about Bryce as much as he did. There was no jealousy. It was just the way the three of them fit.

"I wanted to do something for you. Make this your home. This is your home, Bryce."

Tate could not stop the smile that broke out across his face. "Yep. Home." He'd thought that same thing just a few minutes before. Pilot looked over at Tate with so much love expressed on his face, it turned his ordinary features into something spectacular. Pilot knew what home meant to Tate, who had struggled with it for so long. He hoped Bryce knew too. "Go on then," Tate prompted him.

He pulled away from Pilot's huge hand and made his way across the floor. He checked out the bike first. Squatting down to look at it, as if afraid it would break if he touched it or got too close.

"You can't do any damage to this thing. I promise. It's for you to practice on. Play with. Whatever you want. Take the whole damn thing apart. It doesn't even matter if you don't get it back together. It's to learn on." Pilot waved an arm toward the machine.

Bryce's smile lit up his face, his eyes sparkled with happiness, and he jumped up and down.

Tate couldn't stand the anticipation of it all. "Check out the toolbox already."

"Okay." Bryce reluctantly turned from the bike to examine the red and black box. It had silver drawer handles down the front and the top lid opened up. He lifted it and peered in. "OhmyGod! What?"

Tate felt joy bubble up from inside and burst from his mouth. Bryce held up the dog tag charm on a silver chain that matched his and Pilot's. "Look!" Tate held his out and Bryce rushed over to read it. They'd had Bryce's name added to both of their charms and all three names engraved on Bryce's new one.

"This is incredible." His mouth hung open.

"You're a part of us. Always. If you want it." Pilot's hand creeped back up to Bryce's shoulder, and then to the back of his neck to finger the hair there that was getting a little too long.

"I want it. So bad. I want you. Both of you."

Tate grabbed Bryce, pulling him and Pilot into a three-way hug. "This is so incredible."

Pilot broke out of the hug first. "Come on. You can play with your new toys later, Bryce."

Tate took Bryce's hand and they followed Pilot through the house and into the bedroom. Tate felt a little nervous. They'd been together for a while, but this seemed suddenly new—real. Pilot's dog tag charms made their commitments into a solid, living and breathing thing in his mind. Tate wanted to jump right back into the hot and heavy sex, but he also wanted to take it slow and savor every second of their time together.

Pilot leaned over and kissed Bryce, reaching for his pajamas, while Tate slid his sweatpants off. For a moment, Tate stood there naked and vulnerable in front of his partners. In the next, Bryce was also naked. Pilot's eyes darted between them, as if he couldn't take in enough of them and couldn't decide which to look at. Tate and Bryce jumped forward at the same time, grabbing at Pilot's clothes. They worked together quickly to pull off his shirt and tug down his jeans. Pilot kicked off his Nikes and let his pants and underwear drop to the floor before nudging them toward the bed. "I need to touch you."

Bryce jumped on the bed, bouncing a little and giggling, so Tate jumped at him, pushing him down to the bed, landing on top of him. Bryce spread his legs so Tate could get in between them. As their bodies lined up, Tate took Bryce's mouth. He kissed Bryce with all the fierce passion he had inside, wanting to show him how much he needed. "Want...you," he mumbled between flicks of his tongue.

Pilot dropped lube and a handful of condoms next to them. "We need to get tested soon, so we can get rid of these."

"Oops." Bryce's eyes grew wide. In the dim afternoon light, Bryce's face with his dark eyebrows and smooth skin, looked like a dream. "We kind of beat you to it. Uh, earlier." Bryce shrugged and Tate tried to hold back a laugh and ended up snorting instead, which set Bryce off too.

"What?" Pilot knelt beside them, stroking his hand down Tate's back, making him shiver. "Well, didn't we just commit to being together? So..."

"Guys, uh...Bryce hasn't been with anyone else." Tate reminded them. "And we've been tested." He nodded between Pilot and himself.

"I'm good without it. I trust y'all," Bryce added. "Obviously."

Tate leaned in and kissed him again. "Me, too."

Pilot grabbed the condoms and tossed them to the floor. "Me, too." He leaned over and kissed Tate's neck. "I want to be inside you."

"Yes." Tate slid his legs out farther, straddling Bryce. Pilot smoothed his palms over Tate's ass. He pulled Tate's cheeks apart, then his hot tongue slid over Tate's hole. Wet and velvety, he pushed inside. Tate moaned and his eyes rolled to the back of his head.

"What's he doing?" Bryce asked. "I can't see."

"Rimming me. OhGodOhGod!" Tate groaned and pushed his ass back, wanting more of that moist, sultry bliss rubbing inside him.

Pilot chuckled, his face vibrating against Tate's skin.

Bryce leaned up and forced his tongue into Tate's mouth, rubbing against his lips and tongue. Tate didn't know how much he could take with one on each side, too much oral stimulation. His hips bucked as if they had a mind of their own and they wanted desperately to fuck something. His cock rubbed against Bryce's hip, and Bryce's cock was trapped between them, making him pant.

"Don't come," Tate said. "I want in you first."

"Yes!" Bryce and Pilot called out together.

Pilot gently shoved Tate over and reached for the lube. "You fuck him while I'm fucking you. Yes!"

"Okay." Tate couldn't hold back his smile. He loved seeing Pilot so excited. It transformed his face from his usual severe gaze into something softer and warmer. "Kiss me, Pilot."

Kisses went all around, mouths fusing against skin, necks, shoulders and more. At one point, Bryce's fingers were in Tate's mouth. All the while, Pilot covered his own fingers with lube and used them on Bryce, sliding in and out until he begged for more. "Push in." Pilot moved Tate, manhandling him, between Bryce's legs. Pilot had to be in control of *everything*, but Tate would never complain about it – at least not in bed.

He lined his cock up and pushed slowly into Bryce, while Bryce held his knees back, giving him maximum access. Once he was all the way in, Pilot told him to stop there, and then slick fingers pushed inside Tate. Pushing and pulling and rolling across his prostate. "Enough. That's enough. I want you."

Once Pilot had pushed all the way inside Tate, it took them a few minutes to get a rhythm down with Pilot leading, fucking into Tate and pushing him into Bryce. As he pulled back, so did Tate.

"I've got the best end of this." Tate fucked Bryce as Pilot pushed in to him. Pure bliss. Tate didn't want it to ever end, yet he could feel his orgasm rolling around in the pit of his stomach, waiting to spring out on him. He wanted, needed to come, but he also wanted to wait, to make it last longer.

Bryce's cock slid against Tate's stomach, trapped between their bodies, giving him the friction he needed. Bryce came in three gushing spouts, but his cock was still pretty hard and slipped between them in his own pool of cum. Bryce groaned and tightened his ass is spasms.

"Oh God, Bryce!" Tate came hard, the feeling of Bryce's smooth hole gripping him like a fiery fist, sent him over the edge. He saw the little white stars of a hard orgasm and his body shook.

Pilot called out behind him and came inside Tate. He could feel it. They'd marked each other, the three of them. Pilot pulled out with a grunt, leaving Tate wanting more, but his own cock softened a bit and he eased out of Bryce, slowly.

Bryce's still hard cock arched up and back, pointing at his belly button. It hardened even more with Tate watching him, so Tate grabbed it. Tate stroked him hard and fast, his hand sliding easily with Bryce's cum making it slick, until Bryce shuddered and came again. This time, he only shot a little trickle, but his body didn't know that. He sighed and practically melted into the mattress with a cocky smile on his face.

"Bryce came twice, Pilot."

The deep chuckle he received as an answer said it all.

"I love y'all." Bryce exhaled his words slowly.

Pilot and Tate echoed the sentiment as they all snuggled up. Tate in the middle for once, as they dozed off.

Chapter 41 – May, After Season, The Ranch

Tate thought his joy might burst out of his chest. Surrounded by his friends and family, he lay back on a float in the pool and soaked in their love along with the sun's rays. He wore a new pair of swim trunks by Onia with a cool black and white palm print and Aviator sun glasses. He gave Bryce his old Michael Kors trunks, while Pilot had on some plain blue no name brand, but they fit him, so Tate didn't complain. Green Day blasted out of the speakers and at the other end of the pool people splashed around and laughed and squealed. So many people, the whole crew really, hung around enjoying the day.

"Hey! Where's Bryce?" Pilot asked, swimming up to him and leaning over his float to get a quick kiss.

Tate smiled. "Where do you think? He's with Tyler in the garage farting around with that old Harley." Of course that had been after spending an hour on the phone with his parents. They weren't suffocating him anymore, but they still had to be in Bryce's life. There was a lot of love there, and Tate had to make sure Bryce kept that. He knew, all too well, what it was like without loving parents. He wanted Bryce happy, to have everything. Tate was relieved that they'd made up. He never wanted to be what they'd fought about in the first place, though he knew that was really an oversimplification of things.

Davey did a cannonball, splashing them all before swimming over and pulling himself up on another float. "Any chance Ty has to get his hands greasy with that thing, he does."

"Yeah, Bryce is the same way." Tate couldn't help smiling at that. Every break they'd had, long enough to go home, Bryce would be in the garage.

"So, Tate. What're you going to do when your career is over?" Davey had thrown this colossal party to celebrate his retirement, as well as the end of the season. Next season, things would be different for him and the Apex team.

Davey went out on top, though. He'd taken first in points and had two red plates to prove he was the best. Everyone had expected that. The season only had one surprise, and that was Tate finishing third in points. Although he wasn't happy with it, everyone else was thrilled that he'd finished so well. Chad Regal was predictably in second and Cole Lindt came in fourth, right behind Tate. Third and fourth had been a very tight race that Tate really had to fight for, but he'd done it, surprising his entire team.

"Over?" He wasn't looking that far ahead. "I don't think I'm ever going to stop riding."

"No, but you'll stop racing. Trust me."

"I've got a few seasons left in me though." He splashed Davey, hoping to end that line of discussion, but Davey just splashed him back.

"Seriously. Bryce is already thinking about it and he's just started."

"Uh...we're supposed to be having fun right. Let's talk about it later, already." He looked at Pilot who had been standing there the whole time, not saying a word. "Right?"

"Davey has a point, Tate."

Tate rolled his eyes, though no one could see them behind his shades.

Davey picked the conversation back up as if Tate hadn't tried to stop it. "Well, I'll tell you a few things. I've seen what you've done with Bryce."

"What?"

"Shut up. I know you've been coaching him. And...uh, we want him on our team next year. We're working out contracts with his team already."

"That's great. I'd rather have him on your team anyway. Right, Pilot?"

Davey laughed. "Yeah, and guess who's getting a bodyguard? Pilot will be Bryce's bodyguard. Feel better now?"

"I'm so good with all of that. I think I need another beer."

Pilot took his empty bottle. "I'll get you one." Tate didn't miss the look he exchanged with Davey as he walked away.

"Tate? I want you on our team, too."

"I have a contract with MSR and they're so fucking happy with me, they are not going to break it."

"Yeah. I asked Oz about it already, but it ends next year and I don't want you to renew it. I'm betting you're going to finish first next year and if you don't it'll be the following year. Only a matter of time really."

"I get it. You want the winners. You want a monopoly."

He waved his hand around. "More than that. I want you to keep coaching Bryce and I want you to do it officially and I want you to, uh...be my partner in this. All of this."

Tate startled and slid off his float, falling under the water. When he came up, he flung his hair back. It was getting too long, but it splashed Davey, who splashed him back with a few curses. "You can't really mean that."

"Of course I do." He grabbed Tate's sunglasses out of the water and handed them back to him.

Tate slid the dark lenses back over his eyes. He didn't know what to say. He hadn't even thought of coaching or any career past Supercross and it astonished and touched him for Davey to be just handing him this. "I'm flattered. I don't know, though. I don't know if I'll be any good."

"Oh, you're good. Bryce is proof of that. You're probably better than me, as far as coaching. Tyler is the only one I've coached and more often than not, he curses me out instead of taking my advice."

Tate had to laugh at that; he could totally picture it. "Well, I'll think about it. I mean the coaching part and the partner part. But, as far as joining your team after my contract with MSR is up, that's a no brainer! I'm totally in."

"Awesome! I'll work it out with Oz." He splashed Tate again.

Not long after that, Tyler and Bryce came back to the party. Food was served and cold beer passed around. Then they had dog fights with Tyler's best friend, Janie, on her boyfriend's shoulders, Bryce on Pilot's shoulders, Johnny was on Uncle Gary's shoulders, and Tony had his girlfriend on his shoulders. Angel tugged on Stewart's arm, trying to get him to play, too. Tate remembered last year's party. While the others played around in the pool, he had his ear plastered to the phone with Donny, arguing. How much his life had changed in a year just amazed him.

"Get her Bryce!" Tate shouted and Janie flipped him the bird. He loved her. She didn't hold back, much like Tyler. He totally got why they were best friends.

Oz sat down beside Tate on the edge of the pool to watch the fun. "Crazy fools." He laughed at their antics.

Tate nudged his shoulder. "Davey told me he's going to talk to you about joining Apex."

"He wants you on their team pretty desperately."

"I'm all for it. Just so you know."

"I figured that."

"Oz?"

"Hm?"

Tate kicked his feet back and forth in the water. "Uh...I want to tell you something."

"Sure. What?"

Tate put his arm around Oz's shoulder. "Thank you. You've been like a dad to me. Thank you. I love you, man."

"I love you, too, Tate." They hugged, but then everyone pulled Tate into the water and a major splash fight began.

Tate ducked under the water. When he came up, he retrieved his sunglasses again, and put them on the side of the pool. "It's on now!" He turned to face the others and splashed them with a swipe of his arm.

Pilot dove under the water and wrapped his arms around Tate's waist, picking him up out of the water. With maniacal laughter, he plunged backwards, taking Tate with him. When they came up, Bryce jumped between them.

"Damn, I love you guys." Tate said.

"Me, too." Bryce kissed him quick on the mouth before diving back in the water, but Pilot pulled Tate closer.

"I love you, too. If I could marry you both, I would. You know?"

"I know, bunny." He kissed Pilot, hot and heavy with his tongue plunging into his mouth. Cat calls from their friends broke them up. Bryce hooted the loudest, splashing them, and Tate knew he now had a home in these two men, and his life would happily never be the same again.

The End.

Holeshot 3 Preview
Fourth of July, Las Vegas

Johnny

Johnny walked into the meeting venue and stopped short. He didn't know what he'd been expecting, but it wasn't all the giant pictures of motocross riders...Davey McAllister and Bryce Nickel, if he was guessing right. The poster sized images dominated the large meeting space. In the front of the room a podium had been set up and red and blue lights bounced around the area, creating an overwhelming feeling of expectation. The crowd seemed to be responding to it, since Johnny could feel the tension building by the second.

Someone stepped in behind him, pushing him farther into the room. He scanned the crowd, looking for his Uncle. There had to be nearly three hundred people in there, but it still felt spacious. Johnny felt overwhelmed.

He pushed his glasses back up his nose. Where was Uncle Gary?

They had been invited to this event, which was a combination of celebrating the fourth of July, a retirement send off for Davey, and a launching of a new Apex sponsorship team for motocross. If Johnny understood that last part, Davey and his team would be recruiting and managing riders at various levels. They'd proved themselves with the 250 rider, Sarah Bolster, the previous season. She finished fifth in points in her class and was expected to do much better in her second year. But that wasn't why Johnny and his uncle were there.

He still didn't see his uncle, and was forced to move into the melee of mingling people. He grabbed a glass of wine from a passing waiter, who was dressed in some kind of uniform that looked like modified racing gear. The young man was cute, and Johnny watched his ass in what looked like track pants as he walked through the crowd. He also wore a 27 race jersey, which was meant to honor Davey's retirement.

Finally, he spotted his uncle across the room. He nudged his way past people he assumed were mainly reporters or Apex staff, until he approached his Uncle. "Hey, when's this thing starting?"

Uncle Gary looked at his watch. "Looks like we still have about fifteen minutes or so."

"Great."

"Relax. It isn't that bad." Uncle Gary clapped him on the shoulder.

He was right and he was not right. It was horrible for the introverted side of himself who dreaded being in large crowds of people he didn't know, but it really wasn't too bad, and Johnny needed to be there. He had to support their company, Trident Security Services or TSS, as they had landed the contract with Apex to work with the entire team. They all felt they needed to continue to present a secure front, since Apex was about changing things in the industry and putting forth the best riders, regardless of race, gender, or sexual orientation.

They were the first team to have an openly gay man ride...hell, Davey was a two time champion. They also had the first female rider with Bolster in the 250s. Their next moves would keep them in the spotlight, and they wanted to ensure their riders and crew were safe. So, TSS would be employing more staff and working to improve security across the board, rather than just provide a couple of bodyguards.

Johnny also needed to support his best friend, Pilot. Although, most of the time his emotions around the man ran hot and cold. He had hoped for more than a friendship at one time, but Pilot shattered that when he fell for not one, but two racers...one of those being Bryce Nickel who would be announcing that he will be joining the Apex team. So, he wanted to support them. Being with Pilot made them family. At the same time, he wanted to strangle them both.

It had been difficult to get over the fact that Pilot chose Tate, the bouncy blond Supercross rider over him. His heartbreak had been monumental, but when he found out that they were also involved with Bryce, who was *barely* legal and still technically a teen, it felt like Pilot was throwing it in Johnny's face. He knew that was irrational, but he felt that way all the same, and if he were honest with himself, he'd have to admit he wasn't over it.

Pilot had been a stabilizing force in Johnny's life. They'd known each other since childhood, and supported each other through the rough years of puberty and coming out. Pilot had been there when his own family, his blood relatives, had not been. Pilot had made it better. The darkest days of Johnny's life had been when Pilot had joined the military and went away, stationed across the world with the Army. Until now.

Now, every day was darker than the last. Because the supercross hot shots, Tate and Bryce, had won a lot more than a race or a championship.

They'd won Pilot—Johnny's world.

He sucked down the rest of his wine. "Let's get a seat near the front." He was tired of standing around waiting and moping.

"Yeah, in a minute. We have some time. I want to talk to some people." Uncle Gary was more extroverted than Johnny. That had helped him build the company into what it was today. Johnny had no idea about security and hated marketing and promotion. He let Gary and Pilot worry about that. Johnny kept the books clean. He did the billing and reconciliations and payments. He also took a huge percentage of both his and Pilot's salary for investing. They planned to buy two thirds of the company. That had been their dream. Technically, it still was, but somewhere along the line, in the back of his head, Johnny had thought that stepping their relationship up to a romantic one would go along with that. He had been so totally wrong.

"J-man!" Pilot called to him, and Johnny cringed, but then schooled his face into something pleasant before turning around.

"Pilot. Tate. Congrats." He hoped they didn't hear how he faked the happiness.

Tate scrunched his nose. "Why congratulate me? This is more about you. Well, Trident. Congrats to you." He lifted his glass of wine.

Johnny felt a little heat rush over his face. He wasn't used to the niceness. "Well. Thanks, uh...it's really Davey's night. And Bryce, so...Where is your other half...uh third?"

Tate smiled sweetly, but Pilot answered by pointing to the front of the room. Bryce stood beside Davey McAllister's former manager, Angel Johanson. Johnny liked her. She didn't put up with any bullshit. "Hope she's still going to be on the team."

"Oh, yeah," Tate said. "Davey wouldn't do any of this without her and Stewart."

The lights in the room dimmed and the red and blue at the front of the room flashed and swirled, grabbing their attention and Angel stepped in front of the podium. She raised her voice loud, not unlike an announcement for a fight or something. "Ladies and Gentlemen! The moment you've been waiting for! The reason you are here with us today. Grab a glass of Champagne and get ready..." At her command the cute waiters in race gear started circling the venue with trays loaded with Champagne flutes. It was an army of alcohol pushing hotties. Johnny smiled and winked at the waiter that presented them a tray and took his own glass.

While they moved through the room, loud raucous music blared over the speakers. Pilot leaned over and barked in his ear. "I think that's *Powerman 5000*."

Johnny rolled his eyes. Pilot probably only knew that shit because he hung out so much with his under aged boyfriends. He knew that thought wasn't fair. They were both over eighteen...barely.

Johnny nudged his shoulder and nodded to the front where Angel took the podium again. The music lowered, but didn't cut off. She raised her glass. "We start with a congratulations and job well done. Two consecutive championships is definitely the way to go out. To the man of the hour...Davey McAllister."

The room full of reporters, business associates, and close friends all cheered and Davey stepped out of a door to the side. He lifted his arms, encouraging the room to cheer more. Johnny had half expected him to come out in his race gear, but no, Davey wore a nice suit that emphasized his tiny waist and broad shoulders, and looked damn good. Johnny could see what Pilot saw in these racers.

When Davey stepped behind the podium, he drew his hand across his throat and the music screeched out. "Thank you. Thank you." He paused as the last of the crowd quieted down. "First announcement. Yes, I am retiring from racing." The room erupted in noise. Davey held his hands out, beckoning them to quiet down. "But not Supercross. I can't. It's in my blood." Once more the room cheered, and Johnny found himself clapping along. "So, I've worked with the Apex team, Angel and Stewart..." He nodded to his former management team. "And together we're starting a new era in racing. We'll be managing and training racers at all levels. Including the elite 450 and 250 Supercross leagues. We'll be keeping Sarah Bolster, the first female Supercross racer to start in the 250 Main Events, and not just one race, but all of them, and she placed in the top five in points." He held up his five fingers. "Her first season. Well...she had a lot of firsts last year, but they won't be the last for her. Sarah."

Sarah stepped forward and raised a hand while the others cheered, but the night wasn't about her and she didn't approach the podium to say anything. Johnny had met her this past season once or twice. She was quiet, reserved. She had long brown hair that she almost always had pulled back in a ponytail or tucked under a hat. Tonight it was down around her shoulders. She had also set aside racing gear for a nice blouse and slacks. He hoped she'd do well next season.

Davey continued. "While Sarah will race in the 250 East division, we've recruited another up and coming *Hot Shot* racer for the West." Bryce stepped forward. His signature purple streaked locks falling in his face. He pushed it back. He also wore a suit. Johnny knew it was a navy Hugo Boss, because he'd helped pick it out. His lighter blue shirt and blue and purple tie made his amazing blue eyes pop, but Johnny couldn't see that from where he stood in the crowd. He knew it from helping the kid get ready in the hotel room earlier. "Bryce Nickel. Welcome to the family."

Bryce stood next to Davey while he listed accomplishments and aspirations. Bryce smiled widely as Davey praised him, his eyes jumping over the crowd until they landed on Pilot and Tate. Johnny didn't completely understand their dynamics, but they did have love between them, regardless of how unfair it was.

The rest of the announcements went on quickly and then soft music played as Davey and his team worked the room. It didn't take Bryce long to make his way through the crowd and right into Pilot's waiting arms. "Congrats, baby."

"I'm so excited to be working with Davey. OhmyGod!"

Johnny had heard that exact line from him about a million times in the last few weeks. He was about over it. He handed off his glass and decided it was time for him to go back to the hotel. He'd had enough of the crowd, the press, the racers...Pilot and his *two* lovers. More than any of that, he'd had enough of his bitter heart being jealous of all of it.

"Excuse me. I'd like to talk with you, Bryce, if I could for a minute." They turned to look at the man who spoke, expecting someone from the press wanting an exclusive interview or something. The man wore an expensive suite and tie and held himself with an air of confidence. His brown hair was cut professionally and his deep brown eyes sparkled with a hint of trouble. "I'm Gavin Peri. I represent BikeMax Toyota." He held out a card to Bryce who tentatively took it and looked down at it. "I know you just signed with Apex, but we're prepared to offer you a better deal."

Bryce laughed and Tate laughed too. Pilot scowled. Johnny couldn't stop looking at this Gavin Peri.

"I'd like to meet with you."

"Look. Mr. Peri," Bryce started.

"We're new, but we have major backing. I know we made a mistake with our previous racer choices—"

"Look. It's not that. But, if you don't have Davey McAllister working with you..."

Tate threw in, "And you don't."

"Then, I'm just not interested." Bryce started to hand him back his business card.

Gavin held his hand up. "No. Keep it. You never know when you might change your mind. And, well, you can't blame a man for trying." He held his hand out and Bryce shook it.

Johnny stood there staring. He loved this man's boldness. Gavin Peri. He rolled the name around in his head.

"Yes?" He turned to look at Johnny. Had he said the name out loud?

He held his hand out. "I'm Johnny Killebrew. I work with the security team."

Gavin cocked his head. "You don't look like security."

Johnny noticed Pilot's trio slowly backed away, leaving him to talk with Gavin alone. On one hand he was thankful because this Gavin Peri was yummy, but on the other...he was out of his element. "Uh...owner. I do finance, mainly."

"Ah...Well. I'm an agent, manager...whatever, but my background is finance. Graduated with a degree from Ohio State."

"University of Colorado."

"Ah...both cold. I live in L.A. now. I love it. The BikeMax team is headquartered there."

Johnny nodded and bit his bottom lip. He didn't know what else to say for a moment. He stared at Gavin Peri's plump lips surrounded by neatly trimmed beard, the same color of his hair, like honey almonds.

"Well, Mr. Killebrew. It was, uh, very nice meeting you."

Johnny didn't want to end the conversation. He nodded, and quickly blurted out the first question he could think of to keep it going. "What? How? Uh...how did you get involved with Supercross?"

"That, my new friend, is a very long story." Did he step a little closer? "Would you like to get a drink...somewhere else? I could tell you all about it." His eyebrows rose in question.

Johnny wanted to do more than just get a drink with the guy. He wanted to see those fabulously lush lips wrapped around his cock. He wanted to rub his hands through that soft hair and scratchy beard...he had to stop thinking like that or he'd pop wood and his pants were cut too well for that. They would show everything. He took a calming breath.

"If you're not interested, I apologize—"

"No. No. I'm...very interested. There's a quiet restaurant here. In the hotel. In this place, it's open twenty-four seven."

"Great. Do you need to tell your, uh..." He waved his hand and looked around, presumably for Pilot's trio, but they were off across the room. Johnny only spotted them because he was used to seeing Pilot's buzz cut sticking out above the crowds with his height.

"Nope. I'm a grown man. I'm single. I answer to myself."

"I'm single too."

"Good." Johnny winked at him. He couldn't wait to get to know this guy. "Come tell me about yourself Gavin Peri."

He took Johnny's arm and leaned close to his ear. His hot breath sent a chill down Johnny's spine as he said in a low husky voice, "I like hearing you say my name."

That was the perfect place to start.

Supercross Schedule

January 5th - Anaheim
January 12th – San Diego
January 19th – Anaheim
January 26th – Oakland
February 3rd – Glendale
February 9th – Atlanta
February 16th – Daytona
February 23rd - Toronto
March 2nd - Detroit
March 9th - New Jersey
March 16th - Indianapolis
March 23rd – St. Louis
March 30th – Foxborough
(break)
April 13th - Arlington
April 20th - Glendale
April 27th – San Diego
May 4th – Las Vegas

Holeshot Playlist

Tate's songs:
"Heart Shaped Box" by Nirvana
"2Heads" by Coleman Hell
"Mess Around" by Cage The Elephant

Pilot's songs:
"A Warior's Call" by Volbeat
"Ganghis Kahn" by Mike Snow

Bryce's songs:
"Tiger Striped Sky" by Roo Panes
"Gone" by JR JR

Davey's Songs:
"Waiting for Superman" by Daughtry
"Kryptonite" by 3 Doors Down
"Crazy" by Kat Dahlia

Tylers's Songs:
"UV Love" by Clinton Sparks
"Nookie" by Limp Bizkit
"Fuck Time" by Green Day

Significant events:

The song Tyler was dancing to in the pit:
"Touch Me" by Kazaky

X-TS Event: "Paralyzer" by Finger Eleven

In the Rain, Atlanta:
"Naked As We Came" by Iron and Wine
"Mad Season" by Matchbox 20

Chapter 33 – Tate and Pilot fight over Bryce:
"Nookie" by Limp Bizkit
"Papercut" by Linkin Park

Chapter 40 – Bryce and Tate:
"Dirty, Sexy Money" by The Struts
"Moves Like Jagger" by Maroon 5 (ft. Christina Aguilera)

After Season Party:
"American Idiot" by Greenday
"Come With Me Now" by Kongos

ABOUT THE AUTHOR

Lynn Michaels lives and writes in Tampa, Florida where the sun is hot and the Sangria is cold. Lynn is the newest addition to Rubicon Fiction, and she loves reading and writing about hot men in love.

Other Work by Lynn Michaels
Can be found on Amazon

Novels:
The Holeshot
Lines On The Mirror
Wanton
Evasive Maneuvers

Novellas:

Universe #1 –Elementals
Universe #2 – Disguises
Shot the Plot
Cupid's Christmas Arrow

Short Stories/Anthologies:

Love is Love (poetry)
Take A Chance/Want You Bad

Made in the USA
Columbia, SC
18 September 2019